Alison Sherlock enjoyed reading and writing stories
from an early age. However, she assumed that being
an author didn't count as a proper job so when Alison
grew up, she worked as a secretary, training administrator and answered an IT Hotline. Once older and
a bit wiser, she realised that she really had to write
her novel. So she gave up office life to sit at home and
panic at what she had done. To fund her dream, Alison
became a cleaner, the experience of which she has used
for this novel. A chance meeting with a literary agent
at Winchester Writers' Conference set her on the road
to publication with her first book, *The Desperate Bride's
Diet Club*. Alison lives in Surrey with her husband
Dave and Harry, their daft golden retriever.

You can follow her on Facebook and on Twitter:
@alisonsherlock

Also by Alison Sherlock

The Desperate Bride's Diet Club

The Desperate Wife's Survival Plan

ALISON SHERLOCK

arrow books

Published by Arrow 2013

10 9 8 7 6 5 4 3 2 1

Copyright © Alison Sherlock 2013

Alison Sherlock has asserted her right to be identified as
the author of this work under the Copyright, Designs
and Patents Act 1988

First published in Great Britain in 2013 by Arrow
20 Vauxhall Bridge Road
London, SW1V 2SA

An imprint of The Random House Group Limited

www.randomhouse.co.uk
www.prefacepublishing.co.uk

Addresses for companies within The Random House Group
Limited can be found at www.randomhouse.co.uk

The Random House Group Limited Reg. No. 954009

A CIP catalogue record for this book is available from
the British Library

ISBN 978 0 09956 237 5

The Random House Group Limited supports the Forest Stewardship
Council® (FSC®), the leading international forest-certification
organisation. Our books carrying the FSC label are printed on
FSC®-certified paper. FSC is the only forest-certification
scheme supported by the leading environmental organisations,
including Greenpeace. Our paper procurement policy can be found
at www.randomhouse.co.uk/environment

Typeset in Palatino by Palimpsest Book Production Limited,
Falkirk, Stirlingshire
Printed and bound by
CPI Group (UK) Ltd, Croydon, CR0 4YY

For Dave – husband, best friend and
chief ice-cream tester.
With love always.

Acknowledgements

A huge thank you to my editor Rosie de Courcy who gave so much time and so many excellent ideas to the dreaded second book! Her advice and passion about the story have made all the difference and I am forever in her debt.

Thank you to the whole team at Preface, Arrow and Random House for their hard work and enthusiasm on my behalf.

Special thanks to my lovely agent Judith Murdoch whose continued support and sympathetic ear are much appreciated.

This story is about friends supporting each other through the ups and downs of life. I've been very lucky with mine over the years, including Jackie Hamilton, Anita Timmings, Elaine Nutley and Sharon Warry. As well as all the new friends I have made through the Romantic Novelists Association.

Special thanks also to Jo Botelle – for the Garfield books, grill story and everything else since.

This story is also about how important a family can be to each other in the worst of times. So a huge thank you to all of mine, especially my dad, Ray Sherlock, sister Gill, Simon and Louise Collins for their continued love and support.

Special thanks also to Ross, Lee and Cara Maidens for bringing so much love and laughter into my life. And to all the other Maidens, young and old, both in England and Australia.

Chapter One

When Charley Summers was eight years old, a girl called Wanda at school made fun of her wild, curly hair. 'You have clown's hair,' Wanda told her.

That afternoon, whilst her mother was making tea, Charley took out the iron from under the stairs and tried to flatten her hair straight. The resulting smoke brought her mother running in to throw a bowl of water over her daughter's head. The next day Charley's hair snapped off, leaving a two inch crew cut in its place.

Thankfully, there are easier ways to fight nature these days if one has the funding.

Charley glanced at her reflection in the salon window. The curly tangle of dark hair that she had been blessed with now hung in a smooth sheet around her face.

With a satisfied sigh, she turned her attention back to the receptionist who was processing the payment. Her husband often moaned about the twice-weekly £30 cost but Charley brooked no arguments on the subject. Professional blow drys were an absolute necessity.

'I'm sorry, madam,' said the receptionist. 'There appears to be a problem with your credit card.'

She placed the gold plastic card on to the counter between them. Charley stared down at it, nonplussed. Had she picked up someone else's by mistake in the clothes shop earlier? No, the name was correct. It was definitely hers.

'Perhaps there's a problem with the network,' she said, trying to remain cool and serene.

'It rejected the card on two attempts.' The receptionist switched on a sympathetic smile.

'I see.' Charley snatched the card from the counter and shoved it deep into her handbag. Aware that another customer nearby was eavesdropping, she felt her cheeks begin to grow pink with embarrassment. She found her purse and finally handed over the cash.

'Sorry about the card,' said Charley, trying to recover her composure.

'Not at all, madam,' cooed the receptionist.

'Well, thank you. And sorry again.'

Charley left a massive tip on the counter and scurried out of the hair salon. Once she was a few yards away, she stopped and drew a deep breath to calm her racing pulse. How utterly mortifying, she thought. Something had obviously gone wrong at the bank.

She whipped out her iPhone and rang Steve. But, as usual, it went straight to voicemail. The new shop was taking up all of her husband's time, so she knew he wouldn't have a chance to call her back. But she would definitely ask him to get the problem sorted out. They had obviously missed their monthly payment.

Deciding she wouldn't let the small matter of the credit-card refusal ruin her afternoon, she flicked a smooth lock of hair behind her shoulder and began to walk down the high street. The February sun shone down from a deep blue sky. It was one of those wonderful late winter days where the air was crisp and sharp, holding the promise of a cold, starry night to follow.

Charley strolled down the street which ran through the centre of Grove Village. She walked past the numerous coffee shops, the florist, greengrocer and chemist. All the basics required for country living, plus a few trinket shops where you could pick up a funky cushion or witty tea-towel.

She stopped in front of the designer lingerie and swimwear shop at the end of the parade. The Valentine's Day display of red silk underwear had been replaced with a beautiful purple bikini. Instead of ties, it had large silver buckles on each thigh. The price tag read £85.

Charley knew she should really purchase any beach-wear from one of Steve's clothes shops. However, although the fashions there were up-to-the-minute, the overall look was cheap. Not quite in keeping with the St Kitts crowd they would be mixing with on holiday in a few weeks' time.

She was tempted to try on the bikini but a quick glance at her reflection stopped her from entering the shop. She knew she wasn't fat but she had gone up a whole dress size in the past year. She really would have to do something about it.

There was a new weight-loss club in the village, run

by a lady called Violet. Charley had seen the advertisement in the local newspaper and had heard good things about it from acquaintances.

However, she didn't have time to lose weight slowly and sensibly. Drastic action was required. Perhaps she would hire a personal trainer instead. Maybe a few meetings with a nutritionist would be helpful as well.

As she walked on, she spotted a few schoolchildren at the other end of the high street. Glancing at her watch, Charley realised time was getting on. Her best friends were coming over that evening for dinner and she wanted everything to be perfect before their arrival.

She turned the corner up the small alleyway to Gino's delicatessen. It was her favourite shop in the whole universe and that included Selfridges. Where else could she buy truffle salt for her steaks? Authentic balsamic jelly to be served with her cheese board? Pistachio cream to be swirled into her ice-cream?

The aroma which filled the shop was Charley's drug of choice. It was a heady concoction of oils, spices and herbs, mixed with fresh coffee.

She chose her purchases carefully, deciding on handmade grissini to start and picking up some black olive pâté to use as a dip. She had already bought a beautiful piece of salmon from the fishmonger's, but it needed the green pesto alla Genovese to give it extra flavour. She added two bottles of Chablis to her basket before heading to the till.

She opened her purse and remembered, just in time, not to use the gold credit card. Instead, she handed over her bank card with a smile.

The wizened old Italian woman behind the counter

placed the items into a carrier bag before glancing at the card machine. She muttered to herself in Italian, then fixed Charley with a hard stare. She shook her head and held out the bank card. Charley's stomach dropped. The bank card didn't work either?

This time she didn't question the failure. Instead she fiddled about in her purse, desperately trying to find the correct amount. When the money came up short, she had to choose what to leave behind. In the end, she handed back the bottles of wine, grateful that they already had plenty at home.

Charley was squirming with embarrassment as she left the shop. It was possible that they had reached the overdraft limit on their bank account. Perhaps that was why the credit card hadn't been paid. Steve had been making ominous rumblings over the last couple of weeks about tightening their belts. Charley knew he was stressed about the opening of their fourth clothes shop, but she hadn't taken it seriously.

She drove the short distance to Upper Grove. The high street divided the village into Upper and Lower Grove. Charley lived in Upper Grove which was mainly inhabited by the rich and privileged. In direct contrast Lower Grove was an unfriendly estate, to be avoided at all costs. She never went there, never dared to. The high street was Grove's Berlin Wall and most of the villagers were grateful it was still standing.

Upper Grove had large houses, wide avenues and neighbours who ignored each other. The only person Charley had ever spoken to there was Julie who lived next door.

Julie was one of the group of four friends who met up once a fortnight for dinner. Each of them in turn would cook a meal to enjoy whilst they caught up on the latest gossip. More often than not, the girls demanded that Charley make ice-cream for pudding and it had become a sort of ritual amongst the group.

She swung her car into the driveway and allowed herself a small smile of satisfaction at the sight of her home. It was still the prettiest house she had ever seen. She had fallen in love at first sight with it, over four years previously. The black timber beams set against the white masonry had stolen her heart. The addition of custom made oak windows and a new front door, after they moved in, had completed the look.

Inside, the fireplaces, original oak flooring and exposed beams were crying out for a makeover. Charley had enjoyed turning the house into their dream home.

The kitchen was her favourite part of the house. It had been poky and dark when they moved in. But the addition of a brand new extension had opened up the room, and light now flooded in from the skylights and the wall of folding windows which led on to the patio. Pale, shiny tile flooring and dark walnut cabinets brought the look up to date. The cream marble work surfaces held tiny flecks of silver which provided just enough bling without being tacky.

Having unpacked her purchases, Charley switched on her Gaggia Gelatiera ice-cream maker. For years she had made her ice-cream by hand but as soon as the money had begun to pour in from Steve's business, she had placed an order for the sleek, silver appliance. Loved by chefs everywhere, the paddles churned the ice-cream so well that it always turned out velvety-smooth.

Charley began to break up a bar of Venezuelan black chocolate into chunks so that it would melt more easily before being poured into the ice-cream maker. She had already made a beautiful rhubarb sorbet but there would be hell to pay later from the girls if there wasn't any chocolate on the menu.

Chapter Two

Samantha Harris was bored. She glanced around the office but no one was taking any notice of her. They were all too busy staring at their computer screens.

She wondered if she could get away with reading her new magazine but decided against it. That cow Miranda would definitely notice and probably rat her out to their manager.

Samantha glanced across the low divide between their desks at the dark-haired woman opposite talking on the phone. She hated her posh voice and perfect hair. She hated her constant references to her double-barrelled friends, all of whom appeared to own country estates. Most of all, she hated the fact that Miranda was her line-manager. She was only a secretary, for God's sake. And Samantha was her assistant.

Not that there appeared to be enough work for Samantha to do. She had all the filing and photo-copying dumped on her, but that barely took up any time at all. So she was reduced to glancing surreptitiously at the internet when nobody was looking and texting her friends, mainly Charley, who had the spare time to reply.

She liked Charley. They had both once worked for a small insurance agency, where they had bonded through boredom and a mutual dislike for the Personnel Manager. They had also shared a love of designer clothes and expensive shoes.

Then Charley's husband had begun to make all that money and she had left the insurance agency. It was all right for some, thought Samantha. No sign of a rich husband for her. Yet, she told herself.

But the pickings weren't rich in Grove Village and especially not in her office. Most of the directors were pensionable. All the other men were either fresh out of university, or dull. Craving some male attention, Samantha had had a few flings with university graduates, knowing that they relished a sexy, older woman like herself. Well, not that old. The big 3–0 was hurtling up towards her next year, but she kept herself trim by keeping a careful eye on her diet and constantly exercising.

'Hi. I wonder if you could help me?'

Samantha spun round in her chair at the sound of the deep male voice and found herself pleasantly surprised. Late thirties, dark hair, blue eyes. Cute . . . very cute.

She crossed her legs, knowing that her black skirt would ride up a little as she did so. His eyes lowered to check out her legs. It was a brief glance but she noted it.

She fixed on her sexiest grin. 'Of course,' she said, lowering her voice into a soft, husky tone. 'What can I do for you?'

'Richard, is it?' Miranda's abrasive voice broke into their exchange.

'Yes,' replied the man. 'I've got a ten o'clock with Matthew Jones.'

'I'll take you in,' said Miranda.

He must be the new Sales Director, thought Samantha.

Just then, Richard glanced around, catching her eye for a second before he disappeared into the next room.

Samantha smiled to herself. Things were definitely looking up.

Caroline Jones didn't have time to be bored. As usual, her mug of coffee was only half-drunk and growing cold while it stood forgotten on the kitchen counter.

She logged into her email on the laptop, cradling the mobile between her ear and neck.

'We have one place left in the Tuesday class,' said the voice at the other end of the line. 'Would you like me to reserve it for you?'

'Yes, please,' said Caroline, relief flooding her voice. 'It's just such a rush on a Wednesday when Flora does ballet as well.'

'I understand. We'll transfer all of the future classes to Tuesday at 2 p.m. and cancel the Wednesday lessons.'

'Thank you so much,' replied Caroline, grabbing her desk diary and placing it on the kitchen worktop.

She flipped over the page to Tuesday of the following week and scribbled 'Mandarin class, 2 p.m.'

Caroline was relieved she had been able to transfer the class to a different day of the week. Flora's Mandarin lessons were so important, now that China had become an international player in the world markets.

But Caroline also knew how valuable ballet classes were to a child. Correct deportment was important for Flora's bone structure, not to mention the benefit to her health and fitness.

Flora had enjoyed disco when she was younger but Caroline disliked the lack of structure in the classes and moved her into ballet as soon as she was old enough.

Caroline glanced at the clock. Four o'clock and still so much to do before supper at Charley's house that evening. She really didn't want to go, reluctant to let Jeff take over the bedtime routine. It was so important, in these last precious months before Flora started school, that her reading skills were brought up to scratch. Jeff was always a little too lax, too willing to give in and read that dreadful *Peppa Pig* book his sister had bought Flora for her birthday. Caroline's preferred option was the Oxford Reading Tree. Flora was already over halfway through level one.

However Caroline had known Charley since secondary school and didn't want to let her down at the last minute. They had been friends after Caroline's parents moved to the village when she was thirteen. Her life had been on an upward trajectory ever since school. She had been a top PA for six years at a firm of solicitors. Engaged at twenty-five to Jeff, married at twenty-seven and pregnant at twenty-nine. Her life was orderly, planned and smooth. Even her titian hair was perfectly straight.

Caroline skimmed her emails. A couple of children's party invites would require carefully worded replies. All her diplomatic skills came into play in weeding out any of Flora's 'friends' whose parents might not share Caroline's ambitions. It was all very well now, but as soon as school began, so did the real work. They had scrimped together enough money for Flora to attend the private school for girls on the edge of the village. Her education needed to be given top priority.

Flora was still in her ballet outfit from that afternoon's class and Caroline's heart warmed as she watched her four-year-old daughter read *Angelina Ballerina*. Dressed in a pale pink cardigan and leotard, her red hair swept back into a tidy bun, she was the image of Caroline as a child.

Except there had been no ballet classes for her then. Her own upbringing had been happy, but modest. She was determined that Flora would do better and to that end she had to be a super mummy, an alpha mum. It was exhausting but it would be worth it.

Julie Gordon unpinned the butterfly brooch from her black jacket and stared down at the gold detail. It had been on her mother's dressing table for as long as she could remember. Not worn very often, of course. Perhaps at her grandmother's funeral, Julie wasn't sure. Anyway, it had felt like the right thing to wear that afternoon.

Julie felt sad that there hadn't been many people attending the funeral but she wasn't surprised. Her mother's social circle had always been small, especially after her husband had been sent to prison all those years ago. Nobody trusted a thief at a party or in the pub. Or the wife of one either.

Julie was grateful that her lovely Uncle Sidney had been able to attend. He had wept a few silent tears over the loss of his younger sister, especially when her favourite hymn was played. Afterwards, Julie had taken him home to his flat above the shop that he could no longer manage to run. With a sigh, she knew it would become her responsibility to sort things out for him over the years to come. After all, she was his only family now.

A few of the mourners had been close friends, supporting her mother throughout her hard life. Friends like dear old Sheila and Daphne, muttering under their breath about how Julie's father had been scum and undeserving of such a special wife.

She hadn't offered any defence of her father. Why should she? His infrequent visits between stays in prison had stopped around the time of her fifth birthday. From then on, it had been just Julie and her mother.

Until Julie had fallen for Clive Gordon at the age of seventeen. He had managed to stick around long enough to see their son's sixth birthday. But then he too had left, deciding life would be much better spent in Spain with the barmaid from their local pub. Or so she had been told.

Clive had left behind a large mortgage for Julie to manage and a young son for her to bring up. She had never wanted the rundown house in fancy Upper Grove. What did they need three bedrooms for? But her husband had made a deal with the owner just after they were married. Another dodgy contract, the details of which Julie didn't want to know.

She had never had enough spare money to do up the house so had never bothered. Its rundown exterior and lack of modern appliances didn't concern her. The real interest for Julie lay in the mature garden at the back of the house.

13

She looked out of the window. Apart from the vibrant red stems of the dogwood, the garden seemed to contain only dead stems or evergreen leaves. It was her least favourite time of the year. But she was filled with hope. The snowdrops had just come out, soon to be followed by early crocuses and then daffodils. Spring brought fresh life to the scene, a blank canvas waiting to be rediscovered. She couldn't wait.

The garden had become Julie's refuge from her marriage, with its loud arguments and painful bruises. After Clive had left, Julie had spent more and more time there, especially when Nick entered his teenage years and began to get himself into trouble.

Nick . . . her nineteen-year-old son. A chip off Clive's block. Another lazy, cheating, lying man in her life. But she had raised him so perhaps it was her fault that he had turned out so bad. He hadn't even bothered to finish school before leaving home at sixteen.

He had visited infrequently ever since, usually when he needed money to get him out of yet another mess. And Julie helped him because that's what you did for your children, wasn't it? It would have been nice if, for once, he had thought of her and been at his grandmother's funeral. But he hadn't turned up.

The house seemed very quiet that afternoon and Julie was looking forward to seeing the girls later on. Upper Grove had become very fancy over the years and many familiar faces had gone. Her only friend there these days was Charley.

She was nice and not at all stuck-up like the other neighbours. Of course, she and Steve had done a beautiful job with the house, but they never seemed to look down on Julie's shabby home. In fact, Charley was easy to talk to and get along with. A bit of a lifesaver when the house felt big and empty as it did that afternoon.

Julie stared down at her mother's brooch in her hands. Thank goodness she was still meeting the girls later. She really didn't want to be alone this evening.

Chapter Three

The salmon had been poached to perfection. The salad was fresh and crisp. The wine chilled to just the right temperature. Now it was time for the ice-cream and gossip.

'This is fantastic,' said Julie, licking the chocolate ice-cream from her spoon.

'I don't even like rhubarb normally,' said Caroline, leaning forward to scoop more sorbet into her bowl.

'Just one more spoonful then don't let me have any more,' said Samantha, helping herself to the chocolate.

Charley smiled inwardly, revelling in her friend's compliments. It wasn't that Steve didn't appreciate her cooking, but to her chagrin a takeaway from McDonald's seemed to give him as much pleasure.

This was her favourite time, sitting around her lovely big kitchen table, eating good food and exchanging gossip.

'So what else do you know about this new Adonis in the office?' asked Caroline.

'He's got buttocks of steel,' replied Samantha with grin.

'That's not what I meant,' said Caroline, shaking her head, but smiling too.

'What's the plan then?' asked Charley.

'Seduce him at the staff party at the end of the month.'

'Does he have any brothers?' asked Julie.

It was her first quip of the evening. She had been quieter than usual, her trademark sense of humour absent after the grief of the funeral earlier that day.

Charley got up from the table to get another bottle of wine, thinking as she did so that she was in awe of Samantha's love life. Charley herself had never had a one-night stand, her first and only date had been with Steve, twelve years ago.

The wine cabinet was hidden behind a dark walnut door. Charley picked up a bottle of Pinot Grigio, chilled to just the right temperature. She loved all the gadgets in the kitchen; the hot water tap, which meant the work surfaces didn't need to be cluttered with anything as mundane as a kettle. The integrated bean-to-cup coffee machine, which produced everything from espressos to large lattes. And, of course, the Gaggia Gelatiera ice-cream maker.

She returned to the table and topped up all the wine glasses, apart from Caroline. She was driving Samantha home.

'Are you sure Nick's all right?' asked Caroline. 'I mean, something must have happened for him to miss the funeral.'

Julie shrugged her shoulders. 'I don't know,' she replied, blowing out a long sigh. 'But it won't be anything serious. It never is.'

'Easy does it,' said Samantha to Caroline who was helping herself to yet more ice-cream. 'Are you going for the world record?'

They all knew that Caroline never overdid anything, especially food.

'Everything okay?' asked Charley.

Caroline tucked a strand of red hair behind one ear. 'It's all been a bit stressful today. Apparently I've left it too late to book Flora the violin lessons with Professor Stratberg.'

'Who?' asked Samantha.

'He's the best violin teacher in the area. Comes highly recommended. I was told to leave it until she was five, so that her hands would be large enough. I figured there was only a couple of months to go until her birthday, so I'd perhaps book some lessons in early. But now the professor is fully booked until Christmas.'

'It's only February!' said Charley.

'Exactly,' said Caroline with a sigh.

'She's only four,' said Samantha, trying not to roll her eyes.

'You do realise that Mozart was five when he wrote "Twinkle Twinkle, Little Star"?' replied Caroline, still stressed.

'Yes, but he'd never been subjected to the *Teletubbies*,' said Julie, a touch acidly.

A while later, they were giggling over Samantha's bitchy descriptions of her work colleagues, when the front door slammed shut.

'Sounds like the Lord of the Manor is home,' said Charley.

'I'd better think about going,' said Caroline, standing up. 'Lord knows what state I'll find Flora in when I get home.'

Julie was also rattling the front-door keys in her hand. 'It's been a long day,' she said, hugging Charley goodbye.

'I'll pop in tomorrow,' Charley told her.

She waved them off from the front door before closing it behind her. The house was quiet, giving no indication where her husband was. She hunted around the ground floor before finding Steve slumped in a chair in the den. It was a snug room with large leather armchairs and a huge 3D television.

'Hello,' said Charley, leaning down to kiss him.

Even after twelve years together, he still looked good to her. His strong jaw and cheekbones had become a little more pronounced over the years but he managed to maintain his muscular body with frequent visits to the executive gym to which they both belonged.

But as Charley inhaled the strong smell of whisky and cigarettes coming from him, she stopped short.

'Have you been smoking again?' she said. 'I thought you'd stopped.'

'Give it a rest,' snapped Steve, suddenly getting up and leaving the room.

Charley trailed behind him, shocked by his harsh tone. Normally Steve was all charm and cheeky smiles. But he wasn't smiling now, as he headed into the kitchen and poured himself a large glass of wine.

'What's the matter?' she asked.

He swilled the wine around in the glass before downing it in one. 'Nothing,' he said, sitting down at the table which was still strewn with dirty bowls and spoons. 'Go to bed.'

'Is it the bank?' she asked, picking up the dishes and taking them over to the dishwasher. 'I had a problem with both the debit and credit cards today. You need to get it sorted out tomorrow.'

As she bent down to load the dishwasher, she could feel an extra roll of fat escaping over the waistband of her designer jeans. She hadn't visited the gym in months and then only for a massage. She really had to go the next day and talk to someone about a personal trainer. She turned round to catch Steve pouring himself another large glass of wine, his mouth a tight line.

Charley walked over to the table and sat down opposite him, suddenly anxious.

'What's happened?'

There was a short silence whilst he swirled the liquid round and around in the glass.

He took a large gulp before replying, 'It's all gone.'

'What has?'

'The business. Our money. Everything.'

'What do you mean, it's all gone? Gone where?'

Steve took a deep breath. 'As of four o'clock this afternoon, we are now officially bankrupt.'

Charley stared at him in horror as he raised his glass to her in mock celebration.

'Cheers,' he said.

Chapter Four

For a minute after her husband's shocking admission, Charley could only sit speechless. At last, she found her voice. 'I don't understand. How has this happened to us?'

She realised his mouth was trembling as he fought tears. So she leant across the table and grabbed his hand.

'Tell me everything.'

'Business hasn't been so good recently.'

'It's a recession. What does the bank expect us to do about it?'

'They expect us to pay back our debts.'

Charley frowned. 'How much do we owe?'

Her husband sighed before speaking. 'Almost £200,000.'

She was aghast, her hand slipping away from under his. 'How can we owe that much money?'

'Unpaid rent on the shops. Stock to pay for.'

Charley frowned. 'Yes, but that still seems a huge amount.'

Steve looked away. 'Things have been tight since we opened the third shop. I sorted out some loans but didn't read the small print. Turns out the interest was sky-high. We've ended up owing almost double the amount borrowed. I'll never be able to pay it back.'

'Wait,' said Charley, dragging a hand through her hair. 'The third shop? That was over a year ago. Why didn't you tell me?'

He shrugged his shoulders. 'Thought I could sort it out by myself.'

She rolled her eyes. 'So have you talked to the bank? What about the Citizens Advice Bureau?'

'It's too late,' he snapped. 'We've got an interview with the Official Receiver on Friday. He wants all our personal papers. Mortgage and all that kind of stuff.'

'Why does he need all that? It's the business that's bankrupt, not us.'

Steve got up from the table to find another bottle of wine to drink. With his back to her, he said, 'Our commercial landlords were given a personal guarantee against the shops.'

'I don't understand what that means.'

He glanced over his shoulder. 'It means that we'll have to use any assets we own to pay off the debt.'

She took a sharp intake of breath. 'We'll lose the house?'

He shrugged his shoulders before turning away again. 'House, savings, the lot.'

Suddenly Charley was angry. She got up from the table and began to pace across the kitchen.

'I don't believe this! I don't bloody believe this!' she raged at him. 'How can you have got us into such a mess and not told me?'

'I told you to calm down on the spending, didn't I?' Steve shouted back.

Charley felt a guilty pang. She had raided the savings accounts recently to pay off some of the credit card bills. She had planned to put the money back, but it seemed she was too late.

'I didn't know things were this bad.'

'No, you never asked. You just kept on buying more and more bloody stuff!'

Charley's face flushed with shame as she realised there was some truth in that. But she retaliated, 'You're blaming me for all this?'

'Fancy holidays to the Caribbean. Expensive furniture.' Steve waved his hand around the room. 'Posh kitchen, for God's sake.'

They glared at each other for a minute before she was able to take a deep breath. She placed her hands on the kitchen counter, drumming her perfectly manicured nails on the imported Italian marble worktop. Charley clenched her jaw and ignored the small voice inside reminding her of the tens of thousands of pounds she had spent on this room. And the rest.

'So we have to go and see this Receiver person on Friday?' she said, deliberately making her tone softer once more.

'Yeah.'

They looked at each other for a beat before she headed around the counter to give him a hug.

'We'll get through this,' she muttered into his chest.

'I know,' Steve replied dully.

Charley waited until he had gone upstairs to take a shower before finally sinking on to one of the kitchen chairs. She had done very well not to scream and rant at Steve . . . but what a mess. She couldn't believe it.

Didn't want to. A tear slid out of one eye and rolled down her cheek.

She brushed it away before standing up again. It would all be fine. Perhaps it wouldn't be as bad as they imagined. Perhaps they wouldn't have to lose the house. They would make it. They would get past this and move on.

She finished tidying up the kitchen, switching the dishwasher on before heading upstairs.

Steve was already in bed, his snores an indication of the amount of alcohol he had consumed that evening. She tried to snuggle in, desperate to be comforted, but he turned away from her, oblivious.

But Charley couldn't find the luxury of sleep. Her mind was racing and she suddenly felt very afraid of what the future held for them.

Chapter Five

Thursday brought a fine drizzle but it didn't stop Julie from pottering down the garden to see if her daffodils were in bud. She was just straightening up when she caught movement out of the corner of her eye. It was Charley.

'Hiya!' she called out, surprised to see her friend at that time of the morning.

Then Julie's heart flipped when she saw Charley's expression. She just managed to reach her before Charley collapsed sobbing into her arms.

'What is it?' said Julie, drawing her friend inside into the kitchen.

'I'm sorry,' cried Charley. 'I know you only had the funeral yesterday but I didn't know where else to go.'

'Don't worry about it,' said Julie. 'Tell me everything.'

She pressed her lips together and kept quiet whilst Charley poured out her heart.

When she'd finally stopped, Julie asked, 'So what happens now?'

'We've got some kind of interview tomorrow with the Official Receiver.'

'Sounds fun.'

'I've got to get all our paperwork together today.' As she spoke, Charley realised that it had been some years since she had really got involved in the business or even looked at the bills. She had left it all to her husband.

'What about Steve?'

'He disappeared first thing,' she sighed. 'I think he's feeling guilty and can't face me.'

Julie patted her on the arm. 'Typical man. They're just like mascara . . . always running at the first sign of emotion.'

The touch of humour caused Charley to disintegrate into more tears.

'What do I tell everyone?' she sobbed.

'You tell them the truth,' said Julie firmly. 'If they don't want to know you any more then tough luck. They're obviously not true friends.'

Charley nodded. 'You're right. But can you tell Caroline and Samantha for me? I'm having trouble getting any words out at the moment.'

'Of course. Do you want to hang out here for a while? I'll be at work until four but you're welcome to stay here if you need time to think.'

Charley shook her head. 'I'd better head home, in case Steve comes back.'

'Okay. But if you change your mind, just let yourself in.'

'Thanks.'

Julie watched Charley walk away and then called Caroline.

'You're kidding!' she said. 'I had been wondering

how their shops would cope in the recession, though. Obviously not wishing them ill or anything. You know, it happened to one of the mums from the nursery. Came home one day to find the house boarded up and the locks changed. Husband had never told her about their debts, until the bank took the house.'

'So Charley's lucky that she knows what's going on?'

Caroline blew out a sigh. 'Not sure I'd use the word lucky. Look, we'd better warn her to get anything of sentimental value out of there, just in case the same thing happens to them.'

'Good idea,' said Julie. 'She can put any jewellery in my safe.'

'Poor, poor Charley. God, what a mess.'

'Poor being the word,' replied Julie, drily.

She called Samantha next.

'Do you think they'll lose everything?' asked Samantha, shocked.

'Probably.'

'Blimey.' There was a short silence. 'Maybe I could buy some of that designer gear off her. I'm sure she's got some Stella McCartney in her wardrobe. I wonder what her shoe size is?'

Julie was amazed by her friend's reaction. 'I think fashion is the least of her problems.'

'I know that,' said Samantha quickly. 'I was just being practical. I mean, she's gonna need the money. And she's not going to need any cocktail dresses in the foreseeable future, is she?'

'I don't know,' said Julie. 'But don't mention any of this yet, will you? She's pretty cut up about it all.'

''Course not. God, I'm just grateful that we can help

her out in some small way. I mean, it's not like any of us have money problems.'

Julie didn't reply, thinking about the poor state of her own bank account. But her friends didn't need to know about that.

Chapter Six

'Charlotte? Is that you?' shouted her mother down the phone. 'I won't have that thing in this house!'

Charley held the phone away from her ear. Only her family called her 'Charlotte' these days.

'Mum,' she said, staring down at the paperwork in front of her, 'I haven't got time for this at the minute.'

'It's your father and his latest, you know, thing. What are you doing for dinner? Do you and Steve want to come over?'

'I don't think he can spare the time either.'

But her mother wasn't listening. 'I'll do chicken, shall I? See you at six.'

'We really can't,' said Charley, before realising that only the dial tone was listening.

She sank back in the kitchen chair, trying not to tremble. Her mother's phone call had been only one of many that Monday morning. Every other call was someone else wanting to be paid. It was horrifying how much money they owed to so many people.

It was also upsetting how many of them appeared

to know her mobile number and were prepared to use it when they were unable to get hold of her husband.

Charley knew how they felt. She had barely seen Steve since their meeting with the Official Receiver the previous Friday. He had spent the whole weekend in his friend's pub. She could hardly blame him. Yes, because of the personal guarantees that Steve had signed, they would have to sell the house. Unfortunately, they had taken out a second mortgage and some additional loans to cover all the renovation work. Therefore any other assets they owned would also have to be sold.

It was still quite sketchy to her at that point. Charley had nagged Steve to talk through everything with her but he was too drunk every night when he finally came home. And she wasn't going to discuss their personal life in the pub in front of his mates. She knew he was avoiding her out of guilt, but she had countless papers to go through for the Official Receiver and could not answer the innumerable questions without him.

She sent Steve a text message telling him about the invite from her parents for dinner but didn't expect a response. Besides, it was probably best he wasn't around when she told them the very bad news about the state of their finances.

Later that afternoon Charley clambered out of her BMW, shivering in the cold air as she walked up the driveway. Her parents had lived in the same house in Little Grove for over forty years. Little Grove was a small hamlet on the outskirts of the main village, with only a cricket green, farm shop, church and post office to its name.

30

Charley turned her key in the lock and stepped inside.

'Hello,' she called out, dumping her car keys in the pale green bowl on the hall table.

It was a family ritual. Like everything else in the house, the bowl had stood in the same place for decades. Charley and her younger sisters had carried on placing their keys in the green bowl long after they had left home.

'Charlotte?' Her mother came rushing out of the kitchen in a whirlwind of smoke. The air was filled with the smell of something burning in the oven.

Maureen Summers gave her daughter a hug before trying to smooth down a wild tendril that had escaped from Charley's ponytail. But they both knew she was fighting a losing battle. Whereas her mother's dark hair was kept under control by being cut short, Charley's long hair had reverted back to its natural unruly state. She had eked out her last salon blow dry as long as she could, but in the end nature had won.

'You look terrible,' said Maureen, frowning to see her eldest daughter's pale face.

'I'm fine.'

'What's the matter? Where's Steve?'

'Busy at work. He sends his love,' lied Charley. She had received no reply from her text earlier. 'So, what's this about Dad?'

Her mother clutched one hand to her heart. 'It came this morning.' She shuddered and pushed her daughter through the kitchen and towards the back door. 'You've got to talk to him. You know he listens to you.'

Charley stepped out of the house alone, clutching her coat around her for warmth as she walked slowly

31

towards the garage at the end of the garden, which had been converted into a workshop a few years previously. There her father could have a quiet smoke, listen to his old music and potter about undisturbed.

She pulled open the metal door and went inside. 'Hi, Dad.'

Her father looked up from the workbench and smiled. A tall man in his early sixties, his silver hair matched his years but his soft grey eyes retained a youthful twinkle. Retired for over a year, his days were now divided between gardening, fishing, and the cause of his wife's despair.

He came over to give his daughter a hug. 'Hello, love. You look tired.'

'I'm fine.'

Charley's eyes moved across the table to the glass case he had been working on. Next to it stood an immobile grey squirrel which was poised in the act of eating a peanut.

'Just finished him last week,' said her father, following her gaze. 'Isn't he terrific?'

'Great,' said Charley faintly.

Taxidermy. The loss of their family cat had started all the trouble eight years ago. Her father had done a bit of investigating and poor old Marmalade hadn't been given the chance of a decent burial in a flowerbed. Instead, she was stuffed and put on show. Now she held pride of place on the opposite wall, curled up on a red cushion.

His collection of immobile friends had grown ever since. Rabbits, squirrels and fish now adorned the walls next to Marmalade. His wife confined her displeasure at his hobby to pursed lips and maintaining a distance from the workshop.

Charley found her eyes magnetically drawn to a large crate standing near the door.

'Ah, come to see what the fuss is about, eh?' Her dad went over to the wooden box and lifted the lid. 'What do you think?'

She peered cautiously inside.

'My first badger,' he said proudly. 'And look at the size of it!'

Still lost for words, Charley took a step backwards.

'Dinner's ready!' came a shout from the top of the garden.

A dozen pairs of glassy eyes watched them head back into the twilight of a cold February afternoon.

'The chicken's been in the oven for hours,' muttered her father in a low tone. 'Don't say I didn't warn you.'

It wasn't that her mother was a bad cook – she was a terrible cook. Charley had grown up believing that food was merely fuel for the body and certainly not to be enjoyed or lingered over. But once she had begun taking cookery lessons at school, a miracle had happened. Suddenly food tasted fresh and full of flavour. Each recipe she followed turned out perfectly. Her mother's culinary genes had, thankfully, skipped a generation.

As she grew older, she began to find individual ingredients interesting. Spices and herbs fascinated her and she sampled as many different foods as she could lay her hands on. Gradually, she stopped following recipes to the exact letter. Instead she used her own instincts and loved to experiment.

The march of time hadn't improved her mother's cooking skills but at least the supermarket ready-meals had become more edible. Unfortunately, Maureen always tried to make an extra effort whenever the family visited. Thankfully misery loves company and Aunty Peggy had joined them for dinner, which was a welcome distraction from the food.

Aunty Peggy wasn't a relation but Maureen's best friend who lived just around the corner. Now they were both retired, their days were spent in a whirlwind of bazaars, jumble sales and WI meetings.

Charley and her father sat down at the dining-room table, struggling with the inedible food on their plates whilst her mother and Aunty Peggy caught up on the latest gossip.

'Ethel Mitford was up at the hospital again yesterday,' said Maureen. 'Visiting the sick, apparently.'

'If they weren't feeling bad before, they'd have felt a lot worse once she arrived.' Aunty Peggy speared a rock-hard potato with her fork. Maureen's food never appeared to trouble Peggy's constitution. Perhaps her stout body was immune to it after so many years of close friendship.

'I told you that Dukan diet was bad for the breath,' replied Maureen. 'Don't you think she looks terrible? Our Charlotte, I mean.'

'It's not morning sickness, is it?' said Aunty Peggy.

Maureen's face lit up. 'Is it?'

Charley gulped back a tear. 'No, Mum. I'm not pregnant.'

She had been desperately putting off telling her parents about the bankruptcy but knew the time had come.

'But I do have some news.'

Her parents glanced at each other, raising their eyebrows.

'Unfortunately it's not good news,' added Charley.

Maureen's face dropped back into a worried frown.

'It seems the business hasn't been going so well,' began Charley.

Three faces stared back at her in silence.

Charley took a deep breath. 'In fact, we're not doing very well at all. We are, actually, erm . . . well, we're bankrupt.'

She exhaled a long breath as her parents and Peggy stared back at her, their eyes widening.

'But we'll be fine,' she quickly added. 'Really, we will. So don't worry.'

She gave everyone her bravest smile. Perhaps she would mention a small loan at a later stage.

Charley had expected many reactions to her words. Tears, hugs, words of worry and concern. But the reaction she hadn't expected was anger. And it wasn't even directed at Steve or herself.

She watched as her mother spun round to glare at her father. 'You idiot!'

The ferocity of Maureen's anger was shocking to her daughter.

Aunty Peggy was shaking her head. 'Terrible it is, how your own family can take advantage. And now what do you do? Cancel that cruise, I suppose. Still, I hear the buffets aren't what they used to be. Sheila Morris said they were rationed to three profiteroles each at suppertime.'

Charley was baffled. 'Why have you got to cancel your holiday?' she said, turning to look at her parents. 'I'm the one that's bankrupt, not you.'

But Maureen was still staring at her husband who was glugging down his glass of red wine in order to avoid her glare. Finally, he put down his glass. 'It just makes things a bit tight for us, that's all,' he told his daughter.

'A bit tight!' snorted Maureen. 'Forty thousand pounds gone! Our life savings! All without any discussion with your wife because you know I would have said no!'

Charley stared at them, trying desperately to follow the conversation.

'We won't get it back,' carried on her mother. 'Not now they're bankrupt. I knew it was a bad idea. Knew it wouldn't turn out well. So now we're stuck with nothing to live on but our state pensions, and they're worthless.'

'Let's not discuss it now,' muttered her father.

'She's got to know sooner or later,' replied her mother, standing up. 'You kept it secret long enough from both of us.'

Aunty Peggy also stood up and put her arm around Maureen as they walked out of the room. Charley just managed to catch her mother's words before they left.

'I knew it was a bad idea the minute he told me. We're broke, Peg. There's nothing left . . .'

Still sitting at the table, Charley's mind felt ready to explode.

'What's going on? What's Mum talking about?' she asked.

'She's just mad because I didn't tell her.'

'Tell her what?'

Charley's father stared down into his empty glass. 'He came to me a few months ago. Said business was tight and could I help him out? He said he would pay us back with interest. A bit of extra money for our

36

retirement.' He looked up into his daughter's eyes. 'He said it was for both your sakes.'

'Who said . . . ?' But Charley knew the answer before he spoke.

'Steve. I lent £40,000 to Steve.'

Chapter Seven

Charley slammed the front door behind her and rushed from room to room in search of her husband.

'Steve!' she yelled.

She could hear movement upstairs so took the stairs two at a time and sprinted towards their en-suite bathroom.

Steve was in the large walk-in shower. She flung the door open so quickly that it almost smacked her in the face.

'Jesus!' he swore, spinning around. 'I thought you were an axe murderer or something.'

'Well, I'm sure as hell ready to kill you,' spat Charley. 'You took money from my parents without telling me!'

'Oh. That,' said Steve, switching off the taps.

'Yes, that! Forty grand! Do you know what that kind of money means to them?'

He pushed past her to grab a towel from the heated rail. 'They'll be okay. They must have paid their mortgage off by now.'

'So?' Charley was shocked by how little he appeared

to care. 'What are they supposed to live on until you can pay them back?'

'I can't pay them back, can I? We're bankrupt, remember?'

'How could I bloody forget?' she shouted into his face.

'Calm down, would you?' said Steve. 'I'll think of something.'

As Charley stood there, incensed, she heard the front doorbell ring and turned around, slamming the bathroom door behind her.

She stomped down the stairs and away from her husband before she could strangle him with his soap on a rope. Perhaps that was why they were so popular. Perhaps they were the last resort of desperate wives looking to kill their husbands. 'The rope got caught around the shower rail, your honour, and he slipped.'

She flung open the door. 'What?' she snapped.

A pair of men held up some ID cards in front of her. 'Mrs Mills?' one of them asked.

'Yes.'

'We're from Blake Collections.'

Suddenly fearful, Charley took a small step backwards.

'We're acting on behalf of Rose Motors,' said the other man. 'Here's our warrant.'

A piece of paper was put in front of her face. It appeared authentic, with official court stamps and signatures.

'I don't understand,' she said.

'You owe too much money on your car,' said the larger man, giving her a pitying smile. 'We're here to take it away.'

Charley glanced across at her BMW convertible. It

had been a present from Steve the previous summer. She couldn't park the damn thing, but it sure looked good driving around the village. She had never thought about how he had paid for it until that moment.

'It's got to go?' she asked. 'Tonight?'

The man nodded. 'Unless you've got thirty grand on you.'

She tried to laugh but it stuck in her throat. 'No, I'm pretty certain I haven't.'

In a daze, she went in search of her handbag and found the car keys.

'Do I have to sign anything?' she asked, handing them over.

'Here,' said the man, holding out an official form. 'And here.'

She scribbled her signature on the paper.

The man ripped off the top carbon sheet. 'Here's your copy.'

The piece of yellow paper rustled as a cold wind swept up the driveway.

'Do you want anything out of the car?' asked one of the bailiffs.

She found she could barely take it all in. 'I don't know.'

'Why don't you come with us and check?'

Charley followed them over to her car. She removed the iPod from the dashboard and scooped up a couple of coins that were lurking in the centre console, but that was it.

She stared down the driveway, watching her car being driven away. When she could no longer hear the engine, she turned and headed towards the front door, still clutching the form and her iPod.

How were she and Steve going to cope with only one car between them? And what if his car was repossessed as well? How would she get to the supermarket to buy food? Even more pressing a thought was what would she use to pay for it? Their current accounts had been frozen by the bank. She only had the cash in her purse and that was dwindling fast.

Steve was standing at the bottom of the stairs when she went back into the hallway.

'Who was that?' he asked, fastening the belt on his jeans.

'They were bailiffs,' she told him. 'They've taken the BMW.'

'Bloody hell,' he swore, picking up his car keys from the table. 'I'm going to the pub. If anyone comes here looking for my Mercedes, tell them you've never heard of me.'

'The pub? Again?' she said.

He shrugged his shoulders. 'No point sitting around here, feeling miserable.'

Charley watched him leave, wishing, despite their earlier row, that he had asked her to go with him. Not that she really wanted to go out. She wasn't in the mood for chatting and laughing with his mates at the moment. She was surprised that Steve was. But it would have been nice to spend a bit of time with him, not to be alone again.

Chapter Eight

Samantha suppressed a smirk as she stared at Miranda's pear-shaped hips. What on earth made her think she could pull off a tight pencil skirt? And nobody over the age of twenty-five could really get away with a pussy-bow blouse. She looked like she was channelling Margaret Thatcher.

Samantha got up from her desk to fetch herself a coffee, grabbing her mobile as she went. She glanced at her own reflection as she headed down the corridor but already knew that her chocolate-coloured shift dress looked good. With black high heels adding a good couple of inches to her legs, she could feel the admiring glance of one of the marketing managers on her as she walked by.

She went into the kitchen and pressed the button on the vending machine for a cappuccino. Her phone rang while she waited for her drink.

It was Charley.

'How's it going?' asked Samantha.

Charley sighed. 'Not so good. The bailiffs took my car last night.'

'My God!' Samantha was shocked. She had always been envious of Charley's BMW and couldn't believe it was gone. 'Are you all right?'

'I suppose.' But Charley's tone wasn't convincing.

'Can I do anything to help?'

'Actually,' said Charley, 'I was wondering if you could take me to the supermarket after work? I need to get a few things and I daren't tell my mum yet. If she hears about the car, she's gonna really freak out.'

'I'd love to,' began Samantha, 'but I've got to stay on tonight for a meeting. They're saying it's going to run late.'

'Oh. Well, not to worry. I'll see if Caroline's about.'

'Sorry,' said Samantha. 'I'll give you a ring over the weekend, yeah?'

She did feel a pang of guilt. The truth was that there was no meeting: Samantha had a whole evening of pampering planned. She knew if she had seen Charley, they would have ended up having a bottle of wine and chatting all night. Then she would have lost her 'me' time.

She would help her friend out later on. Charley had a husband to support her through the bad times. Samantha was still single at the age of twenty-nine.

Mind you, she was hoping the office party in a few weeks would change all that.

Caroline held the phone under her ear as she opened the post.

'Yes, of course I can take you,' she told Charley. 'How about eleven o'clock? See you later.'

As she focussed on the letter she had just opened, her mobile slipped on to the floor. But Caroline didn't

43

pick it up. She was too busy staring at the piece of paper in horror.

For nearly five years she had held on to one dream: sending her daughter to private school. Not that there was anything wrong with the local primary school, but Grove School for Girls was perfect for Flora. It was a vibrant prep school on the outskirts of the village that encouraged each girl to 'find their special gift'. Money meant quality, and Flora was going to have the best education money could buy.

She was going to look so cute in her royal blue pinafore dress, blazer and boater. Even the duffel coat with its school crest made her look adorable. Caroline had been so excited, thinking of that first day at school.

But beautiful royal blue blazers with cream piping came at a price. A hefty one. She and Jeff had discussed the £3,000 per term fees and had decided that they could manage to afford them on his salary. Jeff earned a very good wage in the banking sector of the City and hadn't yet reached his full earning potential. Of course, that had meant a few sacrifices along the way. Camping holidays in France, rather than villas in Tuscany. An updated car, but not with all the top of the range gadgets. Designer shoes that were now a couple of years old. But they were all sacrifices that Caroline had been willing to make.

She took a deep breath and glanced back at the piece of paper in her hand. It was a bright and friendly letter from the school, listing the add-on requirements for the year beginning in September. Requirements that she hadn't even considered.

Caroline had had no idea all the extras would amount to so much. The uniform had already totalled £500. In addition, it appeared they now needed to find the money for music lessons, after school clubs, lunches, book bag, trips and the school bus . . . totalling over £800 per term. And the school was very politely asking for the money by the end of June.

As she bent down to pick up her mobile, Caroline decided that she couldn't talk to Jeff about it. He was already stressed as it was thanks to the financial crisis engulfing the banking sector, spending extra long hours at the office.

She would just have to find the money herself, that was all. She would continue to scrimp and save. A little here, a little shaved off the housekeeping there. Jeff wouldn't even know.

After all, it wasn't as if they were in the same situation as poor Charley. Caroline shook her head, sad for her friend. The least she could do was give her a lift to the supermarket.

She tucked the letter deep into her handbag. It would be her little secret. Everyone else had bigger problems to deal with. Hers were a drop in the ocean.

Julie finished work at six o'clock and drove home, weary after a long hard day. She hadn't slept properly since the funeral and the overcast days didn't help her feel any brighter. She hated February and was glad there were only a couple more days of it to go until March. That meant spring was on the way and she might finally get out into the garden.

In an unusual display of self-indulgence, Julie had placed an order for a rare peony, via a specialist website, the previous evening. The flower had won many awards for its rich ruby-red double petals. Fifty pounds was a hugely extravagant price, but Julie knew it would be worth every penny.

Once home, she let herself in the front door and switched on the hall light. She picked up the post from the doormat, giving the envelopes a cursory glance as she went into the kitchen. It was mostly junk, but one envelope stood out. She opened it to find a letter from the bank. The interest rate on her mortgage was being increased. She would have to find an extra £75 per month.

Julie dropped the letter on the kitchen table and went to find something to eat in the freezer. But she had lost her appetite.

One mortgage she could cope with, but the second mortgage was hitting her purse hard. She had remortgaged the house a year ago to help Nick out of a financial hole. He was desperate to gain his independence and, once he had found a job at the local DIY superstore, Julie had indulged him with the money for a deposit on a flat and some furniture. He had also needed a more reliable car, which she had paid for. A few weeks later he had walked out of the job, telling his mother that the manager was an idiot.

Julie kept extending the loan further and further, until she was struggling to cover the cost of both mortgages each month. She had worked on an IT hotline for Mason & Mason, a large local firm, for almost ten years, resolving technical abnormalities on a large database. She wasn't sure how she had managed to become a database administrator but it was a decent enough wage. Until she had overstretched herself for her son's sake.

But it wasn't as if she hadn't known financial difficulties before. She could still remember how, as a small child, she'd watched her mother cowering in a corner while a couple of burly men took away the rental television because of unpaid bills.

The thought of her mother brought a lump to Julie's throat. Keeping busy was her default way of coping with grief. She had already cleared her mother's small council flat; hadn't kept much apart from jewellery and the odd ornament. Work helped as well, she found. But whilst winter dragged its heels, she was unable to lose herself in her beloved garden.

The thought of it brought a feeling of fresh guilt upon her. She glanced again at the letter from the bank. Paying £50 for a peony was beginning to look very extravagant. She wondered if it was too late to cancel the order.

Chapter Nine

'Why the hell isn't there any hot water?' yelled Steve, as he came into the bedroom wearing nothing but a towel. 'The shower is freezing!'

Charley rolled her eyes. 'I've switched off the hot water and heating,' she explained to him in a tight voice, 'because there isn't any money to pay the bills.'

You would know this if you were ever here, she almost added.

'This is ridiculous,' he snapped, quickly getting dressed. 'It's five degrees out there.'

'So? Wear a jumper,' retorted Charley, before walking out of the room and down the stairs.

She refused to start the day with yet another row but his whingeing was beginning to grate on her. March had already arrived yet still he didn't seem to understand what bankruptcy was going to mean to them. He seemed only to have accepted that the house was going to be sold when the For Sale sign went up a few days earlier. Most of their furniture and house-hold items would have to be handed over to official bailiffs. Their bank account was frozen indefinitely. They might be able to open a new one in the future, but most banks would be giving them a wide berth for years to come.

A lack of hot water was the least of their problems. In fact, Charley was nipping over to Julie's house each day for a lovely hot shower but she wasn't going to let on to Steve. In her eyes, he didn't deserve it. He needed to be punished.

Deep in her heart, Charley knew it wasn't all his fault. She should have taken more interest in the business, then perhaps things wouldn't have got so out of control. She could have intervened, made a difference somehow. But it was too late for that. Nothing was salvageable from this mess. It was about survival now.

She felt sure they would make it through this rocky patch and carry on as before with their marriage. But it didn't stop her being cross with him, especially when he was still ducking out of the house each day to mess about with his mates. The atmosphere between the two of them was extremely tense, and she was secretly grateful that he went out most days. She had even stopped asking exactly where it was he went.

So she was home alone when the satellite man arrived to disconnect their cable system and broadband. He had only just left in his van when two more men arrived to take the large leather sofas back to the furniture store. The dishwasher disappeared the next day, swiftly followed by the tumble dryer.

With every knock on the door she was faced with more people and their forms. These were official, certified bailiffs, acting on behalf of the people from whom Charley and Steve had bought or leased things for their house. The men were polite, just doing their job.

49

She always tried to offer them a cup of tea before they took another part of her home away in their vans.

She didn't cry though. Not until they had left.

The enforcement agents arrived next, looking for anything else of monetary value. There being no cash or bank accounts left to plunder, they began to take goods that could be sold at public auction.

Room by room, day by day, Charley's home was gradually being dismantled. As she watched it all being carried out of the house, she felt ashamed at the amount of money they had squandered over the years. Did they really need four flat-screen televisions when only two people lived in the house? An iPod docking station in most of the rooms? Every conceivable games console? Two computers, a scanner, laptop and a couple of iPads?

Thankfully, Caroline had reminded her to copy their most important files on to memory sticks before all the computer equipment was taken away. Charley had begun to move irreplaceable items to her parents' house for safe-keeping. Unfortunately, this meant running into her family, all of whom she was trying to avoid as the nagging had become incessant.

'You've left Mum and Dad up to their necks in it,' said Victoria, her younger sister. 'They're so upset,' added Elizabeth, the other twin.

'I know!' Charley told them, slumping on to the sofa. 'I've apologised, haven't I?'

'They can't live on apologies, can they?' said Victoria, scowling across at her from her position in the armchair.

'I don't understand where all the money went,' said Elizabeth. 'You were loaded.'

Charley thought about her empty house but said nothing.

'And where's Steve this afternoon?' snapped Victoria. 'He's busy.'

Charley glanced at the clock on the mantelpiece and wondered how quickly she could excuse herself from this interrogation.

Maureen brought in some tea plates and placed them on the coffee table. The imminent arrival of a home-made cake made everyone pause for thought. But not for long.

'What's more important than his wife's family?' said Victoria.

Her husband Adam shot her a look. 'Leave it,' he said, in a quiet tone.

Victoria ignored him. 'I just don't understand why Steve wants to be by himself at the moment. He's still married to you, isn't he? You should be getting through this together.'

Luckily Maureen had to dash back into the kitchen to sort out the cake so Charley made her excuses and followed suit.

'Want a hand, Mum?'

'No, thank you, darling.' Maureen ripped off some pieces of kitchen roll to use as napkins. 'So? Where is Steve?'

Charley gave a theatrical sigh. 'He's trying to get our lives back in order.'

'And then you'll sort out things between you?'

'Yes.'

Maureen raised her eyebrows. 'So you might have time to see about giving me some more grandchildren soon.'

'Aren't two enough?'

'There's no need to feel jealous of your sister. You've still got a few childbearing years left in you.'

Charley glanced at her watch. 'I've got to go soon.'

'Have you had your tubes checked?'

'Mum! Can we focus on one thing a time?'

'I just thought it might be a bit of good news. Lord knows we could do with some.'

Charley gulped back her own tears as she watched her mother's eyes fill. She stepped forward and was enveloped in a hug.

'I'm sorry,' she said, snuffling into Maureen's shoulder.

'I know.'

'And we will repay you. I don't know how long it'll take but we'll get there, I promise.'

Her mother smiled but didn't reply, instead picking up the barely risen chocolate cake and leaving the kitchen.

Charley knew her mother didn't really believe her. That the whole family was expecting her to fail in her promises. But she was determined that every penny would be returned to her parents. She just didn't know as yet how it could be done.

Chapter Ten

By the middle of March, the ground floor of the house was bare. From the lounge, nearly everything had been taken, including the TV, sofas, chairs, glass coffee table, fancy artwork, crystal vases, mirrors, and other pretty things she had picked up over the years. Charley had kept all the photographs, but had to relinquish their expensive silver frames.

The study was now missing its desk, chair, bookcase and all the computer equipment. The den had been stripped of its games consoles, leather chairs and huge television. Even the hallway had lost its table, mirror and hat stand.

The Wednesday night dinners with the girls had slipped whilst Charley's life disintegrated. But as soon as the Sold sign went up outside, she insisted they came to her home. It was left unspoken, but this was probably the last time they would meet there.

The oak table and chairs in the kitchen were now missing so Julie suggested having a picnic indoors. Caroline brought some rugs and cushions to sit on.

'I can't believe they even took the microwave,' said Samantha in disbelief. She lived on healthy ready-meals.

Charley nodded. 'The double fridge-freezer went today as well.'

The only appliance in which they could now keep food cold was the wine cooler because that was built into the kitchen cupboards. Steve had drunk his way through most of the contents, so there was room for the ever decreasing food supply.

The girls had brought a mixture of cold meats, quiches and salads with them. They all felt a little sad when they saw the boxes of home-made ice-creams defrosting on the counter.

'It would have been a shame to let this lot go to waste,' said Julie, licking the dark chocolate from her spoon.

'This praline's fantastic,' said Samantha, before putting down her bowl. 'But I mustn't eat any more. That new bodycon dress I bought for the office party is pretty unforgiving.'

Charley stared down at Samantha's perfectly mani-cured fingernails before glancing at her own. She had already lost four false nails that week. She would have to get rid of the others soon. It looked ridiculous.

She felt sick at the thought of her ice-cream and couldn't bear to taste it. She hadn't cared about the dishwasher or all the silly televisions. But losing her ice-cream was heartbreaking. That was real. Making it was possibly the only real talent she possessed. She had no appetite.

'Where's Steve?' asked Caroline.

'Out.' Charley shrugged her shoulders. 'He's always out these days. Bankruptcy does not make for a happy marriage.'

'It's just all a bit stressful at the minute,' said Julie. 'Once everything's calmed down, you two will be all right.'

'How soon do you think you'll have to move out?' asked Caroline.

'About a month, I think.' Charley looked around the room. 'Not that there'll be much to take with us.'

'They won't take all your clothes, will they?' Samantha felt horrified as she thought of Charley's fabulous shoe collection.

She shook her head. 'We're allowed to keep clothing, bedding, a bed and important kitchen stuff like the kettle and plates. Beyond that, it's all up for grabs.'

The front doorbell rang and didn't stop. They all looked at her. Someone was leaning on the bell.

Charley stood up.

'It's gone eight o'clock,' said Julie, tutting.

Bailiffs were only supposed to visit between dawn and dusk. It was dark when Charley opened the front door.

'Steve Mills live here?'

These men were different. They weren't the sort of people she had become used to dealing with. These were hard men dressed in black. These men were more certifiable than official.

Charley nodded, too terrified to speak.

'He owes us three grand,' said the larger of the men, pushing past her into the hall.

Charley meekly followed as they peered into each room.

'I see we're not the first,' said the other man. 'What's left?'

They went into the kitchen, ignoring the women sitting on the floor. Charley opened up one of the cupboards, where she had kept some appliances ready for the next visit from the bailiffs. The men took a smoothie maker, cappuccino machine, juice extractor, bread maker and food processor.

Before leaving, one of them did a last scout around the kitchen and picked up the Gaggia ice-cream maker.

'B-But . . .' Charley stammered, before her voice trailed off.

What was the use? She didn't even have a freezer any more.

The men slammed the front door behind them. Charley disintegrated into tears.

'It's all right,' said Caroline, giving her a hug. 'You'll get through this.'

'Who the hell wants to bake their own bread anyway?' said Julie, raising a small smile from everyone.

'You'd better hide your shoe collection, though,' said Samantha. 'You don't want all those lovely Gina heels disappearing out the door.'

Julie glared at Samantha. Who cared about shoes at a time like this?

Charley was still trying to rein in her tears.

'So what now?' asked Caroline, gently.

Charley sniffed. 'I'm going to try and get a job. Though God knows, the employment market isn't exactly buzzing at the minute.'

'Perhaps you could try some of the shops on the high street,' said Julie. 'You've got experience from working in Steve's all those years ago.'

Charley smiled, but shook her head. 'Already tried. Nobody's taking on any more staff.'

It had been one of the most humiliating days of her life when she had walked into each of her favourite shops and asked about employment. After all, previously she had spent most of her time in these places, buying glittering tea lights, retro storage boxes and cute cushions. So much money wasted on such fripperies. If only she had saved, instead of squandered, her money. If only she had put a bit of cash aside for a rainy day. If only she hadn't been so stupid, she told herself. So greedy. So spoilt.

Hindsight would have been Charley's preferred superpower of choice at the moment.

She gave them a small smile through her tears. 'But Aunty Peggy knows someone who is taking on new staff.'

Her friends stared expectantly at her, even a little excited.

'It's a cleaning job.'

'A what?' said Samantha, beginning to laugh before swiftly turning it into a cough.

'I need a job,' said Charley. 'And it's cash in hand.'

'Cleaning houses?' prompted Caroline.

Charley nodded.

'Well, you've always kept your home lovely,' said Caroline brightly.

'Absolutely,' said Julie, nodding frantically.

But Samantha couldn't keep her horror hidden. 'I think we'd better open this other bottle of wine, don't you?' she said.

Chapter Eleven

Charley woke up with a throbbing headache. She blamed the bottle of wine that she had finished drinking by herself after the girls had left.

She also blamed it for the massive row she'd had with Steve when he finally came home, equally drunk. To her surprise, he had gone off in a strop and slept in the spare bedroom. She was less surprised to find the house empty when she woke up late in the morning. Now she needed to struggle up and get dressed, because she had a job interview.

She had hoped that Steve would give her a lift but there was no reply to her apoplectic text message, so she gave up and began the long walk to her parents' house to pick up a car which Aunty Peggy was lending her.

Seeing her parents filled Charley with guilt once more. But a new job would certainly help in repaying them and so would a car. Besides, a car meant freedom, a touch of normality in this bizarre new world in which she suddenly found herself.

She glanced at Julie's house as she walked past. To her utmost inner shame, she had always looked down her nose at it. Secretly she could not believe that Julie had never wanted to smarten up the place. Now she was beginning to realise that perhaps Julie had never had enough money. Perhaps living within her means was what mattered to her and, after all, it was Charley's house with the Sold sign outside, not Julie's.

A steady drizzle began, compounding Charley's misery. Pounding the pavements in frustration, she eventually found herself walking up the driveway towards her parents' front door. But her path was blocked by a small car. Charley's mouth dropped open at the sight of it. It looked like the survivor of a demolition derby masquerading as a blue Mini. But the numerous dents had obviously not stopped it from being roadworthy as Aunty Peggy had told her that it was taxed and with an MOT for the next ten months.

Charley gave the vehicle a wide berth before letting herself into her parents' house. But all was quiet. A note told her that they had gone food shopping and that the keys to the Mini were, of course, in the green bowl on the hall table. With a heavy heart, Charley realised it wasn't some cosmic mistake. The car outside was her only means of transport – temporarily, she prayed.

Back outside, she walked slowly around the battered car before putting the key in the driver's door. No remote locking. No smart leather upholstery, she thought, as she gingerly sat down on the heavily stained beige velour seat. She swiftly wound down a window to bring some much needed fresh air to the stale interior. Then she remained seated, wondering what she had possibly done in a former life to deserve such misery in her current one.

She was still sitting there a couple of minutes later when her parents drew up.

'Oh, good,' said her mother, getting out of her car and waving. 'You found the keys.'

Charley nodded dumbly in response, watching Maureen pick up a couple of Lidl bags. That was new too, she realised. They had always shopped at Waitrose before.

Her father headed over to the Mini, sucking on the pipe he had just retrieved from his shirt pocket.

'It's not as bad as it looks, apparently.' He tried not to smirk as he leant in through the open window.

'Nothing is as bad as this car looks,' muttered Charley.

'Lord knows what Peggy's nephew did with it whilst he was at university. She says you can have it as long as you want. He's on a gap year travelling around South America.'

Charley knew she had no choice. There was no point being snobbish about these things. It was a car, wasn't it? Her parents were shopping in Lidl, for God's sake. She owed them £40,000. She was about to be interviewed as a cleaner. It was time to get over herself.

She turned the key in the ignition and the car spluttered into life. With her parents calling out good luck, Charley found first gear and proceeded to bunny-hop down the driveway. The car gave a shudder every minute or so, accompanied by a questionable knocking sound. But at least it would get her as far as her interview without breaking down. Or at least she hoped so.

Peggy's friend Patricia, the head of the cleaning

business, had sounded terribly posh when Charley called her. She wasn't sure how Aunty Peggy had come to mix in those kind of circles.

Patricia lived in a detached cottage on the outskirts of Little Grove, with a beautiful country garden at the front. The cleaning business was obviously flourishing.

'Do come in,' she said, in a cut-glass accent.

Patricia Chalcot was a stout woman in her early fifties. She was wearing a blue silk blouse, matching pencil skirt and court shoes. She led Charley into the lounge, which was all floral fabrics and sparkling white net curtains.

'So, my dear.' Patricia gestured for her to sit down. 'You want to join my team of happy cleaners?'

Charley managed a fake smile. 'Yes, I do.'

No, I don't, she wanted to shout. I want to run away from here as fast as I possibly can.

'Well, you look smart enough. All my girls must be trustworthy, reliable and neat. I won't have untidy cleaners. A messy cleaner is a reflection on Grove Cleaners, which is a reflection on me.'

'I understand.'

'My customers want to come home at the end of their working day to a spotless home. My girls see to it that their dream comes true.'

Charley had thought that the job only required her to dust and clean.

'As a rule, my customers require a weekly service. Normally either a whole morning or afternoon. It can take up to four hours to achieve the dream look.'

The telephone rang.

'Grove Cleaners. Patricia Chalcot speaking. Yes, Mrs Palmer. I saw your application. How are you?

Wonderful. Well, you're in luck, my dear. I have a lovely girl called Charlotte who will be available to start attending to your home next week.'

Charley's eyebrows shot up. This was all going a bit too fast. She hadn't even agreed to take the job yet.

'Nine o'clock sharp on Thursday,' carried on Patricia. 'Super. So nice to talk to you again. Goodbye.' She put down the phone and turned back to Charley. 'Your first customer.'

'Really?'

The phone rang again.

'Gosh, it's busy today.' Patricia picked up the phone. 'Grove Cleaners, how may I help you? . . . I beg your pardon? . . . Fanny, is that you? Calm down, dear.'

She rolled her eyes and sighed in an exaggerated manner.

'I can't understand you. Stop shouting. Fanny . . . can you hear me?'

Then Patricia lost her temper.

'Fanny! What the bleeding 'ell is going on there?' All traces of the cut-glass accent had gone. In its place was pure cockney. 'Well, what do you want *me* to do about it? Empty the bloody Hoover bag, you silly mare! If the blasted guinea pig's not in there, then you're in the clear. If it is, nip down the pet shop and get another. What? I dunno. A tenner? No, of course I'm not going to pay for it. You Hoover up the family pet, *you* bloody pay for it!'

Patricia slammed down the phone and turned back to face Charley.

'These bloody girls! Some of them are so thick . . .' She caught Charley's wide-eyed stare. 'The customers like the posh accent, sweetheart. Makes them think they're not going to get some deadbeat like Fanny cleaning their homes. So, whaddya think? You game for this cleaning lark or what?'

That was it. Interview over. Charley had a job.

Chapter Twelve

'No wife of mine is going to be a bloody cleaner!' shouted Steve.

'For God's sake!' screamed Charley. 'I will not have this row over and over with you. It's a job!' She put her hands on her hips and scowled at her husband. 'Which is more than you've got at the minute.'

He stomped out of the lounge, leaving Charley to finish packing the box in front of her. She had stuck a few photographs on the walls to keep up the impression of normality but with the house now almost devoid of furniture, they looked ridiculous. She plucked the last of the photographs down from the wall and stared at the picture of a happy couple getting married. Steve was looking uncomfortable in his suit; Charley was swamped by a meringue of cheap ivory silk. But they were grinning like idiots, young and in love.

It had been a happy day, if perhaps a little soon after the beginning of their relationship. If you could call six months of sex in the back of his Fiat a relationship.

At the age of eighteen, Steve still lived with his

tyrant of a mother. She was a scary religious nut who went even nuttier when he'd told her that Charley had accidentally become pregnant. One row followed another. By the time she miscarried at eleven weeks, the church had been booked and there was no going back. So they said their vows and got married.

Steve's meteoric rise in the local fashion trade took them both by surprise. On the advice of a mate, he had borrowed some money from the bank and set up a small shop selling knock-off clothing. By some kind of miracle, the clothes were popular and people started to come into the shop in droves. The bottom had begun to drop out of the housing market and customers were looking for cheap ways of staying fashionable.

In those days Charley helped out in the shop at the weekends and it had been fun . . . certainly different from the boring office work she was used to. Steve made all the business deals and she worked the till. Then they had become ambitious and decided to open a second shop. She gratefully gave up her office job as the money began to roll in. Two more shops were added to their empire in as many years.

But when had their ambition turned to greed? Was that when it had all begun to slip away from them? Now they had nothing, she thought as she dropped the last photograph into the box. Nothing but each other. They were back to where they had started.

She carried the box into the kitchen and set it on the floor, next to the counter top. Glancing at the clock on the oven, she realised it was time to leave for her first cleaning job. Patricia had told her that it would take a week or so to build up to a full complement of customers but had already arranged a three-hour clean for that Monday morning.

Charley found herself unexpectedly grateful. The money would give her a chance to top the car up with petrol, and the work would get her out of the house, away from Steve and the risk of yet another row.

The customer lived down a country lane beyond the green in Little Grove. It was a small farmhouse with a stable block tagged on to one side. A large pond curved around the front and one side of the house. It was a beautiful setting with rabbits on the grass, ducks by the pond and birdsong filling the air.

Walking up to the front door, Charley was suddenly wracked with nerves. She had no idea why. It wasn't going to be rocket science. She had cleaned her own home, hadn't she? She took a deep breath. She would just get on with the job, take the money and get the hell out of there. How difficult could it be?

Brushing off her anxiety, she rapped firmly on the front door knocker. A cacophony of barking exploded from inside the house and Charley took a step backwards. She heard the sound of a woman shouting amongst all the woofing and yapping. Gradually, the noise became muted before the front door was opened.

'Are you the cleaner?' boomed the middle-aged woman standing in the doorway.

'Yes. Hello, I'm Charlotte.'

The customer introduced herself as Miss Fuller and went back into the dark hallway.

'Dogs are going mad for their walk,' she said over her shoulder. 'Never had a cleaner before.'

Despite the idyllic setting, the house was a mess of paperwork, boxes, dog baskets and general untidiness. It wasn't filthy but it wasn't pristine either. And the smell of dog was definitely in the air.

'Blasted landlord has told me that I've got to keep

the place tip-top. Can't possibly move away at the minute. I've only just planted a new lot of potatoes.'

Charley glanced out of the window and spotted four dogs tearing around the garden.

Miss Fuller threw open the back door. 'Leave those cabbages alone!' she roared.

She slammed the back door shut and led Charley on a tour. Front room, dining room, utility room, a couple of bedrooms which were mostly used for storage. And a grim bathroom which hadn't seen a drop of bleach for decades.

By now, Charley was seriously worried. She had only been allocated three hours. This house looked as if it needed three years spent on it.

Back in the kitchen, Miss Fuller told her all the cleaning materials were under the sink. 'Hoover's in the hall cupboard. We're off for our walk. Should be back in an hour. Just start wherever you like.'

She left through the back door, calling the dogs as she went. 'Herbert! Mozart! Come on, you lot! Desmond, I told you to get away from my cabbages!'

Charley watched them recede out of sight and then turned to face the inside of the house. It was weird being alone in a stranger's home. She felt unnerved, as if she were an intruder.

With a sigh, she opened up the sink cupboard, grabbed a duster and some furniture polish and made her way to the front room. An hour later, she had dusted, scrubbed and cleaned as much as she could downstairs and was already exhausted.

She trudged her way upstairs to the bathroom. Grimacing, she squirted cleaner around the dark rim inside the bath and stood well back to avoid the toxic aroma of bleach and chemicals. Then she scrubbed at the places where the chemicals had done their job, giving the bath a streaked effect. She was running out of time, with the bedrooms and vacuuming still to do. She would just have to get the bits she'd missed the following week, and hope Miss Fuller wouldn't notice.

Charley heard the back door slam and some movement in the kitchen.

'Want a cup of tea?' came a holler.

'Yes, please,' she shouted back, hoping the offer was for her.

Next she heard the sound of scrabbling paws on the tiles in the hallway, followed by pounding on the carpeted stairs. Something was coming for her and there was nowhere to hide. Charley drew herself up to her full height and braced herself.

A blur of yellow labrador rushed around the corner into the bathroom and leapt into her arms, knocking her down on to the floor. Pinned to the lino, she had no choice but to endure his rough licks and bad breath.

'Herbert!' came a shout from the doorway. 'Stop that! Leave poor Charlotte alone.'

The dog instantly abandoned Charley, leaving her free to struggle to a sitting position.

'Sorry about that,' boomed Miss Fuller. 'Have your cup of tea.'

'Thank you,' she stammered, checking for broken bones as she stood back up and Miss Fuller strode downstairs again.

Charley brushed herself down before catching her reflection in the mirror above the sink. What a mess! Her t-shirt was damp and appeared to have new white blotches where the bleach had splattered it. Her hair had escaped from its ponytail and was now framing her face in wild black curls. She peered closer and found one small curl coated with a dew drop of doggy saliva.

She sank on to the side of the bath, staring down at her ragged hands. No longer manicured, no longer pristine. Slave-to-money hands. Cleaner's hands.

After gulping down her tea, she finished dusting the bedrooms and went downstairs to find the Hoover. She opened the hall cupboard and was greeted by a mess of coats, brooms and boxes.

Pinning the ironing board back with one elbow, she held a broom high out of the way in order to make way for the Hoover. However, the broom handle dislodged a plastic tub on the top shelf and a large number of shoe-polish tins and brushes tumbled down around her. Charley shouted out in surprise and then pain as the tins bounced off her head. She screamed at the messy cupboard, screamed at the pain in her scalp and then screamed at her own wretched life.

She sank to the floor. Wracking sobs appeared from nowhere, and once they started Charley found she couldn't stem the tide. Her tears were dripping on to the lid of an old ice-cream box.

She thought back to her lovely Gaggia Gelatiera ice-cream maker. To when her beautiful home had been filled with expensive things, as well as laughter and smiles. A time when it had been filled with the love between her and Steve.

That all felt a very long time ago.

Chapter Thirteen

The club had once been a large rundown pub in the High Street, but now it was the only cocktail bar in Grove. After its makeover, it was frequented by Upper Grove clientele who relished the long leather sofas, soft lighting and sophisticated atmosphere.

Not that there was much sophistication amongst her work colleagues, thought Samantha, staring across to the dance floor with disdain. There was nothing worse than watching middle-aged people trying to be cool. Moves like Jagger? More like David Cameron, she thought.

God, she was bored. All the oldies were bopping on the dance floor. All the youngsters were downing tequila shots at the bar. She had already had to endure a soggy pizza in the Italian restaurant down the road, stuck between snotty Miranda and the head of Human Resources who kept talking about work. Was this night never going to end?

Or even begin, she wondered, her eyes flicking around the club trying to pick out Richard, the new

Sales Director. She noted a few men looking in her direction but avoided making eye contact. She knew she looked fabulous. Her hair had behaved itself; the new blue bodycon dress clung to all the right places. Modesty was for other people. She was looking good.

But it all felt such a waste. She took a sip of her Cosmopolitan, to relieve the boredom. Not that she ever got drunk. Samantha liked to be in control. She wasn't going to let go and make a fool of herself like the others.

'Hello.'

The voice was so close to her ear that when she spun round, she found herself, finally, face to face with Richard.

'Hi,' she said, giving him the full benefit of her smile.

He was standing very close to her. 'Enjoying yourself?'

I am now, thought Samantha. But she wasn't going to rush this.

'I was just watching the floor show,' she said, nodding at their dancing colleagues.

He followed her gaze. 'Do you think they know how bad they look right now?'

She gave a low, soft laugh. 'I don't think so.'

He turned back to sweep his eyes briefly over her before bending forward to whisper, 'And do you know how good you look tonight?'

She locked eyes with him before smiling. 'Of course.'

He smiled as he straightened up. 'Well, I'll probably take off soon. No rest for the wicked and all that.'

She took a sip of her cocktail as he continued to watch her. Stay cool, she told herself.

'Do you want to share a taxi?'

She tried to contain her excitement as she shook her

71

head. 'Thanks, but someone's got to show them how it's done, don't you think?'

She put down her glass on the nearest table and walked towards the dance floor. Once there, she forced herself to relax into the beat, her body swaying in constant, fluid motion.

Finally, she moved her head to flick her hair behind her shoulders and glanced across to where she'd been sitting. Yes, he was still standing there, watching her, his eyes heavy with what she was certain was desire.

She was desperate to share that ride home with him, knowing what would happen next. But a drunken kiss after the office party, followed by the inevitable embarrassment, wasn't good enough for Samantha.

Slowly, slowly, she told herself. Let him do the chasing. He'll be worth the wait.

Apparently the average four year old will ask over 400 questions a day. It was only ten o'clock in the morning and Flora was already on number 300. Or so it felt like to Caroline.

'Why is it raining?'

'Because the clouds have got moisture in them and need to let some of it go,' replied Caroline, peering at the recipe book.

'Why have the clouds got moisture?' asked Flora.

'Because some warm air has passed over the sea and made a cloud.' Caroline stared down at the mixing bowl. She was certain she had measured the ingredients correctly, so why was her pastry congealing into a soggy mess?

'Why was the air warm?'

Perhaps if she added some more flour . . . or would that make the pastry too dry?

'Mummy! Why was the air warm?'

Caroline blinked and stared across at her daughter. 'Because it was a lovely warm day. You know, like in summer when we go to the beach.'

'Can we go to the beach?'

She shook her head. 'Not today.'

'Why not?'

'Because it's raining!' Caroline took a moment to calm her agitated tone of voice. 'It wouldn't be much fun, would it?'

'But why is it raining?'

Thankfully Jeff came into the kitchen at that point. 'Hello, lovely ladies.'

'Daddy!' shouted Flora, running up to him. 'Can we go to the beach?'

'Not today,' replied Jeff, pouring himself out a mug of coffee. 'Daddy's got to work.'

'But only this morning,' said Caroline, with a smile.

Her husband shook his head. 'Just got an email requesting a full report. It's going to take most of the day.'

She frowned. 'But we were all going out this afternoon.'

'To the beach!' shouted Flora.

'No, not to the beach,' said Caroline. 'But maybe the park.'

'Perhaps tomorrow,' said Jeff, turning to leave.

Caroline marched up to him, her hands covered in raw pastry dough. 'I thought you were going to spend some time with us this weekend,' she said in a low voice.

'Work's got to come first,' he said, shaking his head. 'You know how tight it is out there at the minute.'

Caroline suddenly felt very weary. 'But I could do with a break too.'

'Well, switch the TV on,' he whispered.

'It's not good for her,' she replied, also keeping her voice low.

'Didn't you ever watch any Disney films when you were growing up?'

'Yes.'

'So why is it so bad for Flora?' Jeff gave her a small pinch on her bottom. 'After all, you didn't turn out so bad.'

With a wink, he left the kitchen.

Caroline sighed as she turned around. There was no way that pastry was going to turn out well. She smiled at her daughter. 'How about a trip to the supermarket?'

'Yay!'

Julie finished work at four o'clock and headed home, looking forward to spending a couple of hours in the garden now that the evenings were becoming lighter.

Perhaps once she had finished, she could sit down on the little wooden bench on the patio and admire her handiwork with a nice cup of tea. Or something even stronger.

But as she swung her car into the driveway, she realised there was another one already parked up. Her son was home. She told herself she should be pleased but found, in reality, that she was filled with dread. She didn't want an argument, or to listen to Nick's lies that evening. She just wanted to potter in her garden undisturbed.

'Nick?' she called, as she opened the front door and walked inside.

'Hello, Ma,' he said, coming into the hallway.

His black hair was long, almost to his shoulders. He was a tall, lanky lad – the same build as his father.

Facially, he was like him too, with his large nose and pale complexion.

Julie stared at her son for a moment. There had been no message, no contact from him since his grand-mother's funeral. The funeral which he had omitted to attend. She briefly considered voicing her anger but knew it would only lead to him spouting some excuse.

'What are you doing here?' she asked.

'Aren't I allowed to visit my dear old mum?' he said, sweeping her into an awkward hug.

'You're a bit late. Mother's Day was last Sunday,' she told him, once released.

It had been a struggle, visiting her mother's grave so soon after the funeral. Julie had placed a large pink rose on the newly dug ground and said a prayer for her mum. How she missed her.

'I was gonna call,' said Nick, following her into the kitchen. 'But I didn't have any credit.'

'Cup of tea?' she asked, filling the kettle.

'We could always have something stronger to celebrate.'

His words hung in the air as she dropped tea bags into the mugs.

'Celebrate?'

Julie's heart sank. Her mind reeled as she tried to pick from the various options running through her head. Had he just escaped a lengthy jail term? Got a girl into trouble?

'Look, I've been thinking,' he said. 'I know you've been blue since we lost Nan.'

How would you know? thought Julie.

'You're rattling round this old house on your own.'

Julie braced herself. She realised now what was coming.

'So I'm gonna move in and keep you company for a while,' said Nick.

She nodded and smiled as she filled the mugs with hot water.

Her Prodigal Son had returned. Unfortunately Julie wasn't at all happy about it.

Chapter Fourteen

On Wednesday morning, Charley braced herself for her next cleaning job. After the horror of cleaning Miss Fuller's dog-filled house on Monday, she'd believed it couldn't get much worse.

But as the door opened she realised how wrong she had been.

'Hi, I'm Charlotte. Your new cleaner.'

Her words faltered as she stared at the blonde woman standing in front of her.

'Don't I know you?' said the customer whose name was Mrs Benedict.

Charley sighed. 'I think we've met at the golf club. My husband was a member.'

The woman's eyebrows shot up as high as her Botox would allow. 'Really?' Mrs Benedict coolly appraised her. 'Yes, I remember now. You're the one with the shops, aren't you?'

'Yes.'

'Did I hear something about bankruptcy?'

Charley's humiliation was complete. She was now

a cleaner for someone with whom she used to share drinks at the golf club. Not that Mrs Benedict, or Martina as Charley had previously known her, had been a close friend. But they had been of equal social standing. Until now, that was.

'How's Gerry?' asked Charley, as they went into the hallway.

The woman glanced over her shoulder. 'I think we'd better keep it as Mr and Mrs Benedict, don't you? I'm not sure I want to be on first name terms with my staff.'

Charley blanched at the word 'staff' before meekly following Mrs Benedict towards the kitchen. Once there, she was shown the cleaning products and quickly set to work.

But each time she went into a new room, she found Mrs Benedict would quickly follow her. Charley would smile, silently willing her customer to leave her to get on with her work. But the woman wouldn't budge and obviously expected Charley to carry on cleaning in front of her.

She was wiping down the sink in the downstairs bathroom when Mrs Benedict appeared once more.

'Have you everything you need?'

'Yes, thanks.'

Charley found she hated anyone watching her whilst she cleaned, especially the toilets and bathrooms. It felt so degrading. She wondered if there would ever be a time when she didn't feel that way.

The silence was unbearable so she made an effort at some small talk whilst she attacked the taps. 'How old are your children?'

'Bethany is six and Felix is eight. We've just taken him out of the local school. He's showing intelligence far superior to the other children in his year so he's gone private.'

'Great.'

'Bethany is more of a creative child.'

Ah. So she wasn't blessed in the brains department, translated Charley.

'She's a natural actress, though. Always the star of the school plays. Last term she shone as part of the forest in Narnia.'

The child had been in the star role of a tree?

'How lovely,' said Charley, with a fake smile. She was an actress too.

'You will wipe down the tiles, won't you? And polish them?'

Thankfully Mrs Benedict didn't wait for any reply and left the room. Charley could then allow herself the exasperated eye rolling which she had been saving herself from.

Eventually she had finished the majority of the rooms downstairs and headed up to the bedrooms. She felt exhausted. Cleaning was so much harder than it looked. She had renewed respect for poor old Cinderella, not least because she'd had an enormous castle to clean.

She'd expected to enjoy cleaning the children's bedrooms but these particular ones were slightly creepy. Although toys and drawings were in evidence, they were outnumbered by the amount of embroidered pictures hung on every wall. *Love Thy Mother and Father*, said the majority. Perhaps the kids needed reminding, thought Charley.

She had been hard at work for three hours when she finally began work on the kitchen. No offer of a refreshing drink had been forthcoming. *Love thy parents but never the cleaner*.

Charley continued to scour, bleach and wipe every surface until her head was thumping from the heady smell of chemicals.

She had just finished the kitchen floor when Mrs Benedict appeared.

'My husband's been in the en-suite and thinks the shower glass is looking a bit streaky. You will have another go at it before you leave, won't you?'

Charley couldn't prevent herself in time from shooting her customer a long look. Although she had managed to fix a smile upon her face, her eyes must have betrayed her as Mrs Benedict quickly left the room again.

Charley trudged back upstairs, hoping not to bump into the man of the house. Gerry Benedict had always invaded her personal space whenever she had met him. His reputation as the club's resident creep was assured, as far as she was concerned.

Charley went into the en-suite to discover that the shower door was only slightly smeared. It was streaky from cleaning products, not dirt, and the next time it was used, it would become spotty from the water again. But she polished and rubbed the glass until the shine was bouncing off the walls.

With a loud sigh to herself, she went back into the hallway to head downstairs when she unexpectedly bumped into Gerry Benedict, who was wearing only a dressing gown. Charley had no idea where he had been hiding all this time and didn't really care.

'Hello,' she said, eager to leave before he recognised her.

'Hello,' he said, breaking into an oily smile. 'You must be the new cleaner.'

He didn't know who she was, Charley realised. Out

of her designer dress, to him she was just the cleaner. She found herself quite grateful not to have explain her circumstances once more.

But when she tried to move around him to go downstairs, Gerry Benedict blocked her path. She watched in slow motion as he slowly untied the belt on his dressing gown and opened it up to reveal his naked glory.

The creepy smile remained fixed on his face as he asked, 'What do you think?'

Charley took a beat before replying, 'I think it looks like a penis only smaller.'

She quickly brushed past him and headed downstairs.

She spotted Mrs Benedict in the kitchen, eating her lunch and leaving crumbs all over the counter Charley had only just cleaned. But she didn't care. She just wanted to get the hell out of there.

'I've finished,' said Charley, grabbing her handbag.

'There's your money,' mumbled Mrs Benedict through her full mouth, pointing a finger at the kitchen table.

Charley picked up the notes and stuffed them into her bag.

'We'll see you next week, I hope. For some reason we seem to have terrible trouble keeping cleaners from one week to the next.'

Charley stared at the woman. 'Well, if your husband keeps flashing at them all, I'm not surprised.'

And she quickly ran out of the house.

Later on, she received a phone call from her new boss.

'Look,' said Patricia with a sigh, 'you're gonna get perverts. But they're paying perverts, okay?'

'I can't go back there,' said Charley, still feeling somewhat hysterical. 'I won't and you can't make me.'

'All right. Keep your knickers on.'

'Thank God I did,' replied Charley with a shudder.

'Men!' grunted Patricia down the line. 'From monkeys to morons in four million years.'

Charley put down the phone, grateful that her husband's only shortcoming was his business sense.

Chapter Fifteen

'So? How's the first week of cleaning gone?' asked Samantha, as she topped up everyone's glasses.

It was her turn to be hostess. The flat was modern, with wooden floors, big white sofas and lots of glass tables. The kind of place where no mummy could ever bring her toddler.

'Exhausting,' said Charley, slumping back on to the leather sofa.

She could feel every muscle in her body aching, and she had only cleaned for four hours that day. Patricia hadn't warned her how tiring it would be. Lord knows what it would be like the following week when she would be cleaning for eight hours every day.

By the time she had arrived home, she could barely walk. Then she had had to endure a freezing cold shower because Nick was now living with Julie and secret showers there had become a thing of the past for Charley.

Samantha wrinkled her nose. 'I don't know how you can do it, what with all that scrubbing and vacuuming.'

Charley sighed. 'It's money. That's the only reason I'm doing it.'

'Yes, but it must be so humiliating,' carried on her friend. 'Cleaning people's toilets, I mean.'

Samantha's tactlessness had always been one of her worst faults, thought Caroline, who had spotted Charley squirming in her seat.

'Your new cushions are lovely,' said Caroline brightly.

'They're only IKEA,' said Samantha, stroking the fluffy fabric. 'But I wanted to give the place a bit of an update, so I've replaced the curtains and bought some new tea lights too.'

'Teal is very in this year,' said Caroline.

'I presume this makeover isn't just meant for our eyes?' said Julie, raising her eyebrows.

Samantha grinned. 'Hopefully not.'

'What's the plan?' asked Caroline.

'There's a conference coming up that includes an overnight stay at a hotel.' Samantha's eyes went dreamy. 'I'm gonna see how things progress there.'

'So he's good-looking?' asked Julie.

Samantha nodded. 'Plus smart and funny.'

'Sounds too good to be true,' said Caroline.

'Yeah,' agreed Julie. 'Why isn't he married if he's that great?'

Samantha shrugged her shoulders. 'I don't know. Perhaps he is.'

Caroline frowned. 'Shouldn't you find out, before you invest too much time and effort in him?'

'I've got to get him hooked first,' said Samantha, breaking into a smile.

'That Richard sounds like bad news,' said Julie on the way home.

Charley struggled to get the car into third gear.

'Samantha's pretty strong-willed. You'll never talk her out of it.'

'Well, it's her heart she's in danger of breaking.'

Charley turned the car into Upper Grove, the Mini spluttering all the way. Home. It didn't feel like it any more. At one time she had imagined the bedrooms filled with a large, noisy family. The memory of her miscarriage before the wedding still remained raw, but Steve had kept urging her to be patient. Children would come in time, he'd said, and he wanted to concentrate on the business for a few more years. And hadn't that turned out well? thought Charley, rolling her eyes.

She pulled into the driveway, noticing a strange car there. The lights were on inside, but there was no sign of anyone about.

'Is it Steve?' asked Julie.

'I don't know,' replied Charley, suddenly fearful.

What if the bailiffs had come back? There was surely nothing left for them to take. She opened the front door cautiously and crept in, with Julie close behind. The place felt so different these days, unlived in and unloved. It was nothing but an empty box.

There was the sound of movement upstairs.

'Maybe it's squatters who think the place is already empty,' whispered Charley. 'Should we ring the police?'

Julie shook her head. 'They'll take too long. Besides, I've dealt with enough scumbags over the years to sort out whoever's up there.'

So she took the lead, with Charley following. There was movement in the master bedroom so they crept in.

In hindsight, Charley thought that perhaps she should have made a noise to announce their presence in the house. Then maybe her husband would have received some kind of warning.

Instead Steve and an unfamiliar woman continued their lovemaking on the bedroom carpet in blissful ignorance.

Charley wanted to run, but her feet wouldn't move her away from the shocking scene. She wanted to scream, but found herself unable even to speak.

'You'll want to get some cream on those knees later,' said Julie, in a loud voice. 'That carpet burn's murder on the skin.'

Steve's steady rhythm came to an abrupt halt, but he remained on all fours as he stared in horror over his shoulder at Charley.

It briefly occurred to her that this was the second naked man she had come across unexpectedly within the past twelve hours. It was just a shame she was married to this particular one.

Chapter Sixteen

'I've got a cup of tea for you,' came a shout through the bedroom door.

Charley rolled over to face the window. She hadn't slept, hadn't eaten. Hadn't spoken to anyone.

She glanced at her mobile but there were no messages. It was ten o'clock. It had been over twelve hours since she had found Steve with another woman. Twelve hours since she had picked up the last of her boxes and brought them to her parents' house. Twelve hours since the end of her marriage.

Steve had rung every hour until she finally switched off the phone at three o'clock in the morning. She listened to his apologies. Listened as he told her that he hadn't known what he was doing. That he was scared after the bankruptcy. That he wasn't thinking straight.

Charley listened in silence to his excuses, cutting the line whenever she couldn't cope with any more. As the night wore on, Steve's tone became harder. She hadn't supported him, he told her. She had carried on and not paid him enough attention.

She turned on to her back and stared at the ceiling. Perhaps he was right. Perhaps it was her fault.

She had turned the phone back on at six o'clock in the morning but there had been no further calls. No messages. The phone stayed quiet.

The bedroom door opened.

'Come on, love,' said her mother. 'You've got to get up for work. You've got a cleaning job this afternoon, remember?'

'I don't want to go,' whined Charley, pulling the duvet over her head.

She just wanted to stay in bed for the next decade, if not for ever.

'I'm sure you don't,' replied her mother, flinging the duvet off the bed. 'But jobs are scarce, so you'd better keep yours. Besides, you need the money, don't you?'

Charley closed her eyes. She might have fled to her parents' house but the safe haven came with a side order of guilt.

Eventually she got dressed and trudged downstairs into the kitchen.

'How about some lunch?' Her mother held out a plate of blackened toast.

Charley shook her head.

'Your father went and picked up the little car for you,' said her mother.

Charley sat at the table, staring in a daze around the small kitchen. She realised she wouldn't see her lovely big kitchen ever again. She didn't live in Upper Grove any more. Somebody else would soon live in her house. She wondered how long it would take her to get over losing her home and husband in the same day. Then she wondered whether she would ever recover.

That afternoon, she drove to her customer's flat and let herself in. She had been given a key as the owner was at work and felt quite grateful that she wouldn't have to make any polite conversation that afternoon.

With no one else at home, Charley was able to wander around the stylish flat in silence. But her mind was reeling with questions. How long had Steve been cheating on her? What could she have done to prevent her life crashing down around her?

And how on earth was she going to get this wretched stuff off the bath tiles? An inspection of her customer's bathroom shelves had revealed a plethora of St Tropez lotions. Charley could only presume she was the same orange colour as the splash marks up the walls.

She scrubbed at the tiles, but even with the bathroom spray it was hard work. After ten minutes, the brown stains were still there but a little less vivid. She would just have to keep at it week after week.

Charley rubbed her aching arms. Nobody had warned her how physical the job would be. Or how out of shape she really was.

She went into the lounge and sank on to the leather sofa with a sigh. She felt exhausted.

Her mobile rang and she picked it up, assuming it was one of the girls. But it wasn't.

'Charley? Hi. It's me.'

Her heart lurched at the sound of Steve's voice and she felt the tears welling up in her eyes.

'You all right?' he asked.

'I've been better,' she told him in a small voice.

'I know. I'm sorry. I really am.'

After a short silence, she asked him, 'How long has it been going on?'

'Only a couple of weeks.'

She had been hoping it was a one-night stand. Now it sounded like a relationship. Something serious. 'Who is she?'

'Just Susie from the pub.'

Well, thought Charley, that's great. 'Susie from the pub' had just ruined their twelve-year marriage. But she didn't say anything.

'I handed back the house keys this morning,' said Steve.

She tried to think about all the happy times they had enjoyed in their lovely house. But she drew a blank. She was too tired to think straight.

'Are you staying at your folks' place for now?' he asked.

'Yeah.'

'I can't go to my mum's,' Steve told her. 'You know what she's like.'

'Yeah.'

'So I'm staying with a friend.'

'Right.'

The silence hung in the air between them.

'Well, I'd better go,' he told her.

Charley hung up the phone before disintegrating into tears. She had just made it through the conversation without breaking down.

She needed time to think, to adjust, to come to terms with everything that had happened. But she didn't have that luxury. She had to dust and vacuum a stranger's flat before mopping the kitchen floor and cleaning the windows.

Take the money first. Then she could fall apart.

Chapter Seventeen

The following day, Charley again had the morning free. Once more she slept in, craving the quiet of her bedroom. Except it wasn't her bedroom and it was never going to be quiet.

'Time to get up,' said her mother, coming in and flinging open the curtains. 'Caroline's downstairs.'

'I don't want to see anyone.'

'She's your friend. Of course you want to see her. Come on. Up with you.'

As Charley slowly got out of bed, her mother tutted to see the baggy t-shirt of Steve's that she was wearing.

'We must get you a nice nightie. And have a shower before you come down. You mustn't lose your looks as well as everything else.'

Half an hour later, Charley trudged into the lounge.

Caroline stood up and gave her a hug. Only her eyes, widening momentarily, betrayed how bad Charley must look.

'How are you?' asked Caroline.

91

In reply Charley's eyes filled with tears. Her heart ached with emptiness and betrayal.

'I should have guessed,' she croaked, the tears rolling down her cheeks. 'Should have known something wasn't right. I'm such an idiot.'

'No, you're not,' replied Caroline.

'Quite right,' said her mother. 'Now why don't you get some nice fresh air? You could buy the local paper whilst you're out as well, and have a look through the property section.'

'I can't afford to buy anywhere,' said Charley, dragging her hand through her hair. The last thing she wanted to do was go out in public where she might see somebody she knew. At least with the cleaning work she could stay anonymous.

'Not to buy, silly,' her mother told her. 'To rent. You've got to live somewhere.'

Charley was horrified. 'I thought I could spend a bit of time here until I get my act together?'

Her mother turned away and began to tidy a newspaper on the coffee table. 'Well, yes,' said Maureen, avoiding eye contact. 'We were going to tell you, but then all this happened.'

'Tell me what?'

'Your grandmother's had a bit of a shock. Literally, as it happens. She was fiddling about with the electrics and flew four feet into the air. Broke her wrist when she landed on a nest of tables. She can't even manage the kettle, so I've said she can stay with us for a while.'

Charley began to shake. She couldn't handle this. There was nowhere else for her to go.

Her mother walked over and held on to her shoulders. 'I know it feels like the world has fallen apart, but you'll get through this. Do your mourning and then face up to things.'

Huge tears rolled down Charley's cheeks. 'I don't think I can,' she wailed.

'You will.'

'But . . .'

Her mother shook her head. 'No buts,' she said, before enveloping her daughter in a bear hug. 'You know we'll always love you. They can never take that away from you. But it's time to be strong.'

Charley had never felt less strong in the whole of her life. 'But where will I go? What's going to happen to me?'

'You will find your feet and carry on living,' her mother told her. 'It's what women have done for centuries.'

'I'm not sure I can even afford to rent anywhere.'

'Your father's worked it all out for you. If you find a cheap enough place, we'll get the deposit for you somehow. You'll have to take on all the cleaning jobs you can, but a bit of work won't do you any harm.'

Charley and Caroline left the house and walked towards the small shop on the green. Late March sunshine was trying to break through the clouds.

'You know, you could stay in our spare bedroom if you want,' said Caroline.

'Thanks but I'll find somewhere,' said Charley.

She knew that Caroline would try and be the supreme hostess, which was too much for her. And for Charley as well. She loved her friend but she probably didn't want to live with her.

'Julie sent her love,' said Caroline. 'She says you can stay with her. But I don't suppose you want to go back to Upper Grove?'

'Not really,' said Charley. 'Especially not next door to my old house. It's really kind of you both to offer, but Mum's right. I've got to stand on my own two feet.'

She heard the words come out of her own mouth, but didn't believe them.

She bought the local newspaper and took it to the village green, where they sat down on a bench.

'Where's Flora today?' asked Charley.

'Easter holidays,' Caroline told her. 'I managed to persuade Jeff to take a whole day off.'

Caroline's smile was tight, so Charley dropped the subject and opened the newspaper to flick through the property pages. She stopped for a while at a photograph of her own house with the words 'Recently Sold' across it.

'Nice photo,' said Caroline.

Charley sniffed away a tear. 'The loft needed insulating anyway,' she said, quickly turning the page.

They peered at the list of properties to rent. Everything at the cheap end of the market was a flat. That meant no garden, no patio and no barbecue. Charley shook her head. The bailiffs had taken away the huge gas barbecue and who the hell would she be entertaining, anyway, these days?

The cost was surprisingly high as well. Even the bottom three properties were at least £400 per month. How on earth did people cope with all the extra bills on top?

'Studio basement flat,' Caroline read aloud. 'What does that mean?'

'No daylight. No separate bedroom.'

'Where do you sleep?' asked Caroline, horrified.

'In the kitchen probably. What's the next one?'

94

'Studio loft flat.'

Charley sighed. 'I think that means you still sleep in the kitchen, but with the added bonus of a bruised forehead from all the sloping ceilings.'

'This one sounds hopeful,' said Caroline. 'And it's the cheapest. Spacious one-bedroomed flat, short walk from village centre.'

'There must be a catch,' said Charley, ringing the number on the advertisement.

She talked to the landlord who said they could view the flat that morning. But the address of the flat was in Lower Grove.

'Oh dear,' said Caroline. 'That's why it's so cheap.'

They walked back to pick up Caroline's car and drove to the high street. Once across the main traffic lights, the look of the road went down sharply as they entered Lower Grove.

The houses became smaller, less tidy, with no pretty hanging baskets. They took a left under a railway bridge and into the depths of Hill Estate. It was a jumble of tiny council houses, all plain and square apart from the occasional patch of pebbledash and graffiti which distinguished one residence from another.

On the edge of the estate was a large block of flats called Hill View Court. It was three storeys high and there was a burnt-out Citroën in the car park. The flats had been built on the H-block principle, presumably because most of the inhabitants had spent time at Her Majesty's pleasure.

As they waited for the landlord to arrive, Caroline flicked the central locking for the doors. She gave Charley a small smile. 'Just in case.'

The landlord finally arrived. He was a man called

Harvey, with a large beer belly and body odour. He led them through one of the front entrances into a communal hallway and stairwell. At least the main door looked secure. Whether it was to keep the hooligans outside or in was less certain.

The flat was on the ground floor. The overhead light in the communal hallway flickered. Rubbish lay rotting in bags near the door. Music boomed through the front door of the flat across the hallway.

Harvey fiddled with the key before opening the door to number five. He flicked a switch as there was no natural light. The dim lightbulb showed the patches of damp in their full glory.

A brief inspection of the bathroom confirmed Charley's opinion that yellow, black and mirrored tiles weren't a fashion statement that should ever be repeated. The bedroom was tiny, but at least it had a built-in wardrobe. But when Caroline opened the wardrobe doors, there was an overwhelming odour of decay and the walls inside were covered in mildew.

The lounge was barely big enough for a sofa, which was good news because the bailiffs had taken them all away. The tiny kitchen housed an oven and washing machine, both included in the rental. Neither was new or modern, but Harvey said they worked. Caroline swung open the oven door and immediately closed it again.

'It only needs a bit of a wipe down,' grunted Harvey, sounding as if this wasn't high on his list of priorities.

Charley peered out of the kitchen window, which overlooked the car park. 'At least I can keep an eye on my hubcaps.'

'So? You gonna take it?' asked Harvey, picking his thumbnail.

Charley glanced across at Caroline, who was violently shaking her head in reply.

But Charley shrugged. The way her life was at the moment, it was a perfect match.

So she shook hands with Harvey and agreed to move in at the weekend. He wanted to be paid in cash for the rent, which was handy as she didn't have a bank account.

As they drove away, Charley realised she had both a job and a home. She should be thankful for that. But she didn't feel it. She was pretending to be strong, but inside she was quaking with fear.

She just wanted her husband and her old life back.

Chapter Eighteen

Samantha sat down at the chest press machine and settled herself into position. As she ruthlessly worked her upper arms into submission, she darted her eyes around the gym to see who was there.

It was Saturday on Easter weekend, so the place was packed with people working out. All the stereotypes were present and correct. Marathon Man was sprinting away with no intention of relinquishing the running machine. Midlife Crisis Man was on the rowing machine in his brand new sportswear, desperately trying to shed his beer belly, no doubt on the advice of his doctor. Bench Press Guy was flexing his pectoral muscles, with weights so heavy that his veins were bulging.

All were considered and then quickly dismissed. These weren't viable options for someone as good-looking as Samantha. Her toned body was looking great in its tight-fitting Lycra and she had just enough waterproof make-up on to look as if she was naturally gorgeous.

Her eyes finally settled on a man doing sit-ups on an exercise ball. His gym wear of shorts and t-shirt was trendy enough without being too self-consciously sporty. He was sweaty after his workout without being disgustingly wet. He was in his early thirties and nice enough to look at. Not classically handsome like Richard was, of course. But certainly someone she could mess about with for a while.

In Samantha's eyes, all men were toys to be played with and teased. She had adored her father and at an early age learnt to wrap him round her finger, using her big brown eyes and wide smile to charm him into submission.

But not even Samantha's charms could keep him at home. It was all her mother's fault, Samantha knew. Her mother with her sniping and nagging. Never making herself look pretty. Of course her father was going to cheat on her with someone far more attractive. Why wouldn't he?

Other women never seemed to like Samantha. But that was fine because the feeling was entirely mutual. Apart from the others in their foursome, of course. But even they were a teensy bit dull, she had to admit to herself.

She thought about Richard with whom she had enjoyed a marvellous flirting session the previous day. He was the small spark of glamour in an otherwise very tedious village. Something to brighten up her dull days.

But that would have to wait. In the meantime she had a long bank holiday weekend to endure, and no one to share it with.

Samantha got up and walked slowly over to the exercise mats where the good-looking guy had just completed his sit-ups. She allowed him a small smile before she began her own stretches. She could feel his eyes on her, feel his appreciation of her taut body.

They would have a drink in the sports bar afterwards. And then? Well, he was just another man to be played with and discarded, like all the rest.

Caroline had spent all week devising an Easter egg hunt that made the Da Vinci Code look simple. She had been secretly hoping that Flora would be able to work out all the clues by herself and was frowning therefore as she watched Jeff lead their daughter into the corner of the garden where the next clue lay.

She sighed, checking her watch. They only had half an hour until her parents arrived. Caroline ran through the checklist in her mind. The Easter biscuits and simnel cake were made. The lamb was in the oven, filling the house with a divine aroma.

Even the display on the dining table was perfect. She and Flora had spent many hours painting blown eggs. Although, Caroline had to admit to herself, not many of those hours had been happy. Flora was a heavy-handed child who had destroyed many fragile shells with one stab of her paintbrush. Therefore, Caroline had spent most of the recent evenings painting the damn things herself.

'Mummy!' cried Flora, running up to her. 'Look what the Easter Bunny has left me!'

She held out a *Junior Illustrated Dictionary*.

'How super!' said Caroline, with a big smile. 'You'll have to show Nanny and Grandad when they arrive.'

She watched Flora rush off into the house to read her new book.

'A bit of chocolate wouldn't have killed her,' muttered Jeff, coming to stand next to his wife.

100

'You know it makes her hyper,' replied Caroline. 'Besides, if she's inherited my soft teeth we'll have to be careful, otherwise she'll end up with a mouth full of fillings before she's eighteen.'

Jeff sighed. 'I just think we should let go once in a while. Let her be normal.'

Caroline spun round to face her husband. 'She *is* normal.'

He shrugged his shoulders. 'Then let her eat chocolate, for God's sake. She's not overweight. She's not a faddy eater. She's just a kid.'

'I know that,' snapped Caroline, stung by his criticism. 'But don't worry. I'm sure my parents will have bought an egg for her, so she can gorge herself on chocolate all afternoon.'

'Good,' retorted Jeff.

Caroline marched back into the kitchen, feeling hurt. Flora was a balanced, healthy child. Of course she led a normal life. Hadn't she just had a treasure hunt? Wasn't wanting to educate your child well normal?

Jeff was just stressed, as usual, and taking it out on her. Everything was fine.

All Julie wanted to do was to sit on the sofa, watching *Easter Parade*. Preferably whilst eating her own body weight in chocolate.

But the lounge was full of strangers, there wasn't any chocolate left in the house and the music on full volume was rap music. Judy Garland and her Easter bonnet it most definitely wasn't.

Julie shuffled into the kitchen and stared around at the mess. Dirty plates and mugs were piled up in the sink. Butter and cheese had been abandoned on the kitchen tops. Spilt drinks. The oven on, but nothing inside.

She sighed as she switched it off. Nick had said he wanted to support her in the weeks following her mother's death and initially she had been grateful for the company. But she'd known it had been too good to last.

In fact, it had only taken three weeks before the real story came out. Another job gone, apparently through redundancy. The subtle hints about his lack of funds. Her purse missing a £10 note she had been certain was in there.

And now his so-called friends were in her house. Suddenly Julie craved the solitude she normally hated. At least if she was lonely she could escape into the garden. But here there was no escape. Her garden was being used as a convenient ashtray for Nick's frequent cigarette breaks.

It was no use. She would have to ask him about finding another job once Easter was over. The inevitable row would ensue, closely followed by her feelings of guilt. But they couldn't go on like this.

Raucous laughter filtered in from the lounge causing Julie to grab her car keys and handbag. She had to get out of there, if only to visit the garden centre.

'I'm going out,' she shouted through the lounge door, which had remained worryingly shut most of the afternoon.

There was no response.

Julie shut the front door behind her, trying not to worry about what lay on the other side of the lounge door. Yet another day spent tidying up beckoned tomorrow. But not now. Now she would go and look at plants, even if she could not afford to purchase any.

She stopped short in front of her car. Nick had borrowed it that morning, claiming his was out of petrol. But he had failed to mention the small dent which had suddenly appeared in the rear door.

Julie glanced at the junk-food debris which was strewn across the passenger side.

It was her own fault. She had forgotten one of parenting's golden rules. Never lend your car to anyone to whom you have given birth.

Chapter Nineteen

The whole of Charley's family turned out for her move into the flat on Easter Monday. Her parents' hallway was filled with boxes and suitcases. Her granny was moving in as Charley was moving out.

She took a long look around her mother's spare bedroom. Charley didn't want to leave, but knew she couldn't stay any longer. She picked up her handbag and an empty mug before heading downstairs to the kitchen which was crowded with family members. The chattering stopped. She was obviously number one topic that afternoon.

Through the crowd, Charley could see her mother standing in front of the grill which was on full blast, despite the warm spring sunshine outside.

'Don't let her see me crying,' her mother was sobbing, trying to dry her eyes in the heat. 'I must be strong for my brave little girl.'

Victoria nudged Maureen in the ribs. Their mother spun round and looked at Charley for a second, her mouth trembling, her cheeks shiny with tears. Then she drew herself up to her full height and strode across the kitchen, cannoning members of the family into the wall units.

She swept her eldest daughter into her arms. 'I'm going to miss you.'

Charley began to tremble in her embrace. She never wanted to leave this hug.

'Now who's going to take your father his morning coffee?' carried on Maureen. 'You know I won't go near that workshop of his.'

Charley smiled through the tears. 'I'm only ten minutes down the road.'

Her mother released her grip and stroked Charley's hair. 'You'll be all right.'

She nodded hard, trying to convince them both.

'Is someone going to get me a cup of tea or shall I just expire from thirst?' Everyone looked up to see Granny standing in the doorway. 'What's going on in here? Maureen, why are you a bitter, sobbing heap?'

Granny was tiny but wasn't a woman to be messed with.

Elizabeth, Victoria's twin, rolled her eyes. 'Charlotte's just a bit upset, that's all.'

'Nothing to be upset about,' barked Granny, coming to stand in front of them. 'So you got yourself in a bit of a state . . . are you going to let that man ruin your life?'

Charley shook her head, more out of fear than honesty.

'Then turn that frown upside down, my girl. I'll have that cuppa in your new abode.'

Charley opened her mouth wide in horror. She'd had no intention of letting her family see the ghastly flat, especially her mother and grandmother.

But Granny wasn't about to take no for an answer. 'You've got a kettle, haven't you? Maureen, pack the tea bags and milk. And some decent biscuits. The good ones that you've been keeping back, not them economy packs you've been dishing up. Don't think I haven't noticed.'

The procession of cars left Little Grove and made its way into Lower Grove. A short while later they were all parked in front of Hill View Court flats.

'Bloody hell,' Charley heard Victoria mutter as they got out.

'Mummy said a bad word,' said one of her young nieces.

'Quite right,' said Granny, taking her great-granddaughter's hand. 'But this is your Aunty Charlotte's new home, so let's be nice about it. We should all be grateful for having a roof over our heads in this day and age.'

Charley put the key into the front door and stepped into the flat.

'The hall's on the small side,' she said over her shoulder, bracing herself for the inevitable guffaws. But they never came.

'Never seen the point of hallways,' said Granny, striding past. 'Waste of good space, if you ask me.'

Charley showed them into the bedroom. 'It's a bit musty.'

'Nothing that a good airing won't cure,' said her mother, opening a window.

They all peered into the kitchen. 'It's tiny,' Charley told them.

Her mother ran a finger along the worktop. 'You don't need a lot of space. It's only you.'

Finally they went into the lounge.

'Quite cosy,' said her father, sucking on his pipe. 'It'll save you a fortune on heating because you're insulated by all the flats around you.'

They were being so kind, so positive, that Charley could feel the sobs welling up inside her. She hid her face as she followed her mother back into the kitchen.

'You can keep the coffee and tea bags,' Maureen told her. 'I'll take most of the mugs back with me, but I bought you some washing up liquid and a few other bits.'

'I know what you're thinking,' said Charley, leaning against the counter. 'And it's true. The flat is horrible.'

'You need to start somewhere,' said Maureen with a shrug.

Charley's father and brother-in-law brought in the mattress that had been strapped on to the top of Dad's Volvo. This was followed by an ancient armchair, a portable television, a small nest of tables and a chest of drawers for the bedroom.

'Feels more like a home now it's got furniture in it,' said Granny, sitting down on the only chair.

Charley realised this was true. With the family sprawled across the lounge, plus her suitcases and boxes beginning to fill the hallway and bedroom, it felt less empty. Less bleak.

Her twin sisters sidled up to her.

'I know we've given you a lot of grief about the money,' said Victoria.

'And we're still really cross about that,' added Elizabeth.

'I know,' said Charley, with a sigh.

'But you got yourself a job,' said Elizabeth.

'And this place,' said Victoria, with a small shudder.

'So we just want to say, you know, that we can see you're doing your best and we're proud of you.'

'You are?' Charley's eyes filled with tears. 'Thanks.'

She let them embrace her, grateful for having such a supportive family. But all too soon they began to wend their way home.

'I'll be over next week to see how you're getting on,' said Granny, giving Charley a stiff hug. 'Make sure you eat properly. I'll not have you wasting away.'

'Victoria's left you a spare telephone,' said her father, attempting to appear normal though his watery eyes betrayed him. 'It's plugged in and ready to go. Give us a ring tonight, so we can get the number.'

'Your dad's switched on the fridge but it's not cold enough yet so I've left you some dinner in the cool bag.' Charley's mother kissed her on the cheek. 'Thirty minutes in the oven should do. Drop the bag off when you're next round. I'll need it for the church picnic next month.'

She squeezed the air out of Charley's lungs with a massive hug before leaving.

Finally, Charley was alone. She stood trembling in the hallway for a minute before getting busy. She avoided the kitchen, deciding to concentrate on the bedroom first.

The inside of the wardrobe and chest of drawers needed wiping and then drying before she could start to unpack. She realised that she had far too many clothes for an average wardrobe, most of which were unnecessary in her new circumstances. When was she going to wear an evening gown again? Or any of her beautiful high heels?

In the end, she unpacked her jeans, t-shirts and casual tops and left all her smarter clothes in two suitcases, which she then placed at the back of the wardrobe. She unpacked her flip-flops and trainers, leaving all her expensive heels in a black bin liner, which she placed at the bottom of the wardrobe next to the suitcases.

She glanced at the bag which held her fancy under-wear. These weren't bras to wear under t-shirts, or sensible cotton pants. This was silky, sometimes flammable, underwear, that she had worn only for Steve. Gulping back tears, Charley carried the bag out of the flat and shoved it down the communal bin chute.

Back in the lounge, Charley slumped into the armchair and looked around her. The flat was riddled with damp, the wallpaper was peeling off the walls and the bathroom was a kaleidoscope of yellow and black. There really was no place like home.

But it was hers, sort of. She had sole ownership of the remote control at any rate. Later on, she could read for an hour in the bath, if she could face those mirrored tiles. She could even hog the whole of the mattress, instead of lying perched on the edge whilst her husband lay diagonally across the middle, snoring loudly.

The thought of Steve put a stop to any further positive thoughts. What was he doing now? And with whom? Was he snuggled up with whatshername somewhere? Or down the pub, laughing with his mates, having forgotten his wife?

Charley hugged her knees into her chest, wishing they were back in their lovely house, before all the trouble had started. The only thing she wanted to do right at that moment was to switch on her ice-cream maker and start mixing batches of strawberry sorbet or chocolate pecan mix. But that wasn't possible. Charley suddenly felt very alone.

Her mobile tinkled into life. She thought it would be her mother, reminding her about the cool bag. But she was wrong. It was Julie.

Hope you've unpacked already! she read. *Don't forget we're coming over on Friday night for a housewarming. Keep smiling!*

Later that evening she also received a text from Caroline, as well as one from her mother about the cool bag.

Charley allowed herself a small smile. She wasn't entirely alone. She still had her friends and family.

Chapter Twenty

At least it had only been a short working week, thought
Charley as she drove to her last cleaning job on Friday
afternoon. Though that meant only four days' wages
too, which made the amount of money in her purse
seem perilously paltry.

But for now, she only had one more house to clean.
Just get through the afternoon, she told herself, and
then it was the weekend. Of course, that meant too
much time spent in her ghastly flat. It still felt alien
to her, and certainly not like 'home'. She was scared
to be living alone for the first time in her life, and
frightened by the weight of responsibility that it
brought.

Charley got out of the car and hurried up to the
front door of the large house. She took shelter from
the April shower that had begun and tugged the old-
fashioned bell pull. She waited for someone to come
to the door. And then she waited some more.

She glanced around the grounds. The driveway was
bordered by an overgrown lawn. Box hedges had

grown out of shape. Weeds filled the flowerbeds.
Nature had run amok.

She was about to ring the bell again when the heavy
oak door began to open, revealing a tiny old lady. She
was about four foot tall and her frailty was further
emphasised by faux auburn hair which was obviously
a wig.

'Hi. I'm Charlotte. I'm your new cleaner.'

'Hello, dear,' said the pensioner. 'I'm Mrs Wilberforce.'

Charley stepped into the hall and straight back in
time. The house was lovely. Or at least it had been
eighty years ago. And that looked to be the last time
anyone had dusted. If nature had run amok outside,
dust and dirt had overtaken the inside of the house.
Everywhere she looked, thick cobwebs stretched across
from picture frames to the ceiling, from the grandfather
clock to the floor. Most surfaces were thick with dust
and there was a smell of mould and decay in the air.

Charley followed Mrs Wilberforce's slow progress
through the entrance hall to the doorway at the far
end.

'Have you ever had a cleaner before?' asked Charley,
assuming she knew the answer to the question.

'Yes, but Irene retired last month. Been with us thirty
years.'

And not done a decent day's work in all that time,
thought Charley.

'Where would you like me to start?'

'I thought you could do the drawing room today.
And then the kitchen next week.'

Charley frowned. 'But that's only one room. Are you
sure you don't want me to do more than that this
week?'

Mrs Wilberforce shook her head. 'I don't want to

wear you out, my dear. That was all Irene could ever manage. You're only here for two hours. Shall I show you around?'

Charley thought it was the kind of tour they should include at Universal Studios. 'Step right up, folks. The new haunted mansion ride has just opened. Admission includes free cobwebs and moths to take home with you. Scary chamber music for an additional charge.'

She shook her head in dismay. How did anyone live like this? Why weren't her family getting this nice lady into a sunny bungalow?

'Have you a large family?' she asked.

'No. Since my husband Ernest passed away there's just my son now. He's a hairdresser living in London. Very busy, of course, so he can't come down here very often.'

Back in the hallway, Charley was shown the cleaning materials, such as they were. A tin of scouring powder, one of furniture wax and a couple of rags.

As she went back into the drawing room and surveyed the damage, Charley thought that Mrs Wilberforce was really very sweet. The room was a large one overlooking the garden. Some battered sofas and armchairs were positioned around the large fireplace. Various pieces of china were on display on occasional tables. It was a good thing that this was the only room to be cleaned today. It would take all of two hours to get it into a reasonable state.

Charley felt her lips press together and her back straighten. She was experiencing a feeling she hadn't felt in any of her cleaning jobs so far: determination to do a good and thorough job. Normally she just wanted to get by without breaking down into hysterical tears, but this afternoon she was going to make a difference to someone's life. She didn't care how long it took. This nice little old lady was going to sit in a clean, dust-free drawing room tonight.

Charley mentally rolled up her sleeves as she appraised the room before deciding to start on a little table by the door. She carefully removed the photo frames and pill boxes from the top and placed them on the carpet.

She went back into the kitchen and dampened one of the rags, before wringing it almost dry. Back in the drawing room, she wiped the table top. A stripe of beautiful walnut veneer appeared. Then another. Once all the dust was clear, she buffed the table top using the furniture wax. Her arms were already beginning to ache but she kept going as the table began to gleam. Who needed aerobics and hand weights when you could tone your arms by polishing furniture instead?

Once the ornamental frames and boxes were also cleaned, Charley placed them back on the table and looked at her handiwork. The table shone out in a room full of dust. She allowed herself a small sigh of satisfaction, before moving on to the next piece.

An hour had flown by when Mrs Wilberforce pottered in.

'Goodness!' she exclaimed. 'How super!'

She beamed with delight as she stared at all the wooden furniture, now gleaming and full of colour.

But with an hour to go, Charley still had to dust the paintings, take down the china plates from the walls and wash them, as well as vacuum the carpet. If she had enough time, she also wanted to clean the windows.

'You've worked so hard, my dear,' said Mrs

Wilberforce. 'Would you like a cup of tea? I've just made one for the new gardener.'

Charley followed her into the kitchen and watched it being poured out of an ancient teapot.

The back door suddenly opened and there, filling the doorway, was a figure from her past.

Mike Shearer had been in the same year at school as Charley, from the first day at primary school right through to the age of sixteen. He hadn't been one of the trendy boys like Steve, exuding cocky confidence and flirting with the girls. Instead Mike had chosen to stay on the periphery and quietly watch the action. Like Charley, he had also stayed in the village, carving a career for himself as a gardener.

But she was surprised and extremely embarrassed to be discovered by him in her new role as domestic staff.

'Hi,' said Charley with a shy smile.

'Hello.' Mike looked equally surprised to find her there.

They had occasionally bumped into each other in the village but never exchanged anything more than a passing nod and greeting. Working together would mean having whole conversations with each other.

'This is my new cleaner,' said Mrs Wilberforce, pouring out the tea. 'It's the first day for both of you.'

Mike stared at Charley for a few seconds before lowering his eyes and going over to the counter to pick up his cup of tea.

'Thank you,' he said. His huge hands made the cup look doll-sized, she noticed.

'How are you getting on?' Mrs Wilberforce asked him.

He took a long swig of tea before replying. 'You've

115

lost a couple of roses but I've pruned the rest back hard. Should come on a treat this summer.'

'Well done,' she told him. 'Let me fetch you a chocolate biscuit. I think I left them by the bed last night.'

There was a silence as she began her slow journey upstairs, leaving them alone.

Charley glanced at Mike, thinking how rarely she actually saw him, despite the fact that they both lived in the village. Mike lived in a small cottage on the outskirts, nowhere near Upper Grove and the life that she led. Or rather, used to lead.

She had forgotten how tall he was. He had to be well over six foot. Perhaps it was all the fresh air.

She found herself blushing as she realised he was studying her in return with his dark eyes.

Charley shuffled from foot to foot under his scrutiny.

'So you're a cleaner?' He was unable to hide the surprise in his deep voice.

'That's right,' said Charley, suddenly feeling defensive. 'Just one of many personal goals I've achieved so far this year.'

'What are the others?' asked Mike, a small smile playing at the corners of his mouth.

Was he laughing at her? At the ghastly situation she had found herself in?

'Bankruptcy, losing my house and finding my husband with another woman,' she snapped in reply.

His smile faded. 'Really?'

Charley sighed. 'Yes.'

'I'd only heard about the house and bankruptcy.'

Charley waited for words of commiseration and comfort, especially about the demise of her marriage. But they didn't come and the silence stretched out between them.

Thankfully they were interrupted by the arrival of the chocolate biscuits. 'Here we are,' said Mrs Wilberforce, holding out the packet to them both.

Charley took a couple of digestives with a smile of thanks. They were stale but chocolate was chocolate.

'I'd better get on,' said Mike, finishing his tea in one swift movement.

He grabbed a couple of biscuits before heading back out into the garden, without so much as a backward glance in Charley's direction.

She felt rattled as she went back to the drawing room to finish cleaning. Okay, so she and Mike weren't exactly close, but they had known each other since they were five years old. They used to play at each other's house when they were very young. A little sympathy wouldn't have gone amiss, she thought. After all, she would have done the same thing if the tables were turned. Not that she knew that much about Mike's love life or finances.

Enraged by his unsympathetic attitude, she cleaned furiously and an hour later her work was done. The room was a warm inviting place once more.

'What a wonderful job you've done,' said Mrs Wilberforce with tears in her eyes. 'I haven't seen the place look this good for years.'

Charley sighed with a small sense of satisfaction. She had survived her first week at work and made someone happy. If only she could say the same of herself.

Chapter Twenty-one

The girls came over to see the flat on Friday evening, the idea being to give her new home a housewarming. Charley figured it would be better to set light to the whole place. It seemed a lifetime ago that she had prepared for a girls' night in by purchasing expensive roses and scented candles to set the mood. It was hardly the same in her damp-ridden flat. But then, nothing was the same for her any more. The most upsetting thing was that she hadn't been able to make any ice-cream.

Charley had found out to her cost that wooden floorboards had been installed in the flat above. Every noise was magnified tenfold. Footsteps, furniture scraping along the floor, dropped objects.

'What are they doing up there?' asked Julie, walking into the lounge. 'Auditioning for *Riverdance*?'

'You get used to it,' lied Charley, turning up the radio for some background noise.

'This is, er . . .' Samantha stopped and looked

around her. She was unable to disguise the horror on her face as she took in the flat. Finally she broke into a smile. 'Let's unscrew that wine, eh?'

Once poured, they clinked their wine glasses together and tried to act normal.

'To the future,' said Caroline.

'And may Steve's be absolutely rotten,' said Julie.

Charley sighed.

'It must have been horrible for you, finding them together like that?' said Caroline.

Charley shrugged her shoulders. 'It wasn't a Kodak moment, that's for sure.'

'I hear the Caribbean is rubbish this time of year anyway,' said Samantha.

'Start of the hurricane season, isn't it?' said Julie. 'The hotel will probably be as flat as a pancake by now.'

'And real tans are out,' said Caroline, whose pale skin never went dark, thanks to Factor 50. 'Better to fake it anyway.'

Samantha just managed to stop herself from telling them about the long weekend in Ibiza that she'd booked with some of her female work colleagues.

'So how's the cleaning?' asked Julie.

Charley rolled her eyes. 'Exhausting.'

The others shook their heads in sympathy.

'With the added joy of bumping into old school chums,' she said with a groan.

Caroline frowned. 'Who?'

'Mike Shearer, of all people.'

'Aww!' cooed Caroline. 'He was always so sweet at school. You were too busy getting off with Steve behind the bike shed to notice.'

Charley's reply caught in her throat at the mention of her husband's name.

'Mike went to agricultural college, I think,' said Caroline. 'Got his own business now. Doing really well, from what I hear.'

'He must be the same Mike I know at the gardening club,' said Julie. 'Tall and dark-haired?'

Caroline nodded. 'And with a great body!'

'Oooh,' said Samantha, her eyes lighting up. 'Handsome?'

'No,' said Charley at the same time as Caroline and Julie said, 'Yes.'

'Come on,' urged Caroline. 'You must at least admit he's good-looking?'

Charley shrugged her shoulders. 'He doesn't really compare with Steve.'

The others exchanged glances before looking at Charley sympathetically.

'You'll get over him,' said Julie in a gentle tone. 'In time.'

'I'm not so sure,' replied Charley.

'Ice-cream will help,' said Caroline. 'Have you made any?'

Charley shook her head. 'Too tired, too broke, and the freezer section at the top of the fridge is too small.'

'Just enough room for a small taster,' urged Julie. 'How about it?'

But Charley had no inclination to do any kind of cooking. Most evenings she slumped in her armchair, staring at the small television. Tired from a day's cleaning, she normally cooked herself a bowl of pasta with a tin of tomatoes poured on top. It was hardly nouvelle cuisine, but she didn't care. What was the point of making an effort when there was only her to cook for?

Besides, her lovely ice-cream maker had left along with the bailiffs.

No, her ice-cream days were definitely behind her.

Chapter Twenty-two

Back at Miss Fuller's house, Charley had just finished mopping the kitchen when a small dachshund called Desmond trotted through the back door and across the floor, leaving a perfect set of dirty pawprints behind him.

Charley thought it was a good thing that she was an animal lover otherwise Desmond could easily have ended up in her father's workshop.

On Tuesday morning she had to drive into Upper Grove, although thankfully to a different road from the one on which she had lived until a few short weeks previously.

The reminder did little to lighten her mood, especially when she met her new customer. It hadn't been instant dislike on Charley's part. It had taken as long as thirty seconds perhaps.

She didn't know why Mrs Smith irritated her so much. Perhaps it was the ridiculous new home which had been built in the style of a Spanish villa. Maybe it looked all right when the sun was shining, but on a dismal April morning the pristine white villa appeared as fake as Mrs Smith's generous chest.

And then there had been the name. 'It's pronounced Smythe.'

Charley watched Mrs Smith swan off to her fitness class and was about to close the back door when she spotted someone striding across the garden. With Grove Village not being the largest place in England, perhaps Charley should have expected that trained gardeners would be thin on the ground. But she had not reckoned on coming face to face with this one so soon after their last meeting.

'Hello again,' said Mike, with a nod.

Charley stood aside as he stepped in through the back door. 'Hi.'

'I thought I recognised your Mini on the driveway.'

Charley rolled her eyes. 'Oh, yes. There's only one like it in the world. I hope.'

Mike followed her into the kitchen. Most customers were happy for Charley to help herself to a hot drink. Some days it was the only thing that kept her going.

Mike nodded at the empty garage viewed through the kitchen window. 'Where's she gone this morning?'

'Pilates.'

He gave a snort of derision. 'Isn't that some kind of Greek bread?'

Charley smiled as she poured hot water into two mugs. 'So the gardening business is going well?'

'Thanks,' he said, taking the mug from her. 'Yes. Can't say it was easy in the early days, but I'm doing okay.'

She didn't offer any information about herself. She was cleaning other people's houses. Her situation was obvious enough.

Thankfully her mobile rang so Mike gave her a nod and headed outside while she answered it.

'Hey. It's me.'

Her heart lurched at the sound of Steve's voice. It was the first time they had spoken in a couple of weeks.

She tried to keep her voice level. 'How are you?'

He gave a sigh. 'Not great.'

'That makes two of us,' she snapped, before instantly regretting her words. Now wasn't the time for nagging. Especially if he had missed her enough to call.

'The doctor's put me on antidepressants,' said Steve.

'Oh dear.'

Charley was trying to work up the strength to feel sorry for him, but all she could think was that he hadn't even asked about her, about how she was.

'You're not making this easy for me,' her husband told her.

Charley tutted in exasperation. 'What do you expect?'

'I did apologise, if you remember.'

'No. I don't, as it happens.' Her tone began to harden. 'I don't think you ever said sorry for anything. For the money you borrowed from my parents. For losing the roof over our heads. For any of it.'

He heaved a theatrical sigh. 'This obviously isn't a good time for me to have called.'

'I haven't had a good time since you spent all of our money and then cheated on me,' she snapped.

'Look . . .' he began.

'No, you look!' Charley's voice had risen above shrill. 'I'm here, slogging my guts out cleaning other people's toilets, for God's sake! I'm trying to make enough so I can pay back the money you took from my parents. And I'm having to do it all by myself, because *you're not here!*' Her voice was now so high it was possible only dogs could hear her. 'You haven't even asked about me, have you? No, as always it's all about you. It's always been about you! You broke my heart, stole my parents' life savings, wasted all of our money . . . and now you've got the nerve to ring up because *you're* the one that's depressed!'

Charley gave a frustrated scream and threw the phone across the room, narrowly missing Mike who had come back into the kitchen to drop off his empty mug.

He raised his eyebrows at her and opened his mouth as if to speak. But seeing her irate expression, he quickly changed his mind and left.

Charley was left to stomp about the kitchen in a rage, before grabbing the mop and bucket to clean the floor. She slopped the damp mop against the tiles with a smack, shaking with fury as she swished it to and fro.

Steve was a liar, a rat, and she wanted nothing to do with him ever again. He and that trollop deserved each other.

Halfway across the floor she stopped and let the pain wash over her for a moment. He was still her husband and she missed him, despite his many faults. She missed him so much she ached.

Her tears splashed on to the floor. She began to move the mop around once more until they had disappeared.

Chapter Twenty-three

By the end of the week, Charley felt as low as she had ever done. The fresh misery caused by Steve's phone call hung over her like a cloud. The cleaning had been exhausting and demeaning. Her husband had not called her back or even sent a text. She had hidden from Mike in the downstairs bathroom that afternoon at Mrs Wilberforce's house, not able to face any questions about Steve.

Charley blinked away a tear and pulled down the kitchen blind before washing up her solitary plate. She missed her dishwasher, her six-ring hob, even the microwave. She missed everything from her previous life, but especially the food.

Having bought some basics and topped up the electric meter, she only had £14.50 left in her purse to last her the weekend. Everything was now paid for in cash, including the rent. Using an electricity meter had been an eye-opening experience. Now she made sure that every wall socket was turned off when not in use. She could see the meter count rising if even her mobile was charging, so nothing was left on standby.

Being paid in cash did make it easier to keep to a budget, she had learned. Whatever amount of money she had in her purse was final. There were no hidden accounts, no cash stashed away. Once it had gone, there was nothing else.

Charley was still using up the drawerfuls of shower gels, lotions and potions that she had purchased months or even years ago. They were all expensive, in total contradiction to her current circumstances. But at least her skin felt and smelt nice.

It was a different story with the food she ate. All the store-cupboard basics such as pasta, rice and anything tinned were fine. She had lots of those, but it was all easy, bland fare. Her beloved special ingredients, the magic touches she had once used to make her ice-cream and other favourite recipes, were still boxed up untouched in the hall cupboard. She hadn't yet been able to face unpacking them.

The phone rang at eight o'clock on Saturday morning. There was only one person who would call her at that time of the weekend.

'Charlotte? It's Mum. What are you doing today?'

Charley stifled a yawn. 'Not much.'

'It's the second day of the May Day Fête and I'm manning the cake stall. Why don't you come down later and sample my rock cakes?'

Charley grimaced at the thought. 'I'm a bit tired, actually. Thought I'd rest today.'

'Well, come over for lunch tomorrow. I know! You can make some ice-cream for pudding.'

'I haven't got the ice-cream maker any more,' said Charley, feeling herself sink into melancholy.

127

Her mother tutted. 'Then make it the way you used to, lazybones. You don't need those fancy gadgets . . . What's that? . . . Your grandmother says a bit of your ice-cream will go down a treat before she heads home next week.'

Charley thought Granny would probably be grateful for the opportunity of some edible food.

'I haven't got any ingredients in the house,' she whined.

Didn't her mother realise how painful this was for her? How painful everything was these days?

'Get yourself down the market then. You'll get some cheap fruit there.'

'I don't know if I can, Mum.'

'You've promised your grandmother now, you can't let her down, and I forgot to pick up a dessert for tomorrow. Come round at twelve. It'll be fun.'

She hid under the duvet for a while, desperate to go back to sleep but the conversation with her mother had woken up the dormant chef inside. With a sigh, Charley threw off the duvet and stumbled out of the bedroom and into the hallway.

She flung open the door to the tall cupboard and stared down at the pile of boxes. 'Sugar and Syrups', she had written on one. The word 'Spices' was written on another.

Charley recalled the day when all her precious cooking ingredients had been packed away. Bottle by bottle, packet by packet, she had picked them out of her enormous built-in larder and put them into the appropriate cardboard box. Some of the ingredients had barely been touched; some were old favourites that she'd used time and time again. Her precious collection of cooking ingredients had been tucked out of sight if not quite out of mind. Charley had often found herself thinking about her cardamom pods or kirsch liqueur. She had even found herself standing outside Gino's delicatessen and inhaling the fragrant aroma in deep breaths. But she no longer went inside. Couldn't bear to.

Now her precious ingredients were in front of her again, just waiting to be touched, tasted. She reached up to the box on top of the stack and brought it down. On the side she had written 'Recipe Books'. She ripped off the packing tape, opened up the box and stared inside. There they were, her books, all with well-thumbed pages and creased spines. She had given away the ones she never used to the charity shop. But these were her favourites, her old friends that she could never give away.

She knew which particular book she was searching for and dug deep until she found it. It was a book on desserts, in which she had found a basic ice-cream recipe many years previously. To that classic base, any number of flavourings could be added.

Charley knew she had the sugar but she was going to require cream and fruit. She found herself pouting like a sulky teenager. She didn't want to make ice-cream. It was too painful a reminder of how far she had fallen, of how happy she had been with Steve and how lonely and miserable she was now.

Ultimately, though, she knew that the pain of making ice-cream would be nothing compared to the pain she'd endure if she turned up at her mother's house the following day without it. Besides, she still owed them £40,000. A bit of ice-cream was nothing compared to that debt.

She ate her breakfast in front of the television and

remained there until she knew she could put it off no longer. After getting dressed, she walked out of Lower Grove towards the end of the high street where the market was held every Friday and Saturday.

In the heady days when she'd had money to spend, Charley had bought all her fruit and vegetables in the farmers' market which was held in Little Grove on a Tuesday morning. There she had bought produce which was fresh, local and organic. A little bit pricy but it was top-quality food.

By comparison, the main Grove market was less organic fair, more flea market. In a small car park at the back of the cinema about fifty stalls jostled for space. Amongst the fruit and vegetable stalls were imitation handbags, knock-off DVDs and dodgy mobile phones.

Charley strolled around, enjoying the calls of the market traders and the smell of fresh produce. There were lots of imported bananas and melons, but in the end she chose a large punnet of early strawberries. She also picked up some new potatoes and a cabbage. The whole purchase came to £2. In the good old days, the only thing that had cost her less than a fiver on her supermarket bill was *Vogue* magazine.

She wandered away from the stalls, swinging her carrier bag and feeling a rare glimmer of something approaching contentment. On the way back she popped into the corner shop and picked up a large pot of whipping cream, which was about to go out of date. It was going to be frozen that afternoon so it didn't matter.

Her silent flat was in stark contrast to the noise and bustle of the market. Anticipating the loneliness about to engulf her once more, Charley brought out the small radio that her father had lent her. Her iPod and CDs had all been sold by Julie on eBay the previous week, which had brought in a few more precious pounds.

She placed the radio on the kitchen counter and switched it on. Every pop song was either about being happy or unhappy in love. She didn't need reminding of either, so fiddled with the dial until she came across some classical music. No words meant no reminders and the tunes were quite jolly, so she was able to start making her ice-cream.

She washed and hulled about half of the strawberries, before cutting them up into tiny pieces. Normally she would have puréed them in a blender, but the bailiffs had taken both the blender and food processor. Instead she mashed up the strawberries with the end of a rolling pin. There were a few small lumps remaining, but Charley figured that they would add a bit of texture.

She whipped the sugar into the cream until it was just thickened, another task that took a lot longer without her precious food processor. Her arms were aching by the end.

Then she folded in the strawberry mush, giving it a ripple effect, and poured the whole mixture into an old Tupperware box, ready to freeze. Without her ice-cream maker, she had to remove the box from the freezer every half-hour to give the mixture a stir and ensure it remained smooth.

At least it kept her busy. By the time the ice-cream was frozen, Charley had managed to lose a couple of hours and it was the middle of the afternoon. She looked down at the mixture and felt impressed with herself. Without any kitchen gadgets, she had made this.

Still, she felt she should have made a bit more of an

effort. Perhaps a touch of strawberry jam to bring out more of the fruit taste. Or making a chocolate base would have been a nice twist. But she was exhausted by the cleaning and by the mental strain of the week, so she put the ice-cream back into the freezer and went into the bedroom for a nap.

She tossed and turned before curling up on the bed in a tight ball. Without anything to distract her, her imagination ran wild. She daydreamed of Steve arriving unexpectedly at her door, apologising, sobbing that he'd make a terrible mistake and that they should be together, for ever.

Unable to sleep, Charley groaned in despair. She was tired but knew that keeping busy was going to be the key to survival. So she dragged herself off the bed and went back into the kitchen to begin making another batch of ice-cream.

Chapter Twenty-four

On Sunday afternoon, Charley found herself sitting at her parents' dining table, looking at their new double-glazed patio door.

'It's lovely,' she said to her mother, hoping her tone was enthusiastic enough. It was hard to become animated about a sheet of glass at any time of the day.

'They've made a right mess on your father's decking, which we'll have to fix somehow.'

'But how can you afford it?' said Charley.

'They couldn't cancel the order, could they?' said Granny, who was sitting at the head of the table. 'The fools paid in advance.'

'All those dodgy cancellation policies these companies have,' added Aunty Peggy, who had also joined them for lunch. 'Disgusting it is, how they can rip off good people.'

Charley hung her head, once more feeling the burden of guilt for her parents' current financial status.

'Wasting the last of their money, when the roof's got

a leak and the washing machine's up the creek,' carried on Granny.

Charley looked across the table at her parents. 'Is that true?'

'It doesn't matter,' said her mother quickly. 'It's been a nice change going up the launderette.'

She didn't look her daughter in the eye and Charley knew she was lying. For a start, the launderette was in Lower Grove.

'Anyway, Peggy's giving us her old one when her new machine comes at the end of the month.'

They were both being so cheerful, so plucky, despite the fact that they had nothing much to live on. Charley looked down at her plate, which looked worse than normal. Her mother appeared to have bought the smallest chicken in the world for the roast dinner. Plus they had been given only two small roast potatoes each. The meal was inedible as usual, but there would never have been as little of it on offer as this in the old days. Charley felt wretched.

'Lovely chicken, Maureen.' Aunty Peggy's faulty taste-buds were legendary. 'Charlotte? You not eating any?'

Charley glanced down at her plate of burnt offer-ings and undercooked poultry. 'I've got a bit of a headache.'

'That'll be all those chemicals you're using in that new job of yours. Your lungs are probably hardening up. Plus all those filthy houses . . . Goodness only knows what kind of skin complaints you'll pick up! Those dust mites can be nasty little buggers. It wouldn't surprise me if you ended up covered in eczema . . .'

Charley suppressed a wave of nausea and hoped it was only the chicken.

'And as for other people's beds,' carried on Aunty

Peggy, 'I shudder to think about them. Don't you, Maureen? Once you've got bed bugs, you're stuck with them. They're dirty little devils too. Luckily, my mother swore by her home-made potions. I can always knock up something for you, if you end up with a tapeworm.'

'Shut up, Peggy,' said Granny, with a fierce glare. 'The girl's gotta work, hasn't she? And she's working a damn sight harder than you ever did, in that cushy office job of yours.'

Aunty Peggy stuffed a potato in her mouth. She would never have dared contradict Granny. Charley also received a hard stare from her grandmother.

'Eat up your food, Charlotte,' she snapped. 'None of us can afford to let good food go to waste.'

The trouble was, the food here was never good, which was probably why the strawberry ice-cream went down so well.

'Give us a second helping,' said Granny, holding out her empty bowl. 'You were a bit stingy with the first serving, Maureen.'

'Very tasty,' said Aunty Peggy, also on her second helping. 'Did you hear about Grove Castle?'

'I know!' replied Maureen, turning to tell the rest of the family. 'He's only gone and married her!'

Grove Castle had been yet another English stately home struggling for survival before the last Lord Beckenham had passed away. His fifty-year-old son, who was rumoured to be a playboy, had just caused a scandal by installing his glamorous and very young new girlfriend as Lady of the Manor.

'I heard she wants to reinstate the Valentine's Ball,' said Aunty Peggy.

'She never does!' replied Maureen.

135

'I met your grandfather at the Valentine's Ball at the Castle,' Granny told Charley. 'He looked so handsome in his demob suit.'

'What were you wearing?' asked Charley.

'A pair of curtains.' Granny smiled.

Charley was shocked.

'It was just after the war. There wasn't a decent dress to be found anywhere. Plus we had no money, did we? So your great-grandmother got down the rose-printed curtains from the front room, cut out a pattern on them, and I wore that once she'd stitched it together. It had tiny little red rosebuds on it. Ever so pretty.'

'I didn't know that.'

Charley suddenly realised her family had been through a whole host of bad times before the present crisis. Post-war rationing, three-day weeks, recession after recession. If they could survive all that, why couldn't she do the same? If her grandmother could wear a pair of curtains to a fancy ball, why couldn't Charley clean other people's houses to keep a roof over her head? It wasn't her dream job but she was still surviving, wasn't she?

She reached across the table to give her grandmother a kiss on the cheek.

'What's that for?' asked Granny, with a smile.

'Kisses are free, aren't they?' replied Charley.

A few good things were. She just had to find them.

Chapter Twenty-five

Samantha checked her appearance in the bathroom mirror. Not bad . . . not bad at all. Her hair was a little messy but in a good, sexy way. Her eye make-up had stayed intact. She peered closer. The blusher had disappeared from her cheeks but they still had colour in them.

She smiled a wicked smile at her reflection. Tonight had finally been the night. The weeks of flirting, the subtle gestures, the secret smiles . . . It had all been worth it.

She walked back into the bedroom. Only a single light was switched on next to the bed but even in the semi-darkness she could see what great shape Richard was in.

He was lying on his front, his bare back smooth and thankfully hair-free. As he stretched out one arm, she saw the muscles flex inside it. She walked quietly to the bed and reached out her hand to stroke his ruffled hair. But she managed to stop herself just in time and sat down on the edge of the bed instead.

'Hey, you,' she said in a husky tone.

'Mmm,' he murmured, reaching out to pull her down on the bed with him. He kissed her on the lips before moving his mouth down her neck.

'Uh-uh,' she told him, pulling away. 'It's time for you to get back to your room, before anyone finds out.'

'Why don't I leave early in the morning instead?' He drew her close and began to kiss her again.

'Because someone will see.'

God, but she really wanted him to stay, to keep touching her. But she had to be strong if he couldn't.

'Come on,' she said, her voice a little firmer, as she managed to escape from his arms to the other side of the bed.

With a groan, Richard threw off the covers and began to tug on his trousers. She remained on the bed, holding the sheet over her demurely.

Once dressed, he bent down towards her.

'Damn, you look so sexy,' he told her, before giving her a rough kiss. 'I'll call you.'

Samantha nodded. 'Yes, please.'

One last goodnight kiss and he was gone, closing the hotel door quietly behind him.

She sighed and sank back on to the pillows. She was right to be sensible. The last thing they needed was some nosy work colleague spotting him wandering through the hotel corridors early in the morning.

And this affair was going to be on her terms, no one else's. Samantha allowed herself a smile of pure satisfaction. She was in total control and loving it.

* * *

Caroline took a long gulp of her chilled white wine.

'I thought we'd got past the toddler-tantrum phase.'

Jeff refilled his own glass. 'We have. She's just going through a growth spurt before school. You know, finding her own little way in the world.'

Caroline raised her eyebrows in surprise. 'Have you been on Mumsnet again?'

He shook his head. 'No, but I have actually read some of those parenting books you bought.'

'Go on then,' she said, relishing the relaxing effect the wine had on her. 'Why don't you tell me which level of competency Flora should be at before she starts school?'

Jeff laughed. 'Competency? She's four years old!'

'I know, but in terms of social and physical skills, what do you think we should be concentrating on?'

Jeff tried not to despair over his wife's perfectionism when it came to their daughter. He just wanted to relax after a hard week's work, not run through more parenting checklists.

He looked at Caroline sitting on the sofa next to him. She was gorgeous, kind and generous, but she could stress for England. And a discussion about school was the last thing on his mind at that moment.

He reached out to play with a long lock of titian hair that had escaped from her ponytail.

'Jeff? Did you hear what I said?'

He smiled at his wife. 'Do we have to talk about this tonight?'

'When else do we get the chance? You're at work all week until late and we can't talk about it when Flora's about.'

'What about tomorrow night?'

139

Caroline frowned. 'What's wrong with tonight?'

'Because I don't want to talk about Flora tonight.' He shuffled closer to her on the sofa. 'Tonight is going to be all about us grown-ups.'

'Jeff . . .' she protested as he began to nibble her ear lobe. 'This is important.'

'You're right about that,' he murmured.

'That's not what I meant,' she told her husband.

But the couple of glasses of wine were beginning to relax her. Perhaps the conversation about their daughter could wait.

Caroline was smiling as she leant over to kiss Jeff.

'You look awful,' said Sidney.

'Says the man with the hacking cough in May,' Julie told her uncle.

'It's nothing.'

Julie wasn't so sure. Her uncle Sidney was in his mid-seventies and that cough had been hanging on since late March.

'So have you been out on the town with your friends again?' he asked, cupping the mug of tea Julie had made him between his hands.

'No such luck,' she said. 'Nick had all of his mates over last night.'

Sidney shook his head. 'When are you going to throw him out?'

She was aghast. 'I can't!'

'Why not?'

'He's my son.'

'So? Might do him a bit of good rather than all this smothering.'

'There's no work out there for anyone in their late teens, you know that.'

140

Sidney fixed his niece with a stare. 'Has he even tried looking?'

Julie sighed. 'He's all I've got.'

'Yes, but he knows that and takes advantage of you. Always has.'

'I know.'

After they'd finished off a packet of biscuits, Sidney showed Julie out. His progress down the stairs from his flat was painfully slow. She knew that eventually they would have to make a tough decision, but he had lived here all his life. The flat was above the sweet shop which had been in Sidney's family for many years. These days, though, the shop was closed.

She drove home, yawning. She really would have to have a word with Nick about the late nights. That morning, she had almost fallen asleep at her desk.

'Nick?' she called, as she opened up the front door.

'In here,' he shouted from the kitchen. 'Where've you been? I've got a surprise for you.'

Julie sent up a silent prayer. Nick's surprises were never good news.

She took a deep breath and walked into the kitchen.

'Got something to cheer you up,' her son told her, opening the back door and heading outside.

For a fleeting second, Julie wondered whether he had actually bought her something for the garden. But she quickly decided that wasn't possible. Nick never gave her gifts like that.

She raised her head as her son returned. But he wasn't alone. Her motherly instincts had been spot on.

'This is for you.'

Nick held out a small, wriggling puppy.

Chapter Twenty-six

By the time she arrived at Mrs Wilberforce's house on Friday afternoon, Charley didn't think it was possible to feel any lower.

The cleaning job was wretched, but the ongoing effects of the bankruptcy hung over her like a black cloud. She had nothing left but the money in her handbag, and that wasn't much.

As she passed through the kitchen, she glanced at Mrs Wilberforce's purse which had been left on the sideboard. Charley stopped short and stared down at it. All she needed was a little bit of money, she thought. Just enough to put in the electricity meter for the weekend and to buy some food. How easy it would be to turn to a life of crime.

She took a deep breath and began to turn away. She would never sink that low. She had nothing left but her morals and she was going to cling on to them as long as she could.

She gave a start as she saw Mike standing in the back doorway, watching her. His eyes darted to the purse and then back to her face. Blushing, Charley quickly left to return to the drawing room. Could he tell what she had been thinking? She shook her head and switched on the ancient Hoover.

At the end of the afternoon she bumped into him once more as they both waited patiently for Mrs Wilberforce to pay them.

'That's peculiar,' said the old lady, frowning. 'I could have sworn I had another £20 note in here.'

Charley watched as Mrs Wilberforce checked and rechecked the pockets of the purse once more.

'Well, I don't know,' she said, shaking her head. 'Let me just pop upstairs. I would hate not to be able to pay you both for your hard work today.'

Charley watched her make her slow progress up the stairs. The last thing she needed was not to be paid. She had no food for the weekend and had been relying on this money.

In the silence that followed, she gradually became aware of Mike's eyes upon her. He said nothing but her cheeks began to flush under his scrutiny. She forced herself to glance back at him, their eyes locking for a moment. Then she looked away.

His dark eyes betrayed nothing but she knew what he was thinking. Knew what his silent accusation meant. And the embarrassment slowly changed to anger. What kind of a person did he think she had become? She hadn't stolen anything.

Mrs Wilberforce reappeared on the landing.

'Here it is!' she called, waving the £20 note in her hand.

Charley flashed Mike a smug smile before turning her attention to the old lady coming down the stairs.

'I must have put it to one side last night,' said Mrs

Wilberforce, arriving in front of them. 'There you are.'

She handed different notes to Charley and Mike.

'Thank you,' said Charley, putting the money in her handbag. 'Well, I'd better go. Have a nice weekend.'

'You too, dear.'

Mike caught up with her as she walked towards the Mini.

'What was all that about?' he asked, grabbing her elbow. 'That look you gave me. What's going on?'

Charley spun round as he spoke, gazing up at him accusingly. 'You know exactly what it was. You thought I'd taken the money, didn't you?'

He rolled his eyes. 'Of course not. How stupid do you think I am?'

'Is that a rhetorical question?' she snapped back.

'I don't understand you at all these days,' he told her, shaking his head.

'Because you obviously think the worst of me. And what's worse than being a thief? But you were wrong, weren't you? I would never steal from anyone, regardless of any temptation to do so.'

'It sounds like you're arguing with yourself, not me.'

But Charley wasn't listening to him, too intent on venting the resentment that had been building inside her for so long.

'Go on,' she said, goading him. 'Admit it. Tell me what you really think of me.'

He stood in front of her, their bodies almost touching. His disdain was almost overpowering as he glared down at her. When he finally spoke, his voice was scathing.

'I try not to think of you, to be honest. You're so self-obsessed. So wrapped up in your own little world of woe. It's all about you, isn't it? God save me from

144

women like you who are only interested in money.'

Shocked by his words, Charley gave him a hard shove so she could pass by him. She opened the car door and sat behind the wheel. She wanted to close the door but found Mike was hanging on to it.

'Let go,' she told him, tugging at the door handle.

He didn't. 'For the record, I never thought you had stolen that money.'

She wrenched the door away from him and slammed it shut. The car started with a puff of grey smoke and a squeal from under its bonnet. Charley crunched it into gear and drove off.

Chapter Twenty-seven

On the way home she received a phone call from Caroline, telling her to drive straight to Julie's house after work.

All the women were enchanted by the fluffy golden retriever puppy as he charged around the garden chasing Flora, who was giggling with joy. The puppy's short thick legs gambolled in all directions. Once in a while he would come to an abrupt halt and stare up at them with his deep black eyes. His rapid panting seemed to make him smile as his pink tongue lolled out.

'He's adorable,' cooed Caroline, reaching out to stroke the puppy's soft fur.

'He's a menace,' said Julie, scowling at the low branch of one of her favourite rose bushes which had lost a tug-of-war and was now lying on the ground.

She was not enchanted by the puppy. She was as mad at her son as she had ever been.

'I got it from a man in the pub,' Nick had told her. 'Thought it would cheer you up.'

'Why would I need cheering up?' she'd snapped.

'Jeez,' said Nick, puffing out a large sigh. 'Thought you'd be pleased.'

'Well, I'm not,' said Julie, before trying out a more gentle tone of voice. 'Look, I'm grateful. Honest, I am. But I don't need one. I don't want one. You'll have to take it back to wherever it came from.'

She knew she didn't have time for a dog. She had her work and her garden. When would she find the time to walk the damn thing? What possible reason did she have to keep it? It had whined in the kitchen all night and there was pee all over the floor.

'Come on,' urged Samantha. 'Aren't you even a little bit tempted to keep him?'

'For what reason?' said Julie.

'Perhaps he would be a bit of company for you,' said Charley, who was discovering how lonely it was to live on her own. Maybe Julie had been lonely all these years as well.

'Look, you can have him if you want,' she said.

Charley shook her head. 'No pets allowed in the flat.'

Julie turned pleading eyes towards Samantha and Caroline.

Samantha shook her head. 'Allergies,' she lied.

'And I've got far too much on my plate,' added Caroline very quickly.

'Poor thing,' said Charley. 'It's only a youngster. Fancy Nick not buying anything for him, like food or a bed.'

'No surprise to me,' said Julie.

She had already had to make a swift trip to Pets R Us the previous evening and had ended up spending £100 on food, bowls and all sorts of doggy

147

paraphernalia. She wondered whether some of it might be returnable.

She was convinced Nick would get it sorted. For once, he wouldn't let her down.

Chapter Twenty-eight

The next Friday started badly for Charley when the Mini shuddered to a halt in the high street in the middle of rush hour. Turning the key over and over again didn't make the engine start. Nor did the strident horns of everyone stuck behind her.

Eventually a white van man pulled over to help push the Mini on to the side of the road. He had a quick look under the bonnet, fiddled with a few wires and got the car started again, but explained that this was only a temporary measure and it would take quite a bit of work to get the problem fixed. It sounded expensive so Charley decided not to think about it for the moment.

She was barely scraping through the month and had already had to sell the last of her jewellery that she had kept hidden from the bailiffs to meet the rent.

She had unearthed her jewellery box from the back of the wardrobe. It mainly held big gaudy pieces bought by Steve. They looked, and probably were, expensive but had never been to her taste. She kept her great-grandmother's ring and pearls but, apart from a few earrings and necklaces, took the whole lot to the new Sell Your Gold shop that had opened up in Lower Grove.

By Friday afternoon she had had enough and was grateful for the fact that once she had cleaned Mrs Wilberforce's entrance hall, she would be finished for the week.

Now that she had thoroughly cleaned the drawing and dining rooms, they only took half an hour to dust and vacuum. She was still building up to the horror of the kitchen, so had set herself the task of transforming the entrance hall and stairwell first.

The woodwork and windows were no trouble. However the entrance hall included a vast fireplace which was a blackened mess. It took her a whole hour to clean it thoroughly. Then it took a further ten minutes to wash all the soot from her face and hands.

Drying her hands and wishing she were anywhere but here, Charley allowed herself a loud sigh.

'Hi,' said Mike, suddenly appearing next to her.

She had opened the back door to let in some fresh air and hadn't heard him come in. She grunted a reply, still rattled by his uncaring attitude towards her the previous week. Plus her own embarrassment at having accused him of thinking her a thief.

'What's up?' he asked.

She glanced down at her t-shirt which was smudged with black soot. 'I'm filthy.'

'So? I am too.'

She rolled her eyes. 'You're a gardener. You're allowed to be. It's expected.'

'It's only dirt.' Mike shrugged his shoulders. 'It's a job. You should be grateful.'

She barked out a humourless laugh. 'Oh, yeah?' she said, sarcastically. 'Grateful for the fantastic time I'm having? Do me a favour.'

He stared down at her. 'Many people would be grateful for your job. You only beat the rest of the competition because Peggy had a word with that Patricia.'

'How do you know?'

'My mum heard it from Peggy.'

Charley sighed again. The village telegraph was obviously still working well. But suddenly she felt irritated. On top of everything else, she had to stand here and listen to someone tell her she should be grateful for the mess she was in. Thankful, even, that she was broke and alone.

'Listen,' she snapped. 'You don't know how hard it's been for me. In fact, you don't know anything about me and my life.'

'I know plenty,' he told her. 'Fancy clothes, fancy car, fancy house. Now it's all gone and poor little Charley hasn't got any toys left to play with.'

She flinched.

'It's not just that,' she told him, tears pricking her eyes.

'Yes, it is. You feel humiliated. Well, get over yourself.' He changed his tone of voice to a slightly softer one. 'Did you hear about Tommy Flynn? Threw himself in front of a train a month or so back.'

Tommy had been in their year at school too.

She nodded. 'I heard. But he had suffered from depression for years.'

'Cheryl Mann? Her husband walked out the very day she had her baby.'

This bit of news hadn't reached Charley and she was surprised.

'And what about Greg Baker? Just back from Afghanistan with his leg amputated from the knee.'

She held up her hand to stop Mike from going on. 'So what's your point?'

'My point is, you're healthy and you're alive. You've got all your limbs and most of your brain cells.' His eyes twinkled before he became serious once more. 'You never used to be a snob at school. You never used to care what people thought or lust over the most expensive car or house.'

A tear finally escaped and rolled its way slowly down Charley's cheek. He reached out and wiped it away with his rough hand. He had gardener's hands.

Mike stared into her eyes for a beat before saying, 'There's nothing wrong with being humbled once in a while. Get over yourself, Charlotte Summers, and I might start to like you again.'

She recoiled at his words but he was already walking back out into the garden. Charley was left alone with a swirl of emotions and a whole lot of anger.

How dare he talk to her like that? How dare he even think that about her? She wasn't a snob. She wasn't a bad person. She didn't deserve all this.

But a very small voice deep inside wondered if his words might be true.

Chapter Twenty-nine

Samantha held the phone under her ear as she picked up the set of matching underwear.

'Bloody man!' raged Charley.

'Absolutely,' murmured Samantha in agreement.

Perhaps red was a bit too trashy? Maybe the pale blue was better. Virginal, even. Samantha smirked to herself. Her two previous meetings with Richard had proved that she was anything but.

'So what if my clothes are designer?' carried on Charley. 'What does that matter to anyone?'

'Every woman should have pretty things,' said Samantha, now looking at a lace body before putting it back on the rail. Richard was classier than that.

She glanced at her watch. Half past four. She had already ducked out of work early, pretending to have a dentist's appointment, but really she just wanted to go shopping for something lovely and new, to bolster her confidence when she saw him later.

She couldn't stop thinking about him and this was bad. Bad for her self-control. Bad for staying on top in this relationship. If it was even to be a relationship.

He had come over to her flat twice since they had slept together at the conference. Yes, he was definitely married. No, he probably wasn't going to leave his wife any time soon. A couple of kids had made sure the wife was going to hang on to him as long as she could.

But that was fine with Samantha. She wasn't looking for love and marriage. Just a bit of fun with absolutely no strings attached.

The reason she couldn't stop thinking about him was that the sex had been phenomenal. It had been a long time since anyone had made her feel like that in bed. So they would continue to enjoy the sex and leave the messy relationship love stuff to others.

She was nearing the tills when she saw a pair of fluffy black handcuffs in the 'hen night' section. Samantha threw them into her shopping basket. Just in case he had a kinky side. She wanted to be his perfect fantasy.

Nothing on the outside of Caroline's beautifully kept house was anything less than perfect. The four-bedroomed detached cottage had been recently repainted. The front lawn was immaculate. The box hedge was clipped regularly to prevent any irregularities from ruining the line. There was even a white picket fence along the front of it.

The back garden was equally neat, until you reached a narrow path leading around the back of a hedge. Home-grown vegetables had seemed such a good idea at the time. Jeff wanted to do the manly thing and had dug over the whole area before collapsing in a heap in front of the Sunday football match on the television. As far as he was concerned, that was the only contribution required.

Caroline had readily agreed with him and speedily researched which vegetables would suit their soil, climate and aspect.

Jeff had joked the previous evening over dinner that soon all their fruit and vegetables would be brought in from the garden. Caroline had smiled and nodded along with him. But her heart was speared by fear. Fear that he would discover her guilty secret. Fear that her husband would find time in his hectic schedule to saunter down the garden path and find that things were not so rosy there as he thought.

For some reason, the green leaves of the early potatoes were a sickly-looking yellow. The onions she'd pulled up were barely bigger than a shallot. The strawberry and raspberry plants showed absolutely no signs of life.

In a final act of rebellion, the tomato plants had shrivelled up within a couple of days of being planted. It was these that Caroline had just been pulling up, to replace with healthy new plants she had bought from the garden centre.

Except Charley had rung to rage on about Mike's words to her earlier.

'Did you know about Cheryl Mann?' she asked down the phone.

'Yes,' said Caroline. 'Very sad. The husband's gone off with some bimbo.'

'Must be catching,' said Charley.

Caroline thought of Jeff. Thank God she trusted him. She knew she should confess to him about the vegetable plot and that he would just laugh. After all, he wasn't like Steve, the lying, stealing cheat. Caroline had more faith in her husband than that. But these little lies weren't in the same league. She just wanted everything to be perfect for him and Flora, that was all.

'Look, don't upset yourself,' she told her friend.

'I didn't become a snob, did I?' asked Charley in a small voice.

'No,' said Caroline, firmly.

She was bending down to place the rotting plants in the bottom of a garden rubbish bag when she found that she felt dizzy and a bit nauseous. Caroline staggered over to a low wall and sank on to it, trying to breathe deeply and keep calm.

'Are you sure?' said Charley.

'Sorry but I've got to go,' said Caroline. 'Nothing major, just a problem with Flora.'

'Is everything okay?'

'Oh, yes,' said Caroline, trying to control her breathing. 'I'll ring you tomorrow.'

She hung up the phone, feeling the prickling of tiny beads of sweat on her forehead. 'Mummy!' called Flora, coming around the corner. 'I've planted my sunflower seeds.'

'Good girl,' said Caroline, fixing a bright smile on her face.

'Where's the watering can?' she asked.

Caroline stood up, suppressing the sickness and forcing herself to carry on. She had no time to be sick. There was work to be done.

'So what if my house was large?'

'Charley, you're talking to the wrong person,' said Julie. 'Mine's covered in dog hair.'

She let her friend rant on for a couple more minutes

but in the end had to hang up. She knew she had to face whatever was waiting inside for her.

Julie cautiously turned the key in the lock. She crept inside and closed the front door softly. There was no sound, no movement. She sighed and felt herself relax as she turned around . . . but then stopped in her tracks. There he was. The enemy within.

The fat, golden retriever puppy sitting in the middle of the hallway gave a short, delighted puppy bark at seeing Julie. She glared back at him. He was sitting next to a pool of pee on her oak floorboards.

'Nick!' she hollered, but already knew he wasn't at home. His car wasn't in the driveway.

Julie went to find some wipes from the kitchen. The cupboard under the sink was stuffed with wipes and disinfectant since the puppy had arrived.

But when asked, 'How are you getting on with finding a new home for the puppy?' each morning and evening, her son would merely shrug his shoulders and reply that he was waiting for a phone call.

In the meantime, Julie was stuck with them both. Her son had told her that he was 'between jobs'. She was secretly praying for a swift employment offer as her quiet routine had been totally disrupted. Contrary to all promises, Nick hadn't fed or cleaned up after the dog since they had both arrived. The puppy whined when left, had chewed every sock and shoe available, and appeared never to have been toilet trained. Julie's home had become one massive lavatory, or so it seemed to her.

Even her beloved garden was starting to look a little battered. The pots of herbs around the back door had been pulled up in some kind of canine frolic. Julie had had to move them up high out of reach.

Every night she would fall exhausted into bed and then listen to the puppy whine. Nick said he couldn't hear a thing and that she must be exaggerating.

Julie couldn't wait until her life reverted to normal once more, when it would be just her and her beloved garden.

Chapter Thirty

It wasn't the first time the boy had pointed the pistol at Charley but it was the first time she'd known he was going to shoot her.

Mrs Smith's stepson was home from boarding school for the holidays. Alexander was a ghastly child who wasn't due back at school until late September.

Charley wasn't sure if he should return to school or be sent straight to prison.

'Put it down,' she told him, looking around the kitchen for an escape route.

There wasn't one. He was blocking the doorway.

'Think of the trouble you'll get into if you shoot me,' she said.

'I don't care.'

The eight-year-old boy broke into a grin and squeezed the trigger.

Water came rushing out of the water pistol and splashed against her chest and face. Ker-pow. She'd been hit.

Mrs Smith rounded the corner a second too late.

'Oh dear,' she said, taking in Charley's dripping face and sopping wet top. She turned to face her stepson. 'That was very naughty, Alexander. Say sorry to Charlotte.'

'Sorry,' he sing-songed. 'Can I have some chocolate?'

'No,' snapped his stepmother. 'We're going to Isabella's birthday party in a while. You can have some there.'

'But I want chocolate now!' he wailed, stomping around the kitchen and kicking over the bucket of water with which Charley had been mopping the floor.

'Alexander! Stop that!' Mrs Smith clutched her Botoxed forehead, which was straining unsuccessfully to scowl.

'I want chocolate! I want chocolate!' he chanted, going round and round the kitchen table, all the while kicking spilt water up the kitchen cabinets.

'I said no!'

'I'll tell Daddy!'

'Enough!' she cried. 'We'll get some on the way to the party, okay?'

Alexander finally stopped stomping. 'And a new Playstation game?' he said, an evil grin on his face. 'Then I can tell Daddy how nice you've been to me today when he gets home later.'

Mrs Smith gave her stepson a smile which suggested she would like to gouge his eyes out with her false nails, but merely said, 'Of course, darling.'

They departed a short time later, leaving Charley with a thumping headache and a hell of a mess in the kitchen.

'I thought you were supposed to be cleaning up

the mess, not making it,' said a voice from the back door.

She turned round and shot Mike a glare. She hadn't forgotten his previous harsh words, which had left her stewing all weekend.

'Any chance of a coffee?' he asked.

She ignored him as she began to mop up the water.

'Charley?' he prompted. 'Hello?'

She squeezed the mop head into the bucket before looking at him. 'I'm not speaking to you,' she told him.

'Thank God for that. I thought I'd gone deaf.'

'You were very mean to me.'

He shrugged his shoulders. 'Only for your own good.'

She sighed. 'Why do you hate me?'

'I don't hate you. However, I still haven't forgiven you for breaking my yellow pencil.'

She looked up, puzzled. 'On Friday? I don't remember.'

He shook his head. 'No. I mean when we were twelve.'

'Twelve years old?'

'Yeah. In Mrs McClusky's class.'

Charley stared at him in utter bewilderment. 'What on earth are you talking about?'

'We used to sit next to each other. You stole it out of my pencil case for something, used it and then broke it. You were trying to impress Steve because you had a huge crush on him.'

Charley blew out a long sigh. 'And look how well that turned out.' She glanced at Mike. 'Well, sorry about the pencil.'

'That's all right.'

With that, he left.

Charley shook her head. Who would harbour a grudge about a pencil after all these years? Men. There was something wrong with each and every one of them.

Chapter Thirty-one

Charley had a secret.

The weekdays weren't a problem. She would clean all day and then stagger back, exhausted. Her evenings were then spent slumped in front of the television, before a quick shower and into bed. But at least keeping busy meant that she didn't have time to think about her ex-husband any more.

She didn't really bother about making a fancy dinner either. She still felt embarrassed and guilty about the sheer amount of food she used to waste by buying too much and then letting it go uneaten. Let alone how much money she used to squander on takeaway coffees, sandwiches and cakes.

Now she checked how much money she had in her purse before she went food shopping, and tried to spend around half what she used to. She bought food from the basic supermarket ranges. Some of it tasted fine. Some was dreadful. Trial and error taught her which to avoid.

Some food was horribly expensive, she realised.

Especially meat and fish. So the majority of her meals were jacket potatoes or pasta. She no longer bought bottled water either. It tasted just fine coming out of the tap so she made do with that, refilling a spare bottle each day to take with her to work.

Carbohydrates were abhorred by Dukan dieters, but Charley now weighed less than she had done for many years. The combination of physical work and reasonably healthy meals meant her extra pounds had just dropped off. All those years of worrying about her weight, when all she'd had to do was follow the bankruptcy diet.

But the weekends dragged. So much time and nobody to spend it with. She did pop out and see the girls sometimes, but most of her time was spent in solitude. It was then that her mood deteriorated, as she mulled over mistakes made in the past.

Even cleaning was better than sitting around with nothing to do all day. In hindsight she could see the tediousness of her previous existence. Not that she wouldn't have given her right arm to go back to a bit of luxury now and then, and to her wonderful kitchen in particular.

More often than not, out of sheer loneliness, she would let her mother persuade her to come to Sunday lunch. Anything to get out of the flat.

'Bring some ice-cream,' Maureen would say.

And Charley would sigh, huffing and puffing that she didn't really have time, knowing she did. So she began to keep a couple of pounds aside each week for ice-cream ingredients, as well as one or two pounds extra to save up towards repaying her parents. It would take years, she knew. But she would pay them back.

The bankruptcy was being taken care of by the

Official Receiver. It was just a matter of time and survival until it was dissolved in a year's time.

In the meantime, she would wander down to the Saturday market, buy some fruit and knock up a batch of strawberry or raspberry ice-cream. Punnets of in-season strawberries and raspberries were relatively cheap. The tiny ice box in the top of her fridge could hold only two slim Tupperware boxes, but that was all she needed.

Soon she had begun to grow bored with the plainer recipes, lovely as they tasted. So one Saturday afternoon in the middle of June, she had opened up the hallway cupboard and stared at the cardboard boxes filling most of the space there.

She had already opened up the recipe book box but that wasn't what she was interested in now. Instead she picked up another box and took it into the kitchen. Placing it on the small counter, she ripped off the packaging tape and opened up the cardboard flaps.

She stared down for a long time before reaching in and grabbing one of the clear bottles. She knew which one it was before she had even read the label. It was rosewater. She slowly unscrewed the top before inhaling the sweet scent. Charley knew instinctively that a few drops of this would add a subtle new flavour to her raspberry ice-cream.

She carefully pulled out a tall bottle of elderflower cordial. In the past she had mixed it with sparkling water to make a refreshing summer drink. Elderflowers, she knew, had a natural affinity with gooseberries. Now it would add new depth to a refreshing sorbet.

Charley's hand twitched to grab the next bottle but she stopped herself, carefully folding the cardboard back over the bottle tops and replacing the box in the hallway closet. The other ingredients would wait until next week. She wanted to pace herself and keep the excitement building within her.

When she returned from the market later that morning, Charley was laden with fresh raspberries and gooseberries. It was the height of the season when all the summer fruit was at its cheapest.

It took her the rest of the day to whip up two separate ice-creams. The raspberry and rosewater mix was creamy and rich, dotted with dark pink. The gooseberry and elderflower sorbet was light and refreshing, a delicate pale green that was perfect for summer.

Whilst the desserts set in the freezer, Charley opened up one of the still-empty kitchen cupboards. She carefully placed the bottles of rosewater and elderflower inside.

Half an hour later, she peeled off the Tupperware lids and tested both the mixtures. She checked the texture and colour of each ice-cream before leaning down to inhale their scents.

The two desserts smelled fresh in their own different ways, one exotic and one comforting. How extraordinary to realise that she did not need her wonderful machine in order to turn out beautiful ice-creams. That she had had just as much fun making them in her tiny, grotty little kitchen as she'd had in her £30,000 emporium.

Charley inhaled the ice-cream scents one more time and realised what they had triggered, the feelings they evoked. They smelt like home.

Chapter Thirty-two

Samantha was ready for her hot date. She was waxed, exfoliated, moisturised, painted and shining. It had taken many hours to make her beauty look this natural.

She was wearing a mini-skirt and a top with a wide neckline, which would gradually slip off her shoulder during the evening to reveal the new underwear beneath.

All this and she had cooked too.

Well, she had opened the packets, put them on her own baking trays and hidden all the evidence in the bin. As far as Richard was concerned, she would be a domestic goddess.

Especially when he tasted Charley's ice-cream, which Samantha was going to pass off as her own. She checked the time and brought out the block of passion fruit sorbet. It needed about twenty minutes to soften up properly, so she placed it on the side.

The chicken and roasted vegetables smelt delicious. Everything was ready and primed, including Samantha.

The only thing missing was Richard. Where the hell was he?

At that moment, her phone bleeped with a text. She groaned. Dinner would be burnt to a crisp if he was going to be late. She headed into the lounge and stared at the screen.

Sorry, she read. *Going to have to cancel. One of the kids is sick. Will call soon.*

She stared at it in a daze. Couldn't his wife deal with the children? Why the hell did he have to do anything? How dare he treat her like this?

She considered calling him but knew it would turn into an argument and she couldn't risk that. Best to play it cool.

That's fine, she replied. *No worries. See you soon, I hope.*

She was pleased. The reply was cool, a grown-up response. He would be the one to suffer. He was the one who would be upset tonight. Not her.

She padded back into kitchen and switched off the oven.

Then she picked up the box containing the ice-cream and threw it against the wall, screaming as she did so.

Caroline came out of the bathroom and went down the stairs, somewhat pleased to find her daughter still sitting on the bottom step. Flora might be on the naughty step but at least she had remained on it.

It had been a stressful morning and Caroline's daily score was already in the negative. She had never confessed to Jeff or any of her friends about her scoring system. Jeff was always telling her to relax, but it was all very well for him, she thought. He didn't carry the full weight of their parental responsibility on his shoulders.

So Caroline had come up with her perfect ten-point system. A point added for every educational outing, play session and spell of fresh air. A point deducted for each half hour of television watched, or *Disney Princess* magazine read. Food was also included in the running total. The one day that Flora had eaten at McDonald's with Jeff for a treat, the score had been minus twenty.

Each night before going to sleep, Caroline would consider the daily score and think up new ways to get the score back to ten. She knew she was placing too much pressure on herself, but when Flora went to school, she told herself, she would relax a bit. Even take on a part-time job during school hours perhaps. In a small way, she was looking forward to being her own person again.

The money would come in handy as well. She had already given up talking to Jeff about it. The last time she had mentioned his Christmas bonus, he had snapped, 'And what if I don't get a bonus? Have you seen the news? It's not exactly boom time in the City at the moment.'

Perhaps the part-time job would help to make him feel a bit more secure. She had already seen a few advertised on-line that looked encouraging.

Caroline patted her daughter's head as she passed by her on the stairs. Perhaps she was being a little harsh on Flora. It was only a small tear to the cover of her book.

When Caroline came back down again perhaps they could play her favourite board game. Flora was a competitive child, which would stand her in good stead at her new school.

She went back into the bathroom. Five minutes had nearly passed. She took a deep breath before looking at the white plastic stick in the sink.

There was no mistaking the blue line. Caroline was pregnant.

Julie was tired. The hotline had been manic because the whole network had crashed the previous night. Then some idiot had reversed into her car in the car park and driven off, leaving a massive dent in the boot but no note.

On top of everything, the puppy had whined and howled like a banshee for at least an hour last night after she had gone to bed. Eventually she had shouted at Nick to go down to the kitchen and sort the dog out. It was about time he learnt that his actions had consequences. She didn't like the puppy, but it was a living, breathing thing. It needed taking care of.

Julie was determined to get things sorted over the weekend. She couldn't go on like this. She just wanted to go home each night and relax, preferably before a decent night's sleep.

She parked her car in the driveway, noting that Nick's was missing. Perhaps he had listened to his mother for once and taken the puppy out somewhere. The poor thing hadn't left her house since it had arrived. It was shut in the kitchen most of the time. Luckily, Julie's kitchen was nothing like Charley's former modern masterpiece. Interior design had never been a priority for her.

She went inside, relishing the peace and stillness. Until she heard a small noise from the back of the house. A whimper. Julie walked through the house and took a deep breath before opening the kitchen door. The puppy looked up and wagged its tail.

Julie sighed and put down her handbag on the counter, just as her phone rang with a text. It was from Nick.

Gotta job up north, she read. *See you in a month or so.*

She stared at the screen for a few seconds before calling Nick's number. But it rang out. He obviously didn't want to talk to her.

She sent a text back. *What about the bloody puppy?!!!*

But after five minutes there was still no reply.

She glanced down at the dog who was watching her with his big, black eyes. 'Now what?' she asked.

The puppy began to waddle around the kitchen floor. Julie watched him in a daze, realising that she would have to take responsibility for rehoming him. The puppy continued to stagger round and round before coming to a sudden halt. He swiftly squatted, before Julie could understand what was happening. A second later he was up and trotting into the hallway, leaving a small but stinky pile behind him.

Julie sighed. 'You and every other male in my life,' she muttered.

Chapter Thirty-three

Charley had finally confessed that she was making ice-cream again and the girls had insisted she bring some over to Julie's house at the weekend.

She was trying out her brown bread ice-cream. It was a rich vanilla base dotted with crunchy clusters of caramelized brown bread. The name might not have sounded great but the taste was like cookies and cream. It was certainly going down well with the girls.

'I'd better not have any more,' said Samantha, pushing away her bowl. 'Richard's popping by later and I don't want my stomach to be all bloated.'

'What's the point in worrying what you look like?' said Julie, between mouthfuls. 'He's married, isn't he? He won't care if you're twenty stone.'

Samantha tried to look wounded. 'It's not just about the sex.'

Julie snorted and almost choked on her ice-cream. 'Of course it's about the sex. Do you ever spend the whole night together? Go out in public?'

Samantha took a deep breath. She knew the girls

wouldn't understand how special her relationship with Richard was. But soon they would realise. Soon everyone would know how much he loved her.

Besides, he had sent her a huge bouquet after cancelling their last date. She had accepted his grovelling apologies but kept him at arm's length, in ice-queen mode. He was now desperate to see her, so she had decided she would allow him to later that afternoon and let him beg some more.

The puppy gambolled into the lounge at that point. Julie scowled at the focus of her current bad mood. Then she looked at Caroline.

'Can you ask around at school and the playgroups for me?' she asked. 'I don't want him going to a rescue centre. I think it's best he goes to a family home.'

'Of course,' said Caroline. 'What have you been feeding him?'

'I think Nick picked up whatever was on special offer at the supermarket,' said Julie with a shrug.

Her friend frowned. 'You've got to be careful, especially with puppies' sensitive stomachs. What did the breeder recommend?'

'I have no idea.'

'Didn't Nick say?'

'He didn't even say it was from a breeder.'

'Right,' said Caroline, tapping the keys of her iPhone.

Charley stared, realising she had never even thought that she could be capable of phone envy until that time.

'What are you doing?' asked Samantha.

'Seeing which is the best food for puppies.' After a short while, she found the answer. 'This website recommends turkey with rice.'

Julie's eyebrows shot up. 'For a dog? He's going to be eating better than me.'

Caroline ignored her. 'The rice is very good for puppies' delicate stomachs,' she read. 'Plus they need lots of protein for growth. Look, all the measurements are laid out week by week so you don't over- or under-feed the puppy. How many weeks old is he?'

Julie stared at her. 'I don't know,' she said.

'What did the vet say?'

'What vet?'

Caroline was visibly shocked. 'A puppy needs injections. I think it's around the three-month mark. You can't take him out for a walk until he's properly protected against disease and infection.'

Julie was about to retort that she had no desire to take the puppy out anywhere. That would be Nick's job when he returned. Instead she just sighed. What did everyone else see in the dog that she didn't?

'What are you going to call it?' asked Samantha, trying to move her feet away from sharp canine teeth.

Julie looked blank. She hadn't named the puppy because then he would begin to become a proper presence in her life, something to care about. And she didn't want that.

'It's got to have a name,' said Charley. 'What about Andrex?'

'Or Scooby-Doo?' said Caroline.

'You must be joking,' muttered Julie.

'I know,' said Caroline, with a sigh. 'Blame it on the hormones. I'm pregnant.'

'That's wonderful,' squealed everyone else, rushing over to give her a hug.

She nodded, a little tearfully. 'I'm feeling permanently sick, but hopefully my blood pressure won't rocket like it did when I had Flora.'

174

'I tell you what would help,' said Julie with a smile, 'a nice family pet to take your mind off the stress.'

Caroline shook her head. 'Nice try, but a puppy and morning sickness is not a good mix.'

Julie sighed.

'What about Fluffy?' asked Samantha.

'It's got to be a proper name,' said Julie. 'I couldn't bear something like Pluto or Digby.'

'I know!' said Caroline, picking up her iPhone once more and showing them *The Times* newspaper app. 'And he looks exactly like him!'

She pointed to a story about the London Mayor. They all looked at the picture of Boris Johnson and then back at the puppy. It was a perfect fit.

'Boris it is!' declared Charley, before sweeping up the puppy in her arms. 'What do you say, eh, Boris? Do you like your name?'

The puppy's tail thumped at all the excitement.

'He likes it!' said Caroline.

And so it was official. Of the four women, Julie was the only one not smiling.

A while later, they were getting back into the car to leave. Caroline sat in the driver's seat and glanced across at Samantha, who was tapping into her mobile.

'There's a woman at work who might want a puppy,' she said. 'I'll text her.'

'Don't send it!' said Caroline, trying to snatch the phone out of her hands.

Charley leant forward from the back seat. 'What on earth's the matter?'

Caroline glanced back at the house but thankfully the front door was closed. 'That puppy could be the best thing ever to happen to Julie.'

'But she hates it.'

Caroline shook her head. 'Only because she thinks it will hurt her, like the men in her life have. But dogs aren't like that. They're faithful and loyal. When was the last time she was given unconditional love?'

'Know the feeling,' muttered Charley, before shaking her head. 'Sorry. Not about me today. Other people have problems too. Got it.'

Mike's words of criticism were haunting her day and night.

'We'll just keep telling Julie that we're putting the word around,' said Caroline. 'But we won't, okay?'

'What if she doesn't get used to the dog?' asked Charley.

'If she's still fed up when he's six months old, then we'll rehome him otherwise it's not fair on the puppy,' said Caroline. 'But I think we should give Julie time.'

And so the pact was made.

Chapter Thirty-four

It was late on Sunday afternoon and the sun was glinting on the trout. And the squirrel. Thankfully the badger had been returned to wherever it had come from.

Charley's mother had cooked Sunday lunch for the whole family. The warm weather had helped them through it.

Charley's nieces were playing with the garden hose in the garden, soaking themselves and everything else in sight. Her twin sisters were on the patio arguing. Aunty Peggy was drunk on sherry, and her mother was in the kitchen trying to burn something.

Teatime and all was well in the land of the Summers family.

Charley handed her father his cup of tea.

'Thanks, love.'

They sat together in silence for a while as she watched him slot together a wooden frame and tried not to think about what was going to fill it.

She had always found his workshop a comforting

place, despite the glassy-eyed audience. The windows were open and they were alone together. Birdsong filtered through from the garden. The sound of sandpaper smoothing down a piece of timber was oddly soothing.

For the first time in a long while she felt herself relax.

'Charlotte! Daddy!' her mother called down the garden. 'Teatime!'

'I've heard rumour of home-made carrot cake,' said Dad.

Charley's mouth dropped open in horror.

'The quicker we eat it, the quicker it'll be over.'

They reluctantly left the workshop and ambled down the garden, getting splashed with water as they went past the children.

'Love the hair,' cooed Victoria as they reached the patio.

Charley's hand flew up to her head to touch the frenzied curls that she now had to put up with.

'What happened to your hair straighteners?' said Elizabeth, running her hand over her own sleek blonde hair.

Charley shrugged her shoulders in reply. It was too nice a day to talk about the bailiffs.

'Have you started paying Mum and Dad back yet?' asked Victoria.

Charley blanched before retorting, 'Yes. Of course I have.'

She had saved up a whole £10. It was a ridiculously small amount of money but it made her feel slightly better.

'And very grateful we were too,' said her father, sitting down at the outside table before giving Victoria a glare.

Charley escaped into the kitchen just in time to see her mother jostle a burnt cake on to the counter. Maureen grabbed a carving knife from the drawer and stood over the cake before glancing at her daughter. 'You look a bit down today.'

'I'm fine.'

'Well, here's something to cheer you up,' said her mother. 'A party.'

'I think I'm too old for a bouncy castle.'

'No, silly. It's our silver wedding anniversary at the end of the month.'

'I know. Where are we going for the party?'

Her mother's smile dropped slightly. 'We're having it here, darling. At the house. What with money being short and everything.'

Charley's eyes pricked with tears. She knew her mother had always dreamt of a special party for their twenty-fifth wedding anniversary. And the dream certainly hadn't included a dull affair in their own back garden.

'I mean, it'll be more fun here, won't it? A lovely afternoon tea party. I've invited all our friends. Everybody's bringing something to eat.'

Charley smiled and nodded along with her mother, but felt the weight of guilt hang over her. It was all her fault that they were having to do without. That her parents were having to relinquish their dreams.

'I know!' Her mother waved the knife around in an alarming way. 'Hopefully it's going to be hot so why don't you knock up some of your ice-cream? There'll probably be quite a few kiddies there.'

'Of course,' said Charley. It was surely the least she could do?

She ended up poring over her recipe books late into

the evening, determined to provide the most stunning ice-cream ever for her parents.

Unfortunately, she then overslept on Monday morning, having forgotten to switch on her alarm. Swearing under her breath, she dashed around the flat. It was too late to grab either a coffee or a shower, but at least the aroma of dogs would compensate for that.

It was only when Charley arrived at Miss Fuller's house that she remembered her employer was out that morning. Luckily she had a spare key and was still able to get inside. The sound of barking from within indicated that not all the dogs had gone with their owner.

As Charley put the key in the front door, she tried to ignore the blond blur pacing to and fro behind the glass panels. As she opened the door, a hairy nose appeared through the gap, followed by the body of a labrador. It seemed Herbert had been left behind and was looking for company.

He threw himself at her and Charley staggered under his weight. She was only freed when he spotted a rabbit in a nearby bush and jumped off to chase it. Knowing he wasn't usually allowed out of the house unless on a lead, she then began to chase Herbert to try and get him back indoors.

No one warns you about this kind of thing at the beginning of a job, thought Charley as she ran. Can you dust a room properly? Yes. Can you use a Hoover? Yes. Do you have experience in handling animals, including obedience training and dog psychology? Er, no. Perhaps she should call Julie for advice.

Eventually, she managed to drag Herbert by his collar into the house and shut the front door. He shot her a low 'woof' in disgust and went off to sulk in the lounge.

Later, when she switched off the Hoover, the sound of chomping filled the silence. Charley headed out to the hallway to find Herbert happily filling his stomach with a light snack. It was a good thing that she had never liked those flip-flops and thanks to her previous shopaholic existence, she had plenty back at the flat to replace them.

Chapter Thirty-five

Samantha let him peel the top off over her head. She shook her head to make sure her hair settled back on her shoulders. He gave a gasp of delight at the sight of her lacy black bra and leant forward to kiss her neck.

A warm summer breeze wafted the curtain, letting in a shaft of evening sunshine. After he had arrived, they had enjoyed a couple of glasses of wine. All too soon he had begun to make his move, putting his arm along the back of the sofa and moving closer.

They had intended to go out to dinner and were unlikely to make it to their eight o'clock reservation now.

'Mmm,' she murmured as he moved his mouth along her shoulder.

But Samantha's heart wasn't in it. It was no use. He wasn't Richard.

She had met Gareth at the gym a week or so previously. He was good-looking and reasonably fit so she had agreed to have dinner with him.

She hadn't been surprised when he had made his move so early in the evening. After all, what was the point in going out to a restaurant to make small talk when they could have the main reason for their date over and done with?

He moved the bra strap from her shoulder, following it with his mouth. She knew Gareth didn't want a serious relationship with her. After all, you didn't make a move like this if you were in it for the long haul.

And nor was Samantha serious about him. Gareth was being used to prove a point. That she could still pull any man she wanted, that she had no need to rely on Richard for male company.

The trouble was that she was beginning to miss Richard when he wasn't around. That Gareth's lips on hers didn't have the same magical effect.

He moved his head up to hers and kissed her mouth.

'Okay, baby?' he murmured.

'Yeah,' she replied.

But Samantha wasn't all right. She was scared that no man could ever match up to Richard.

Caroline had told the others that she was pregnant but hadn't actually told her husband. She knew she could never tell the girls what she had hoped would happen in the past couple of weeks. It was too awful, too shocking, to admit. But her prayers weren't answered. Her period had not arrived. The doctor had confirmed that morning that she was definitely pregnant.

Caroline checked the salmon on the griddle pan. It was beginning to look a bit dry.

'Jeff!' she called once more.

She knew he was on the phone about work but it was gone eight o'clock at night. If she didn't eat soon she was going to feel nauseous again. But then she knew she might feel sick after dinner anyway.

The classical music wasn't helping to soothe her nerves. She knew it was better for Flora's development but sometimes Caroline yearned for pop music. Sometimes she put her Take That CD on in the car when she was alone but would never confess to doing such a thing.

'Bloody hell,' said Jeff, coming into the kitchen. 'The whole house stinks of fish.'

Caroline sighed. 'It's good for us,' she told him, flipping the fish steaks off the pan and on to their plates. A green salad had already been placed on the dining-room table, along with a bowl of couscous.

'It's Friday night,' said Jeff, pouring himself a large glass of wine. 'Couldn't we have a takeaway?'

'Friday is fish night,' said Caroline.

'Yeah, yeah,' he muttered. 'I know.'

Caroline sipped her water whilst she watched her husband push the fish around his plate.

'I thought you liked this dish.'

'Just once in a while couldn't we have fish and chips instead?' he said.

'It's too greasy.'

'There's always an excuse with you,' snapped Jeff, becoming riled. 'I work hard all day, come home late and I have to eat this organic rubbish. I'm a man! I want a real meal!'

'Well, what about me?' shouted Caroline. 'I wanted something healthy. Something nutritious, not full of toxins and rubbish.'

Jeff's looked shocked. His wife never shouted.

Her anger subsided as quickly as it had flared. 'Sorry,' she said. 'It's the hormones.'

'Ah,' said her husband. 'Time of the month, is it?'

'No,' said Caroline. 'I'm pregnant.'

'You are?'

Jeff flung back his chair and raced around the table to hug her.

'That's fantastic! When?'

'The baby's due on the first of March.'

'We've got to ring my parents,' said Jeff, his face flushed with joy. 'And yours. Wow, this is great!'

Caroline forced a smile, wishing she could share his excitement.

Julie had her hands on her hips and was scowling down at the puppy.

'You're a hooligan,' she told him. 'A lout. All you need is a hoodie top.'

She tried once more to wrestle the ruby-red peony from Boris' mouth but he ran off, thinking it was a game.

'It was £50!' she shouted after the retreating dog. 'I won't be able to afford another one. It took me months and months of research to find the right one . . . and now look!'

She drew a deep breath and picked up the petals that had scattered in the puppy's wake. The peony was the latest casualty in a long line of destroyed items that included numerous pairs of shoes and socks, any long cardigan that Boris could leap up and nip at, and her dressing gown.

But the worst damage of all was to her beloved garden. The lawn was scattered with yellow patches from the dog's numerous calls of nature. He had also begun to dig holes from which came earth, clumps of grass, dirt, and bulbs that had remained hidden for many years.

Boris had been caked in dirt himself for most of the week until Julie hadn't been able to put off the inevitable. He needed a bath.

It was hard to work out who ended up the wettest. Julie was soaked from trying to control the puppy who had been frightened by the shower head. She found herself feeling slightly sorry for Boris, who shivered in terrified response to his first bath. He did look a very sad sight.

But then she had picked him out of the bath, placed him on the floor, and he did that dog shake thing which meant both she and the rest of the bathroom were showered as well.

Julie chased him through the bedrooms to try and towel him dry. In the end she closed the bedroom door and turned the hairdryer on him. Unfortunately that resulted in a panicked wee on the carpet. In the end, she gave up and let him run around the house and garden to dry off.

'You're not my dog!' she shouted after him.

But every strop she threw, every word she shouted, none of it seemed to matter to Boris. To him she was everything: his mother, his carer, his feeder. He trusted her implicitly.

Julie remembered when she had been that young. And possibly more stupid. She didn't want to let him down. But she also didn't want to let him into her heart. There was no more room in it for any further disappointment.

Chapter Thirty-six

The Saturday of the anniversary party dawned fine and sunny. Fluffy cotton-wool clouds scudded across a bright June sky.

Charley stared out of the kitchen window. The garden was packed with people she didn't know. There was the odd distant relative or friend of her parents but mainly it was just strangers.

Her parents had managed to cobble together various umbrellas and parasols to put up around the garden and at three o'clock in the afternoon the majority of people were huddled underneath them, trying not to look sweaty in their smart outfits. Only the very young were skipping around in the blazing sunshine, decorated with coloured stripes of high-factor suntan lotion.

'Come on,' said Aunty Peggy, coming to stand beside her at the window. 'You can't hide in here all afternoon.'

Charley wondered when Peggy had become so perceptive. She was indeed hiding from the glances of her parents' friends, who were no doubt blaming her for this drab garden party instead of the glamorous celebration her mother had been planning for years.

'I'm making up some ice-cream for the kids.' Charley picked up a packet of wafer cones and ripped it open with her teeth.

'Your ice-cream is too good for them brats. Have you seen what they've done to your father's pond? Your mother's livid.'

Charley scooped up a ball of chocolate ice-cream and pressed it into place on top of a cone. She leant out of the open kitchen window and handed the ice-cream to a young lad who was loitering outside.

'My brother says can he have one?'

She gave him a wink and handed him another chocolate cone.

'That's his third,' said Aunty Peggy, pointedly.

'He's only young,' said Charley. 'Let him have his fun.'

'As long as he's not sick anywhere near me,' she said. 'Now, what have you got for the more mature palate? I know you've got the good stuff stashed somewhere in here.'

Charley opened up the freezer and took out a couple of Tupperware boxes. 'Coconut ice. A taste of the Caribbean for you, madam? Or watermelon sorbet? Very refreshing, I've been told, when the mercury is high.'

She waved both the boxes in the air but Aunty Peggy merely raised her eyebrows in reply.

'You win,' said Charley, opening up the freezer once more to bring out a third box. 'Rum and raisin, and it's heavy on the rum.'

'That's my girl. Give us a large one.'

Charley filled her paper bowl with a couple of scoops and waited for feedback.

Aunty Peggy smacked her lips together after the first bite. 'Smashing. You've a real talent, girl. Don't let it go to waste.'

'There isn't much call for ice-cream on the cleaners' circuit.'

After Peggy had left, Charley carried on serving up the ice-cream through the kitchen window, which was now acting as a food counter. Once all the children were dripping with chocolate and strawberry ice-cream, she washed up the empty Tupperware boxes and looked around the kitchen. The majority of the adults' ice-cream had also been wolfed down so she put the last remaining scoops in the freezer before they melted.

She decided to escape her bolthole via the drinks table as her wine glass was empty and there was no way she was going through this party sober.

She was just contemplating the wine bottles when her father came to stand next to her.

'Want a refill?' he asked.

Charley stared down at her empty glass. 'I'm wondering if I should stay sober in the hope of a quick getaway.'

'In that car? You'll be lucky.'

She nodded in agreement and let him refill their glasses.

Charley took a brief moment to walk into the sunshine on the patio and let the rays shine down on her.

She was just about to make a bolt back for the security of the kitchen when a cry of 'Charlotte! Yoo-hoo!' came from across the garden. A battleship of a woman loomed into view. It was Mrs Trimble, head of the Mothers' Union.

'My dear, I must congratulate you. I've just heard from Peggy that you made all the ice-cream yourself,' she boomed. 'I had quite forgotten how good the home-made stuff can taste. What's your secret?'

Charley shrugged her shoulders. 'To give it a good stir every half an hour until it freezes.'

'And you didn't even use one of those new-fangled machines? How extraordinary.' Mrs Trimble took her elbow and led her on to the lawn. 'I was wondering, my dear, if I could ask a little favour of you.'

Charley thought that she really didn't want to do any more cleaning. She was barely getting through each day without collapsing with exhaustion as it was.

'I'm having a small soiree for some old school friends in a fortnight and was contemplating serving up some of your marvellous ice-cream for afters.'

'You want me to give you the recipe?'

'Oh, no! I've not got time for that. There's an Annual General Meeting coming up plus the monthly beetle drive. No, I was thinking you could knock up a batch for me.'

Charley blinked a couple of times. 'You want me to make the ice-cream? Aren't you better off buying some from the shops?'

'Best not to, I think. One of my girlfriends says she's Cordon Bleu so there's always a bit of one-upmanship. Mind you, I swear last time I spotted a load of M&S packaging in her recycling box when we left.'

'What did you have in mind?' asked Charley.

'Something creamy and wicked, I think. And organic, obviously.'

'Obviously,' she parroted, still in a daze.

'And I'll pay you for your time as well as all the ingredients.'

Charley's mind was reeling but the idea of extra money was appealing.

'Marvellous,' boomed Mrs Trimble, taking her silence for agreement. 'I'll give you a call this week, if I may? And mum's the word, eh? You'll keep it strictly between us?'

Charley nodded. 'Yes, I will.'

'No, she will not,' thundered Granny, storming up to them.

'I beg your pardon?' said Mrs Trimble, as they both stared at Granny in astonishment.

'You can beg all you like, Gladys Trimble, but you're not taking all the glory for my granddaughter's talent,' snapped Granny.

Mrs Trimble looked like thunder. 'That wasn't what I meant, Elvira Sweeney, and you know it.'

'That was precisely what you meant, Gladys, and I'm not standing for it. Nobody takes advantage of my family.'

'I wasn't taking advantage. I was going to pay the girl.'

'And then take all the credit, as per usual. The whole village knows that fruit loaf which has won you first prize for the last two years at the summer fête is shop-bought.'

Mrs Trimble's face was purple by this time. 'How dare you! That recipe has been handed down from generation to generation.'

'Whose generations were they? Tesco's?'

Both women had planted their court shoes squarely, faces drawing closer and closer. For a fleeting moment Charley enjoyed a daydream of seeing fists flying between her grandmother and the head of the Mothers' Union. But her own mother had now arrived to referee.

'Mum, what's going on here? Mrs Trimble . . . anything I can do for you?' She looked from one stony-faced pensioner to the other and back again.

'You can write down our Charlotte's telephone number,' said Granny, not taking her eyes off Mrs Trimble. 'Gladys wants her to make up a batch of her ice-cream.'

'You do? How wonderful,' said Maureen, giving her daughter a quick hug. 'I keep hearing how good everyone thinks it is.'

'Gladys is going to pay her a good price for her time and effort, as well as telling everyone that our Charlotte made it.'

'Super!' said Maureen, trying to ignore the atmosphere and glaring eyes. 'I'll jot down that number for you, Gladys.'

Mrs Trimble nodded in reply and forced a smile on to her face as she looked at Charley.

'And that is acceptable to you, I hope?'

'Yes, of course,' said Charley quickly. Anything to keep the peace.

She let her grandmother lead her away.

'You make sure she gives you a good price,' she hissed at her granddaughter.

'Yes, Granny.'

'Don't let her walk all over you.'

'Yes, Granny.'

'And if she gives you any lip, you tell me. I'll give her what for.'

'Yes, Granny.'

As Charley climbed into bed that night, she was still basking in her small victory. Someone thought she had talent. Someone actually wanted her ability as a cook rather than a cleaner. Still in shock, she fell fast asleep without crying beforehand for the first night in a long time.

Chapter Thirty-seven

'So what's everyone doing for holidays this year?' asked Samantha who was bronzed after just returning from a long weekend in Ibiza with her single friends from work. It had been fun, picking up various men and getting drunk, but something had been missing. She had a horrible feeling that it was Richard.

'Nothing,' muttered Julie. She hadn't had a holiday in years.

'Me neither,' said Charley, wistfully thinking about the Caribbean trip she had once planned.

'You could always come camping with us,' said Caroline in a hopeful tone.

'You must be joking,' said Julie. 'But perhaps you could take the puppy. He'd love all that fresh air.'

'Nice try,' said Caroline, breaking into a smile. 'But not a chance. Besides, he hasn't had his inoculations yet, has he?'

'Vet's appointment made for tomorrow, boss,' said Julie.

Caroline peered at the dip. 'Is this unpasteurised, do you know?'

'No idea,' said Samantha.

Caroline decided to leave her breadstick plain, rather than take a chance.

'Are you worried about the mayo?' asked Julie. 'I ate loads when I was pregnant with Nick so you needn't worry. Or perhaps that was where it all went wrong.'

But she knew Caroline would spend the next eight or so months fretting about every bit of cheese or spread. Why did she always worry about the small stuff that wasn't important?

'Maybe we should forget about the main course and go straight to dessert,' said Julie with a gleam in her eye. 'What flavour have we got?'

'Chocolate ginger,' said Charley.

The jar of crystallized ginger had been the latest find from her box of treasured ingredients. She had also opened up another box to dig out the chocolate she knew was in there somewhere.

'I thought the ginger would help your stomach,' she told Caroline.

Her friend nodded and said a grateful thanks.

Mrs Trimble had rung Charley to confirm the order for ice-cream. As the dinner party was a gathering of old school friends, Charley had decided to make hokey-pokey ice-cream, an old-fashioned recipe using caramel and condensed milk. She had spiced it up with a smattering of pecan nuts but it was still reminiscent of school puddings and childhood.

Her nerves were jangling though. Someone she barely knew was paying for this ice-cream and she needed an impartial opinion. The girls were hardly impartial but it was the best Charley could do.

Caroline and Julie were still licking their spoons. The silence was killing her.

'Well?' Charley finally asked.

Caroline broke into a smile. 'It's the best thing I've tasted in ages. And you're talking to a woman who's been throwing up for the last fortnight.'

'This woman is paying you?' said Julie, dipping her spoon into the Tupperware box for another tasting.

'I hope so.'

'I think it's fantastic,' said Caroline, ever supportive. 'And a bit of extra cash for you too.'

Either way, they all enjoyed the ice-cream except for Samantha who was on yet another diet and refused to eat even a spoonful.

Charley told her it didn't matter though secretly she was hurt.

The following afternoon after work a clean and presentable Charley was standing in front of Mrs Trimble's mock-Tudor mansion.

Clutching her Tupperware box, she walked up to the front door and pressed the doorbell. Mrs Trimble opened the door and gave her most gracious smile.

'My dear, thank you so much for doing me this tiny favour.'

She led her through the vast hallway and into the kitchen which was about the size of Charley's flat. Placing the ice-cream in a vast freezer, Gladys turned to her with another wide smile.

'Coffee?' she said.

She looked tense, her smile just a little too wide. Granny had obviously scared the living daylights out of her so Charley decided to let her off the hook.

'I'm afraid I can't,' she replied. 'I'm meeting some friends for lunch.'

'Oh, dear,' said the other woman, her shoulders dropping with relief. 'Let me just give you what I owe you.'

She took some notes from the counter and handed over £15 in cash.

'It's too much,' said Charley. The ingredients had only come to about £5.

'The rest is for your time,' said Mrs Trimble, pushing away her hand. 'Please. You've done me a great favour.'

Charley's cheeks were burning and she made her exit shortly afterwards.

'Perhaps I'll tell my friends about you,' called Mrs Trimble from the front door.

Charley sincerely hoped not, as she had visions of Granny threatening women all over the village that unless they paid her a decent wage they would be beaten to death with one of her mother's scones.

But it was £15 that she could put aside to give to her parents. With the money she had already saved, that only left £39,975 to go until the debt was fully repaid. Charley shook her head. She would never manage it.

Chapter Thirty-eight

Julie was late for the vet's appointment. She had come home to find that her housetraining wasn't working at all and that Boris had weed on the newspaper she had laid down on the kitchen floor before then ripping it to shreds. By the time she had tidied up, it had all become a bit of a rush.

She hurried up to the reception desk, holding the puppy in her arms.

'Hi,' she panted. 'I'm so sorry. I'm late for our 4.30 appointment.'

'Name?'

'Julie Morgan.'

The receptionist arched an eyebrow. 'Is that the dog's name?'

'No,' replied Julie. 'He's called Boris.'

'Boris Morgan,' repeated the receptionist. 'Take a seat.'

It was only whilst Julie waited in the seating area that she realised that only the names of the pets were called out, not those of the owners. She rolled her eyes, pretty sure that 'Fluffy Jones' wouldn't be picking up the bill.

The W. J. Seymour veterinary clinic was packed in the post-school rush. An assortment of guinea pigs, cats, dogs and rabbits eyed each other up. It was a pet apocalypse just waiting to happen. Julie clutched tighter at Boris' collar.

'Boris Morgan,' called the receptionist. 'Room One.'

Julie stood up and headed towards the back of the clinic. Finding the door to Room One closed, she knocked softly and went in.

She found herself gulping. The vet was enormous, a mass of muscles that seemed to fill the room. With his shaved head, he wouldn't look out of place in a wrestling ring.

'Hello there,' said the man, suddenly breaking into a smile. 'I'm Wes.'

'Hi,' said Julie, only giving him a small smile in return.

This wasn't about making friends. This was about getting the dog his injections and getting the hell out of here.

'And this little fella is Boris?' said the man, picking up the puppy and placing him on the table.

The pronounced accent was definitely antipodean. Julie took a guess at Australian as it was quite strong.

'So . . . what can we do for you this arvo?'

Julie blinked. 'This what?'

'Sorry,' said Wes. 'I mean afternoon. It's the Aussie in me. You'd think I'd have lost some of it after being here a couple of years.'

'Oh. Well, I thought the puppy should have a check-up,' she replied.

She watched as he began to feel all over Boris' body,

his huge hands remarkably tender as they felt for any abnormalities.

'How old is he?'

'I don't know,' replied Julie eventually, in a small voice.

'Do you know his date of birth?' asked the vet.

'No.'

His smooth forehead briefly creased but he continued the examination. 'I would put him at approximately ten weeks. You've never had anyone check him over?'

She shook her head. 'He was given to me as a present.'

'With no history? No paperwork?'

'Nope.'

'I see.' His initial warmth had cooled down to distinctly frosty. 'Look, I'm not gonna ask you where you got this dog, but I feel it's my responsibility to tell you that getting a pet without any kind of health history is just asking for trouble.'

Julie remained silent, sick of having to defend Nick over and over to everyone she met.

'I mean,' carried on the vet, 'I've just had to put down a six-month-old pup because he didn't have any inoculations and had contracted the parvo virus.'

Again, no reply from Julie whose cheeks were growing pink.

'So, I'll give him his first injection now. You'll need to come back here in two weeks' time for his second bout of jabs. I'm also going to recommend a worming treatment, to be safe. Until his second lot of injections have taken effect, which will be about a week afterwards, you can't allow Boris here to come into contact with any dogs that have not had their injections. He's at huge risk right now of all kinds of infection. He's okay at home and in the garden, but that's it.'

It was like being ticked off by a school teacher, thought Julie as she stared up at the vet's craggy face. His nose had been broken on at least one occasion. Obviously someone had come to a similar opinion of him as Julie had.

'Listen,' she said in a quiet but tense tone, 'my son gave me this dog with the stupid idea that it might help cheer me up after losing my mother. So I'm stuck with the thing until I find it a better home. I am not cruel to the dog. I do not starve the dog. I'm trying to make the best of what was hopefully the last of many bad ideas that my son has had. No, I don't have the first clue what I'm doing, but will you please just give me a break, all right?'

She stopped and found herself breathless, tears stinging her eyes. When she eventually dared herself to look up at the vet, she found he had a hypodermic in his hand.

'Don't worry,' he told her, breaking into a smile. 'It's not for you. Can you hold Boris for me?'

Julie reached forward and held on to the puppy. Boris whimpered a little when the needle went into the roll of skin that the vet was holding but it was over in moments. The vet rubbed the puppy's furry head with a gentle touch before straightening up.

'I'm sorry about your mum,' said Wes.

Julie stiffened. 'Thank you.'

'Dogs can be a great source of comfort during difficult times,' he carried on. 'They're very loyal and loving.'

'I'm sure,' replied Julie. 'And I'm sorry about my ranting before.'

'No worries,' he said with a shrug.

'This dog stuff just isn't for me,' she told him. 'My

friends are trying to find him a family home to go to. In the meantime, I'll keep up with the injections and treatments.'

The vet nodded. 'We'll see you in two weeks' time.'

'If he's not rehomed by then,' said Julie, before picking up Boris and quickly leaving the room.

Chapter Thirty-nine

It was Tuesday morning and Charley was crouched down cleaning kitchen cupboard doors. Perry Como could sing all he wanted to but this most definitely wasn't a magic moment.

Thankfully she was almost finished and just had the floor to clean. On her hands and knees, of course. She threw open the back door to let some air in. July was turning out to be humid and cloudy. Water shortages and a breakdown of public transport loomed.

She headed towards the cupboard which housed the bucket but nearly bumped into Mrs Smith who came into the room with a strange man. He looked startled to see Charley. She was equally surprised. She had never seen a bald man in tight, electric blue leggings before. She tried not to stare at his bare torso. He had the chest of an eight-year-old boy.

'I've left the money on the side for you.' Mrs Smith gestured towards the kitchen. 'I'll be in the conservatory with my prayer teacher for the next hour so I'll see you next week.'

As they turned away, Charley saw the bald man raise his eyebrows in a query.

'She's just the cleaner,' she heard Mrs Smith stage-whisper to him.

That was Charley. Just the cleaner.

They disappeared soon after that. Spirituality was the latest thing in seeking peace from the hectic world beyond. Her world wasn't very hectic but Charley knew what Mrs Smith was praying for. She was praying that her husband didn't find out how much the prayer tutor cost.

As she filled up the bucket with hot soapy water, she thought it had been a very strange couple of weeks.

Mrs Trimble had placed another order for ice-cream. Then another. Then a couple of other women had called, citing Mrs Trimble as their secret source, asking to buy it from Charley. It was all very puzzling but at least her bank balance was looking slightly healthier than of late. And it had given her a small thrill of excitement that people thought her ice-cream was that good.

As she wiped the floor, Charley's mind drifted towards her recipe books. She enjoyed running through the different ways she could include her favourite ingredients or give a new twist to an old classic.

She would have loved to have returned to Gino's delicatessen and stock up her cupboard with Limoncello, to add an alcoholic depth to her lemon sorbet. Or perhaps some Calvados to add to an apple granita she had dreamt up.

Her weekly food bill was low but she always kept back a little bit of money to pick up a different ingredient to experiment with. Nothing expensive, just something that would make a difference. Last week it had been coconut milk, which made the ice-cream lovely and creamy.

In a reverie, she didn't hear Mike come in through the back door until he was almost a third of the way across the kitchen.

'Stop!' she shouted. 'I've just cleaned there!'

'Sorry,' he told her, reversing towards the back door.

Charley sighed, staring at the dusty footprints. 'This house is difficult enough to clean without having to wash the same tiles over and over.'

'I know and I did apologise.'

To be fair, she only needed to bend down and quickly wipe where he had been. The ground outside was dry from the lack of rain so the mess wasn't too bad.

'By the way, I meant to tell you what a nice job you've been doing on Mrs Wilberforce's house,' said Mike, in a casual tone. 'The place looks much better these days.'

Charley knew she was doing well at her job as she was getting good feedback from all the customers via Patricia. Apparently nobody understood the demands of wealthy women better than an ex-wealthy woman.

But she stared at Mike for a beat. 'Wow. A compliment,' she said, feigning surprise. 'Is it a leap year? Or perhaps I'm just high from the expensive perfume I'm still using up.'

His eyes crinkled with amusement. 'Still not forgiven me yet?'

'Nope,' she said, tiptoeing back across the floor and out of the kitchen.

And yet his words had hit home. She had been complacent, smug even, with her fancy car and all the fripperies of modern living. But with her life stripped down to the bare bones, she'd found there wasn't much left. Certainly not the strong marriage she'd once thought she had. No skills either, except her ice-cream making.

Perhaps that was why she had experienced a slight lift in her spirits recently. At least she still had one string to her bow, one talent that marked her out as different. She just didn't have a clue what to do about it.

Chapter Forty

Samantha stared at the diamond drop earrings glinting in their box.

'They're beautiful,' she said.

'So are you,' said Richard, leaning forward to kiss her. 'Put them on.'

She smiled as she took off her own small stud earrings and placed them on the coffee table. She picked up the box, noting with pleasure that they were from the very expensive jeweller in the high street.

Samantha stood up and took the box over to the mirror above the mantelpiece. She put the earrings on and flicked her hair back over her shoulders so she could see them properly.

Richard came up behind her and kissed her neck. 'I knew they would suit you,' he told her.

She stared at their reflection. God, but they made a stunning couple.

She had been right to play it cool recently. He couldn't keep messing her about like he had been. There had been too many last-minute cancellations.

Too many meetings that he apparently couldn't duck out of. So Samantha had begun not to pick up his calls or answer his texts, which had grown increasingly frantic.

So tonight he had arrived with roses and diamonds. In time, she would need promises as well. Promises that their future lay together. That he was hers and only hers.

Richard turned her around and begin to kiss her fervently, ardently. Her body ached with need as his hands roamed over her. She had missed him so much.

But for now she was reassured to see how much she meant to him. All he had needed was a little reminder of how much he stood to lose.

'Can I take Benjamin?' asked Flora, hugging the toy rabbit close to her chest.

Caroline frowned. 'I'm not sure about that, darling. What if he gets covered in mud?'

Flora stomped out of the bedroom, taking her beloved stuffed toy with her.

Caroline sank on to the spare bed with a sigh, staring out at the rain pattering against the window. Why on earth had she suggested camping in England at the end of June?

She knew why. Money was a little tight and it was the perfect excuse to try out a proper, family holiday. Caroline stared at all the bedding she'd piled up in readiness and wondered how they were going to get it into the car in a week's time. When they had gone camping in France a few years ago, the tent and equipment was already set up for them. This time, though, they were doing it themselves. Caroline wasn't even sure that Jeff knew how to pitch a tent.

They could have managed a cheap bucket and spade holiday in the Mediterranean. Various acquaintances were heading off to Tuscany, France and Greece. But no, as usual, Caroline had worried about what everyone else would think. They were going to have an old-fashioned holiday with old-fashioned values and fun.

She had been planning it for months, looking up reviews of various attractions, making sure they all had wellington boots and proper camping equipment.

But now she was pregnant, the thought of lying down each night on an inflatable bed filled her with horror. Let alone coping with morning sickness in communal bathrooms.

Caroline suppressed the taste of nausea in her mouth, wondering whether a ginger biscuit would help. But she knew it wouldn't. She had suffered from terrible morning sickness with Flora, and baby number two was causing equal amounts of nausea and headaches.

In the heady days of first pregnancy, Caroline had managed to cope with the nausea by taking it easy when she got home from work. She had even managed to have the odd day off sick. She wondered, not for the first time, whether the intervening five years had faded the horror of morning sickness from her memory.

It was vital that she should keep going. So, as usual, Caroline was running herself ragged, sorting out school clothes for her daughter and checking on Charley. Even picking up a puppy book for Julie to read through.

The rain was coming down harder now against the window. Caroline snorted a mirthless laugh. At that moment she would even sacrifice herself to the horror of Disneyland if it meant a chance of sunshine and someone else to do the cooking, tidying and cleaning, in a hotel with walls and en-suite bathrooms.

Pushing aside the tempting thought of lying down on the bed for five minutes, Caroline got up and went to sort out the food and cooking equipment for the holiday.

Julie had managed to steel herself to face the vet once more as Boris' twelve-week injections were now due. She was still mortified about the way she had carried on the last time she had taken the puppy to the vet's. But with no one to take Boris off her hands yet, she had to carry on keeping his inoculations up to date.

Thankfully, she saw a different vet this time and Boris behaved himself as he received his injection.

She'd thought she heard an Australian accent as she left and had picked up speed out of the front door.

On the way home, she parked in front of Sidney's Sweet Shop and sighed to see the neglected shop front. The window was full of faded posters, most of them hanging on to the glass by shreds of Sellotape. The posters were cheap advertisements, probably sent out from the sweet manufacturers and at least ten years out of date. Julie wasn't sure some of the sweets advertised were even available any more.

She walked past the shop and pressed the doorbell to the flat above. Her uncle welcomed her with a hug.

'Sorry I haven't seen you for a while,' she told him. 'It's all been a bit hectic.'

'Doesn't matter, love. It's nice to see you and this little fellow here.'

Sidney bent down to stroke Boris, who was sitting on his feet. There is no such thing as an unfriendly puppy, thought Julie. Sidney's worn face creased into a smile. He was looking a bit thin, she thought. She knew his pension didn't stretch far and was pleased she had remembered to bring a packet of biscuits with her.

'I'll make us a cup of tea,' he said. 'I've just got to check the post first.'

He brought out a set of keys and opened up the front door to the sweet shop. The bell above the door rang out, instantly transporting Julie back to her childhood. The brass bell was a signal to Sidney and his wife Doris that school was out and the children were desperate to spend their pocket money. Julie had found a visit here extra special because she was allowed to go behind the counter and help measure out the sweets.

Most afternoons the shop was full of children, laughing and chattering, the bell constantly ringing with more and more kids packing into the shop. Julie recalled paper bags full of hundreds and thousands, cherry drops and fizzy cola bottles, and the huge plastic tubs of sweets packed on to shelves that seemed to reach up to the sky.

But not today. And not for a long time, it appeared. The shop was empty and dark, with a musty smell in the air. This place hadn't been full of laughter for a very long time.

There were still tubs of sweets on the shelves but they looked dusty and well past their sell-by date. No one would take pleasure in buying their sweets in here and it looked like the customers had deserted it many years ago. A sense of gloom hung over the place.

Sidney lit up a cigarette as he looked over the shop. It had been closed for some years, with nobody seemingly wanting to take it over during the current economic climate.

'I used to love coming in here when I was little,' Julie told him. 'I can still remember all the sweets I used to buy.'

Her uncle gave her a sad smile. 'Don't know what happened, love. They just seemed to stop coming.'

He took a deep drag on his cigarette and some ash dropped into an open tub of liquorice that stood on the counter.

'Yeah, it's a real mystery,' said Julie, rolling her eyes. 'And you shouldn't be smoking.'

'Let me have one bit of pleasure, love.'

The truth was that once his wife Doris had passed away, the place had fallen into disrepair. The same could be said of Sidney. Julie and her mum had kept an eye on him but eventually the shop had become too much of a burden, too much work for a widower in his early seventies.

'You're not still paying rent on it, are you?' asked Julie. Perhaps that was where all his pension was going.

Sidney gave a rasping laugh that turned into a cough. 'Lease?' he said, still struggling for breath. 'I own it, love.'

Julie was astonished. 'You own it? How? Since when?'

His face split into a smile. 'I bought shares in Apple long before that iPhone. I'm loaded, love!' He fixed her with a look. 'It's all yours, you know. When I go.'

'I don't need a shop,' she told him. 'Besides, you're not going anywhere.'

She had already attended her mother's funeral that year. She had no intention of losing anyone else.

212

'It's your inheritance, love. You're my family. The last of it.'

Julie briefly thought about Nick. He was technically the youngest member of the family but he had turned out like his dad.

She wandered through to the back of the shop and stared at the large larder and ancient refrigerator and freezer. They were huge.

She went back into the shop. 'I told you about Charley's ice-cream, didn't I?' she said.

'I'm still waiting for my tasting session,' Sidney replied with a cackle.

'She's beginning to get a few orders and needs somewhere to store it.'

'She's welcome to use the back room,' he said. 'You've got a spare set of keys, haven't you?'

Julie nodded, a smile forming on her face.

As Sidney bent down to pick up the post that had come through the mailbox, she ruffled Boris' fur. 'What do you think, boy? Are you thinking what I'm thinking?'

He stared up at her, long pink tongue lolling from his mouth. But he seemed to be smiling so Julie took that for agreement. She couldn't wait to tell Caroline the news.

Chapter Forty-one

'It's me,' said Julie down the phone. 'Where are you?'

'Just finished work.' Charley opened up the door of the Mini, letting out the stifling heat. 'What's up?'

'Meet us in front of my uncle's sweet shop on Lower Green Road.'

Charley drove the car into the village and parked in front of the small parade of shops which were a stone's throw away from the busy high street. Lower Green Road might eventually lead into Lower Grove but, at this far end, it still clung on to Upper Grove respectability by its fingertips.

She got out of the car to find both Julie and Caroline waiting for her.

'Samantha wanted to come but she's meeting her fella,' said Julie before gesturing at the front of Sidney's sweet shop. 'So . . . what do you think?'

'I'd prefer a coffee, to be honest,' said Charley. 'I'm shattered.'

Julie shook her head. 'Imagination, girl. That's what you need. Come on inside.'

She led them both into the gloom of the shop. It smelt musty, unused. Unloved.

'What's this all about?' asked Charley, spinning around to face them both.

'The shop is lying empty these days,' said Caroline.

'And my uncle just isn't up to running it any more,' added Julie.

'So why doesn't he sell it and retire in Spain or whatever?'

Julie shook her head. 'He can't. He loves this place, needs it. It's the only link he's got left to my aunty.'

'So what has this got to do with me?' said Charley. 'Do you want me to clean it up? Make it smart again?'

'Sort of,' said Caroline, breaking into a smile.

'We think you should open up the shop for the summer and sell your ice-cream here,' said Julie.

Charley was astounded. 'Here? Me?'

They were both nodding frantically at her. 'Yes.'

'They used to sell it,' explained Julie, walking over to a filthy glass cabinet, full of the empty metal tubs which once held ice-cream. 'Think of all your lovely flavours in here. All home-made with none of the chemicals they put in nowadays.'

Julie had a point there. Charley had looked at the list of ingredients on a tub of ice-cream in the supermarket recently. Locust bean gum? And what on earth was anhydrous milk fat? The mind boggled and the stomach turned.

'Think about it,' urged Caroline. 'It would only be for the summer. Just something different from that wretched cleaning job.'

'Yeah, but that wretched job pays the rent,' Charley told her.

'Then work through your lunch hour and finish

earlier so you can open up by mid-afternoon. And you can open every weekend too. It could be a great business opportunity.'

'Or a complete disaster,' muttered Charley.

She walked slowly around the shop, taking in the dirt and the dust. She stopped for a while to peer out through a gap between the posters to the village green. It was a nice setting that would be even better with lots of people taking their ice-cream tubs and cornets there and sitting on the grass in the summer months.

She carried on her tour, eventually coming to a halt in front of the ice-cream cabinet. It was empty now, but for the moths and spiders. But imagine it full of ice-cream again. Her ice-cream.

She swung back to face her friends.

'This is mad,' she told them. 'It'll never work.'

Caroline and Julie walked over to her.

'So in September you go back to your cleaning full-time,' said Julie.

'The only thing that matters is that you give it a try,' said Caroline.

Charley stood still for a moment. It was a huge gamble and it wasn't as if her business instincts had been exactly spot on in the past few years. But somehow, despite all the doubts, it felt right. And her friends seemed to think it was right for her too.

So from somewhere deep inside, she found herself saying, 'Okay, I'll do it.'

Chapter Forty-two

'I don't understand how you can run a business when you're bankrupt.'

Charley sighed. 'Mum, as I've told you before, it's Julie's business. She's inherited it from her uncle and she's only loaning me the shop for the summer. Just to make a bit of cash.'

'It's quite seasonal, isn't it?' added her father. 'As a business, I mean.'

Charley nodded.

'So you probably won't make any real money?' Her mother's tone was full of concern.

Charley dragged a hand through her wild hair. 'I don't know until I try. But maybe. I mean, they're talking about a heatwave this summer, aren't they?'

'Aren't they always?' said her father, with a wry smile.

Charley bit her lip. She couldn't really blame them for being so negative. After all, the last business she had been involved in had crippled them all financially.

'Look, do the figures add up?' said her father.

'The ingredients don't cost too much. There are already freezers and tubs in the shop, they just need a good clean. And, apparently, Caroline says the mark-up is quite significant.'

Unsurprisingly, it had been her organised friend who had found the time to investigate the business side of the idea. She had showed Charley flow-charts and profit projections.

'But I can't own any business whilst I'm still bank-rupt,' Charley had told her.

'You've got to think long-term,' said Caroline.

Charley couldn't even dare to think beyond the following week.

'And there's no competition to speak of,' said her father, nodding thoughtfully.

'Apart from that ghastly ice-cream man,' said her mother.

They all shuddered in unison. Wayne's Whippy was a new ice-cream van which had suddenly appeared at the beginning of summer. Wayne was a rough guy from the depths of Lower Grove whose business style was somewhat aggressive. The police were already handling dozens of complaints about his extra loud music and forceful selling technique.

'But what about the money for ingredients?' asked Charley's father. 'Surely the initial layout will be expensive.'

'It's already covered,' she said.

Julie was doing a roaring trade on eBay with Charley's collection of designer handbags and shoes. As she had ransacked her wardrobe, Charley had been ashamed to find that most of them were barely used. So she collected up all the items she knew she was only keeping because of their designer label and bagged them up. It was a gamble because this really was the end of it. After that, there was nothing. No savings. Nothing else to sell. She was just hoping that people would come in to buy the ice-cream and that the mark-up that Caroline had proposed would repay the outlay.

But before any ice-cream could be made, the shop needed a complete overhaul. Julie had made her a set of keys so Charley had let herself in one Saturday morning and stood in the middle of the floor. She turned in a slow circle, realising the place was in a far worse state than she had remembered.

She let her shoulders slump, suddenly overwhelmed by the dirt and frightened by the responsibility. This had been a stupid, terrible idea. Who was she to think that this would work, that people would want to come in here and buy her ice-cream? Who on earth would want to bring their family into this dirty, filthy place to buy food of all things? What if her business skills were worse than Steve's? What if she failed?

Charley wrapped her arms around herself, desperately willing optimism back into her bloodstream. She took a few deep breaths. People would want her ice-cream, she told herself. Hadn't Mrs Trimble and her friends already raved about it? Surely they wouldn't buy it if it tasted bad?

She walked over to the window and tore down the layers of posters from the glass. Down came the faded, brown paper and in came the warm July sunshine. She turned round to find the room bathed in light. The sun may have accentuated the dirt and cobwebs but it also made her see the potential in the place. At once, the room felt bigger, wider and more inviting.

And then she got to work. With Julie stuck at home with the puppy, Samantha obsessed with her boyfriend and Caroline stricken with morning sickness, it was down to Charley to get the place spick and span. It was exhausting, filthy work but there was something satisfying in taking such a woeful place and seeing it slowly come back to life.

That weekend, she'd spent the whole time scrubbing and cleaning the shop counters, floors, walls and ice-cream cabinet. By Sunday night, it was at least sanitary. She would keep wiping and disinfecting it at every opportunity until she was happy to allow her food into the shop.

During the evenings and following weekend, Charley then scrubbed every inch of the kitchen including the fridge and freezers. Both were a good size and would be large enough for her to make up significant amounts of the ice-cream there.

It was thrilling, fun and totally exhausting. She cleaned for her customers each day and then cleaned and scrubbed the shop every evening.

Once the place was ready, she invited the girls back.

'It looks bigger now,' said Julie.

'You've done a great job,' said Caroline. 'You must be shattered.'

'I thought the two ice-cream counters should be back here, in a right-angle.' Charley led them towards the rear of the shop. 'The big one along this side wall and the smaller one along the back. Another counter over on that side for weighing sweets, and the cash register. I still want all the tubs of sweets stacked on to shelves up the wall behind the till.'

'Absolutely,' said Julie. 'That's how it's always been.'

'What about the rest of the place?' said Caroline, looking at the front half of the shop. 'You've still got quite a bit of space.'

'I was thinking of a few tables and chairs against that far wall. You know, for when the weather turns bad.'

'We've got some plastic chairs and tables you can borrow,' said Caroline. 'They're only for the garden anyway.'

'We just need the ice-cream and we're away,' said Julie, with a smile.

Charley nodded. She was shattered but knew they had to open up before summer passed by. It was nearly the middle of July but that still gave her two months of summer trade. Then who knew what would happen? But she didn't dare plan that far ahead.

Chapter Forty-three

Now that the shop was clean, Charley's biggest dilemma was which flavours of ice-cream to serve.

'Okay,' said Caroline, sucking on the end of a pen whilst running through the list she had written. 'I've got the plain versions of vanilla, strawberry, raspberry, chocolate and white chocolate.'

'Ooh, and toffee,' said Julie.

'Right,' said Caroline, adding it to her list. 'Then I've got the sorbets: strawberry, lemon, passion fruit and mango.'

'I've been thinking about experimenting with a chocolate sorbet,' said Charley. 'You know, so it's not so heavy.'

'Maybe you could play around with the flavours at a later stage,' said Caroline.

'Yeah,' agreed Julie. 'Because the private schools are finishing this week and you want to catch the start of the school holidays.'

'What about some different flavours?' asked Caroline.

'Rum and raisin,' Charley told her. 'Chocolate ripple,

coconut, coffee, and the chocolate ginger recipe I made for you.'

'What happened with that chocolate rocky road flavour?'

Charley grimaced. 'Bit of a disaster, actually. The marshmallows froze solid. It was very bad. Best leave that off the menu until I've got the hang of it.'

'Well, the rest sound great,' said Julie, glancing across to Samantha. 'What do you think?'

She looked up from her iPhone. 'Yeah,' she said. 'But . . .'

'But what?' said Charley sharply.

'It's all a bit boring, isn't it?'

The others took a deep intake of breath.

'What do you mean?' said Charley, her fledgling confidence waning. 'Boring?'

'I mean, couldn't you have a few more interesting flavours? You know, other than for the kiddie market. When I was in Ibiza, they had Red Bull flavour and bubblegum. That kind of thing.'

Caroline made a face. 'Sounds gross.'

Samantha shrugged her shoulders. 'But at least it's not too old-fashioned. I mean, you've got to cater for everyone, haven't you?' She glanced at her phone. 'Sorry, I've got to go. I've a hair appointment.'

She kissed them all on the cheek before heading out.

Charley sighed as she peered over Caroline's shoulder at the list. 'She's right. They're all a bit boring.'

'Traditional,' said Caroline in a firm tone of voice.

'Look,' said Julie, 'you've got to cater for your target audience and that's families. Kids are picky and they'll want nice, safe flavours.'

'Exactly,' said Caroline, nodding. 'Besides, I was reading recently on-line about premium brands and how you should never dilute them down. The idea is quality, not quantity. That's what people will warm to.'

'Home-made and delicious,' said Julie. 'But throw in a few wacky ones, if you want. Just to mix it up a bit.'

'You've got thirty tubs to fill in that counter,' said Caroline. 'You can always mix and match.'

Charley nodded, making a mental note to research a couple of unusual flavours.

'I've got the whiteboard in the back of the car,' said Julie.

She had managed to save one that was being thrown out after some recent office renovations at work.

'I've got the posters for the shop windows,' said Caroline, waving a folder. 'And the tubs and cones are on order and should be arriving tomorrow.'

They were both doing so much for her. Charley had no idea how she was ever going to repay them. Free ice-cream for ever?

After they had left, Charley went back into the kitchen. She had a few more days left to make the stock and then that was it. It had been announced in the local paper that the ice-cream shop would open the following Saturday.

There was no going back now.

Chapter Forty-four

The more Julie read through *How to Take Care of Your Puppy*, the more out of her depth she found herself.

She wasn't just taking care of a puppy, it seemed. She had responsibility for a living, breathing thing whose brain was fully formed at six months. After that, any new information or instructions were open to failure so the first six months were crucial. And it was up to Julie to get the puppy up to speed before handing it over, preferably to the first available person.

Caroline had insisted that she was still checking out the families who were willing to take Boris into their home, but that these things took time. In the meantime, he was Julie's responsibility.

At nearly four months, all of Boris' energy was going into a massive growth spurt. He was changing shape weekly, gradually becoming larger. His legs were getting longer which meant he could now reach new and exciting places, such as the sofa, the stairs and, consequently, Julie's bed.

'Get off!' she found herself shouting, finding Boris sprawled there.

He had stared up at her, his large black eyes as sad as he could make them as he crept down on to the floor. A coating of fluffy puppy fur remained on the bed behind him.

Each day she practised the sit command and, very slowly, Boris began to be trained. He would now sit whilst being handed his meals and when waiting for his lead to be put on, instead of leaping up in a frenzied playful attack.

Walking on the lead took more time but, with the help of some cold hot-dog sausages, she could at least walk down the road without him bucking like a rodeo horse.

Letting him off the lead to run about was a little more problematic. The puppy book told Julie that it would be all right, but she wasn't convinced.

'What if he runs off and I can't find him?' she said.

Caroline didn't reply as they walked towards the heath, watching Flora scamper ahead.

The heathland was an open space full of the heather, pine and birch coppices over which much of Upper Grove had been built. But the council had insisted on a couple of miles of heath remaining as a sanctuary for the local wildlife.

Julie liked the ease of access, as one of the many entrances to the reserve was at the end of her avenue. But she worried about taking the dog somewhere unfenced and had roped in Caroline to help bring Boris back, in case he made a bid for freedom once off the lead. Charley was still frantically making ice-cream in time for the grand opening of the shop.

Boris scampered through the woods, the long cord

of his retractable lead getting wrapped about bushes and trees. In the end, Julie knew she just had to be brave.

'Set the beast free,' said Caroline, looking around. 'There's no one in sight.'

Julie nodded. 'Okay. Let's do it.'

She brought Boris closer to her and released the catch on his lead. At once the dog began to gambol around the woods in utter joy and abandonment.

'Aww, he's so sweet,' said Caroline.

She glanced at Julie who was not smiling, however. She was glancing around in total panic in case there were any other dogs, other owners, or just anything that could entice Boris away from her.

But as they gradually began to walk a little further into the heathland Boris kept trotting back to her, lured initially by the treats in Julie's coat pocket then by some inner instinct. Eventually she began to relax.

Caroline suddenly stopped and began to go pale.

'Are you all right?' asked Julie, touching her shoulder.

'Just feel a bit sick again,' muttered Caroline, bending over. 'This is the worst pregnancy ever.'

'Do you want to go back?'

She nodded.

'We'll come.'

Caroline shook her head. 'Don't ruin your first walk with Boris. I'll be fine. I just don't think I can go any further.'

'Okay. If you're sure. I'll text you later.'

Julie waved at Flora as they left and then she was alone. She walked slowly along the path, glancing around her, but Boris kept within sight. She was just relaxing when she turned round a bend in the track and almost bumped into Wes the vet.

'Hi,' he said, just as surprised as she was to be meeting like this.

'Hi,' mumbled Julie.

'I see you've got the little fella off the lead,' said Wes, nodding at Boris who was nearby chewing on a leaf.

Julie nodded. 'First time.'

'Wow,' he said, with a smile. 'Pretty scary, huh? I remember the first time I let Cadbury off the lead.'

Julie glanced over at the dark brown labrador sniffing around nearby. Cadbury seemed an apt name for him.

She glanced back to make sure Boris was within reach.

'I'm just worried that he'll wander off and won't come back,' she told him. 'Any tips?'

'Let me show you something,' said Wes.

Suddenly, he took her by the arm and led her around the trunk of a large oak tree. He pushed her up against the bark and put a finger to his lips.

'He'll follow you because you're effectively his mum,' he whispered. 'Call out to him.'

Julie took a gulp to refresh her suddenly dry throat. 'Boris,' she croaked before clearing her voice. 'Boris!'

She peered around the tree trunk and saw the puppy looking all around for her. Then he spotted her and bounded over.

'See?' said Wes, taking a step away. 'You might look a bit foolish hiding from your own dog but it does work.'

He broke into a grin. Julie smiled shyly in return.

'Just watch out for him eating anything untoward,' he added. 'Especially because you've got a retriever and they're just dustbins for any food they can find.'

Julie frowned. 'What kind of things should I look out for?'

'Wild mushrooms on the heath are probably the worst hazard.'

'Right, thanks.' Julie had a sudden thought. 'What about in the garden?'

'Rhododendron bushes can be toxic. Daffodils, especially the bulbs. Larkspur. Mistletoe. All of them can be fatal to dogs.'

Julie was horrified. 'But I've got rhododendron bushes all along the back of the garden.'

She thought of her beautiful garden, though it seemed suddenly not so beautiful as it had.

'You're either going to have to cut them down or put up some kind of netting that he can't get through.' Wes smiled. 'Don't fret. I don't have that many cases of poisoning from gardens. It's usually chocolate that causes panic.'

'Chocolate? As in a Mars Bar?'

'Absolutely,' said Wes. 'Especially dark chocolate. Too much can be fatal. As can onions and grapes.'

'God,' groaned Julie. 'I'll have to babyproof the kitchen.'

She thanked him and they went their separate ways across the heath.

Later on, the puppy staggered into the lounge. He was shattered after his first big walk and collapsed on to her feet with a big 'whoomph' of air. As he slept, Julie studied him. She watched the way his pale stomach went up and down with each quick breath. The way his ears and paws twitched as he dreamt.

She reached down to stroke one of his floppy golden ears, but quickly changed her mind and took her hand away.

Chapter Forty-five

At eight o'clock in the morning on the last Saturday in July, Charley let herself into the shop. She walked through to the kitchen, nodding to herself in satisfaction as she glanced around. The shop was finally ready for its grand reopening.

The whiteboard behind the counter was filled with lists of flavours and prices. The shelves were stocked with brand-new boxes of tubs and cones. All that was needed was the ice-cream. And customers, she added before sending up a silent prayer. Please God, let there be customers. Please don't let this be a disaster. It *would* work. It had to. She needed to prove to everyone that she could be a success.

As Charley switched on the lights in the kitchen, she heard the bell tinkle into life. Someone was coming in.

'Hellooo!' called her mother.

'In here!' shouted Charley in reply.

'Hello, darling,' said Maureen, as she entered the kitchen. 'Isn't this exciting?'

Charley nodded, even though her stomach was in turmoil.

'Did I show you this new skirt? Oxfam, of all places. Only one pound and it still had the label in it. John Lewis . . . very fancy. I thought it looked appropriate, being in this bright pink. I've invited all of my friends to come in . . .'

Charley let her mother witter on as she went back and forth, switching on the ice-cream counters in the shop and beginning to load them with different boxes from the freezer. She had already worked out the layout in her head and just needed to see it in reality to make sure it worked. It seemed to take a long time but finally she was done.

'What's the time?' she asked.

'I forgot to put my watch on,' replied her mother.

'It's on the clock radio in the kitchen,' Charley told her.

Julie had given her an old radio so she could play music whilst she was cooking.

'I can't see properly,' said Maureen. 'It's flashing on and off.'

Charley frowned and went over to stand next to her. 'That's odd,' she said, pressing a few buttons. 'It must be on the blink.'

'It says five to nine on my mobile,' said Maureen, checking the screen.

Charley took a deep breath and walked around the shop one last time, checking that everything was switched on and in place. Then she crossed the shop floor and turned the sign over in the door so that it read 'Open'. She turned round to survey the shop. Her shop. Or rather, theirs. It was a joint venture for her friends and herself.

231

As Charley headed back behind the counter, her mother grinned at her. 'Isn't this exciting?'

Charley smiled back. 'Very.'

She spun round at the ringing of the brass bell above the door. Their first customer!

But it was only Julie. 'I've just abandoned Boris with Caroline for an hour or so. I couldn't stay away!'

She too joined them behind the counter and they stood in silence. But Charley's prayers were answered as slowly the shop began to fill up. Julie sat down at one of the tables, watching and beaming with pride. Charley's father stopped by with his newspaper and sat down at one of the other tables with a cup of coffee.

But in between all the family and friends there they came, slowly but surely, real customers. Local people, some of whom Charley recognised, others whom she didn't. They bought cups of tea, coffee, and yes, they bought her ice-cream.

By lunchtime, the smile on her face was genuine and relaxed. Her mother had been replaced by Aunty Peggy who was on the lookout for the food critic from the local newspaper who had promised to make an appearance.

'Charlotte!' called Aunty Peggy. 'This lady says she's got an allergy.'

Charley fixed on a smile. Aunty Peggy's customer skills weren't exactly top notch.

'Can I help you?'

'As I said to your staff,' said the woman, glaring at Peggy. 'I have dairy intolerance.'

'How about a strawberry granita?' said Charley, still smiling. 'That's got no dairy in it at all.'

'Okay,' replied the customer.

232

But just as she was bringing out her purse to pay, another woman pushed to the front of the counter.

'Excuse me,' she said, in a loud voice. 'This tastes odd.'

She held out a dripping cone filled with toffee swirl ice-cream.

'What do you mean, odd?' said Aunty Peggy, squaring up for an argument.

'Hello,' said Charley, pushing in front of Peggy. 'Can I help you? I make all the ice-cream myself.'

'It tastes nasty,' said the woman as Charley took the cone from her. It looked the right colour but it had been a bit hard to scoop, not as soft as she had previously found. Had something gone wrong with the recipe?

She threw the cone into a nearby bin and plucked out one of the little wooden spoons to taste the toffee ice-cream from the tub for herself. Immediately she knew something was wrong. It tasted rancid, like milk that had soured after its sell-by date.

'I'm so sorry,' she said to the customer. 'You're quite right. Can I get you a replacement?'

'I wouldn't bother,' said a man, coming to stand next to them. 'This chocolate one doesn't taste very good either.'

Charley was horrified as she took a sample from the chocolate ice-cream, which also tasted off. What on earth had gone wrong?

Then she realised. There had been brief power cuts throughout the week due to some problems at the local power station. What if the ice-cream had defrosted and then refrozen? That would explain why it was more difficult than normal to scoop. And why some of it definitely did not taste right.

As Charley stared at the customers in horror, a man elbowed his way through the crowd to stand in front of them.

'What the hell do you think you're doing?' he roared.

The whole shop came to a halt to stare at the man in the white coat which was emblazoned with the name 'Wayne'.

'My ice-cream van has stood on this green all summer,' he shouted. 'You can't just start selling ice-cream now. It's not right, stealing all my customers.'

'Don't worry about it,' said the woman who had returned the toffee ice-cream. 'Her stuff tastes foul.'

'I think it's the power cuts,' said Charley, trying to maintain some semblance of control.

'Wayne's Whippy is just outside,' the man shouted. 'And there's nothing wrong with *my* ice-cream.'

'We want our money back,' came a shout from near the door.

'Yeah,' came another voice. 'Me too.'

Charley looked at her aunt. But Peggy was too busy staring wide-eyed at a woman with elaborate glasses who was scribbling on to a notepad nearby.

'She's the food critic from the local paper,' hissed Aunty Peggy.

Charley closed her eyes at the horror unfolding in the shop. This was a disaster.

Chapter Forty-six

Julie and Caroline did the best they could, rallying around Charley with hugs and tissues to mop up her tears. Her parents told her that it would be okay, that she should soldier on and get past the catastrophic opening of the shop.

But Charley liked her own plan better. Get up, clean, come home and get drunk. Repeat as necessary.

Monday morning arrived and she went to work as normal, keeping her head down and cleaning like a demon at each house. Then she went home and consumed most of her daily calories via a bottle of wine. But it didn't blot out the bad memories of the previous Saturday. Nor did it help her sleep.

At Mrs Smith's house on Tuesday morning, she cleaned the house, avoiding Mike whenever he appeared to be heading near her. She just knew he would be waiting to laugh at her like everyone else in the village was probably doing.

Towards the end of the morning, Charley was vacuuming the hall carpet when the post thudded through the mailbox. She picked up the many envelopes, glancing briefly at the headline in the local newspaper which had arrived at the same time.

It wasn't until she was placing the post on the kitchen table that the words in the headline sank in.

'Dairy Disaster! Cones at Dawn!'

Charley stared at the article which had exaggerated all the problems from the grand opening, including the 'mouldy ice-cream'. It made very upsetting reading. The words swam in front of her eyes as she spotted the sub-heading, *'How Not to Run a Business!'*

'Hi,' said Mike.

Charley gave a start as she hadn't even heard him come in at the back door.

'Look,' he carried on, 'you haven't got time to be standing around reading the paper. Shouldn't you be out shopping for handbags or something?'

Charley slowly lifted her head until she locked eyes with him. The wide smile he had been wearing quickly faded as he saw her expression.

'Can we have the discussion about how useless and spoilt I am another day?' she said, her voice breaking. 'Okay? Any day but this one, all right?'

She turned her back to him, not wanting him to see the tears that had begun to roll down her cheeks. But her feet wouldn't move, couldn't take her away from the tell-tale sound of the newspaper rustling as Mike picked it up to read the story.

She didn't know how long she stood there, letting the humiliation wash over her. But it gave her time to brace herself for the inevitable sarcasm about her business skills that he would no doubt throw at her.

But no scathing words came, just a large hand touching her shoulder and, turning her round before she found herself crushed against his chest in a hug. She tried to resist but Mike's strong arms held her tight until she finally let go and began to sob.

He held on to her for many minutes until finally she was spent and could cry no more. Mike released her then before reaching out and tearing off a piece of kitchen paper which he held out for her.

'Thank you,' she managed to mumble before wiping her eyes.

'Sit down,' he told her in a gentle tone, watching her as she sank on to one of the fancy bar stools. Then he sat down next to her. 'What happened?'

'The power cuts,' she said in a small voice. 'The ice-creams had all defrosted and then refrozen so they were rancid. I had no idea . . . hadn't tasted them beforehand.'

'Well, that's a hard way to learn that particular lesson for next time,' he said.

'It doesn't matter,' said Charley, with a shrug. 'There won't be a next time.'

'Why not?'

'You saw the newspaper, didn't you? Who the hell's going to come into the shop after reading that article?'

'Maybe not everyone reads the local paper,' Mike told her. 'Maybe some people want to form their own opinion and not believe some idiot reporter.'

Charley sighed. 'It wasn't supposed to be a serious thing anyway. It was only going to be open for the summer.'

'It's the first of August today. There's still a lot of summer left.'

'What's the point?' she muttered.

He reached out to cup her chin, bringing her face level with his. 'The point, Charlotte Summers, is that

237

you've still got time to convince everyone that you can do this.'

'What if I can't?'

'You won't know unless you try.'

She stared into his dark eyes for a beat. 'Since when did you start being nice to me?'

'I'm hoping for a discount when I come in next Saturday.' He gave her a small smile. 'Is there anything I can do to help?'

Charley blew out a long sigh. 'Can you whip up a batch of rum and raisin ice-cream for me? In fact, I need to replace most of the stock so any flavour would do.'

'No can do, I'm afraid.' Mike stood up. 'But I can make you a coffee, if you want.'

She watched him as he made the drinks. Of all the people to show her true emotions to, she would have put Mike last on the list. But he hadn't judged her, hadn't mocked her. Just listened and advised.

She thanked him as he handed her a coffee. 'You can be quite nice, you know.'

'You sound surprised,' he replied, with a wink.

Charley gave him a small smile.

Keep it quiet though, will you?' he said, over his shoulder as he headed out of the back door. 'It'll ruin my reputation.'

Chapter Forty-seven

Feeling a tiny bit brighter after Mike's encouraging words, Charley let her hair down from its ponytail on the way home and allowed the warm breeze to waft through the car. With the music on, she even managed to sing along to the lyrics.

But as she drove into the car park for the flats, her voice caught in her throat. Steve was leaning against the bonnet of a car, his arms folded in front of him. She just about managed to pull into a parking space without crashing the Mini.

Her legs shaking, she slowly stepped out of the car. He looked good, thought Charley. Really, really good.

'Hi, babe,' her husband said, breaking into his trade-mark cheeky grin.

'Hi,' she managed to croak in reply.

But the grin was swiftly replaced with laughter as he took in her appearance. 'Blimey! Was your hair always this curly? You look a fright.'

Her hands shot up to her head, knowing that the combination of wild curls and an open window would automatically ramp up the volume tenfold. She quickly tucked it back into a ponytail, feeling both embarrassed and cross.

'What do you want?' she snapped.

'Saw your photo in the paper,' said Steve. 'Didn't know you were starting up a new business.'

'I wasn't,' said Charley, with a sigh. 'I was just trying to make a bit of money during the summer.'

'Still, you could have told me. I felt like an idiot when everyone started talking about it.'

She frowned. 'What does it have to do with you? We're getting a divorce, aren't we?'

He shrugged his shoulders. 'Just thought you would keep me up to date. Anyway, I see you had a bit of a nightmare.'

'That's an understatement.'

'Look, take it from me. You're always going to get teething problems with any new business.'

This was the last thing she needed. Charley wanted to shout and scream at him but the fight had gone out of her. She was too hot and too tired to be bothered.

By now Steve was in full flow. 'I can help, you know. I know a few people. You should be thinking of franchising. That's where we went wrong. Let someone else take the strain out of the renting and all that. It's common sense.'

'Unfortunately sense doesn't seem to be very common around here.' She shook her head. *'You're* giving me business advice? After bankrupting us?'

'I was a good businessman. It was the overheads that killed it.'

'No, Steve. We killed it. With our greed. With our ridiculously expensive lifestyle. We should have stuck to one shop. We didn't need all the rest.'

His eyebrows shot up. 'You've changed your tune.'

'I've changed a lot since our marriage broke up.' She blew out a sigh. 'What are you doing here, Steve? I mean, be honest for once. What do you want?'

'I wanted to help, so you could try being a little nicer to me.'

'I'll try being nicer if you'll try being smarter,' she told him. 'What makes you think I would even accept your help? You disappear for months on end, leaving me up to my eyes in debt, then you suddenly reappear and insult my hair. For some reason, you think that I should be falling down on the floor and kissing your feet because you're generously giving me business advice. Hah!'

He watched as she brought out the keys to the flat from her handbag. 'Is that it? You don't want to hear what else I've got to say to you?'

Charley shook her head. 'No. I'm tired. I need a shower. It's been a long week. Thanks but I've got this far on my own.'

She managed to get through the front door and close it before she changed her mind.

Chapter Forty-eight

Charley was still having a crisis of confidence on the Wednesday after the not-so-grand opening.

Not that she was getting much sympathy from her mother.

'At least nobody died,' Maureen told her when she rang.

'From my ice-cream? Gee, thanks, Mum. You've picked me right up there.'

'No. I mean, Mrs Courtney from Pine Oaks . . . you remember her? Collected teapots. Anyway, I was in the hairdresser's yesterday and it wasn't until the dryer started to smoke that anyone realised she hadn't moved for three hours.'

Charley stared around the bedroom but the only audience to roll her eyes at was a pile of cuddly toys.

'Terrible shame,' her mother carried on. 'She'd always had such lovely hair. They said they can do something with a wig if it's an open casket.'

Charley had barely hung up on her phone before it rang again. This time Samantha was calling.

'Hi,' said Charley, in a dull tone. At least she would get a bit more sympathy from her friend.

'I'm so angry, I could kill someone!' shouted Samantha down the line.

Charley sighed. 'What's the matter?'

'He's only gone and booked a week away with his family for the end of the month! He's going to be away for my birthday.'

'Well, it is the school holidays.'

'So? I mean, it's not as if I haven't hinted heavily enough!'

Samantha ranted on and on for so long that in the end, Charley had to lie and say that her customer had just returned home.

So it was with a heavy heart that she drove to Sidney's shop to carry on remaking her ice-cream. But the back door was unlocked when she tried it and, upon entering, she found Caroline and Julie waiting for her.

'Thought you might need a hand,' said Julie.

Charley was so grateful to see them that she gave in to the misery inside and gratefully let Caroline envelop her in a hug.

'I feel so bad,' said Caroline, also a little teary.

'You and your hormones,' said Julie, nudging her in the arm.

'It's not that,' cried Caroline. 'It's all my fault.'

'What is?' asked Charley.

'The shop. It was all my idea and I should never have told you about it.'

'Don't be ridiculous,' said Julie, shaking her head with a smile at Charley. 'Besides, it was my idea.'

'But that wretched woman wrote such a shocking article in the paper.' Caroline sniffed. 'I've a good mind to sue her for slander.'

'Take it easy,' said Julie, drawing her over to a chair to sit down. 'Otherwise you'll give yourself another headache.'

'It's not your fault,' Charley told her as she knelt down in front of Caroline. 'I should have checked the ice-cream. As Mike said, it's a lesson worth learning.'

'Who?' asked Julie.

'Mike from school,' said Charley.

Caroline wiped away a tear. 'Our Mike? He said that?'

Charley nodded. 'I know. Who'd have thought? A man saying the right thing, for once.'

'So you're not going to give up?' asked Julie.

Charley shook her head. 'No way. I mean, I had hoped this would be a way of earning a bit of money to repay my parents.'

'And who cares what that woman wrote?' said Julie. 'We'll show her, eh?'

'I've got just what you need,' said Caroline, fishing around in her handbag before bringing out a small paper bag. 'I saw it this morning and thought of you.'

Charley opened up the bag and reached inside, bringing out a fridge magnet that read 'Keep Calm and Carry On'. She smiled and gave Caroline a hug.

'Thanks,' she told her. 'I shall look at it every time I feel like giving up.'

'That's the spirit,' said Julie. 'Right. Where do we start?'

They spent a couple of hours helping Charley remake some of the ice-cream until Julie had to get back to the puppy and Caroline had to pick Flora up from her playdate.

But the pact was made. The shop would reopen on Saturday.

Charley was praying that it couldn't be any worse than the previous weekend.

She glanced at Caroline's fridge magnet, smiled to herself, and began to melt more chocolate for the next flavour.

Chapter Forty-nine

'We never go out anywhere,' Samantha found herself blurting out one Friday night.

Richard laughed as he propped himself up on the pillows. 'What are you talking about?'

'It would be nice to get out of the flat once in a while. Maybe we could go out to dinner for my birthday?'

He frowned and crossed his arms across his bare chest. 'But I'm away on your birthday, as you have reminded me many, many times.'

'Yes, but when you get back.' Samantha gave him a wide smile. 'With a large present for me, of course.'

'You know why we can't go out,' he told her, reaching out to run his fingers up her arm.

Samantha shivered at his touch but was determined to speak her mind. 'But maybe we could go away somewhere. Far away from Grove. Where no one will know us.'

Richard leant forward to kiss her bare shoulder. 'I've got to be careful. You know why.'

'It's just not a very equal relationship at the minute,' carried on Samantha. 'I was supposed to be helping my friend tonight but I cancelled so I could see you.'

'And didn't I show you my appreciation?' he murmured, pulling the sheet away from her.

'Yes, but it's always at the last minute. I have a life too.'

Richard moved away from her with a heavy sigh. 'I can't plan on seeing you. I never know what's going on at home.'

'I just feel like you're taking me for granted,' said Samantha, after a pause.

'For granted?' Richard's handsome face flushed with annoyance. 'You knew the deal when we got together. Said you were happy with just a casual thing.'

'Yes, but it's got more serious, hasn't it?'

Samantha waited for words of reassurance. Waited for him to agree that their relationship had deepened, meant something to him.

But instead Richard swung his legs out of the bed and got up, picking up his clothes from the floor.

'I get this at home,' he told her, pulling on his trousers. 'I don't need it from you as well.'

Samantha realised she had just crossed the fine line into nagging territory, the most dangerous of all for the mistress of a married man.

And, to her horror, he walked out of the flat.

Caroline crossed the road to the hospital car park, holding the mobile to her ear.

'Did you find out the sex of the baby?' asked Jeff.

'No,' she said, trying to find her car keys in her cavernous handbag.

'Why not?'

Caroline was about to snap that if he had been that interested to know about the baby then perhaps he should have taken the day off work to accompany her. But, no, work came first. And he was more stressed than ever.

'We didn't find out with Flora,' she said, reaching the car. 'I thought it would be the same this time.'

'Right. Have you got a photo of the scan?'

'I've tried to get it on my phone but it's not very clear. Maybe it's better that you see it when you get home.'

Her husband sighed at the other end of the phone. 'I suppose. Okay, I'll try not to be late.'

Caroline hung up, thinking that tonight wouldn't be any different. She had taken to having tea with Flora at five o'clock, especially as Jeff wasn't coming home until nearly nine each night. He would then grumble about the hot and sweaty commute. She would nod and pretend she was interested when all she wanted to do was sleep.

She wouldn't tell him what the doctor had said about her blood pressure being high. It wasn't important. She was just stressed. The summer had been so busy already.

'Try and rest,' the midwife had told her.

Caroline had thought of having to get Flora ready for school in a month's time, let alone the regular washing, ironing, housework, gardening and everything else, and just smiled at the midwife and nodded her head.

On the way home she picked up Flora from playgroup. She really wanted to get some housework done but her head was threatening to explode. She couldn't take any painkillers so ended up lying down for an hour. She woke up with a start, feeling her heart pounding.

'Mummy!' said Flora who was standing next to the sofa. 'You promised we could do some painting.'

Caroline nodded as she struggled to sit up. She couldn't wait for this pregnancy to be over with.

On the heath, Julie found herself in a dog walking community she'd never known existed. Some people said hello and wanted to chat. Others just nodded and walked on. Julie came to recognise which dogs were happy to play with Boris and which of the older dogs would give him a low 'woof' before walking on.

Occasionally she spotted Wes from far away but Julie would always abruptly turn in a different direction, to avoid having to make conversation. He unsettled her and she didn't know why.

At home, Boris was now fully housetrained which meant Julie was less stressed about the inside of the house. The carpets remained clean and dry but she still had to watch what was left within his reach. As his teeth came through, Boris entered a second chewing phase, which meant no abandoned shoes or socks were safe. She had already lost her last pair of flip-flops to his sharp teeth.

He needed constant vigilance and she was just too tired, what with working full-time then trying to help out Charley as much as she could. Julie felt just as guilty about the disastrous opening as Caroline did. It was her uncle's shop and reopening it had actually been her idea. All in all, she was tired. She hadn't heard from Nick either for six weeks, which was setting her nerves on edge as well.

Every evening she just wanted to come home and

relax but the dog needed attention, to play and be walked. Bored at being left for hours at a time, Boris was slowly chewing his way through the wood-laminate flooring.

Except that day he had found something else. He had managed to reach up to the kitchen counter where Julie had left her mother's favourite bud vase, ready to be replenished with sweet peas. The sheepish expression on his face when Julie came in and found the vase in pieces on the floor said it all.

Something snapped in her then. She had reached the end of her tether.

The girls had told her that nobody could afford the upkeep of a golden retriever because of the recession. But Julie knew somebody must want this dog more than she did.

So she rang the local newspaper and placed an advert for the following week, that read, 'Puppy For Sale'.

Chapter Fifty

All week, Charley had been praying for a miracle. Something that could turn her business around. Anything that could help. And on Saturday morning, she got the first sign that someone was listening.

The weather had been mixed so far that summer, the odd sunny day but no endless sunshine as had been forecast in advance. But that was about to change. She had received a couple of text messages already that week from Caroline, telling her that the weather forecasters were predicting a heatwave.

And, for once, they were right.

Friday had been a bright day, the summer sunshine finally breaking through the fluffy white clouds. But by Saturday somebody had turned up the thermostat. The weather was going to top the mid-eighties and stay that way for the foreseeable future. Surely that would encourage customers to come into the shop?

But Charley felt no excitement as she turned over the 'Open' sign on the front door. No anticipation of the day ahead. She was going to thank her lucky stars if she got through it in one piece.

'Hi,' said Julie, rushing in a while later. 'I picked up the hundreds and thousands you wanted.' She came behind the counter and dumped her handbag on a seat. 'My God, the supermarket is packed. There's a real scrum. Everyone's trying to get stuff for barbecues.'

Charley nodded and attempted a smile.

'You're gonna have to do better than that,' said Julie. 'Smiles all round as the customers flood in.'

'What customers?' said Charley, gesturing at the empty shop. 'They've all read the review and are staying away.'

'Keep the faith,' Julie told her. 'Somebody somewhere's got to want lovely ice-cream, haven't they?'

And she was right. As the temperature soared, the customers flocked in. Thankfully, Caroline and Aunty Peggy were on hand to help out later that afternoon.

'Coo, I needed this,' said Peggy, helping herself to a couple of scoops of vanilla-and-fudge-flavoured ice-cream.

Caroline frowned. 'Isn't that your third helping?'

'I'm quality control,' said Peggy, grinning. 'Gotta make sure the stuff's up to scratch.'

Charley and Caroline locked eyes but said nothing.

'Excuse me,' said a woman in upper-class tones. 'Is your ice-cream fairtrade?'

'It certainly is,' said Peggy, in between licks. 'Fairtrade, organic, free-range, recyclable, you name it.'

Caroline subtly moved in front of Peggy and smiled at the customer. 'Can I help you?'

But the woman's reply was drowned out by the chimes of an ice-cream van parking right outside the front door. The tinny sound was on full volume as the tune played on and on.

'He's got a cheek!' shouted Julie, who had just returned from taking Boris for a quick walk.

'He's blocking out the sunshine,' said Peggy, scowling through the window.

To Charley's horror, Wayne of Wayne's Whippy entered the shop as he had done the previous weekend. He had left the chimes playing on the loudspeaker fixed on top of the van.

'Can't believe you've got the cheek to open up again,' he scoffed, elbowing his way past the queue. 'Especially after the dog's dinner you made of it last week.'

Charley slowly took in his tattoos, beer belly and grubby t-shirt. 'If you're not here to purchase anything, please leave,' she said, in her loudest, snootiest tone.

'I'm doing a special offer,' he announced to the queue of waiting customers. 'Buy one, get one half-price.'

'More like buy one, get a stomach upset,' snapped Julie. 'You and that van are a health hazard.'

'Hah!' laughed Wayne. 'I wasn't the one serving dodgy ice-cream last week.'

Charley was dismayed to see a few of the customers glance at each other in concern. They obviously hadn't read the disastrous review.

'It wasn't dodgy,' she quickly told them. 'The power cuts affected some of the flavours.'

But one customer took her child's hand and left the shop.

'All the ice-cream is brand new this week,' said Charley in a bright tone. 'There'll be no further problems.'

'So she says,' sneered Wayne.

Another customer left the queue and headed back out into the sunshine.

Charley felt tears begin to prick her eyes. It was all going wrong again.

'Listen, mate,' said Julie. 'I see no problems here that wouldn't be helped by your departure.'

With that, she gave Wayne an almighty shove towards the door. He took the hint but left his van parked outside, the music playing over and over.

'Free ice-creams,' shouted Julie over the din.

There was a rush to the front of the counter. Charley was horrified, thinking that any profit she'd made was disappearing fast.

But, to her surprise, Caroline agreed with Julie's actions when she popped in later on.

'That was absolutely the right thing to do,' she said, nodding furiously. 'Think of the repeat business.'

'Nobody's going to want to come in with that music playing over and over,' said Charley, shaking her head.

'The important thing is that the ice-cream was good. Really good.' Julie gave her friend a hug. 'That's a start, isn't it?'

Charley tried to smile but knew they weren't out of the woods yet.

Chapter Fifty-one

The heatwave continued throughout the first two weeks of August. As Charley opened the door to the shop, she glanced over at the green opposite where the grass was now faded and brown.

She let herself in, relishing the cool of the shop compared to the heat outside. But the weather had at least been good for business. School holidays had meant a brisk trade each afternoon and she had ended up leaving the shop open until the evening. Some of her cleaning customers had gone on holiday so she had taken advantage of the free hours to make more ice-cream.

But the previous evening she had noticed that the darkness had drawn in by eight o'clock. Autumn was just around the corner and then the shop would have to be closed once more. After all, who was going to want to buy an ice-cream cone in October?

Charley knew she should be grateful for having had the chance to earn some extra money, and that now perhaps she would get the opportunity to rest after such a busy summer. The previous morning, Mike had found her asleep on the back doorstep of Mrs Smith's house.

'Hey,' he had said, gently touching her on the shoulder.

But Charley had nearly jumped out of her skin and instantly sprang to her feet. 'What?' she said, blinking at the bright sunshine.

'Were you asleep?' he asked with a laugh.

'No,' she said, somewhat embarrassed. 'I just closed my eyes for a minute.'

'I see.'

'It was only for a second in the sun. If I spend any more time indoors I'm going to get scurvy.'

He suddenly sat down on the back doorstep and pulled her down next to him.

'I've got to get back to work,' she protested, shuffling her bottom on the hard concrete.

'Five minutes,' he told her, leaning against the back wall. 'Besides, she's gone out shopping so I've made us a cup of coffee.'

Charley realised she must have dropped off to sleep as he would have had to creep past her to make the drinks. She shook herself with a sigh as she gratefully took the mug from him. It was too hot to get bothered about anything. She finally relaxed and sat back with a sigh, the warmth from the sun quickly spreading through her.

'How's things?' asked Mike.

'Good,' she told him. 'Apart from Wayne's Whippy, of course.'

Mike frowned. 'Is he still giving you trouble?'

Charley sighed. 'That van is permanently parked outside but it means I get some of his passing trade, so it's not all bad. I'm just tired, that's all.'

'Can't you drop a few of your cleaning jobs for the time being?'

She shook her head. 'Need the money too much.'

'But the shop's going well?'

'So well that I barely have time to make the ice-cream. It's a juggling act to make sure we're always fully stocked.'

He took a sip of his drink. 'Can't you get someone to help?'

'I should but I'm enjoying it. Whenever I get some free time, I mooch around the market and buy whatever fruits are in season, then I head home and add a touch of cinnamon or walnuts or honey. Sometimes it tastes disgusting and I have to start all over again. But sometimes I get it just right. I found the most fantastic recipe in an old cookbook I got for a pound in the second-hand bookstore. You wouldn't believe . . .'

Her voice trailed off as she realised Mike was smiling at her.

Charley felt her cheeks redden. 'But that's enough from Nigella for now.'

She took a long swig of coffee from her mug but managed to spill most of it down her chin. She wiped it away with her hand, avoiding his look.

He gave a low chuckle but said nothing, instead closing his eyes and turning his face up to the sun. It gave her a rare moment to study him. The dark hair was ruffled, as always. The eyelashes lying against his cheeks were similarly thick and black. Her gaze drifted downwards to his arms which were muscly and brown from working in the summer sun. She looked briefly at his broad chest before moving her eyes upwards once more to his face.

It was then that she found him watching her with

a smile. In a slow movement he reached out one hand towards her. She had a sudden vision of being pulled towards him and kissed, right there in the sunshine.

But his hand went up to her hair instead, plucking something out of her ponytail.

'I think it's a money spider,' he said, bringing his hand back so he could study the tiny creature he was holding.

'It must be lost,' she told him, quickly getting up and heading back into the kitchen.

That afternoon, having opened up the shop as quickly as possible, Charley's spirits sank once more as the familiar chimes of Wayne's ice-cream van rang out from the pavement.

Business was slow that afternoon, which unfortunately gave Wayne the opportunity to visit the shop once more. Only a few customers were inside this time.

'Not many in here, are there?' he cooed, giving her a wink. 'I'd give up if I were you.'

'Haven't you got better things to do?' snapped Julie, glancing at Charley's fading smile.

'Aww, don't feel bad about it,' cooed Wayne, ignoring Julie and continuing to grin at Charley. 'A lot of people ain't got no talent.'

Charley bowed her head. She should never have opened up the shop again. There were some things that were out of her control.

'What's going on?'

She looked up to see Mike moving to the front of the crowd, which appeared to be building in anticipation of a showdown.

'Is he giving you trouble?' said Mike, taking in Charley's stricken expression.

She glanced at Wayne before replying, 'It doesn't matter.'

But Mike had turned back to face Wayne. He had straightened up but Mike towered over him.

'What's up, Wayne?' he said, keeping his tone light. 'Can't take a bit of healthy competition?'

'This is my patch,' muttered Wayne.

'Well, it was,' said Mike. 'Until you were done for illegal street trading last year.'

Wayne shrugged his shoulders. 'So what?'

'So I thought you were banned from ever trading again?'

'Nobody cares about that.'

Mike smiled at the queue who were agog at the stand-off in front of them. 'But I think they'll care about the food poisoning outbreak. What was it . . . listeria?'

'Was never proved,' said Wayne, beginning to sidle away.

'Go on,' said Julie, moving to stand next to Mike. 'Hop it. And take that disgusting van with you.'

'Your only purpose in this life is to serve as a warning to others,' said Mike, taking Wayne by the shoulders and marching him out of the shop.

'Blimey,' said Julie, turning to face Charley. 'Who ordered the bouncer?'

The chimes of Wayne's van soon faded into the distance and the women quickly served their customers.

Mike waited until the queue had died down before going up to the counter again.

'Thanks,' said Charley, with a grateful smile. 'Now, this one's on the house. What do you want?'

'Chocolate fudge brownie and toffee sundae,' said Mike, with a grin.

Charley put a scoop of each into a large cone before handing it over.

'So?' she asked, as he took his first bite.

Mike nodded. 'Fantastic,' he told her.

'Let's hope everyone else agrees with you,' she said.

'They will,' he replied. 'And as long as I can rely on my staff discount, I'll be one of your most frequent customers.'

Charley stared at him for a beat as a smile spread across his face.

'Don't push your luck,' she told him.

But with Wayne's Whippy finally out of the way, she began to relax and hope that everything would be all right from now onwards.

Chapter Fifty-two

'Mummy!' whined Flora, shuffling her feet impatiently on the pavement.

'Just one more photo,' said Caroline. 'I promise.'

She was trying not to cry as she looked at her daughter through the camera lens. Flora was so grown up in her school uniform. It seemed like yesterday that she had been a baby in Caroline's arms. Now it was September and she was going off into the world on her own.

'There,' said Caroline, putting down her mobile phone. 'I'm done.'

She took Flora's hand in hers, with the school satchel in the other, and they walked towards the school gates.

Caroline had had a normal upbringing, which had been fine at the time – but she wanted only the best for her daughter. Grove School for Girls would give Flora the best start in life, regardless of the price per term.

She squeezed her daughter's hand tight, both in dread of leaving her and at having to introduce them both to the clique of parents already gathered at the school gates.

Caroline had read about the one-upmanship that went on there regarding parenting, fashions and cars. She could multiply that one-upmanship by ten she knew, when the wealth of parents with offspring at private school was factored in.

There were various groups of women and children standing around and chatting. There was the thin, suntanned group, all with expensive highlights and sunglasses on even though it was an overcast day.

Caroline gave them a wide berth and walked slowly towards another group where the girls all seemed to be of the same age as Flora.

'Hi,' said one of the women, giving her a wide smile. 'First day?'

Caroline nodded. 'Hello. Yes, it is.'

She found her voice wavering, and her eyes beginning to fill with tears.

'Sorry,' she said, fishing in her handbag for a tissue. 'It's the hormones. I'm pregnant.'

'Congratulations,' replied the woman, whose daughter was tugging at her arm. 'Anyway, don't fret. It'll be half term before you know it.'

'God help us,' drawled another of the women. 'Did you book that Euro Disney trip?'

'Arabella's father hasn't come through with the child-maintenance payment yet. Probably too busy bonking his mistress.'

Caroline tried to stop her eyebrows from shooting up but wasn't sure she was entirely successful.

'Poor you,' cooed the other mothers.

'She's an actress too, apparently,' the woman drawled on. 'Just starred in the latest Disney film . . . *Finding Nympho*.'

Caroline joined in with the laughter but felt the

conversation was a bit inappropriate with their children still by their sides. It was their daughters' first day at school. How could they all be so laid-back and stand around and gossip like this?

All too soon, the time arrived to say goodbye. Caroline just about managed not to cry as she hugged Flora. Her daughter seemed unfazed by the new environment and followed the others into the classroom.

Caroline said a quick goodbye to the other mums and was halfway home in the car before she really began to sob. She made it back before calling Julie.

'So? How bad was it?' said her friend, picking up the call.

'Dreadful,' said Caroline, voice breaking at the other end of the line.

'I was the same,' said Julie.

'What do I do now?' said Caroline.

'Relax and enjoy the peace and quiet,' Julie told her. 'Watch daytime television. Read a book. All the things you can't do when Flora's at home. You're pregnant. Put your feet up.'

'It's just so quiet,' said Caroline.

'I know,' said Julie. 'I'll see you tomorrow night?'

'Of course.'

Caroline wandered around the house, unable to sit still. Her mind was racing, watching television unthinkable.

So she grabbed her car keys and headed back out, anything to avoid the silence the house was now filled with.

Chapter Fifty-three

Once her friends had been reassured that the noisy neighbours upstairs had finally been thrown out of their flat, Charley persuaded them to return to her home for the next meet-up.

Unfortunately, she was hideously late getting home as the Mini had broken down on the way home from the shop. Unable to get it going, she rang her dad who had come out with a mechanic friend to look it over.

The mechanic gave the engine a rueful look once he had fiddled with the electrics for a while.

'Well? What do you think?' asked Charley.

He exchanged looks with her father.

'Can it be easily fixed?' Charley persisted.

'Only if I jack up the roof and run a new car underneath in its place.'

She sighed. Everyone had to be a comedian.

Her father managed to establish that the Mini could be sorted out that weekend, ready for work on Monday morning. He dropped Charley off at her flat. She rolled her eyes when she saw her friends' cars already outside in the car park.

'Sorry!' she exclaimed, rushing up to them as they huddled in the communal hallway. 'Bloody car.'

'Maybe your Aunt Peggy will take it back,' said Julie.

Charley grunted. 'Would you?'

She let them into the flat and they all breathed in the glorious smell. Julie had lent Charley her old slow cooker as she said she never used it. Charley could at least afford to buy the cheaper cuts of meat. A couple of mornings each week, she would quickly brown whatever bargain she had bought, throw in some vegetables and stock, and leave the slow cooker to bubble away during the day. It was wonderful to come home to find an appetising smell wafting out of the kitchen. And it was nice to eat meat again as well.

Charley switched on the kettle to heat up the couscous she was going to serve with her sun-dried tomato and chicken dish.

'It's not a very glamorous meal,' she told her friends. 'But it's healthy.'

'Did you hear about Grove Castle?' asked Caroline, once they each had a drink.

'You mean the Valentine's Ball?' asked Charley.

'So romantic,' sighed Caroline.

'I don't know,' said Julie. 'I've never suited evening dresses.'

They all glanced at Samantha who would normally have raved about the fashions but she was looking tired. She had just endured the longest fortnight of her life. Richard hadn't called her before going on holiday with his family.

She had been desperate and miserable, spending

many hours on the phone to her friends to talk about the relationship. Charley, Caroline and Julie had all in turn tried to persuade her to give up on Richard. That he wasn't worth it and was only using her.

But Samantha didn't listen, couldn't bear to think that it was over.

Finally, the previous evening, he had turned up on her doorstep. She had jumped willingly into his arms, grateful that he had come back to her.

Charley frowned as she watched Samantha texting someone who could only be her lover, ignoring everyone else in the room. It was always the same, but it was beginning to grate on Charley.

Samantha was a great friend during the good times, always up for a laugh and ready to party. But she was absolutely lousy during the bad times. She expected the world to revolve around her, but she would be more of a friend if she deigned to listen to someone else's problems for once.

'What's going on?' asked Caroline.

Samantha grinned. 'It would make you blush if I showed you what he's just written.'

Charley made her excuses to attend to the dinner.

Whilst she was stirring the couscous, Caroline joined her in the kitchen.

'I was just in search of another glass of water,' she said.

Charley watched her. 'You don't look very well.'

'I feel a bit rough still.'

'Have you talked to the midwives? Can't they do anything?'

Caroline shrugged her shoulders. 'I'll feel better when the baby comes.'

'Can I do anything?' asked Charley.

'Carry the baby for me?'

Charley gave her a brief hug before saying, 'How about a bit of dinner?'

'That would be great.'

She dished up and handed everyone their plate, realising that Samantha was still going on about Richard.

'He's promised me he'll throw a sickie on Monday. It's the only time we can get to be together now his wife's growing more suspicious.'

Charley stayed quiet. She had never given much thought to Samantha's being a mistress before. She'd known about the affair of course, but now it seemed wrong. Because somebody, somewhere, was as unaware of her husband's affair as Charley had been of Steve's.

'Lovely meal,' said Caroline, obviously trying to change the subject.

'How was the cleaning today?' asked Julie.

But Charley never got a chance to answer as Samantha had suddenly swung round to face her.

'I know!' she said. 'How about we make up a foursome?'

'For what? Badminton?'

'No, silly! You can come out with me and Richard. He must have loads of good-looking friends.'

Charley's heart lurched. Trying to make small talk with some stranger in a bar? Her battered confidence wasn't ready for that.

She shook her head. 'Thanks but it's way too soon.'

'Come on,' said Samantha. 'You need to get out more. It'll be fun.'

'I can't afford it.'

'The men will buy the drinks.'

Charley gave a heavy sigh. 'I don't want to. I'm not ready.'

'Steve cheated on you,' said Samantha. 'He's with her now. He's moved on. It's time for you to do the same.'

'That's all it takes to move on, is it?' snapped Charley. 'A quick shag with some stranger and that'll have me as right as rain? Is that what you do? Is that why you shag everything in trousers . . . so you can forget about your man lying there with his *wife*? Maybe you're right. Maybe that'll help me forget. But it doesn't seem to have helped you, does it?'

They glared at each other for a minute whilst the other women exchanged looks.

'Besides, have you seen the blokes in town on a Friday night?' said Julie in a bright voice. 'Talk about grim.'

'That's what I've been telling you lot for years,' said Samantha. 'The pickings aren't exactly rich out there in single-man land.'

She gave Charley a sheepish grin.

Charley couldn't fight any longer and began to gather up the plates. 'I'll get the ice-cream,' she said.

They all enjoyed the elderflower flavour. Charley served scoops of it inside small pastry cases.

'This is great,' said Julie.

'Thanks,' replied Charley. 'I thought it might perhaps be a bit too sophisticated for the shop customers.'

She was actually itching to make some different recipes but there was never any time to spare. But come the autumn, her life would be her own once more and then she could start to experiment.

There were so many people suffering in the current economic climate. She had been so lucky to have had so much, and then she had thrown it all away. Before that she had never once considered the possibility that she might lose it all. Never thought everything in her life could change so drastically.

She wondered if that were the reason why she didn't want to start dating. She had got to a stage where she was as happy as she could be, considering her current circumstances.

Change meant things could get unpredictable again. That she could become unsure about herself once more.

Charley had only just found her feet. She really didn't want to trip over them at this early stage.

Chapter Fifty-four

Julie stared out of the kitchen window, watching Boris gleefully pulling up clumps of grass and chewing on them. She sighed and looked back down at the note she was holding.

It was from the veterinary practice, reminding her that Boris was due for a six-month check-up and suggesting that he be micro-chipped. That would be another £40 to add to the rest of the expense of having a dog. The food bill alone was creeping up month on month as Boris became bigger.

Things were already tight as it was. The newspaper advert in which she had tried to sell him had not appeared as the debit card charge had bounced. She was beginning to receive stroppy emails from the bank regarding her overdraft. The second mortgage was causing her no end of financial heartache.

It had all been for Nick's sake, to help him towards a more stable future. But that hadn't happened. He had rung her only the previous week to ask for some more money to be wired to him.

Julie called Boris into the house. The last thing she wanted to do was go for a long walk in the oppressive heat of the late afternoon but she knew he would be hyper all evening if they didn't go out.

She put on his lead and set off. The sun had disappeared earlier in the day, leaving a muggy atmosphere in its place. The clouds were definitely getting darker. Perhaps they would finally get some rain after so many weeks of summer heat.

She turned on to the heath and released Boris from his lead. He joyfully bounded off, free at last to explore.

Julie followed him in a bit of a daze, mulling over her financial woes. Something was going to have to give. She had just been paid and finally had a bit of extra money in her account to pay for the newspaper advert.

Not really concentrating on where she was going, she glanced at her phone and realised that they had walked for a lot longer than usual. Julie called out for Boris so that they could turn and head for home. She felt sweaty and hot, desperate for a refreshing shower.

As she waited for him to finish sniffing around a tree trunk, she looked up and realised the sky was becoming darker and darker, the threat of a storm growing ever closer.

'Come on,' she called out to the dog.

But Boris was too busy having fun.

So Julie decided to walk away without him, which normally induced the dog to follow her, in case he was left behind. But she had only gone a few paces when there was a loud rumble of thunder.

She spun round but it was too late. Boris had scampered off in a panic at the alarming sound and was heading across the heathland towards the trees at the outer edge. Julie began to run after him just as thick drops of rain began to fall.

'Boris!' she called out, trying to keep her voice cheerful and light.

But a louder crack of thunder meant he kept on leaping across the heather, far in front of her.

'Come back!' she called, the rain now falling heavily.

In the middle of the heath there was no cover. She was quickly drenched as she ran as fast as she could after the dog.

By the time she reached the trees, she could barely see through the torrential rain. There was a flash of lightning as she stared around the small coppice, but she couldn't see Boris anywhere.

She called out his name once more and tried to listen out for a bark or whimper but the sound of the storm was drowning out everything else.

Julie didn't know how long she searched the woods for signs of his cream-coloured fur but there was still no sign of him and she began to get increasingly upset. He was still so young. What if he had run on to a road or got stuck somewhere?

She had no idea what to do.

Just as she was beginning to shed tears of fear, wondering what might have happened to him, there was movement to her right. She whipped round her head and saw Wes coming through the trees, holding Boris in his arms. His own dog Cadbury was trotting along beside them.

'G'day,' said Wes, coming to stand in front of Julie.

His white t-shirt had become transparent in the rain and was showing the hard muscular torso underneath. Rain was dripping off his face but he was still smiling.

'You found him,' said Julie, her voice still tremulous as she reached out to stroke Boris' fluffy head.

'Poor little guy came rushing past us in a real panic. But I managed to get close enough to grab him.'

The sky lit up once more with a flash of lightning but Wes had Boris tight in his arms.

'Have you got your lead?'

Julie nodded and attached it with shaking hands to Boris' collar.

'You all right?' asked Wes, as he put the dog back on to the ground.

'I couldn't see him anywhere,' she told him. 'Do you think we should wait it out?'

'Nah,' said Wes. 'It's only water. Besides, there's some clear sky on the horizon now.'

Julie glanced across the heath and realised that he was right. The storm was continuing its journey onwards and away from them. The rain hadn't yet eased, though, and there were still a few rumbles of thunder, which made Boris run between her legs for cover.

So they walked back together, the dogs remaining close as the rain continued to pour down. Julie was soaked to the skin and patted her hair, feeling it plastered to her head.

'I don't have to worry about that,' said Wes, rubbing his bald head and smiling.

It lit up his face, she thought. It was such a nice, happy face. A friendly face.

She glanced at his wet torso when she hoped he wasn't looking. Lord, but what did they feed them on in Australia? Growing beans? He was the size of a house, all hard muscles and bulging biceps. Julie and the two dogs could easily have sheltered underneath him for cover from the elements.

The rain was finally easing off as they reached the outskirts of the heath.

'Thank you so much for catching Boris,' she said, as they made their farewells.

'No worries,' said Wes, bending down to rub the dog's head. 'He's a bonzer little guy.'

Julie said goodbye and headed home, more than ever determined to place the advert. Temporarily losing Boris had been dreadful. She didn't need that kind of stress. There was too much else for her to worry about.

Chapter Fifty-five

With the end of the summer heatwave came a lull in the frantic pace of Charley's life. All the children were back at school and so she reduced the opening times to just weekends. Suddenly she had her late afternoons and evenings free once more.

She found herself unexpectedly bored, though, almost grateful for the cleaning job which kept her busy during the rest of the day. It made her wonder how empty her life had really been when she hadn't worked during the latter years of her marriage.

That didn't mean she loved her job, she just got on with it. But once rested she found herself in a relatively good mood. At least until she received a text from Samantha.

The date's set! it read. *Next Saturday night!*

What are you talking about? replied Charley.

The foursome, stupid! Our hot date! came a swift text.

Charley was horrified and immediately called her.

'You've set me up after I specifically told you not

to? After I most definitely said that I didn't want to go on any dates at the moment?'

'It'll do you good,' said Samantha, adopting a soothing tone. 'You'll change your mind once you're there.'

'Anyway, how can you go on a date? What about Richard's wife?'

'She's away,' said Samantha. 'So it'll be us, you and Keith.'

'Keith?'

'His friend from work.'

'No.' Charley was violently shaking her head. 'I'm not doing it.'

'Please!' begged Samantha. 'You'll be my cover. Richard and I can't go out on our own, you know that. And you never know, it might be fun.'

Charley pressed her lips together.

'It'll do you good as well,' Samantha added. 'When was the last time you went out on the town? Had a bit of male attention?'

Around the year 2002, Charley figured.

Samantha took her silence for agreement. 'Good! That's settled then.'

Charley didn't want to go out with some man she didn't know. She certainly didn't want to meet Samantha's married lover. But she found she couldn't bear her friend's whining if she refused, so she said yes. Anything to get it over with.

But she was cross at having been forced into a corner and took it out on the ironing at Mrs Smith's the following day.

'I must have the wrong place,' said Mike, finding her behind a cloud of steam. 'I was wanting the cleaner, not Widow Twankey.'

Charley sighed before finishing off the shirt on the ironing board.

'Cup of tea?' he said, stepping in to switch on the kettle. 'Or shall I just put you into the freezer and leave you there to cool off?'

Charley put the iron down. 'I thought she had someone to do all this for her.'

Mike leant against the counter whilst he waited for the kettle to boil. 'Perhaps they had to give the ironing lady the heave ho. I've heard they've got a few money problems.'

Charley didn't reply as she hung the shirt up on a hanger.

She turned around to find Mike studying her. 'What?'

He cocked his head to one side, still looking at her. 'You don't moan so much.'

'What do you mean?'

He walked over to her. 'Before the summer it was all woe-is-me, but now you seem calmer. More settled.'

'I hope you don't think it's because of your influence that I'm happier in myself?'

'But just think,' he said, putting his hand on the doorframe beside her, 'if we didn't work together you wouldn't be having all the fun you have now.'

Charley raised her eyebrows in mock surprise. 'We have fun, do we?'

He leant in close. 'All the time. Didn't you notice?'

She noted the softer tone of his voice. The close proximity of him as he towered over her.

'Talking of fun,' he continued, fixing her with his dark eyes, 'do you want to go out for a drink on Saturday night?'

'I'd love to but I can't,' she told him, lowering her eyes to avoid his gaze. 'I've got a date.'

Mike pulled back slightly. 'Really?'

She nodded.

'Who?'

'Just a guy. Friend of a friend thing.'

Charley squirmed in the short silence that followed.

'Well,' he said, straightening up and moving away, 'I'm glad things are working out for you.'

'Thank you.'

The mood between them had abruptly become polite and stilted.

'I'd better get back to work,' he told her, walking towards the back door.

'What about that cup of tea?' called Charley after him.

But there was no reply as the door closed softly behind him.

Chapter Fifty-six

Caroline headed across the hospital car park, glancing around her but seeing nobody she knew. She should really have told someone else about the appointment, but after all it was bound to be okay.

Although what the midwife had actually said was, 'Your blood pressure is far too high. It could be a sign of pre-eclampsia.'

'But you just told me that the tests are fine,' Caroline had replied.

'Even so, you've got to rest. Can your husband help out more around the house and with your daughter?'

Caroline had tried not to laugh in reply. Jeff was barely home these days, working all hours and most weekends. Her parents were spending autumn and winter in their villa in Spain.

Every time she asked, Jeff reassured her that he was overjoyed by the news about the baby, but she wasn't so sure. After all, his mood had rapidly deteriorated since she had announced she was pregnant.

When he was home, he was stressed and snappy at everything she said. The previous Sunday it had been about Flora's homework, which had taken up most of the afternoon.

'She's only five!' Jeff had protested, his voice loud with strain. 'Why the hell does she need to do so much?'

'It's the school,' Caroline had replied, trying to stay calm. 'They think it's better to push the girls as much as they can from an early age.'

'It's ridiculous. She should be out playing, not studying.'

It was a beautiful late-summer day and Caroline had silently agreed with him.

But instead she said, 'Then why don't you help her?'

'I've got work to do. I think that's a bit more important, don't you?'

As he stalked back into the study, Caroline sighed and rubbed her head. The onset of another headache threatened.

She glanced over at Flora who had been watching the argument and was now trying not to cry.

'It's all right, darling,' Caroline said, going over to give her daughter a hug. 'Let's get a biscuit and then have a think. I'm sure we can create a nice collage together.'

Caroline longed for a bath to ease her backache. Longed for a lie down on her bed. Longed for a happier atmosphere in the house.

She hadn't yet brought up the subject of the invoice for Flora's next school term, which lay hidden under a pile of papers in the kitchen. No wonder her blood pressure was so high. But hopefully Jeff would be in a better mood the following week. She would broach the subject then.

She sipped from her cup of tea and began to cut out a picture of a happy family from a magazine which Flora wanted in her collage.

Chapter Fifty-seven

Julie had been inundated with phone calls after successfully placing the advert about Boris in the local newspaper. She had arranged to see a couple of callers on Friday evening after work.

'It's for the best,' she kept repeating out loud all week to herself, avoiding eye contact with Boris' big black eyes.

She arrived home from their evening walk and went straight to the pantry, grabbing the filter coffee and setting the machine on. Then she went upstairs and enjoyed a lovely long shower before changing into her jeans and t-shirt and coming back downstairs.

'I know,' she told the puppy who was lying on the kitchen floor. 'You want your dinner. But you'll have to wait until all the visitors have been and gone.'

She glanced at Boris who wasn't moving. That was odd. Normally, as soon as she went anywhere near the kitchen, he would be shadowing her, desperate for his dinner.

As she stared down at him, he was suddenly and very violently sick.

'Oh God,' she swore, going to get some kitchen paper to mop up the mess.

This was the last thing she needed, with people coming round to see him. She had no chance of selling him if he had eaten something dodgy on his walk.

But Boris kept on being sick. Julie began to grow worried and reached out to stroke his head, to try and reassure him.

That was when she spotted some specks of blood in the latest vomit that he had produced. She rushed away to find the book on dogs that Caroline had given her and flicked through the pages, desperately hoping she was remembering her facts wrong.

But when she arrived at the doggy illnesses page and quickly scanned it, she was proved right. Blood in a dog's vomit was never a good thing. In capital letters, the book told Julie to go to the vet's. Right now.

Despite his weight and size, she quickly swept Boris into her arms and ran out to the car. She placed the whimpering dog in the passenger seat before rushing round to the driver's side. Later on she had no recollection of the journey. Whenever she could, she reached across to stroke him.

She abandoned the car outside the vet's surgery, picked up Boris and rushed in.

'Please help me!' she cried.

Wes was standing behind the counter, talking to one of the veterinary nurses. 'What's happened?' he asked.

'He's vomiting blood.'

Wes strode over in three short paces and took the dog from her.

'What's he eaten?'

283

Julie half-ran to keep up with him as they went into one of the rooms. 'I don't know!' she cried. 'Maybe something on his walk.'

He gently placed Boris on the examination table before turning to wash his hands at the sink. 'How long ago was that?'

'About half an hour.'

'Anything in the house he could have eaten when you got home?'

Before Julie could reply, Boris began to vomit once more.

She looked up at Wes. 'Do something!'

'I will,' he told her. 'But was there anything he might have eaten? Poisons? Food? Think.'

Julie frowned in thought. 'I don't know,' she said eventually.

'Can you check?'

So she quickly rang Charley who was on her way home from work and was able to take a detour.

Julie paced up and down the room whilst she waited for her friend to call back. In the meantime, she watched as Wes took Boris' temperature and checked him over for any abnormalities.

After what seemed like an age, Charley called back. 'The pantry door is open,' she said, somewhat breathlessly. 'There's bits of what looks like chocolate wrapper. Could it be that?'

'Oh God,' said Julie. 'Can you see a really big bar of cooking chocolate anywhere?'

'No.'

Julie quickly hung up. 'He's eaten loads of chocolate. The really dark cooking stuff. I must have left the door open when I went upstairs.'

'I'll need a washing-soda crystal,' Wes told the nurse.

Both he and the nurse left the room and Julie was briefly left alone with Boris.

'Please don't die,' she whispered to the shivering puppy on the table. 'I can't lose anyone else this year. Please don't die.'

The nurse returned with the treatment, closely followed by Wes. Julie hugged her arms around herself as she watched the vet force the washing-soda crystal into Boris' mouth.

'Hopefully this will make him vomit up the rest of it,' Wes told her. 'Do you want to wait in reception?'

Julie shook her head. 'I'm not going anywhere,' she told him in a tremulous voice.

She watched as the poor dog was sick and then sick again. It was all her fault, she kept thinking. She couldn't believe she had been so stupid.

Once they were sure that his stomach was empty, Boris was given a form of charcoal to ease his intestines. He was also attached to an intravenous drip, to steady his heart rate and give him much-needed fluids.

All the time that she could, without getting in the vet's way, Julie stroked Boris' front paw.

'You'll be okay,' she told him softly, over and over again.

Eventually, once the dog was settled, Wes found her a seat so she could sit next to the dog, and the nurse produced a cup of tea. Julie found the mug shook in her hand as she took a sip.

Wes crouched down in front of her.

'Will he live?' she asked, the tears beginning to run down her cheeks.

'It's possible,' he told her in a gentle tone. 'There wasn't much time between him eating the chocolate and you finding him. That gives him a better chance.'

'What kind of chance are we talking about?' asked Julie. 'Tell me the odds.'

He rested one large hand over hers. 'It's a fifty-fifty survival rate in most cases of chocolate poisoning. Especially if he's eaten a lot.'

Julie suppressed a sob.

'It's a waiting game now,' Wes told her, squeezing her hand. 'There's not much you can do. We'll get him transferred to the recovery room for now.'

Left alone for a brief minute, Julie leant forward in her chair, stroking Boris' soft silky head.

'I'm sorry,' she told him, the tears spilling from her eyes once more. 'I don't mean to snap at you all the time. You're not a bad dog. I'm just not used to you, that's all. Just get well and I'll be better, I promise. Please don't leave me.'

She brought her lips down on to his head and gave him a soft kiss.

'I love you,' she whispered, just before the door opened.

'Julie?' said Wes. 'We've got to move him now.'

She nodded, unable to speak.

'I'll ring you tonight, okay?' he told her, briefly putting one arm around her shoulder. 'If there's any change, I'll ring you as soon as possible.'

Julie picked up her handbag before giving Boris one last look. Then she left in tears.

Chapter Fifty-eight

Samantha was very unimpressed when Charley rang to cancel the double date for the following night.

'Why the hell can't you come?' she snapped.

'Julie needs me,' Charley told her. 'She's distraught.'

'It's only a dog, for God's sake,' said Samantha.

'Well, he means a lot to Julie,' said Charley sharply in reply.

Samantha put the phone down in a huff.

She needed to go out with Richard, had to. They had just about recovered from their argument before his holiday but it was important to keep going, to start pushing for him to get rid of the old ball and chain.

The fun relationship, the brief flirtation she had envisaged, had long since disappeared. Now it was love. Wretched, awful, undeniable love.

But there was hope.

The previous week, Richard had promised he would leave his wife.

'When the time is right,' he had quickly added.

'Of course,' said Samantha, nodding.

It was going to happen. Of that she was certain.

'Poor Boris,' said Caroline, near to tears on hearing the news after Charley called her.

'He'll be okay,' replied her friend, not sounding at all positive.

'Of course he will,' sniffed Caroline.

Poor Julie, she thought as she put down the phone.

Flora would be distraught as well if anything happened to the puppy. It had even made Caroline think about getting a dog but she had decided to wait. There was too much else going on. Flora had to concentrate on her schoolwork, and Jeff was hardly ever around to help out with a young puppy. Let alone the cost of the pedigree breed that Caroline wanted.

Money was becoming a pressing issue. She would have to see to the invoice for the next school term, especially as a charming but more insistent reminder letter had appeared the previous day in the post.

Then there was Flora's birthday at the end of the month. Her presents wouldn't be cheap and there was the added stress of the birthday party to arrange. Children's parties had gone stratospheric in cost, especially at the private schools. It was one-upmanship gone mad.

Caroline rubbed her forehead. Yet another headache was beginning.

Julie had told Charley she was fine and didn't need any company. But upon finding Charley's clapped out Mini in the driveway once she was home, she rushed inside the house.

'It's all my fault,' she sobbed, falling into Charley's hug.

'Don't be stupid,' said Charley, squeezing her tight. 'It was an accident.'

'I shouldn't have left the door open. He must have seen the chocolate and grabbed it.'

'He's a dog!' Charley told her. 'He'll take any food that's going! It wasn't your fault.'

'What if he dies?' whispered Julie. 'What will I do?'

'He won't,' replied Charley in a firm tone. 'Now, let's get the kettle on. Or have you got something stronger?'

In the end, Charley made Irish coffee for them both. And then they waited.

'Did I tell you I've shut the shop for good?' she said. 'Not much business about now we're into autumn. Remind me to give you the key back.'

Julie didn't reply, merely hugging her coffee closer.

And so Charley went prattling on about this and that. Anything to fill the void as they waited for news.

Finally, after what seemed like the longest two hours in history, Julie's mobile rang.

'Hello?'

'It's Wes,' said the vet. 'The recovery is going well. I'll keep a close eye on Boris overnight but I think he's going to be fine.'

Julie was near to tears again as relief swept over her. 'Thank you,' were the only words she was able to muster.

'I'll ring you first thing in the morning. Try and get a good night's sleep.'

She put down the phone and broke into a watery smile as she told Charley, 'The vet thinks he's going to be okay.'

'Thank God,' said Charley. 'Do you want me to stay the night?'

Julie shook her head. 'I should be fine.'

But she wasn't. The house seemed very empty without Boris. Everywhere she looked there were his toys, his bed, his bowls, and the odd half-chewed shoe. The house seemed too quiet without his snuffling, scratching and constant movement. Julie's house wasn't a home without her dog.

Her phone rang again that evening. She had a sudden moment of fright, thinking it was Wes to say Boris had taken a turn for the worse.

But it was a man replying to the advert, wanting to arrange a viewing time the following evening.

'I'm sorry,' replied Julie, her voice still a little shaky. 'The dog is no longer for sale.'

Chapter Fifty-nine

Two days later, Julie went to the vet's after work to pick up Boris. The nurse brought him through from the recovery room and he was straining at the lead to get to Julie. He sat on her feet, tail thumping in excitement to see her. Julie couldn't stop herself from bending down to give him a hug before roughing up his fur.

'You soppy thing,' she told him. 'Shall we go home?'

She paid the bill with the last of her savings and thanked the staff. She was told Wes was on an emergency call out, but the receptionist said she would pass on Julie's thanks.

Under strict instructions to keep Boris quiet over the next few days, Julie wandered around the house with him that evening whilst he explored the place. He had a lost a little weight and was very clingy. Eventually he sat on her feet, staring up at her.

'Come on then,' she said softly, lifting him up on to the sofa next to her. The puppy snuggled into her side; one soft ear flopped onto her leg.

Finally, she fell asleep with Boris beside her.

On Saturday morning, Charley and Caroline popped in to see how the puppy was.

'He's great, aren't you, Gorgeous?' cooed Julie, stroking Boris' head.

The other women exchanged looks.

'I'm worried that she's changed into a completely different person,' whispered Caroline.

'Yeah,' replied Charley. 'A doggy person.'

They watched Julie fuss over Boris, and exchanged smiles.

'So,' said Charley. 'Are you all set for Flora's birthday?'

'No,' replied Caroline, sounding stressed. 'It's bad enough she was born on the thirty-first of October. Now she wants a Hallowe'en-themed party.'

'Well, the stuff's cheap enough in the shops,' Charley told her.

Caroline took a sip of water.

'You okay?' asked Julie, who had been watching her.

'Been better,' replied Caroline. 'It's all so stressful, trying to think up something original for the party. Like the cake, for instance.' She closed her eyes for a brief second before opening them wide. 'You know what? I think Charley should do it. In ice-cream form!'

'I can't,' said Charley, aghast.

'It's perfect,' said Julie, suddenly looking excited. 'An ice-cream cake! It's definitely original.'

'But still perfect for kids,' carried on Caroline.

'And you'll know where all the ingredients have come from,' said Julie.

'Great!' said Caroline, breaking into a smile. 'That's sorted.'

'Hold on,' Charley said. 'I haven't said I'll do it yet.'

'What about this in ice-cream?' said Julie, who had grabbed a magazine to flick through for ideas.

'No,' said Caroline. 'It'll never survive the car journey. What about this?'

'Hello!' called Charley. 'Do I get any say in this?'

The women looked at each other before looking back at her.

'No,' they replied in unison before continuing to ignore her.

Charley gave up and began to stroke Boris' back. This was a bad idea, was her first thought. Why not? was her second. She enjoyed making ice-cream. Kids plus ice-cream was always a good combination.

Julie rang her the following day. 'I've thought of just the right place for inspiration,' she said.

An hour later, Charley was in hell. The tannoy in Toys R Us blared out, fighting to be heard above the chiming, crashing and crying hordes around them.

Charley clutched her aching head. 'Why are you torturing me like this?'

Julie was rifling through a large bin of hats. 'Because we're friends and Caroline is drowning under all this party stuff.'

She lifted out a small witch's hat with wiry green hair attached on the inside. She rammed it down over her head. The hat stayed there for a whole second before popping off into a nearby display of Dracula teeth.

'Hmm. Maybe not.'

She drew out a larger hat and put it on. It was so large it covered her whole face down to her chin.

'I prefer that one,' Charley told her.

Julie threw the hat back into the box and continued to rifle around. She pulled out two more and threw one at Charley. 'There's yours. All the helpers are dressing up.'

'You've got to be joking?'

'You promised.'

Charley blew out a long sigh. 'I thought I was just making the cake, which I didn't have any choice about.'

'Flora will be heartbroken if you don't come.' Julie put on her most pitiful look. 'It's only one afternoon in the village hall. There are hardly any adults available. You can't leave Caroline to cope with all that on her own.'

'What about Samantha?' said Charley.

'Oh, yeah,' drawled Julie in reply. 'She's not exactly a children lover, is she? Do you know, she never even called me to see how Boris was?'

'I think she's still in a strop with me about cancelling that double date.'

Julie pulled a face. 'Sorry. That was my fault.'

Charley shrugged her shoulders. 'It doesn't matter.' She shoved a hat on to her head and checked her reflection in a nearby mirror.

'Don't hate me but that really suits you,' said Julie, who was watching her. 'You should hear my idea for a costume.'

'Mine's going to have to be black jeans, a black top and this stupid witch's hat.'

'That's the spirit.'

They paid for their goods and left the air-conditioning for the October wind outside. The sun was out but the warmth had gone from its rays. Autumn was here and the heat of the summer seemed an eternity ago.

Chapter Sixty

'All you have to do is come up with something creative for Flora's birthday cake,' Caroline had told her.

Trouble was, thought Charley, she wasn't feeling a creative vibe at all, especially having spent the day inhaling fumes from the limescale-remover spray that one of her customers insisted she used.

She slumped in her armchair, thinking about the Hallowe'en theme. She wondered about buying a big pumpkin and carving a face on the front. That was all very well but what would she do with the ice-cream? Fill it to the brim and let the kids scoop it out with their hands? Not very hygienic or practical.

She glanced at her watch. It was nearly four o'clock. The market would be finishing soon. She leapt out of her chair and grabbed her jacket on the way out. Perhaps she would find inspiration wandering around the stalls.

The leaves had already begun to turn on the trees, giving everything a golden hue in the late-afternoon sun. The wind was whistling around the car park so Charley hugged her jacket close as she mooched around the stalls. The bright colours of the summer fruits had gone, to be replaced by earthy vegetables such as carrots, parsnips and turnips.

There were loads of pumpkins as Hallowe'en was only a fortnight away but Charley still wasn't sure. There were a few baby pumpkins, but those were terribly expensive. Besides, pumpkin and ice-cream didn't really go, did it? Charley wasn't sure that pumpkin and anything went well together.

She was just beginning to lose heart when she passed one of the last fruit and vegetable stalls. She stopped in the middle of the path and backed up a few steps, staring down at the box of fruit.

'How much?' she asked the trader.

'How many do you want, darling?' His cheeks were bright red from the cold wind.

Charley did a rough count in her head. 'Thirty. No, you'd better make it forty.'

'Forty oranges? You're keen, aren't ya? You making marmalade?'

She gave him a slow grin. 'I hadn't planned to but it's a good idea. How much?'

He blew out a long breath. 'Go on, then. I'll never get them sold now. You can have the whole lot for two quid. They're just on the turn, you know.'

It was such a bargain she nearly leant over and kissed him. 'That doesn't matter.'

She handed over a £2 coin and carried the box all the way home. On the way, she popped into the corner shop and picked up four large bars of chocolate and some tubs of cream.

Staggering through the front door, she heaved the box on to the kitchen top and then allowed herself a small smile. This was going to be fun.

Charley decided to make the ice-cream first, one batch of chocolate and one of plain vanilla. An hour and a half later, the tubs of ice-cream were beginning to crystallise in the freezer.

It was almost dark outside so she had to switch on the overhead light in the kitchen. She plucked one of the oranges out of the box and stared at it for a while. Then she grabbed one of her carving knives and waved it in front of the orange whilst her mind tried to shore up its initial idea. If this didn't work then she had just bought forty oranges for nothing.

In the end, she decided to be brave. The expensive carving knife had been one of a set that she had hidden from the bailiffs. She had been very grateful for that afterwards, especially now when it pierced the rough skin of the orange so cleanly.

She sliced all the way across the orange about a quarter of the way from the top. Then she placed the 'lid' to one side and carefully began to scoop out the inner fruit, trying to leave the remaining skin intact.

Charley sucked on a juicy segment of orange whilst she stared at the empty shell. Then she took the knife once more and carefully carved out two small eyes and a jagged mouth. Stepping back, she beamed at the orange. It looked just like a tiny pumpkin all dressed up for Hallowe'en. She repeated the process with a second orange before bringing the chocolate ice-cream out of the freezer.

It was almost frozen so she was able to spoon some into the empty orange. The darkness of the chocolate from behind emphasised the scary face she had carved out of the skin. She popped the lid back on and stepped away.

There it was. A smiley, scary Hallowe'en dessert.

Charley alternated between the chocolate ice-cream filling and the plain vanilla one, which looked equally as good emphasising the scary face. It wasn't a birthday cake as such, but it was different, individual, and in keeping with the Hallowe'en theme. And each one could have a candle placed on top of it.

She glanced at the clock on the front of the oven. It was nearly eight o'clock and she had at least a couple of hours' work still to do on the desserts, but she didn't care. She wanted to finish the job before the oranges deteriorated. And besides, she was having too much fun to stop now.

Chapter Sixty-one

Charley rushed around at Mrs Wilberforce's house and was out to the car on the dot of four o'clock.

'Another hot date?' called Mike, coming across the garden.

'I haven't had the first one yet,' she told him before briefly explaining about Boris.

'So where are you off to now?'

'A birthday party for Flora, Caroline's daughter.' Charley sighed. 'What is the collective noun for a room full of five year olds?'

Mike broke into a grin. 'An uproar,' he replied.

She drove home smiling at his dry wit. Steve, she thought, had had barely any wit, and absolutely none of it dry.

Charley had just changed into her black jeans and top for the Hallowe'en party when there was a knock on the door.

She had to laugh at the sight of Julie, who had wrapped herself up in bandages, from her head all the way down her torso and legs to her feet, looking just like an Egyptian mummy.

'Did you drive here like that?' asked Charley.

'Of course. I'm hoping being mummified will help stop the ageing process.' Julie stepped into the hallway and watched Charley place a witch's hat on her wild black hair. 'You could have made more of an effort.'

'I'm on a budget.'

Julie breathed in deeply. 'This whole place smells of oranges.'

'I know. Isn't it lovely?'

'It certainly takes away that hint of damp.' Julie followed her into the kitchen. 'Let's have a look then.'

Charley lifted the lid on one of the cool boxes that Caroline had lent her to keep the desserts as cold as possible.

'Blimey!' Julie stared down at the scores of smiling faces on the oranges lined up within. 'Looks like a freak show in there.'

'You think they look scary enough?'

'They're giving me the creeps, sitting there smiling at me.' Julie poked at one of the faces. 'What are they made of?'

'Oranges with chocolate or vanilla ice-cream inside.'

'I'm impressed. I didn't know you had been keeping your artistic talents hidden. But what happened to all the insides of the oranges? Don't tell me you ate them all?'

'Not all of them, but I don't think I'm in danger of getting scurvy any time soon. Right, let's get these in your car before they melt.'

The inside of Little Grove village hall was festooned with fake spider's webs and pumpkins lit from within

300

by candles. The lights were turned down low to scare the children, who were scaring the adults by eating too much sugar and becoming hyperactive. But the sight of Julie doing her Egyptian mummy impression with arms held rigid in front of her sent a shiver down everyone's backs.

Caroline had laid out a few games for the children. In one of them they had to guess the body part by sticking their hand into a covered box. The brains made from spaghetti and blood made from tomato ketchup went down particularly well.

After the children had worn themselves out whacking the piñata-witch to smithereens, everyone adjourned to the big long tables set out for tea. Once the majority of the food had been wolfed down, everyone received one of Charley's Hallowe'en-face desserts in a paper bowl. There were even enough for the adults to have one each.

'The puddings were great,' said one of the women to Caroline, once teatime was over and the kids were tearing around the hall once more. 'Where did you get them from?'

Caroline pointed wearily to Charley. 'My friend made them.'

'Are you all right?' asked the woman.

'I just feel a bit drained,' she said, dropping on to a chair.

It wasn't long before Julie and Charley took charge, organising a lift home for Caroline and reassuring her that the party would be fine without her. Caroline had protested at that but they had promised her that Flora would have a lovely time and would tell her all about it when they brought her home.

A couple of hours later, the party was finally over.

The hall was in a state of devastation and the tidy-up began.

Except that Charley found herself surrounded by people, all eager to hear the details of her creative genius.

She was just telling them about having to stir the ice-cream every half hour to ensure it stayed velvety-smooth when Julie barged her way through.

'Excuse me,' she said. 'Can I have a word?'

She led Charley to a quiet corner.

'Thanks for that,' Charley told her. 'It's hard to make ice-cream sound interesting. So what's up? Your ex-husband come back to haunt you?'

But Julie wasn't smiling and her eyes looked troubled.

Charley clutched her hand in alarm. 'What is it? Is it Nick?'

Julie shook her head. 'No. It's Caroline.'

Chapter Sixty-two

The glare of the fluorescent lighting in the Accident and Emergency department of the hospital painted everything with a green tinge.

Charley and Julie had received a few chuckles and stares as they arrived in their full Hallowe'en get-up, but they weren't the only ones. Sitting in silence and sipping the dreadful vending-machine coffee, they both watched as a small boy was pushed through the waiting room in a wheelchair. He was dressed up in a black cloak and pointed hat and clutching what appeared to be a child-sized Hoover.

'Just 'cos Harry Potter can fly, don't mean you can,' said his mother, walking alongside the wheelchair.

'If we'd had a broomstick, I could have done,' the boy said, scowling at the Hoover.

Charley and Julie watched them go through the swing doors before giving each other a small smile. Julie clutched Charley's hand briefly and squeezed it before letting go.

They had been in the waiting room for nearly an

hour when Jeff appeared through the swing doors. He was pale and had obviously been crying but he gave the hint of a smile as he took in their costumes.

'How is she?' asked Julie, having given him a quick hug.

'Weary, but I told her you were both out here and she said she'd like to see you. The nurses said you could only stay for a couple of minutes, though.'

He led them through the doors and past a line of small rooms, each occupied by two patients. At the end of the corridor was a single room where they found Caroline lying in bed with her eyes closed. They crept in and hovered by the bedside, staring down at her.

'They're going to move her up to the ward in a minute,' said Jeff. 'Charley and Julie are here, love.'

Caroline opened her eyes and gave them a smile but Julie noticed it didn't extend to her eyes.

Charley sat down on the bed and gave her a kiss. 'What happened?'

'It's pre-eclampsia.'

'That's why your blood pressure was so high?' asked Julie.

Caroline nodded. 'And all those headaches.'

'What happens now?' said Charley.

'They're going to keep me in for a couple of days and then, if I'm very good, I can go home.'

'No more running around for you,' said Julie, sternly.

'No more anything,' said Jeff, who had stayed nearby. 'They've said she must have complete bed rest.'

'Otherwise I'll lose the baby,' said Caroline, her voice suddenly tremulous with tears.

'Flora's gone home with Molly and her mum,' said

Julie, looking at Jeff. 'They said she can always stay the night.'

He nodded, looking exhausted.

Caroline looked very small in the bed. So very pale with only her beautiful red hair spread out across the pillow to lend her any colour.

Charley took hold of her hand and squeezed it.

'How was the party?' asked Caroline.

'Flora had a lovely time. We got lots of photos and Julie did a good job of scaring everyone.'

They all looked at Julie who was beginning to unpeel, a long strip of bandage dangling down from her arm. 'I aim to please.'

'You gave us a scare too,' Charley told Caroline. 'I hate that we can't do anything for you.'

'Just being here's enough.'

For a moment none of them said anything, listening to the hubbub from the hospital corridor. Jeff started to sniffle in the corner and Julie went across to hug him.

'It's all my fault,' he said, beginning to break down. 'I was made redundant.'

'When?' asked Julie, shocked.

'Just today,' he said. 'There's been round after round of redundancies but each time I was okay. I worked harder and harder, trying to make sure I was essential, but it didn't matter in the end. The whole office is going.'

'Poor you,' said Julie, shaking her head.

'What are we going to do?' said Caroline, beginning to cry.

'You'll survive,' said Charley, squeezing her hand. 'After all, if I can do it, anyone can. How good are you with a mop?'

It raised a small smile from Caroline.

They gave both her and Jeff a hug before the porter came to take Caroline up to the ward.

Charley and Julie managed to hold out until they had got back in the car and then they allowed themselves a little cry.

They used Julie's bandages to mop themselves up before heading home.

Chapter Sixty-three

The last thing Charley wanted to do after Caroline's near miscarriage was go out on the re-arranged double date. But Samantha was insistent that it should go ahead and arrived promptly at the flat at 7 p.m.

'Is that what you're wearing?' she asked, her face wrinkled up in dismay.

'Yes.' Charley glanced down at her outfit. She was wearing a white camisole top, jeans and some high heeled boots. All were expensive items that she had dug out from the back of the wardrobe. The top still had the sales tag on it. 'Why?'

Samantha shrugged her shoulders. 'You might have shown a bit of leg.'

Charley threw on her aviator jacket, also barely worn. 'It's November and going to be ten degrees later.'

'You don't think you could have made a bit more of an effort?'

'I spend my life in old jeans and tops covered in dust and dirt. I've washed my hair and painted my toenails. Believe me, I have made an effort compared to how I usually look.'

But Charley now felt even more nervous.

Richard and his friend Keith were waiting for them in the bar. They were almost hidden from view in one of ten booths that lined the far wall. Samantha seemed to sense where they were and zoomed ahead of Charley.

As they reached the last booth, both men stood up to greet them. In a room packed with glamorous people, Richard fitted in well. He adopted the nonchalance of someone who knows they look good.

He gave Samantha a friendly hug. It all looked very innocent, but Charley saw him quickly brush his hand against her bottom as he kissed her on the cheek.

Meanwhile, Keith caught Charley's eye and gave her an awkward smile before an even more awkward handshake.

'Hi,' he said, in a deep voice, his hand crushing hers.

'Hello. I'm Charlotte. Charley to my friends.'

'I'm Keith, and I hope we will be.'

It was cheesy but broke the ice as her nervous laughter was interpreted as the real thing.

Keith gestured for Charley to take a seat next to him whilst he removed his jacket. It gave her the opportunity to take in his appearance when he was distracted. Older than her, possibly in his early forties, he had a cheerful, round face. His body was also round, but one glance at the cattle market of the bar told her that she should be grateful he was even vaguely presentable. Dozens of girls wearing next to nothing vied for the attention of dim-looking guys standing around sipping beer and talking football. Everyone looked to be about seventeen.

The thump-thump of the rap music was ear-piercing.

'Isn't it depressing?' shouted Keith in her ear. 'Do you think they're allowed out without their parents' permission?'

She nodded. 'And are they deaf as well?'

He offered her some of the wine which had been standing in an ice bucket at the end of the table. She mouthed 'yes, please' at him and noted, with pleasure, that the wine was at the top end of the scale. Then Charley remembered that she might have to buy a round at some point and decided to drink very slowly.

They smiled at each other and clinked their glasses together.

Samantha and Richard had abandoned all pretence of small talk and had gone straight on to the necking stage. Charley felt embarrassed, for her friend as well as herself. Didn't they ever talk? Was this all Richard wanted from her?

She tried to keep her eyes away from their groping and concentrated on Keith instead. He turned out to be quite fun and they whiled away the next hour talking, or rather shouting at full volume, about the latest books and films. Charley had had no spare money to buy any books or go to the cinema but was able to keep up thanks to a regular look at the Sunday newspaper at her parents' house. But it was a pleasure to talk to a man who was vaguely intelligent.

She excused herself a little later to visit the ladies' and studied her reflection in the mirror. Contrary to her pre-date feeling of dread, she found she was enjoying herself. Keith wasn't anything special to look at but he treated her like a lady and was a witty companion. She had had worse evenings over the past few months.

Finding her way back through the crowds to the booth, she sat down before realising Samantha and Richard had disappeared. She turned to look at Keith.

He shrugged his shoulders before leaning forward to say, 'Samantha said she'd be in touch tomorrow.'

Charley raised her eyebrows at him before she could stop herself. 'They've left?'

She couldn't believe it. Samantha was so wrapped up in herself sometimes!

'Ah, *l'amour*,' he said, before draining his wine glass. 'Do you want to go somewhere else? I know a charming little place just down the road where you don't have to shout to hear yourself think.'

Charley bit her lip for a moment. Was this the wisest thing to do? She hardly knew him.

Suddenly she felt his hand on her arm and looked at him.

'I'm not a serial killer, woman beater or psychopath,' he told her with a warm smile. 'Just a lonely old man who's enjoyed our conversation this past hour.'

She followed her heart and chose to believe him.

A short while later they were in a cosy little café which had comfy sofas to sink into and served delicious Irish coffee. It felt safe and comfortable. And, if truth be told, it was nice for her to be out again, after the loneliness of the flat.

They whiled away another hour making small talk before deciding to wend their way home. Even though he lived in the opposite direction, Keith insisted on coming back in the taxi with Charley. The knot of dread in her stomach tightened as they neared home. She wasn't ready for a full-blown relationship yet, let alone having to offer him coffee and hoping that, if he accepted, he wanted only the coffee and nothing else.

But it turned out that Keith was just a gentleman who wanted to see her home. He didn't want a coffee nor did he comment on her dubious accommodation. Nor the car at the bottom of the road which had been set alight by some local hooligans.

He merely kissed her on the cheek and asked if he could call some time. So Charley gave him her mobile number and closed the front door behind her, feeling relieved that her first date in over a decade had gone so well.

Chapter Sixty-four

Caroline had finally been allowed to come home, with the hospital insisting on bed rest once she had. Otherwise she would have to spend the next five months of her pregnancy in the maternity ward in order to ensure the safe arrival of her baby.

Charley thought her friend still looked pale and drawn as she lay on the sofa. Julie was holding up various items of the bed-rest survival pack that they had all put together for her. The box contained romantic novels, CDs full of chill out music, silly or romantic DVDs to watch, and some ice-cream from Charley.

'It's a new flavour, but don't worry if you can't face it.'

'No, the good thing is the nausea has finally gone,' Caroline told her before sighing. 'But this is going to be a nightmare. I'm not allowed to do any unnecessary walking, apart from to the loo and upstairs to bed at night. I can't lift anything, including a kettle. I'm going to go mad.'

'You've got a laptop to surf around on,' Jeff told

her. 'Though I'm going to limit you to two hours a day.'

'He's such a meanie,' Caroline said with a small smile.

'I'm going to make a few phonecalls before picking up Flora from school. So I'll leave you girls alone to gossip in my absence,' he said.

Julie waited until Jeff had left the room before asking Caroline about his job-hunting.

'There's not a lot around at the minute,' she told them. 'But the redundancy package should tide us over until Christmas. I don't know about after that.'

'So Keith was a proper gentleman?' Julie asked Charley. 'I didn't think they existed any more.'

'Nor did I.' She fumbled around in her handbag and brought out her mobile. 'Look at the text he sent me this morning.'

She handed over the phone to show them.

'*Good morning,*' Julie read aloud. '*"Twas a glorious evening spent with a fair maiden last night that has put a spring back in my step. If you would do me the pleasure of meeting me again for dinner, I would be honoured.*'

Caroline raised her eyebrows at Charley. 'Sounds promising.'

'More promising than the chances of Richard leaving his wife for Samantha.'

'I can't believe they just abandoned you like that,' said Julie.

Charley sighed. 'I know. Not the friendliest thing to do. And she didn't even ring to make sure I'd got home okay.'

'I suppose she's still loved up with her married man,' said Julie.

Charley kept quiet. She didn't care how busy or

loved up Samantha was. She didn't care too much about being abandoned with a stranger the previous evening, but found she was more upset that Samantha hadn't even rung to see how Caroline was.

'Tell me about the Hallowe'en party again,' said their friend, leaning back on the sofa cushions. 'I never heard how your little oranges went down with the kids.'

'Amazing,' said Julie, before Charley could speak.

'They did look good,' said Caroline. 'And nearly all the phone calls I've had from the other mums at the party asking how I was, have also been to ask if they can buy some ice-cream from you. For parties and Christmas.'

Charley was speechless.

'That's great,' said Julie.

'I've got their numbers so you can give them a call,' said Caroline.

'You think this is a good idea?' Charley asked her friends.

'What have you got to lose?' said Julie. 'The shop is shut but you can still use the back kitchen, can't you? How about a little sideline in party cakes?'

Caroline was frantically nodding in agreement.

Charley sat back in her chair. Well, perhaps it would bring in a bit more money. Then who knows where it might lead?

Chapter Sixty-five

Back cleaning for Mrs Smith, Charley was in a world of her own. She had spoken to a couple of the mums who had been at Flora's birthday party and they all seemed keen to order a batch of ice-cream from her.

Somebody had ordered a couple of boxes of chocolate ripple. Another woman wanted some rum and raisin. But a woman called Andrea had rung, asking whether Charley was able to provide some kind of ice-cream dessert cake for a dinner party she was throwing.

Charley had already decided that the easiest thing might be to make some sort of ice-cream bombe, where the soft creamy ice-cream was hidden under a layer of either chocolate or iced fruit.

She was desperate to experiment but had to get through the day's cleaning first. It was all very well for Mrs Smith, she thought. She didn't work, the kids were at school, and the only schedule she kept was for her next manicure.

Charley shook her head at herself. Apart from the

kids, she had just described her own empty life until the bankruptcy.

These days her life was packed, barely leaving her with time for her second date with Keith.

La Scala wine bar was surprisingly busy on Friday night. It had opened a couple of months ago and quickly become extremely popular. The combination of good but cheap food, flattering low lighting and hunky Italian waiters was always going to be a winner in Grove Village.

Charley couldn't see Keith so sat on a bar stool to wait. Staring down at her foot which appeared to be jiggling nervously, she was horrified to hear a very familiar voice speak to her.

'Hello. What are you doing here?'

Charley looked up into the face of her soon-to-be ex-husband.

'I'm, er, meeting someone.' She couldn't believe her own dumb luck. 'What are you doing here?'

Steve nodded his head at a group of his mates with whom she had never got along, a bunch of neanderthal, knuckle-dragging lowlifes who could only grunt out monosyllables about football and women. 'Out with the boys.'

'I see.'

He ran his eyes over her. 'You're looking good.'

Charley straightened up a little on the bar stool. She had been especially pleased with her appearance as she was getting dressed that evening. She wore a V-neck sweater teamed with a black skirt. Her waist and stomach had shrunk so much that she now had an old-fashioned hourglass figure.

As she had gazed at her reflection earlier, Charley had considered the amazing effect on the female figure when a husband cheats whilst running up thousands of pounds' worth of debt.

But she didn't say that. She just replied, 'Thank you.'

Steve leant in close. 'Honestly, you're looking really good. You've let your hair grow long as well. Suits you.'

'Thank you.' Charley was keeping her side of the conversation short and polite.

'I rang you a while back and you never returned my call,' he said, trailing a finger across her hand.

She moved it away. 'I've been busy.'

'I sent a couple of texts as well.'

'I know.'

'I've missed you.'

Was he actually flirting with her? She stared into his eyes. 'Susie not with you tonight?'

He remained close. 'No. Just me. And you.'

'And me,' said Keith, materialising next to them. 'Sorry I'm late. Nightmare day at work.'

Steve withdrew and gave Keith a once over. Charley inwardly groaned, knowing how he would feel on seeing her date's large belly. Then she berated herself for thinking such shallow thoughts.

Steve turned back to her with a smile. 'Your date for the evening, is it?'

'Keith Reynolds,' said Keith, holding out his hand. 'And you are?'

'Steve Mills. Charley's husband.'

'We're getting a divorce,' she said quickly.

Steve's eyes narrowed briefly.

'Nice to see you, Steve,' said Charley, in a firm tone. 'I'll see you around sometime.'

He picked up on her dismissive manner and gave a nod before walking back to his friends.

317

'Are you all right?' asked Keith.

'I'm fine,' she replied, smiling through clenched teeth.

'Want to get out of here?'

'Yes, please.'

They went into yet another Italian wine bar, but thankfully this one didn't have her husband lurking inside. Instead it had lots of large, squishy leather sofas, perfect for reclining and snuggling. The lighting was low and yellow, making everyone's skin look golden and healthy.

Keith got the drinks in whilst Charley found a spare sofa. He set the wine and glasses down on the table. 'Premier cru,' he said, as he poured out the wine.

Keith took off his jacket and sat down, loosening his tie. He unbuttoned his top shirt buttons and picked up his glass.

'Cheers!' They clinked glasses and sipped the cool wine.

'Lovely,' said Charley.

But she didn't feel lovely. Just when she'd thought she was getting stronger, seeing Steve had disconcerted her and it was hard to shake the memory off.

'Do you want to talk about it?' said Keith as he leant back, resting his arm along the back of the sofa behind her.

'Just my cheating, lying ex-husband, who didn't exactly have a fine business acumen either.'

'But it's still hard seeing him?'

She shrugged her shoulders. 'I think the train wreck of my marriage is best left in the past.' She took a huge gulp of wine. 'So how was your day?'

He went on to explain the intricacies of the project he was working on. It was some kind of computer

318

thing that Charley didn't really understand but she was happy to let him chatter on about office politics whilst she drank one glass of wine after another.

Some time later he stopped and looked at her. 'You should have told me I was going on for too long. I must be boring you.'

She shook her head and was surprised to find everything went a bit fuzzy when it moved. 'I just don't know a lot about computers.'

'I shouldn't let that worry you,' he said. 'President Clinton only sent two emails from the White House and that was during the internet boom. He sent one to John Glenn, the astronaut who went into space at the grand old age of seventy-seven. The other was a test.'

Charley laughed harder than his words would normally have merited.

'I think we'd better order something to soak up all this wine otherwise I'll be under the table soon,' he said.

Keith ordered some food but it was probably more for Charley's benefit than his own. Unfortunately he'd only ordered hunks of bread and dips which weren't especially filling – especially as he'd had another bottle of wine brought over too. Charley pounced on the bread as soon as it arrived, dipping it in olive oil before wolfing it down. But it didn't appear to make much difference to her level of sobriety. By this time she had drunk at least a bottle of wine and her head was beginning to swim.

Keith offered her the last piece of bread which she dipped into the saucer of olive oil. As she brought it up to her mouth, oil dripped from the bread on to her chin.

He leant forward and caught the drip with his finger. Wiping her chin clean with it, he then drew his finger back and put it in his mouth. It was such a surprise that Charley let her mouth fall open. Keith took the opportunity to lean forward and kiss her.

His tongue went in almost immediately and appeared to do a full exploratory. So he wasn't a good kisser. So what? At least she wasn't spending another night on her own.

Finally, he pulled away. Charley tried casually to wipe her chin free from the saliva which was now running down it.

He gave her a wink before taking a sip of wine. She drained hers at a gulp.

'Tell me more about your work,' she said, grateful for the respite.

He gave her a smile and obliged with small talk until last orders were called.

They shared a taxi home. She wondered about inviting him in. She wasn't sure quite what he would expect of her or what she wanted from him either.

But Charley needn't have worried. He told the taxi driver to wait and helped her to the front door. The fresh air had hit her hard and she was more than a bit wobbly.

She was having trouble getting the key into the lock when she felt Keith stand close behind. He swept her long hair aside and started kissing the back of her neck. It should have been a sensuous experience but it wasn't.

She finally managed to unlock the front door and turned around.

He continued his wet assault on her lips and chin before finally pulling away.

'Sleep well, fair maiden,' he said, smiling. 'I'll call you tomorrow.'

'Good night,' she said, swiftly closing the door behind her.

Chapter Sixty-six

Julie stopped off at Charley's flat on the way to work, to drop off some extra Tupperware boxes that she had forgotten to give her.

'Jeez, what happened to your hair?' she asked, her eyes open wide.

'I think I passed out after I washed it last night,' said Charley, clutching her head. 'I'm a little hungover so go easy.'

'You look like you had an electric shock.'

Charley peered at the mirror in the gloom of the hallway. Eeek! She went into the bedroom and scraped her hair back into a ponytail with a hairband. Then she went into the kitchen where Julie was making some much-needed coffee.

'That's much better,' her friend told her. 'I can see the bags under your eyes much more clearly now.'

'Shut up. And make mine a strong one.'

'Kept you up late, did he?' Julie waggled her eyebrows.

'No. I just drank too much.'

'Was it that bad?'

'Which bit? Bumping into Steve or having Keith slobber all over me?'

Julie grabbed the mugs and followed her into the lounge. She put the drinks on the floor and slumped into the armchair. Charley made do with a few cushions on the floor.

'Girl, you gotta get yourself some more furniture. What was that about Steve?'

'He was in the wine bar last night.'

'Talk about how to ruin a good night out! Where was the tart?'

'At home, I presume. He didn't seem to be missing her too much.' Charley took a sip of coffee. 'Told me I was looking mighty fine.'

'Of course you are. Anyone would look good if they didn't have him in their life, ruining it to high heaven.' Julie shot her a look. 'Don't you go thinking about Steve again. He's not worth it.'

'I know.'

'The only reason he wants to be friends and back in your life is because he wants to have occasional meaningless sex that doesn't include staying married to you.'

'I know, I know.'

'Anyway, you've got that nice Keith to worry about now.'

Charley grimaced before she had a chance to stop herself.

'I saw that!' said Julie, lurching forward in her seat. 'What's going on?'

'He's not a good kisser.'

'Tongue down your throat, bad breath, or slobbering like a ninety year old who's lost all of their teeth?'

'Doors number one and three.'

Julie made a face. 'How bad?'

'Grim.'

'If he's an awful kisser, how bad do you think he'll be in bed?' Julie picked up the local newspaper she had taken from the doormat. 'Maybe we'd better find you somebody in the personal ads.'

'I don't think I want anyone else,' Charley told her. 'I'm not even sure I want him. Besides, it's a bit shallow letting someone go just because they can't kiss, isn't it? He's quite good company.'

'You could always wear a bib.' Julie flicked through the pages. 'Here we are. Which side do you want? The lonely hearts or the adult contact ads, otherwise known as the perverts.'

'Neither.' Charley gulped down some more coffee.

'Suit yourself. I'm going for the perverts. They don't mind if I'm old and wrinkly. In fact, some ask for it especially. How about this one? He's looking for voluptuous ladies.' Julie glanced down at her own less than pronounced chest. 'Only if I wear a Wonderbra. Or this one? Oh. He only wants to observe. Don't suppose he'll want to watch me do the ironing. And how about . . .'

'Enough!' said Charley, clutching her head.

But Julie was staring wide-eyed at the paper.

'What?'

'*Keith of Grove*,' Julie read aloud. '*I have returned from my crusade. My lance is still firm. I require a fair maiden to climb my tower.*'

Their mouths fell open at the same time as they stared at each other.

'Perhaps it's not the same Keith,' said Julie eventually.

'How many Keiths live in Grove?'

'Loads. Possibly. Maybe.'

'He calls me his fair maiden,' Charley stammered.

'God! He does, doesn't he?'

'I don't believe it. It can't be him. It just can't.' But she knew with a sinking heart that it was.

At that point, Charley's mobile rang. 'It's him,' she hissed at Julie.

'Let me at him,' said her friend, attempting to grab the phone from her.

'Get off!' Charley pressed the green button, still holding Julie at arm's length with the other hand. 'Hello?'

'Hello, my lovely,' said Keith. 'How are you this morning?'

'Fine, thank you.' Her voice was a bit high. 'And what about you?'

'A bit weary.'

'You must be. I've heard those crusades can be quite tiring.'

There was a short pause. 'I'm sorry. The line just broke up. I didn't quite catch that.'

'The crusades? Haven't you just returned from them? Hang on, let me check your personal ad.' Charley rustled the newspaper down the receiver at him. 'You are Keith of Grove, are you not? And there was me, thinking I was your only fair maiden. Or am I just the only one not climbing your tower at the moment?'

The phone line crackled.

'Lost for words, Keith of Grove?'

'It's not what it seems,' he spluttered.

'I think it's exactly what it seems.'

'You see, I respect you. I enjoy your company. I didn't want to rush things.'

'But in the meantime, you're happy to get your leg over with any other fair maiden who answers your personal ad?'

'It isn't like that. Sex has always been an important part of my life . . .'

Charley was flabbergasted. 'And?' she screeched.

'I'm a man. I have needs.'

'What you need is castration! Don't ever call me again. Goodbye.'

She pressed the off button and threw the phone down.

'I don't believe it!' she shouted, getting up to pace the room. 'I just don't believe it! He's a bloody sex addict! That's it. I'm becoming a lesbian.'

'I think I'm too old for you.'

Charley attempted to laugh but it all went a bit wrong and tears threatened to fall.

'I never want to date a man ever again,' she snuffled into Julie's shoulder.

Julie stepped away to hold her at arm's length. 'Steady, sister. I'm saving myself for Brad Pitt.'

After her friend had left, Charley thought about being single.

Had she stayed with Steve, would she have regretted the wasted opportunities, the chance to lead a different life? In her heart, she realised the answer was yes. They had married too young and stayed together because it was easy, not because they were especially well matched or even loved each other. They had remained married because it was less trouble than admitting it had been a huge mistake.

Apart from the bankruptcy and debts, Charley had little to show for all their years together. Yes, the business had provided her with a beautiful home but that was just a possession, as was all the rubbish with which they had filled it. It hadn't enabled her to grow as a person. In truth, it had held her back. She had been sucked in to a life of manicures and shopping, and it had been so boring. Only in hindsight could she realise the emptiness of her life back then.

And now? This wasn't the life she wanted either but it had at least given her a clean slate. Perhaps she didn't need a man. She certainly didn't want Steve or Keith. If and when she found the right one, then she would know. But until then, she could and would survive on her own.

The future was in her own hands and Charley felt a tiny glimmer of excitement deep inside as she wondered what lay ahead for her.

Chapter Sixty-seven

Caroline was trying to stay calm but it wasn't easy having Jeff at home all the time. Especially when he went out into the garden one afternoon.

'You want to tell me what happened with the vegetable patch?' he asked her, with a grin.

Caroline closed her eyes. She'd forgotten about the compost heap that her vegetable plot had become.

'It didn't work,' she told him, near to tears.

'Hey,' he said, startled to see her so upset. 'It doesn't matter. It's only vegetables.'

'Yes, but we were going to grow them and it would have been so lovely to sit down together for our Sunday roast and say, "We grew those potatoes." And now we can't.'

'So?' said Jeff, drawing her into a hug. 'You and I have many talents but gardening isn't one of them. You're still a great mum and wife.'

Caroline took a deep breath before confessing to him about the scoring system she'd based around Flora's eating and activities.

'You're insane!' exploded Jeff, in shock.

'I just worry that if I bring her up the wrong way then it'll wreck her future happiness.'

'For God's sake!' he said. 'You're a brilliant mother. Stop feeling guilty about the small things. You love and care for Flora. I don't think you should spend every waking minute working out how much time you've spent on the right and the wrong stuff. No wonder you had high blood pressure.'

'I know, I know,' replied Caroline. 'It adds to the stress, I realise it does. But I'm so pleased, feel so smug when I give her a good meal or whatever.'

'Please just enjoy our daughter,' said Jeff, drawing her close once more. 'She will not turn into some freeloading waster or psycho if you get the odd thing wrong.'

'What about the gardening?'

He kissed her on the nose. 'Maybe we'll stick to one of those hanging baskets of trailing tomatoes next year.'

'If we can afford it,' she told him.

'We'll be able to afford it,' he answered in a stern voice. 'I've got a couple of interviews coming up. Things will get better. You'll see.'

They were still hugging when Flora appeared in the doorway.

'Do you want a biscuit?' asked Caroline.

She shook her head and suddenly burst into tears. She had been very quiet when she had come home from school that afternoon.

'What is it?' asked Caroline, pulling her on to the sofa.

'My drawing,' sobbed Flora. 'She said it was bad.'

'Who did?' asked Jeff.

'Mrs Lewis.'

329

The little girl was terribly upset. Caroline held her close as she cried and cried.

'Right,' said Jeff. 'No, you lie there or I'll get my mother over here to keep an eye on you.'

'Where are you going?' asked Caroline as she watched him pull on his coat.

'I'm going to see this teacher. This isn't the first time Flora's been upset.'

Caroline was amazed. Something else had obviously happened while she was in hospital.

'They're putting her under way too much pressure. She's only five, for God's sake.' He grabbed the car keys before bending down to kiss his wife and daughter. 'Put the telly on and relax, both of you. I'll be back soon.'

But it was nearly six o'clock by the time he returned.

'What happened?' asked Caroline, turning down the volume on *Tinkerbell*.

'We can sell the uniform on eBay, can't we?' said Jeff, sitting next to her on the sofa.

Caroline was aghast. 'You've taken her out of Grove School for Girls?'

'Absolutely. And just in bloody time! I asked to see the headteacher and she was really weird. Like something from *St Trinian's*.'

'We never got to see her at the interview, did we?'

'I got to see the teacher as well. I asked about Flora and they both seemed to agree that her drawing wasn't strictly within the parameters they had set. It seems the last thing they want to do is encourage five year olds to have any imagination! So I decided there and then . . . Flora's not staying. Between them they'll destroy her confidence, and I'm not having that.'

'But what will we do?'

'I rang the local primary school. Got a meeting with the headteacher tomorrow. Far more pleasant than that other woman. They've got a spare place because somebody emigrated, so she wants to meet Flora. It sounds promising. And if that school was good enough for me, then it will be good enough for our daughter too.'

A few days later, Flora was enrolled in the local primary school and loved her first day there. Her new teacher had said that they needed help with the scenery for the Christmas play and could Flora help draw the castle for the background?

Caroline watched her daughter happily drawing designs on a big pad of paper before sinking back on to the pillows, a smile spreading across her face.

Chapter Sixty-eight

Julie said 'Sit!' to Boris as they stood at the edge of the pavement.

She still felt smug when the dog sat on command. Of course, he was looking up expectantly for his doggy treat, but still, it looked impressive.

Boris was back to his old self. Julie, however, had changed for ever. She was officially a doggy person. She found herself talking to the dog more and more now that she could finally relax and let him into her heart. She loved coming home to his excited face and hated leaving him when he put on the saddest expression in the universe.

He was company for her, kept the loneliness at bay. He also got her out of the house, even when it was raining and windy.

Boris seemed to grow, week by week, until now at seven months old his body was gangly but powerful. Julie watched him run ahead of her on their morning walk one day and realised he had a childlike brain inside an almost adult body. He was a canine teenager, she felt. He didn't seem to know how to handle his own growing body sometimes and would misjudge the distance between himself and other objects. Such as trees. And people.

Not for the first time that week, Boris made a mad dash towards Julie to grab the stick in her hand. But his attempt to swerve around her didn't quite work out and instead he hit her thigh at full pelt and she slumped to the ground with a dead leg.

She winced as she rubbed it and sighed, though she couldn't help smiling too. What must she look like? Especially since she had discovered she was sitting in a patch of thick mud.

'Are you okay?'

Julie's gaze ran up from the green wellies, past the thick, muscular legs clad in jeans, the bulging sweat-shirt, and finally the face of Wes the vet.

'I'm fine,' she said, mortified that he should find her in this state.

He held out his hand which she reluctantly took. With one heavy pull, she was standing up.

'I saw Boris take you out,' Wes told her.

'He's hopeless,' said Julie, but leant down to give her dog a rub on his head. 'It's the second time this month he's done this.'

'He looks well. No more problems after the chocolate?'

Julie shook her head. 'I keep everything hidden away in the cupboards these days. And the under-sink cupboard has been baby-proofed.'

Wes nodded. 'Good.'

'You've just got to be careful, haven't you, boy?' said Julie to Boris, who was looking up at her with an enormous branch in his mouth. 'Think you're being a

333

bit ambitious with that. There's no way I can throw it for you.'

And then she realised that her habit of talking to Boris had now become public. She glanced at Wes who was grinning at her.

'Yes,' she told him, blushing. 'I talk to my dog.'

He shrugged his shoulders. 'No worries. So do I.'

They carried on walking in the same direction. Julie tried hard to think of something witty to remark on but was found wanting. The problem was that, embarrassing as it was to admit even to herself, she had a small crush on Wes.

It was the accent, she told herself. And the body. Possibly even the bald head. In actual fact, Julie didn't have a clue why. All she knew was that she kept looking out for him on the heath. It was a silly crush and quite ridiculous, she knew.

Julie glanced at her watch. 'Sorry but I've got to get to work,' she told him. 'Well, I'll see you soon.'

'Bye. Have a good one.'

It was only once she got home and glanced at her reflection in the hallway mirror that Julie realised she had a small piece of bracken in her hair, mud all over her jeans and absolutely no make-up on.

What must he think of her?

But Wes Seymour wasn't thinking about the mud on Julie's coat as he put his dog in the boot of the car. He wasn't thinking about how messy her hair was either.

He was thinking about her cobalt blue eyes and the way they flashed whenever she looked at him.

Chapter Sixty-nine

Charley settled into a vacant armchair in one of the coffee houses in the high street. It was late in the afternoon and the place was packed with post-school-run families, their chatter mixing with the hiss and grind of the cappuccino machine.

She had finally rung Samantha after she had left a third message on Charley's voicemail and had agreed to meet her for coffee one evening after work.

She put the cup down on the little table beside her, still bristling at the cost. Two pounds for a cup of coffee? She was barely making enough to last her the week and pay her bills and the rent without wasting money on this kind of luxury.

The coffee was still too hot to drink so she stared out of the window, trying not to listen to the piped Christmas music over the speakers. December had arrived and the retail industry had clicked into hyper-festive mode.

She wondered where the last couple of weeks had gone. It had been so busy, and yet so bizarre as well.

A couple of Caroline's friends had put in orders for ice-cream cakes and then some of their friends in turn. It was all very startling but Charley's bank balance was going to look a little healthier by the end of the Christmas rush.

'Excuse me? It's Charlotte, isn't it?'

Charley looked up at the women who was standing next to her and tried to recall where she had seen her before.

'I'm Emily. We met at the Hallowe'en Party.'

'Of course.' Charley stood up and smiled at her.

'Look, it's a bit of a cheek but I was wondering about your ice-cream. The other parents are all talking about it. It's my son's birthday in a fortnight. Terrible time to have it, in December. He's still going on about your Hallowe'en face puddings. I was wondering if you could do something like that for his birthday party? It's a clown theme.'

Charley was having trouble keeping up with the other orders she had received but Emily looked so tired, and so fretful, that she found herself saying, 'Of course.'

The woman brightened up. 'That's wonderful.'

'Hello,' said Samantha, arriving laden with shopping bags.

'Hi,' said Charley. 'I'll be with you in a minute.'

'Look, I can see you're busy,' said Emily. 'Shall I give you a ring soon to talk about it?'

Charley scribbled down her mobile number.

'Great,' said Emily. 'And thank you.'

'You're welcome,' Charley called after her as she pushed the buggy out of the café.

Samantha was shrugging off her coat and settling

herself down on the armchair opposite. 'What was all that about?'

'She wants me to make some ice-cream for her son's birthday party.'

'Another one? Wow. Well, the money will certainly come in handy for you. You still owe your parents thousands, don't you?'

Charley took a sharp intake of breath. 'I am going to pay it all back as soon as I can,' she said.

However, Samantha wasn't listening. She was too busy rifling through her bags. She lifted up a top for Charley to admire and saw her expression.

'Don't worry about it for now,' said Samantha, all bright and breezy once more. 'So what do you think of these?'

Charley admired the purchases. The new knee-length leather boots gave her a pang of envy but it quickly passed.

Samantha put everything back into the bags and leant forward with a glint in her eye. 'I've got something to tell you.'

Charley took a sip of coffee and waited.

'He's definitely leaving his wife.'

'Who?'

'Richard!' Samantha beamed. 'Isn't it wonderful? We're finally going to be together.'

'What about his kids?'

'He's going to work out access at the weekends.'

'And he's okay with that?'

'I don't see why not. We'll live together at my place until we can find somewhere bigger. Imagine! I'll get to see him each and every day. And I'll never again have to worry about him sleeping in the same bed as

337

her.' Samantha shot Charley a look. 'Well? Aren't you happy for me?'

'Congratulations,' she replied dully.

'Thanks a bunch. I can see how excited you are about it all.'

And she was right. Charley was having trouble mustering up any enthusiasm for Samantha and her life at that moment. 'Doesn't it ever occur to you that I was the woman left behind when my husband left me for his mistress? That this may be a difficult subject for me to cope with?'

'I know that, silly. But this is different. It's not like you and Steve.'

'I'm trying to understand,' she told Samantha. 'But there's a lot of other stuff going on at the moment.'

'Like what?'

Charley sighed. 'Like Caroline. Have you seen her?'

'Not for a while.'

'She could do with support from all of us at the moment. She's having a really hard time trying to cope with Jeff's redundancy and being put on permanent bed rest. She was really ill in hospital.'

'I know.' Samantha sighed. 'And I do feel sorry for her, really I do. But . . . and don't hate me for saying this . . . it's just that I'm so happy at the moment. My dreams are coming true after all this time and I don't want to be around anyone who brings me down. This is my time, my moment in the sunshine.' At least she had the grace to look a bit sheepish after that. 'Does that make me sound selfish?'

'Yes. Actually, it does.'

Sumantha pouted. 'I'll buy her a present.'

Charley shook her head. 'You don't get it, do you? It's not about money or presents, it's about being

338

there, listening, supporting. All the things you're crap at.'

'Excuse me?'

'Stop using me for free counselling,' Charley told her. 'It would be nice if you ever rang me to ask how I am, for a change. But it's always about you. Never about anyone else.'

'That's not true!'

Charley grabbed her coat and stood up. 'You never called when my husband walked out on me. You made it no secret that you consider being a cleaner to be the lowest possible form of work. There's been no support from you so far, and I don't think there ever will be. We all have to mop you up every time bloody Richard leaves you in the lurch, but you don't even try to help us when the tables are turned.'

Samantha was open-mouthed, shocked by Charley's anger.

'You weren't there for me when I was at rock-bottom. You didn't care about Julie when Boris was unwell. Caroline was seriously ill in hospital and still you weren't bothered.' Charley shook her head in disgust. 'And you know what? You can go ahead and live with Richard, but this is a man who has a history of cheating on his wife. What makes you think he won't do the exact same thing to you?'

'He loves me!'

'Yeah, and he probably told the same thing to his wife once as well.'

'I can't believe you're being so cruel. I thought we were friends?'

Charley stared down at her. 'I've decided to measure my friends by the way they support me through the bad times, not the good. I understand

339

that things have been difficult for you, but I believe I'm always going to have to make all the running in any friendship with you. And that's not good enough for me. I need friends I can rely on.'

She shrugged her coat on. 'Goodbye, Samantha.'

And then Charley walked out.

Chapter Seventy

'She's really upset,' said Julie, leaning against the door-frame in the kitchen behind Sidney's sweet shop later that week.

'I don't care,' Charley told her, wiping out the inside of the large freezer. 'I know that makes me sound harsh, but I have to be sure I can rely on people and I just can't rely on Samantha. She hasn't been there for me, you or Caroline. And you know it, too.'

Julie shrugged in tacit agreement. 'It's great that you're getting so many orders,' she said to change the subject. 'Bizarre but great.'

'I know,' said Charley. 'I think my ice-cream is the latest must-have accessory.'

'People seem to like the fact that it's not mass-produced,' replied Julie. 'Is it mainly birthday stuff?'

'There are a lot of Christmas orders too.'

She found herself constantly brimming with ideas and having to write down a list of them for when people rang with the next order. She had already tried out a frozen chocolate yule log, using a fork to create

341

the tree-bark effect before the ice-cream hardened. All it needed was ten minutes out of the freezer to soften up before serving. This was making it particularly popular as a back-up dessert, especially once she had dusted it with edible gold glitter.

'Nothing says Christmas like a bit of sparkle,' Julie had told her.

Another favourite was the ice-cream layer cake. Charley layered together different colours and flavours of ice-cream in a loaf tin, chocolate and vanilla looking especially striking. The clingfilm with which she lined the tin seemed to work well in lifting out the dessert in one piece, ready for eating. That had worked so well that Charley was going to experiment with larger, round tins to make ice-cream cakes more suitable for general entertaining once Christmas was over.

She had created an ice-cream Christmas pudding the previous night. To a plain base, heavily flavoured with cinnamon and mixed spice, she had added copious amounts of dried fruit and cranberries. All it needed was a good splash of alcohol. But that was expensive so she was having a rethink. Or else a begging mission to her parents' house.

She was also desperate to make a gingerbread house filled with ice-cream. But how to get them to stick together? And what kind of mould should she use?

Charley felt a frisson of excitement as they locked up the shop before leaving. It might just be until Christmas was over, but for the month of December she would be making ice-cream every day. And that thought made her smile.

On the way home they popped in to see Caroline. She had been busy using her laptop to organise home deliveries for all of her food and Christmas shopping. And she was organising the girls' as well.

'You shouldn't be doing any of this,' protested Charley.

'Look,' Caroline told them, 'I've watched all the movies you lent me. I've finished the books. I've written my Christmas cards. I'm only lying here doing nothing. Dear God, let me do something!'

If time was in short supply, money was even more so. But they were all finding that if they clubbed together, the cost of Christmas wasn't so high as in previous years.

New decorations weren't necessary as Julie had picked up lots of pine cones during her walks and they were now sprayed gold or silver, depending on the chosen colour scheme. Flora had been let loose with cardboard, glitter and glue. The house was a disaster zone but the decorations were pretty enough and Caroline had shed a small tear on seeing Flora's glittery home-made angel perched on top of the tree.

Unused former presents such as bubble bath and hand cream were being wrapped up for various relations. Wrapping paper was shared and leftover cards cut up to be used as gift tags.

They looked at the wrapped presents lying all around them.

'I see you're getting organised,' said Julie, raising her eyebrows.

'Thank God,' muttered Caroline. 'You know that Coke advert which says the holidays are coming, over and over?'

'I love that one,' said Charley.

'Not me,' said Caroline. 'It panics me into thinking, "What have I got left to do?"'

'Easy,' said Julie. 'Watch your blood pressure.'

'But actually I'm on top of everything this year,' said Caroline. 'Now the presents are packed, I've really nothing else to do.'

'Wish I could say the same,' said Charley. 'I'm drowning in work. And phone calls from new customers. It's great but I just haven't got time to deal with them.'

'How organised are you?' said Caroline. 'You've got to answer the phone otherwise you'll miss out on new business.'

'I can't answer the phone when I'm cleaning,' Charley told her.

'Then give them my number,' said Caroline, quickly shaking her head at the protests from everyone else. 'Just give me a description of all your recipes and I'll deal with them.'

'You should be taking it easy,' said Charley.

'I will be lying down on this sofa when I answer the phone,' Caroline told them. 'Scout's honour.'

Charley looked from friend to friend before finishing with Caroline.

'If there's one blip in your blood pressure,' she told her, 'one tiny bounce, then the deal's off. Okay?'

Caroline nodded. 'Okay.'

Chapter Seventy-one

The pavement was still slippery from the harsh frost of the night before. A couple of times Julie slid on it and slammed into Charley.

'Why are you wearing the only pair of high-heeled boots you possess?' asked Charley.

Julie shrugged her shoulders. 'They still rub so I thought I could wear them in.'

'Did you wear them on your walk this morning?'

'No.'

Charley knew Julie was lying. 'They make your legs look nice and long.'

Julie gave her a shy smile. 'Do they?'

'Yeah. I bet Wes thought so too.'

Julie had finally told Caroline and Charley about her small crush. To her surprise, they were both enthusiastic about the vet.

'So? Did he like the boots?' prompted Charley.

'I didn't seem him this morning, actually,' said Julie, in a haughty tone. Not through lack of trying. Poor Boris had been round the heath twice and was now laid out on the lounge carpet in a state of exhaustion.

As they walked past the village green with the cold chilling their faces, Charley couldn't stop herself from smiling at the splendour of winter. Little Grove village green was still glittering with frost, untouched by any footprints. The pond had a thin layer of ice on it, which would crack when the ducks appeared later that morning for their bread feast handed out by local toddlers. Even the spider's webs which criss-crossed the hedges were objects of beauty in the freezing weather.

They crossed the road. The Saturday morning traffic had yet to build and the roads were empty.

'Tell me again why we're up at the crack of dawn?' asked Julie.

'It's hardly early. It's gone eight o'clock,' Charley told her. 'But the best stuff goes first and I don't want to be around once the Christmas rush gets going. It'll be murder down here in about two hours' time.'

They crossed the near-empty car park and headed through the garden shop. Instantly they were bathed in warmth and the tinny noise of singing, illuminated snowmen who were vying to be heard above the Christmas carols on the main speakers. It might have been early but they weren't the only ones up and about. There were quite a few shoppers, mainly women, already packing their baskets with gifts.

But they weren't there to peruse the Christmas tree decorations or the expensive fudge. They headed straight through and back out into the morning air, across the area which was stacked with Christmas fir trees ready to be sold and into a large marquee.

The earthy smell of fruit and vegetables hit their

noses as soon as they went through the opening. Long trestle tables were covered with piles of fresh produce from the local farms. Potatoes covered in earth bumped up against carrots, parsnips and brussels sprouts that were still on their stalks.

But Charley wasn't interested in the vegetables. She weaved her way over to the tables where the deep red of cranberries shone next to piles of green apples.

'So? What do we need, boss?' said Julie, looking at her.

Charley grabbed the list from her pocket. 'About three pounds of pears. The same of oranges.'

Julie wandered off to harass one of the farmers for a discount whilst Charley mooched along to the table piled high with cranberries. Scarlet, plump and bursting with flavour, as opposed to the shrivelled dried versions in the supermarket, they were ideal for the Christmas pudding ice-cream which was one of her most requested recipes at the moment.

According to Caroline, Charley's voicemail was no longer filled with people looking for money. These days the messages were from people offering to pay for her ice-cream. When Caroline tried to explain that time was running short and Charley might not be able to meet their order before Christmas, they were suddenly offering such outrageous money that she found she couldn't afford to say no.

She picked up the cranberries, some pine nuts and dates. She also added some lemons and walnuts to her load. When she met up with Julie by the entrance, they were each carrying a couple of heavy carrier bags.

Weighed down with their purchases, they had trouble negotiating their way through the small crowd which had begun to form around the Christmas trees for sale. To Charley's surprise, Mike was standing in front of the forest of trees. He was in his normal gardening clothes but with a money pouch slung around his waist.

'Hi,' said Charley, going up to him. 'I didn't know you were working here?'

He nodded. 'Just for this month. It helps pay the mortgage when the garden work gets a bit slow at this time of year.'

'You expecting it to be busy today?'

'Are you kidding? There are nine days until Christmas. It's gonna be hell.'

'Tell me about it. Do you know how much ice-cream I've got to make and deliver before Christmas Eve?'

She took a moment to close her eyes and inhale the lovely pine scent.

'You want a tree?'

Charley shook her head. 'Not in my budget, I'm afraid. I'm only here for the fruit. Besides, I don't think my flat's big enough to hold even a pot plant.'

'Everyone should have a Christmas tree.'

Charley gave him a rueful grin. 'Maybe next year.'

They went back via the shop, picking up some vanilla pods on the way before heading across the village green to Charley's parents' house.

Halfway across, Julie stopped abruptly. 'Tell me again why we couldn't drive all the way to the farm shop instead of leaving the car at your mother's?'

'It's such a beautiful morning,' Charley told her. 'And I so rarely get any fresh air these days. You're just moaning because you're in your fancy boots.'

They arrived at Charley's parents' house and found

them both having breakfast in the kitchen. They dumped their bags in the hallway before sinking on to chairs around the table.

'Was it busy?' asked Maureen. 'I need some more mincemeat and they had some of that organic stuff on special offer. I had a bit of a disaster with the mince pies and need to make a few more.'

Charley caught her father's eye and they briefly exchanged knowing looks.

'They're not that bad,' said Mum, who had caught the exchange. 'They taste fine, they're just a bit well done.'

'I'm sure they'll be lovely with a bit of orange marmalade ice-cream,' said Julie. 'Your daughter says it's the best thing for them.'

Maureen turned to her daughter. 'You will bring some for Christmas Day, won't you?'

'I don't know, Mum. I've still got so much to do . . .'

'Coo-eee!' came a voice from the hallway. 'Anyone home?'

Aunty Peggy came into the kitchen. 'Good morning, all. It's nippy out there today. Not good for my rheumatism. Still, I should be able to struggle across to the bingo tonight, despite the immense pain. You get one free sherry 'cos it's the festive season.' She poured herself a cup of tea from the pot. 'Maureen, I finally got a Christmas card from Ivy in the post this morning.'

'She didn't die then?'

'Just a kidney stone apparently. But you'll never guess what her Harold's been up to . . .'

Charley followed her father's swift exit out of the kitchen, leaving Julie agog at the rumour mill.

'Dad, can I ask a favour?' she said, once they were in the lounge.

349

'Ask away,' he said, putting on his glasses and looking at the sports news on the back page of his paper.

'You know that bottle of brandy Peggy brought you back from her holiday?'

He peered over his glasses. 'You mean that stuff that strips the enamel from your teeth? Bit early for a tipple, isn't it?'

'I was wondering if I could take it off your hands? I need to soak the cranberries in brandy for a recipe and I don't think it matters too much if the booze isn't the best money can buy. Unless you were going to use it?'

'I shouldn't have thought so. I've got all the paint stripper I need in the shed.'

He opened up the drinks cabinet and rifled around until he drew out a large bottle in the shape of the Eiffel Tower. He then went back in and pulled out a smaller bottle.

'She got us this little number the year before last. Cherry brandy, I think. Don't want that as well, do you? It made your mother go most peculiar when she had a drop.'

'It'll be lovely with a chocolate recipe I've got.'

'Done. Glad to get them out the house, to be honest.' He handed over the bottles and sat down in his armchair again with the newspaper.

'Thanks, Dad.' Charley gave him a kiss on the top of his head. 'I'd better be off. Things to do, ice-cream to make.'

'Charlotte?' he called out as she was leaving the room.

She poked her head back round the door. 'What?'

'You're doing really well, you know. I'm proud of you.'

They exchanged smiles before he went back to reading his newspaper.

Charley was still smiling as she grabbed her car keys from the green bowl in the hallway, feeling a little proud of herself as well.

Chapter Seventy-two

Charley spent the last afternoon before the holidays gossiping with Mrs Wilberforce in front of the Christmas tree Mike had brought for her. It was tiny, only about two feet high, but that meant she could easily reach the top to put the angel on.

Charley also noticed that he had placed logs of wood beside every fireplace in the house, as anxious as she was that Mrs Wilberforce should keep warm. He had even made sure the logs weren't too large so that she could pick them all up.

Charley went outside to see him, suddenly realising how dark it was at only four o'clock in the afternoon. She found Mike in the wood shed.

'Are you nearly finished?' she asked, clapping her hands together for warmth.

'You need some gloves,' he said.

'I was too busy saving up this week.'

'Are you sure you're eating enough? You've lost a lot of weight.'

'You sound like my mother.'

Mike held out his own gloves to her which Charley gratefully slipped on. They were far too big for her hands but were soft and warm, probably thermal.

'What are you up to this weekend?'

'Making a ton of ice-cream. What about you?'

'Last weekend of the Christmas tree rush.'

Charley peered outside at the starry sky above. 'It's colder. Might get a frost.'

'So clear you can even see the Pleiades.'

'What?'

'The Seven Sisters. Only six can be seen without a telescope.'

Mike stood close to her and pointed up into the sky. Charley leant in close to trace the direction in which he was pointing. A small cluster of stars was visible against the dark sky.

As they stood there she became aware that she was now very close to him, could feel his breath on her cheek. She slowly turned her head until their faces were inches apart.

'Do you fancy a festive drink?' he asked. 'Between colleagues, as it were.'

She smiled but took a small step backwards. 'I'd love to but I'm so busy with work. Ice-cream work, I mean.'

Mike straightened up. 'Not to worry. It was just a thought.'

Charley smiled before scuttling back to the house, eager to get into the warmth.

Flora was looking very tired, even though she kept telling Caroline there was no way she was going to be able to sleep that night.

'It's Christmas Eve,' Caroline told Jeff as he came

353

into the lounge. 'That means Father Christmas, rein-deer and presents are all on their way!'

'I know but she wasn't like this last year, was she?'

Caroline smiled. 'You were at the office a lot last year.'

'That's going to change with the new job,' he said, drawing her close to him. 'It's local. Not so much pressure.'

Not so much money either, thought Caroline, but she was trying not to worry about that. In fact, she was trying very hard not to worry about anything.

Her six-month pregnancy appointment had gone well. The midwife had said the bed rest was working but that Caroline had to continue with it until the end of the pregnancy, to ensure the baby would be all right. Plus Jeff had been offered a position in a nearby town as Finance Director. It was a step up the career ladder, even if it meant less pay than his previous job.

'We'll get by, you know,' he said. 'I'm going to save a fortune in train fares. I might even cycle to work. It's only five miles away.'

They had already sold Jeff's large estate car and replaced it with a smaller hatchback. Luckily they had never had any credit card bills, never owed any money. They would get by on Jeff's new smaller wage.

Flora came downstairs to curl up on the sofa with them and drink a glass of milk. She sat between Caroline and Jeff whilst they took turns to read *The Night Before Christmas*. The decorated tree twinkled in the corner.

For Caroline it was the best Christmas Eve she had ever had. Some things were priceless.

Julie came into the lounge at the sound of slurping.

Boris hadn't freaked out too much at having a real

tree inside the house, especially when he'd discovered that the tree stand had a well around the bottom which held water. Of course, Julie had not put any chocolate decorations on the branches.

He was proving to be a welcome distraction from not having her mum with her for the first time at Christmas. She planned to visit the grave on Christmas morning before picking up Sidney to bring him over for lunch. He had been suffering from a heavy cold so it wouldn't be a hectic day but at least they would spend it together. And with Boris, of course.

Nick was staying up north with his new girlfriend who sounded as dubious as all her predecessors. The cheque which Julie had sent with his Christmas card had already been cashed.

Having finished work until the New Year, she now had more time on her hands for lengthy walks across the heath. Unfortunately, there was no chance of bumping in to Wes as he had gone back to Australia to visit his family for Christmas.

Julie found she missed their brief conversations and his gentle humour. It was a miserable time of year to be single.

She sank on to the sofa, placing her large glass of red wine on the table next to her. Boris leapt up beside her and spun around until finally sinking into a comfortable position. Julie knew she really shouldn't let him up on the sofa but she'd rather got used to their nightly snuggle. And besides, it was Christmas Eve. Her new next-door neighbour seemed to have fireworks for most occasions. If they went off tonight, Julie wanted Boris close to her.

Love Actually had just begun on the television when the first volley of fireworks rang out from nearby. Boris abruptly woke up and trembled with every bang and whizz from outside.

Julie switched channels, deciding not to put up with a schmaltzy love story which would only make her feel even more miserable. She soon found a wildlife documentary about the African plains. Boris was always fascinated by animals on the television so she switched up the volume and held him close to her.

Eventually they both fell asleep in front of the flickering fire.

Chapter Seventy-three

Charley was slumped exhausted in her armchair when the doorbell rang. She sat bolt upright, panicking as she tried to remember if she had promised to let anyone have their ice-cream that evening. But surely everything had been delivered, hadn't it?

It wasn't a customer. It was Mike.

'Hi,' he said.

'Hi,' said Charley, stunned. 'What are you doing here?'

He reached behind him and lifted up the smallest but most perfect Christmas tree. It was about three foot tall and planted in a red tub.

'Small but perfectly formed,' he said.

Charley's eyes unexpectedly filled with tears. She had deliberately not thought about putting up any decorations; hers were still hidden in a box in the hall cupboard. The few cards she had received, she had stuck to the wall in an attempt to hide some of the damp. A Christmas tree felt like a huge luxury to her.

'Well?' said Mike softly.

She nodded and brushed away a tear, holding the door open for him.

She followed Mike into the lounge and watched him put the Christmas tree in the corner.

'There's a socket there for your lights, I think. You've got some, haven't you?'

Charley nodded but was still a bit weepy.

'And it's rooted so you can plant it out afterwards.'

She didn't have a garden but she wasn't about to spoil his generosity by saying so.

'I don't know what to say.' Charley's voice caught as she spoke.

Mike stood in front of her. 'Like I said, everyone should have a Christmas tree.' He brushed away her tears with his rough hand.

'You smell like a forest,' she told him.

'And you smell of oranges,' he said, smiling down at her.

'It's the marmalade ice-cream.'

'Smells fantastic. I can't remember the last time I ate anything home-made. I tend to live on ready meals.' He held up his hand. 'I know, a typical bachelor.'

'Then you should have something home-made.'

She swept past him into the kitchen and opened up the door of the tiny freezer. She brought out a box and put it on the counter.

'There you are,' she told him, putting it into a carrier bag. 'Christmas pudding ice-cream. It's my number one bestseller.'

'I can't take this from you.'

She held out the bag. 'I can't give you any money for the tree.'

'I didn't want any money,' he said, sounding most affronted. 'It's a gift.'

'And so is this,' she told him, banging the box against his chest. 'Anyway, I need the space in the freezer. You'll be doing me a favour. Just bring the box back after Christmas.'

In the end, he took the bag from her.

'Would you like a drink?' she asked him, smiling. 'I've only got cheap brandy, I'm afraid. I mainly use it for cooking.'

'I'd love to but I can't.' He looked a bit sheepish. 'I've got a date.'

'Oh.'

'A set-up from one of my mates.'

Charley stared up at him and realised he was actually blushing.

'That's great,' she told him, trying to sound bright.

'Yeah,' he replied, sounding like it wasn't. 'Anyway . . .'

'Anyway . . .' she said.

But neither of them finished the sentence.

They went back into the hallway where Charley opened the front door for him.

'Thank you so much for the tree,' she said. 'It's lovely.'

'You're welcome. And thanks for this.' He jiggled the bag in his hand.

'You're not at work this week, are you?'

He shook his head. 'All done.'

'So I guess I'll see you in the New Year?'

'Yep.'

He stared at her for a moment before leaning down. Charley thought he was going to kiss her on the lips but it was just a peck on the cheek, his stubble brushing against her skin.

'Happy Christmas, Charley.'

'Happy Christmas, Mike.'

The smell of pine lingered in the hallway long after he had left.

Chapter Seventy-four

January slipped and shivered its way into the landscape.

'*Glad you're back,*' read the note from Mrs Smith. '*I noticed over the holidays that the shower surrounds were getting horribly dirty. Can you make sure that you give them a thorough going over every week?*'

Charley crumpled up the note and threw it into the kitchen bin. She was having trouble getting back into the cleaning routine. Far too many lie-ins and too much pottering in the kitchen over the Christmas holidays had made her temporarily forget how physical this job was.

She had also assumed that she would have some spare time now that the festive season had finished and everyone would be recovering, both financially and figure-wise. But still the orders flooded in, with her fat-free fruit sorbets doing a roaring trade. She had even had a recommendation from the local diet club, which had brought in extra sales.

Charley began to wonder how much money she

could make if she didn't have the cleaning to tie up her time.

The girls met one evening at Caroline's house. The days of fixed dates every fortnight had long since gone as their lives had changed. Now they saw each other at least three times a week, normally more.

Not that there was much incentive to go outside at that time of year. The short days and long dark evenings made everyone want to hide indoors in the warmth. The tree stems and branches remained bare and spring seemed a very long way away.

They gathered in front of Caroline's wood-burning stove – another money-saving addition to the house. She found she liked the spit and crackle of the flames during the day. She was now seven months pregnant but still bound to the sofa for the duration of the pregnancy.

'So, did you hear anything from Samantha?' asked Julie.

Charley shook her head. She had found, to her surprise, that she didn't actually miss having Samantha in her life.

'What's the new flavour of the month?' asked Julie.

'Orange ice,' replied Charley. 'But it's still creamy because I've added low-fat yoghurt. The diet club can't get enough of it.'

'That's because they're still having puddings, just not fattening ones,' said Caroline. 'And I've had some orders for Easter as well.'

'Already?' Charley was aghast.

'You're still enjoying it, aren't you?' asked Julie.

'Of course,' she replied. 'But there just aren't enough hours in the evenings and weekends.'

'I know,' said Julie, nodding her head. 'By the time

I've finished work and walked Boris, it feels like there's only just about time for dinner, bath and bed.'

Plus she still felt terribly guilty about leaving him alone each day. She would rush back in her lunch hour to feed him and let him run about the garden, but she could feel her stress levels rising.

'I wish I could help,' said Caroline.

'You are,' said Charley. 'You take the orders, work out who needs their ice-cream first. Plus you make sure I get paid as well.'

'I've got to do something,' said Caroline. 'I ended up watching daytime television the other day.'

But she was secretly enjoying her time on the sofa. If only she could do something about the guilt.

'So, what are our New Year resolutions?' asked Julie.

Charley shrugged her shoulders in response but Caroline was beaming at them both.

'Now, I've had a lot of time to think about it, lying prostrate on this sofa day in, day out. I was thinking we should all follow the same resolution.'

'And what's that?' asked Julie.

'I was thinking that this should be the year for us all to be brave.'

'Brave?' repeated Charley.

'Absolutely. And you can't argue with a poorly pregnant woman, can you? Come over at the weekend and we'll make our pledges then. You've got forty-eight hours to decide.'

Charley and Julie stared at each other, wondering what on earth they were going to come up with.

Chapter Seventy-five

The following morning Caroline smiled to herself as she thought of her friends' reactions to her suggestion of a group resolution.

Of course, she had already decided how she would be brave. She would be brave enough to let go. To relax. To let things slide.

So much had happened to all of them over the past six months. Did she really need to fret that Flora wasn't learning Mandarin any more? Especially as her daughter had never seemed to enjoy it. She'd certainly never smiled after the lessons in the way she smiled when she helped Julie take Boris for a walk. Or when she had been playing hide and seek on the heath with her friends from school.

So Caroline was going to relax and give Flora the greatest gift she could think of. She would have the time to dream, to play, to laugh, to run. To be a child.

She would also try not to set herself and Jeff such high standards. Her husband was enjoying his new work, along with the much shorter commute. He was

364

home by six o'clock and therefore able to help with dinner plus Flora's bath-time and story-reading.

He and Caroline had cuddled together on the sofa the previous night. 'I love being with you both,' he'd told her. 'I always felt a bit isolated before. Like I didn't know my own daughter.'

She kissed him on the cheek. 'We love having you home more too.'

'We can make the mortgage payments, but I'm afraid that's the end of our fancy holidays for a while.'

Caroline shrugged her shoulders. 'It doesn't matter where we go, as long as we're all together.'

'Even camping?'

She grimaced briefly before smiling. 'Even camping.'

The favourite part of Julie's day was also the favourite part of Boris' day as well. That first release from his lead on the morning walk caused her dog to run and bounce with glee, his tail swinging round and round with joy. It always brought a smile to her face.

'Someone's cheerful this morning,' said Wes, appearing from the opposite direction.

'Just Boris being Boris,' Julie told him, feeling ridiculously pleased to see him.

'Happy New Year.'

'You too.'

He had a great suntan that shone out from the winter gloom. He looked healthy and hunky. Julie found herself gulping at how attractive he was.

'They're great when they're this age, aren't they?' said Wes. 'I was hoping I would bump into you this morning. I've got a present for you.'

He'd bought her a present? All the way from Australia?

'Proper doggy chocolate drops,' said Wes, bringing

the packet out of his pocket. 'The non-poisonous, doggy-friendly kind.'

Julie found herself having to force out a bright reply. 'That's great. Thank you.'

She felt a stab of something. Jealousy? Of her own dog? She was an idiot. She took the packet, his large fingers briefly brushing hers.

'So you had a nice time in Australia?' she asked.

'It was great. But Mum always cries when we get to the airport.'

'It must be hard for her,' replied Julie. 'She must hope you'll move back home at some point.'

'She knows I'm settled here now,' he said.

Thank God, Julie found herself thinking.

'Well, I'd better be off to work,' she told him. 'No rest for the wicked.'

'I know,' replied Wes. 'I'm always trying to find an extra hour in the day, even if it's just to walk the dog.'

'Well, thanks again for the chocolate,' she told him.

And then they went their separate ways, both deep in thought.

It wasn't until she had walked a short distance that she finally focussed on what Boris was doing, which was eating as much horse manure as he could in a short space of time.

'Boris!' snapped Julie. 'Stop that. Bad dog!'

His ears went down at her angry tone.

'I'm sorry,' she told him, bending down to stroke his head. 'Here, have a wretched chocolate drop.'

He wolfed down a couple of them before giving her hand a lick in thanks. Julie tried not to think about the horse manure.

'Do you know, you're the first male who's loved me just as I am?' she told him. 'You don't care about my lack of money or the fact that I'm not all girly and sexy.'

Sometimes Julie longed to be soft and lovable. One of those women men wanted to protect from all evil. A girly girl. But she knew that wasn't her. Knew she could never be like that.

She glanced at her watch and realised she had to get back to the house to be on time for work. She thought about Wes' words on trying to find another hour in the day.

She finished her walk with her head bent, deep in thought. Something had to give in her life. It was all about being brave, she realised.

Chapter Seventy-six

Charley was also mulling over Caroline's pledge of courage. Be brave, indeed.

'It's hard to be valiant and courageous when you're cleaning other people's toilets,' she told Caroline and Julie the following weekend.

'Well, things can always change,' said Caroline, breaking into a grin.

'What are you talking about?' asked Julie.

'It's about Charley.'

'Me?' said Charley. 'What have I done?'

'Only made such fabulous ice-cream that the new Lady Beckenham up at Grove Castle has got to hear about it.'

'Oooh! La-di-dah!' said Julie, grinning.

'But I haven't made her any' said Charley, frowning.

'Well, she heard about it from someone,' carried on Caroline. 'And now she wants to place an order.'

'Okay,' said Charley. 'Did she have any ideas?'

'Well, seeing as it's for the Valentine's Ball, she thought something heart-shaped.'

Caroline broke into a warm smile as she watched the idea slowly sink into Charley's mind.

'The Valentine's Ball?' she said, now astounded. 'Are you serious?'

'Deadly. And so was she. They want you to make all the desserts for the Valentine's Ball.'

'That's fantastic!' said Julie.

'Isn't it?' said Caroline.

Then they both stared at Charley once more. But she wasn't smiling. She was panicking.

'How many? How many desserts does she want me to make?'

'Two thousand individual desserts,' said Caroline.

'I can't make that many,' replied Charley, shaking her head.

'But you've got to,' her friend told her. 'Think of the money, if nothing else.'

'How much are they willing to pay?' asked Julie.

'A cool £5,000,' said Caroline. 'I got them to up the figure because of the late notice.'

'What am I going to do?' said Charley. 'I mean, I'd love to, but I just haven't got the time . . .'

'Jeff and I were working it out last night,' said Caroline. 'He said the publicity alone will generate you so much business you should be able to set up on your own.'

'What do you mean?' asked Julie. 'You think Charley should do this full-time?'

'Absolutely.' Caroline picked up her laptop which was lying nearby. 'We did a bit of research, working out how many ice-cream cakes and punnets she could make and sell each week. I've got all the figures here.'

But Charley couldn't focus on the columns on the screen. 'What are you talking about?'

'You running your ice-cream making as a proper business.'

'But what about the cleaning?'

'Is that what you really want to do for the rest of your life?' asked Caroline.

'This is mad,' Charley told her friends. 'It'll never work.'

'So you can go back to your cleaning if it doesn't,' Julie told her. 'But think what might happen if it does work.'

Charley bit her lip. 'I don't know. I really don't.'

'Remember what I said the other day,' Caroline told her. 'About our pledge to be brave. You've been braver than anyone I know this past year.'

'She's right,' said Julie. 'You've got through the worst of it. What have you got to lose now?'

Charley gulped. This was a turning point in her life. She could be brave or she could run away. But surely she had done enough penance for her many faults in the past? She had already survived one new start in the last twelve months. Perhaps she could survive another.

So she nodded. 'Let's do it,' she told her friends, breaking into a smile.

Chapter Seventy-seven

Charley handed in her notice to Patricia on Monday morning, with more than a hint of nervousness in her voice.

'Well, I can't say I'm pleased,' said her boss on the phone. 'You're one of our best cleaners. Not that there's a lot of competition, I've got to admit.'

'Thanks for the opportunity,' said Charley. 'It really helped when times were tight.'

'I'm going to the Valentine's Ball so I'll look forward to sampling the ice-cream. But can you work out your notice this week? That would really help me.'

'Of course,' said Charley, wishing she could refuse.

That left her with not much time to plan the desserts for the ball and an awful lot of goodbyes to be said.

Miss Fuller surprised her with the enthusiasm she showed for Charley's new job.

'Something local,' she boomed. 'Splendid! That's what we need around here. Not all that fancy stuff in the supermarkets, full of who knows what. Well, I wish you luck.'

It was a similar theme amongst most of her other customers too.

Prepared to put up with Mrs Smith's sneering one last time, Charley was amazed to find her shuffling around the house in her dressing gown and no make-up.

'He's gone,' said Mrs Smith in dull tones.

'I'm sorry?' replied Charley. 'Who's gone?'

'My husband. He's gone . . . it's all gone.'

She was pale and shaking so Charley sat her down at the kitchen table and made her a cup of tea. 'What happened?'

'The silly sod invested it all in some dodgy shares. We've got nothing! Everything will have to be sold. The house, the cars . . .'

Charley tried not to smile at the irony as she sat down at the table with her employer. 'The same thing happened to me,' she said.

The other woman stared at her, as if taking proper notice of Charley for the very first time. 'You?' she said, amazed. 'You had money?'

Charley nodded. 'We went bankrupt and lost everything.'

'What did you do? How did you cope?'

'I coped because I had friends and family who loved and supported me. And I got a job as a cleaner. No, it wasn't glamorous, and, yes, it was hard work. But it paid the rent and meant I could eat every week.' Charley gave her a smile of sympathy. 'I can tell Patricia if you like. They're always on the lookout for more cleaners.'

Mrs Smith looked horrified. 'I'm not going to be a cleaner!' she cried.

'It's not so bad,' Charley told her.

As she left, she realised her words were true. It really hadn't been that bad. It had been a job that had kept a roof over her head and food in the fridge. What could be more important than that?

Mrs Wilberforce was possibly the most upsetting person to say goodbye to. Charley had already made sure Patricia had organised a suitable replacement.

'I think it's super,' Mrs Wilberforce told her. 'Proper ice-cream. My Ernest used to take me to an ice-cream parlour in our courting days.'

Charley knew she would miss these times with the old lady on a Friday afternoon and found her eyes filling with tears as she tidied the kitchen one last time.

Mike came in, saw her crying and came over to give her a hug. 'Come on,' he said, giving her a squeeze. 'I'll keep an eye on her. Don't fret.'

'I know,' said Charley, with a sniff. 'I don't know why I'm so sad.'

'It's all a bit scary at the minute,' he told her. 'But it's a good kind of fear. It really is.'

She wiped the tears from her cheeks and looked up at him.

'My life's changing again,' she told him.

'Yes, it is.'

'Thank you,' she found herself saying.

'For what?'

'For keeping me going through the darkest of days.'

Mike broke into a smile. 'That's what friends are for, aren't they?'

Charley smiled back. Yes, they were friends.

As she watched him leave, she finally admitted to herself that it wasn't only Mrs Wilberforce she was going to miss.

Chapter Seventy-eight

The girls held a summit meeting at Caroline's house the weekend after Charley had finished work.

'No more cleaning,' she said with a satisfied sigh. 'Unless I fail spectacularly and get myself into more debt.'

'Rubbish,' said Julie. 'You'll be fine.'

'Absolutely,' said Caroline. 'Remember what I said about being brave? So, what have you decided to make for the ball?'

'Chocolate and raspberry hearts,' said Charley. 'Chocolate because everyone loves it, raspberry because it's pink, and hearts because it's Valentine's.'

'You're going to make 2,000 individual ice-cream hearts?' asked Caroline, looking faintly apprehensive. 'In three weeks?'

Charley nodded. 'I tried it out last night.' She leant over to bring a silver object out of her handbag. 'I wrapped tin foil around a long length of card and then made it into a heart shape. Then I just stapled the two ends together at the pointy bottom bit.'

'Then what?' asked Julie.

'I filled the heart-shaped mould with some ice-cream that was just on the verge of setting then I stuck it in the freezer. Once it was solid, I cut the mould away and that was it. Simples.'

'How long did that take?' asked Caroline, glancing at Julie.

'A couple of hours,' said Charley. 'But the heart was a bit of a pain to get right at first.'

'I see,' said Julie, staring wide-eyed back at Caroline. 'So a couple of hours times 2,000 . . . ? Hmm. I think I'd better ask for some holiday in the next couple of weeks.'

'You will?' Charley was amazed. 'Thanks.'

'Actually the time off is the first part of a bigger plan,' said Julie. 'All that being brave stuff you made us think about.'

'Why? What are you up to?' asked Caroline.

'I'm thinking of going part-time,' Julie told them. 'I've had a chat with my boss and he thinks we can work something out. Maybe job share.'

'Blimey,' replied Charley. 'You're going to be a lady of leisure?'

'Hardly,' said Julie, with a grin. 'Look, Sidney's moving out of the flat soon and he's going to need help settling into his new retirement place. And I can't keep leaving Boris on his own all day. It's not fair. And with any extra time after all that, I'll be packing.'

'Packing?' the others exclaimed.

'I'm going to put the house on the market,' said Julie.

'But you've been there years,' said Charley.

'And that's the problem,' said Julie. 'I've got a huge mortgage on it, two if I'm really honest. And what do

I need a big house in Upper Grove for? I don't even like the area.'

'But it's been your home for nearly twenty years,' said Caroline.

'And I've been hiding in there for most of that time. I mean, what do I need a dining room for? Or all those extra bedrooms. I need to get myself straight financially. I was thinking of getting a small cottage in Little Grove.'

'Will you still need a mortgage?' asked Caroline.

'Hopefully not. That's another plus. I held on to the house for far too long. Security blanket, I guess.'

'Long enough that some developers might offer you a small fortune for it now,' said Charley.

'Let's hope so,' said Julie with a grin. 'So what's the plan for Charley and the chocolate ice-cream factory?'

'I was talking to Jeff last night,' said Caroline. 'The financial whizz kid that he is thinks this business could be a roaring success.'

'If I get the Valentine's Ball desserts done in time,' Charley reminded her.

'You'll be fine,' said Julie.

'Exactly,' said Caroline. 'And once you get their recommendation, the world is your oyster. You've already got people who can help you so you don't have the worry of recruiting. The only other overheads are the ingredients.'

'Plus Sidney doesn't want any money for renting the shop,' said Julie. 'He's just happy someone is using it. He loved the rum and raisin flavour, by the way. Said the rum did him the world of good.'

'Eventually you could get your own website,' said Caroline. 'Jeff says he can help you with that. Maybe even open the front of the shop as an ice-cream parlour permanently.'

Charley was beginning to look stressed. 'I can't think about that. If it ever happens, that's way off in the future. Look, I've got to concentrate on making those desserts first.'

'Which is another thing,' said Caroline. 'We were looking on-line last night. There's a second-hand industrial-sized ice-cream maker for sale for £1,500.'

'I don't have that kind of money,' Charley told her, horrified.

Actually, thanks to the recent flurry of business she had about half that amount put away to give back to her parents.

'But you're going to be getting a deposit from Grove Castle,' Caroline reminded her. 'Isn't it worth investing in labour-saving tools?'

'It'll help with the amount of ice-cream you've got to make for the ball,' Julie told her. 'How else are you going to make it all?'

Charley went into the kitchen to make everyone a cup of tea.

'She thinks she's going to fail,' whispered Julie.

'I know,' replied Caroline in a low voice.

'But I think this is just the beginning.'

'Absolutely,' said Caroline.

They nodded at each other in silent agreement. They hadn't finished with the ice-cream making business quite yet.

Chapter Seventy-nine

The large commercial ice-cream maker had arrived within a matter of days. It took another day for Charley to work out the measurements for the ingredients as the balance differed from the smaller batches she was used to making.

She had decided on a dark chocolate ripple flavour, with streaks of raspberry puree running through it. The alternative flavour would be marbled vanilla with swirls of toffee. Finally, she was happy with the look and taste of the recipes.

With only a week to go until the Valentine's Ball, the tricky task of making and filling the moulds was all that was left.

Many hands make light work, thought Charley as she looked around the kitchen at the back of Sidney's shop. Julie had taken three days off which, along with the weekend, made five days in which she would help in the kitchen. Now they were measuring out the ingredients plus preparing the fruit purée and toffee sauce.

Even Charley's mother and Aunty Peggy were helping, although she had decided it was best if her mother stayed away from the food preparation. Therefore, she and Aunty Peggy were in charge of wrapping long lengths of four-centimetre-wide cardboard with tin foil, ready to be shaped into moulds. Which left them free to share their gossip with the others.

'Grove Castle is looking marvellous apparently,' said Aunty Peggy. 'The ball is going to be fantastic. And they're talking about having *Antiques Roadshow* up there next month.'

'You've been there?' asked Julie, who was washing a large bowl of raspberries ready for puréeing.

'We bumped into the new housekeeper,' replied Maureen. 'She was at Bingo for Singles last night.'

Briefly, the activity in the kitchen halted.

'You went to a singles event?' said Charley, looking directly at her mother. 'Both of you?'

'I couldn't let Peggy go on her own,' said Maureen. 'You know what her taste in men is like.'

Aunty Peggy had been widowed ten years previously. It was probably the wisest decision her husband had ever made.

'You should have taken part, darling,' carried on her mother.

'I've been busy,' replied Charley.

Her mind briefly flitted towards Mike before she banished the thought. It had been a fortnight since she had last seen him and she was finding she missed their cups of tea and cheery banter. She missed his encouraging words and dry wit too. Charley wondered if he was still seeing anyone and, if so, would he bring her to the ball?

She shrugged to herself, trying to feign disinterest. It didn't matter to her if he brought a date with him, did it? But her heart kept trying to tell her different.

Chapter Eighty

'Did you manage to deliver all the desserts safely?' asked Caroline.

Charley balanced the phone under her chin as she painted her toenails. 'Yes. They just about fitted in both our cars.'

She was feeling incredibly nervous about the results. What if the new Lord and Lady Beckenham didn't like her work? What if they wouldn't pay and wanted their deposit back?

'I'm sorry I won't be there to see them all laid out,' said Caroline. 'You'll have to memorise every detail of tonight.'

'I'll try,' said Charley.

'Is Julie picking you up on the way?'

Charley swapped the phone to the other ear. 'Yep.'

'I've been thinking about her too,' said Caroline. 'Any chance you can try and glam her up a bit?'

'Julie? Not a chance. Why?'

'She doesn't make the most of herself. Try and do

something with her hair . . . and get some make-up on her.'

'God!' Charley blew out a long sigh. 'I'm gonna have to order us a taxi. There's no way I'm giving Julie a makeover with either of us stone cold sober.'

'Don't go overboard,' said Caroline. 'You're trying to make her look glamorous.'

'I used to be glamorous, a long time ago,' said Charley. 'By the way, I suppose you want me to steer her in the direction of Wes?'

'Of course.'

But Julie didn't sound like she wanted any man in her life when she arrived at Charley's later that afternoon.

'Who cares that we haven't got dates for tonight?' she said. 'It's not a sit-down meal, is it?'

'You're telling me that you don't mind being single?'

'Over forty per cent of people in this country are now single.' Julie put her glass of wine down with a clatter. 'Valentine's Day is so commercial. Basically it's just the majority of the country saying, "Hah! Look at us! We're buying overpriced red roses and having sex tonight – and you're not!"'

'You know,' said Charley, 'you use that forty per cent figure quite a lot.'

'That's because it reminds me that I'm not a freak, just one of society's oppressed minority.'

'You're still a freak though, right?' Charley watched her friend glance at her reflection. 'Although a lovely-looking one.'

Julie was wearing one of Charley's long evening gowns that she hadn't been able to sell on eBay. It was pale gold with a lace overlay, off-the-shoulder and floor-length. It suited Julie's blonde hair and pale skin much more than it did Charley's colouring.

She had managed to persuade Julie that she needed a touch more make-up than usual so had made up her friend's eyes with smoky dark golds, and had brushed her cheeks with blusher to make her look healthy, not ashen. She had fixed Julie's hair with spray and then tied it back in a messy bun to soften the effect.

Julie frowned. 'I don't look like me.'

'Well, perhaps tonight you can be someone else.'

'I think the role of Prince William's wife is already taken.'

Charley quickly got dressed in the only other long dress she owned: a black strapless gown with a heart-shaped neckline. She had always felt this was a little too low for her comfort zone, but she had no other choice. She had also rolled her long hair up into a bun, just in case she had to go near the food preparation area.

'Very nice,' said Julie. 'You look like a busty Audrey Hepburn.'

'Oh, God,' said Charley, rushing to the mirror. 'Is it too low?'

'Can a dress ever be too low?' Julie's phone bleeped. 'Anyway, the taxi's here. It's too late to change your mind now.'

Charley took one last look at her reflection before snatching her evening bag from the bed and rushing out. The Valentine's Ball awaited them.

Chapter Eighty-one

The sky was streaked with a dark pink sunset as the taxi trundled up the long driveway to Grove Castle. The fifteenth-century building had more the look of a stately home, standing in around 1,000 acres of land. The huge grounds were home to a herd of deer and there were aged oak trees lining the driveway which had been lit with fairy lights.

'I'd forgotten how lovely the castle is,' said Julie as they got out of the taxi. 'It's been years since I've been up here.'

The huge square mansion had the look of a golden, miniature Buckingham Palace, lit up that evening with big spotlights set at ground level. Hundreds of people were milling around, getting out of taxis and their cars, gazing up at the beautiful building. The whole village had been invited for a champagne and buffet supper.

Julie shivered. 'Let's go in,' she said, her bare arms getting goosebumps from the cold February night air. A frost had been forecast and the temperature was already close to freezing.

They went into the immense entrance hall, with its grand stone staircase leading up to the first floor. A string quartet serenaded them as they took in their surroundings. To their left was the beautiful ballroom, white-painted, with crystal chandeliers hanging from the ornately moulded ceiling. A DJ played soft music from a secluded corner, trying to set the right ambience for the elegant evening ahead. To their right was another large room, the state dining room, which had been laid out with hundreds of round tables for people to sit at.

They each took a glass of champagne that one of the many waiters had offered them.

'This is the life,' said Julie.

Charley nodded in agreement, already nervous about the reaction her ice-cream would receive.

'Shall we try and find some food?' said Julie, in a bright tone.

They went into the state dining room and helped themselves to the finger food on offer. It was bland but edible fare, puff pastry seeming to be the main ingredient.

'Perhaps all the money is going to the charity fund,' said Julie, peering at the grey mixture inside a vol-au-vent.

'What charity is it for?' asked Charley.

'No idea,' said Julie. 'The whole village is only here for a good nose around.'

'Darling!' came a familiar cry from nearby.

Charley looked round to see her parents and Aunty Peggy bearing down on them. Maureen bent to give her daughter's cheek an air-kiss so that her lipstick stayed intact.

'It's nice to see you out of your washerwoman clothes

for once,' she said. 'I don't think everyone needs to see quite so much of your chest, though. You'll catch your death of cold.'

Charley tried unsuccessfully to pull her dress up a bit.

'I said to your mother, it's all a bit fancy,' said Dad. 'Not sure how comfortable I am with all these upper-class airs and graces.'

'Nonsense. It's easy,' said Aunty Peggy, before bellowing '*Garçon!*' at a young waiter.

Charley cringed and hoped no one was looking. The waiter scuttled over, allowing Aunty Peggy to replace her two empty glasses with full ones.

'I don't want to panic you,' said Julie, craning her neck to see above the crowds, 'but they're just putting out your ice-cream hearts.'

'Oh, God.'

Charley drained her glass in one gulp and grabbed one of Aunty Peggy's full ones.

'And that dreadful food critic is here from the news-paper,' said Maureen.

Charley felt ill. What if she received yet another wretched review? What if her whole ice-cream busi-ness was going to be annihilated before it had even begun?

Feeling even more nervous, Charley drank another glass of champagne. Getting drunk was obviously the only way to get through this evening.

Chapter Eighty-two

Caroline's phone rang out just as Jeff turned the car into the long driveway leading up to Grove Castle.

'It's Julie,' she told her husband. 'She says the ice-cream looks great and people seem to be enjoying it.'

'That's terrific,' he replied.

'Don't go too close,' said Caroline. 'I've only got my baggy old clothes on and no make-up.'

She stared out of the window as the car neared the castle. It looked beautiful, all lit up on that cold winter's evening.

Jeff ignored her protests and took the car past the main entrance where he pulled over in a dark spot underneath some trees.

He turned to face his wife. 'I keep telling you, you're beautiful.'

'I can't believe I let you bring me here,' said Caroline.

'I couldn't have you missing out after everything we've been through.' Jeff glanced at the back seat where Flora lay fast asleep.

He opened the driver's door, walked around the front of the car and opened the passenger door.

Caroline looked up at him. 'What?'

Jeff held out his hand out to her. 'Please, just get out of the car for five minutes.'

She glanced down at the thick sweater which covered her eight-month baby bump, and sighed. But she was smiling as she took his hand.

It was a beautiful night, she thought. The sky was lit with stars, the air fresh and crisp. Jeff led her around to the driver's side of the car where it was darkest. Then he took his wife in his arms and began to sway gently in time to the music drifting out of the castle.

For a moment, Caroline tensed up. Then she told herself to relax. She was in the late stages of her pregnancy. She would be fine. Besides, she realised, she wanted to dance with her husband.

Jeff held her close as they swayed gently back and forth. Caroline snuggled into him, resting her head on his shoulder.

'I love you,' she murmured.

'I love you too,' he replied.

They danced on for a couple more minutes before Jeff gently sat his wife back in the passenger seat.

'Let's get you home,' he said, before closing the car door.

Caroline glanced up at the castle as her husband turned the car around to head for home. She hoped the others were having as romantic a time as she was.

Chapter Eighty-three

Julie glanced around the tables. Everyone was busy eating the ice-cream hearts and none were being left untouched. That had to be a good sign, she thought.

'I'm going to get some fresh air and text Caroline about your roaring success,' she said.

Charley nodded in reply, still furtively glancing from table to table in apprehension.

Julie replaced the empty champagne glass in front of her friend with yet another full one before heading out.

Once outside, she sent a text to Caroline. Then she put the phone back in her small handbag and sighed as she glanced back at the castle. It was all so dreamy and romantic, all so lovely, even the rat pack music drifting out of an open window was adding to the soft ambience.

Except she was alone. As usual.

Julie shook her head. She had been alone for a very long time and had been happy that way, right? And anyway she had Boris now, didn't she? She wasn't alone any more.

Heading back inside to find Charley, she was quickly cornered by a creep who wouldn't leave her alone.

'Baby, where have you been all my life?' cooed the man, who stank of drink and cigars.

Julie grimaced. 'Hiding from you,' she replied, before skirting round him and walking away.

What was wrong with men? Why weren't there any decent ones left?

A face suddenly popped into her mind. A friendly face. A face to be trusted. She had searched each room but hadn't been able to find him. Perhaps he hadn't come.

The dance floor in the ballroom was full of couples dancing close. She swiftly turned and went back across the entrance hall towards the dining room.

Then she saw him, talking to someone at the foot of the stairs. Wes was patiently listening to a story about a hamster when he glanced up and saw Julie. He excused himself and walked straight towards her. Julie found that everything around her had slowed down. The whole world had shrunk until it was just her and Wes.

'Hi,' he said, finally arriving in front of her.

'Hello,' she replied.

'You look beautiful,' he told her.

Julie ducked her head as she blushed. Nobody had ever called her beautiful before. He was looking pretty good too. The man certainly knew how to fill a dinner jacket.

She found herself tongue-tied, unusually so when she normally found him so easy to talk to.

'Dance?'

She glanced up at Wes, figuring that she had misheard. But no, he was gesturing with his head towards the dance floor.

Be brave, she heard Caroline telling her.

So she nodded in reply and they walked together into the ballroom. They inched past the many couples slowly moving around the floor until there was space for them to join in.

She turned to face Wes, unsure what should happen next. But he took control, moving his left arm around her until it came to rest on the small of her back. With his right hand, he picked up hers and held it close to his chest. It brought Julie close against him so she had no choice but to sway with him in time to the music.

Julie's heart was hammering so loud she felt sure Wes would be able to feel it. He was just being kind, that was all. She shouldn't read any more into this dance.

But, oh, it was so wonderful to be held in his arms, to feel his breath on her bare shoulder. She briefly closed her eyes in case they betrayed her strong feelings.

The music had changed and now 'The Way You Look Tonight' was playing.

'Appropriate song,' Wes suddenly said.

Julie looked up at him and found his face very close to hers.

'It's all an act,' she blurted out. 'The make-up. The dress. It's not me.'

He smiled down at her. 'No, it's not. You do look very pretty tonight but I actually prefer the other you.'

She rolled her eyes. 'The scruffy one?'

This was typical. She was only ever herself in muddy wellington boots and windswept hair apparently.

But Wes shook his head. 'The one whose cheeks glow after a long morning walk with Boris across the heath,' he told her. 'The one whose blue eyes sparkle in the morning light.'

Julie looked down, blushing at compliments she was unused to hearing.

But Wes took her chin in his fingers and tilted her face back up to his. 'I couldn't stop thinking about you when I was away.'

'Me?'

He smiled softly. 'You.'

He held her even tighter and they continued to dance slowly, around and around.

Chapter Eighty-four

Samantha was just heading out of the ladies' cloak-room when she saw Julie. She ducked behind a pillar for a moment.

She should have realised that her friends would be there. Ex-friends, she reminded herself. She missed them, though, Charley in particular. But she wasn't going to grovel. So she was on her own again. Trouble was, she needed them, especially at the moment. Richard was still wavering over his decision to leave his wife and she could have done with some advice as to how to get him to hurry up and move in with her.

She peered around to see if Julie was still there. Thankfully, she was putting on her coat. Or rather, a very tall, good-looking man was helping her on with it. Who was he? She must have got a boyfriend. It was definitely serious, from the looks of things. He had taken her hand to lead her outside.

Samantha glanced around but couldn't see Charley or Caroline anywhere. So she walked back into the main dining hall to see if she could spot Richard. She knew he was here somewhere, despite his protestations that he wouldn't be attending the ball.

Trouble was, she was certain he was lying a lot to her these days. The old words of love and flattery had been less frequently used in the past month or so. There had been a change in their relationship and she wasn't sure she liked the way it was going.

Samantha walked around the room, keeping to the back wall. Then she saw him. Richard was always good-looking, but in his tuxedo he was breathtaking.

She stared at him, willing him to turn around and see her. She had spent a fortune on her sexy, backless black dress and knew he wouldn't be able to keep his hands off her when he saw her. If he saw her.

She watched as he stood with a couple of people, roaring with laughter at someone's joke. God but she loved him. She loved him so much it hurt. She wanted him body and soul, every hour of every day. Nothing else would satisfy her, nobody else ever would again.

Samantha made her decision. She would make him see her. She would walk up to him in front of everyone at the ball and show him that she was no longer going to be messed around. That he loved her and was going to spend the rest of his life with her.

But as she began to move through the crowd towards him, she realised Richard had his arm around the petite dark-haired woman standing next to him. Samantha took a deep intake of breath. It was the wife, of that she was sure. Well, it was time she found out that her husband was leaving her.

They were hidden from view for a moment as a group of people passed in front of her. But when the way was clear once more, Samantha stopped short.

Richard and his wife had turned around and were heading for the door. She had a perfect view of them both as they walked away together, laughing softly. The realisation of all his lies and deceit suddenly hit Samantha, causing her to fight for breath.

Richard's wife was heavily pregnant.

Chapter Eighty-five

Charley was unaware of the romantic developments for Julie and Caroline. In fact, she was quite drunk so she was unaware of most things, except that Julie had disappeared a very long time ago and hadn't come back.

She was slumped in a chair, staring at the people around her in a daze.

Her mother peered at her closely. 'Are you all right? Is your dress too tight?'

'No.'

'Your ice-cream is a triumph!' said Aunty Peggy in a loud voice.

'This whole evening has been marvellous!' slurred Maureen.

Her father was designated driver and therefore sober, which might have meant he had a different perspective on the evening. He had been keeping count of the number of glasses of champagne drunk by his wife until it had crept into double figures.

'Shall we go home soon, love?' he said, in a hopeful tone.

But his question fell on deaf ears.

'I'm so proud of you,' said Maureen, patting her daughter on the arm.

'Thanks, Mum. You know I'm still going to pay you back the money, don't you?'

'Don't think about it tonight.'

'I think I'll see if Julie's on the dance floor,' said Charley, slowly standing up. She smiled as she looked around with hazy eyes. 'I love you, Mum,' she said, swaying slightly from side to side. 'Even your cooking.'

'I love you too, darling.' Maureen was looking a little cross-eyed. 'And what do you mean about my cooking?'

Charley staggered off, managing to negotiate her way through the entrance hall and into the ballroom. It was past midnight and the disco was now into pure pop mode, currently playing 'It's Raining Men'. Charley peered through the flashing lights, trying to make out if she could see Julie, but she was having trouble focussing.

Until a very familiar man materialised in front of her.

'Hello,' said Steve.

'Hi,' replied Charley in amazement.

He glanced at her cleavage before breaking into one of his killer smiles. 'You look incredible.'

'Thank you.'

He looked good too in his dinner jacket.

'I hear the ice-cream business is going well,' he told her.

She nodded. 'I think so.'

'Good for you. You deserve it, you know.'

Charley didn't know what to say so just smiled back at him.

To her surprise, Steve suddenly took her in his arms and pulled her close to him. 'I've missed you.'

'Have you been drinking?' she giggled.

He shook his head, giving her a crooked smile. 'Not that much. And not as much as you, by the looks of it. Hey, I've been thinking. We should make a go of it again.'

Charley's mouth dropped open. 'What? Why?'

He shrugged his shoulders. 'I dunno. Could be fun.'

She couldn't believe it. The decree absolut divorce papers had arrived only that week.

'Steve,' she said, shaking her head.

'Look, your business is doing well,' he carried on. 'We won't make such a mess of this one. I promise.'

'What about Susie?'

'She's long gone,' he told her, reaching out to brush her cheek. 'Think about it. We could have our lovely life back. Great house. A couple of decent cars. What about that Range Rover you were always lusting after?'

She sighed. 'That stuff's not important to me any more, Steve.'

'So what is?'

And suddenly she knew. She finally admitted to herself what her heart had been trying to tell her for so long.

She stared at her ex-husband for a long time before kissing him on the cheek.

'Goodbye, Steve.'

Then Charley walked away.

Chapter Eighty-six

She walked back across the entrance hall, deep in thought. Romantic music drifted across from the ball-room, tugging at her heart.

'Charlotte?' came her father's voice from nearby.

She went over to where her family were standing, feeling unsteady on her feet.

'I'm taking your mother and Peggy home.' Her father grimaced as he glanced over to the two women who had linked arms for support. 'Do you want a lift?'

'I'll take her home, if you like,' said Mike, suddenly materialising next to them.

Charley stared at up at him in shock. She had failed to spot him all evening. She glanced around. Was he alone? It appeared so.

'Thanks, son.' Her father sighed before giving Charley a kiss. 'Take care, love. Good night.'

There was a small skirmish whilst Maureen and Peggy were persuaded to leave the party. Having watched them finally leave, Charley spun round to face Mike. But she was a little too quick and swayed at the sudden rush of blood to the head.

Mike reached out to steady her.

'Hello,' he said, but he wasn't smiling.

'Hi,' she told him, suddenly feeling shy. His hands on her bare arms were making her skin tingle.

'Are you all right?'

Charley gave him a bashful smile. 'I might have had a little bit too much champagne.'

'Is that why I saw you with Steve?' His grip on her arms became tighter, harder.

She shook her head, which made the room swim. 'It's over,' she told him. 'It's been over for a very long time.'

He stared down at her before saying, 'Let's get you home.'

'I can't leave yet. I don't know where Julie is.'

Mike broke into a grin. 'I saw her leave with that Aussie vet.'

Charley's eyebrows shot up. 'Really? Wow.' She recalled Caroline telling her to be brave so took a deep breath. 'Maybe we could have a drink to celebrate my success?'

But he shook his head. 'I don't think there's any left. You've drunk the place dry.'

Her head drooped. He had said no. He didn't want her any more. She had waited too long to trust him.

Mike took her hand and began to lead her towards the main entrance. 'Come on.'

She went with him, feeling more miserable than she had done in a long time. They got into one of the waiting taxis. As they were driven away, Charley glanced back at the castle, wondering if tonight had changed anything at all. She glanced across at Mike and, finding him watching her, shuffled in her seat.

'Did you like the ice-cream?' she asked, desperate to break the lengthy silence.

'It was great,' he told her. 'You should be proud of yourself.'

'Let's hope Lord and Lady Beckenham agree with you.' Charley began to unpin her hair and let it down.

'They will. They're surprisingly nice.'

Charley stared at him. 'You know them?'

'I bump into them on occasion when I help out in the gardens.'

An idea was trying to force its way through her champagne-fogged brain. 'Wait,' she said, rubbing her forehead. 'Does that mean . . . ?'

Her voice trailed off. He wouldn't have . . . couldn't have, surely?

But glancing back at him, she saw Mike nodding. 'I was the one who recommended your ice-cream for the dinner tonight.'

The taxi journey flew by in silence after that. All too soon they were outside the flats. The taxi drove off, leaving them standing in silence in front of the building.

Charley walked up to the front door, tripping up the first step before turning to face Mike. She was surprised to find him standing so near, their faces so close.

'I can't believe it was you who suggested my desserts for tonight,' she blurted out.

He shrugged his shoulders. 'Thought it might help.'

She shook her head in wonder. 'Why are you being so nice to me?'

She looked deep into his eyes, which was a mistake. In the streetlight, they were the colour of melted plain chocolate and she found she couldn't look away.

'Because I thought you needed a friend to help you out,' he told her.

Charley felt even more despondent. Was that all they were? Friends?

Be brave, she heard Caroline telling her.

She leant forward and placed her hands against his broad chest. Beneath her fingers, she could feel his heart beating.

'I want you to know that I've drunk a lot of champagne tonight,' she told him.

'What are you saying?'

She moved her face closer to his. 'I've drunk a lot of champagne so I can't be responsible for my actions.' Her gaze dropped to his mouth. 'So don't forget that.'

'I won't,' he told her, looking bemused by her words.

She reached up and kissed him. She had only meant it to be a brief kiss, something that would prove to her once and for all that they were only meant to be friends. That he meant nothing to her after all. But once their lips had met, she found she couldn't stop kissing him.

For a brief moment he kissed her back, strong and hard, and she was lost. But then she found herself being pushed very gently away from him.

'Charley,' he murmured, shaking his head.

Her cheeks were flaming with horror. He didn't want her. He didn't feel the same way.

'It was just the champagne,' she told him, breaking into wide, fake grin. 'I did warn you! Anyway,' she carried on, the words coming out in a rush, 'it's been a big day so I'll say goodnight.'

He watched her until she finally managed on the third attempt to get the key into the lock.

'Goodnight,' he said in a soft tone. °

'Goodnight,' she called over her shoulder, unable to face making eye contact with him.

Closing the door to the flat behind her, Charley leant back against it. She brought her hands up to her lips. The kiss had been, oh, so sweet. But only for her, it seemed.

She put her hands over her eyes and began to cry.

Chapter Eighty-seven

It wasn't possible to feel this bad without being dead, decided Charley.

She had barely been able to drag herself out of bed and had only made it as far as the kitchen so far. She was on her second cup of coffee and her third piece of toast. That helped repair much of the physical damage from the previous evening's champagne. However, the mental wounds were still gaping.

Oh, yes, it was all coming back to her now, detail by horrifying detail. She had rejected Steve, that was good. Her ice-cream had, hopefully, been a success. That was even better. But Mike ... Her lovely, wonderful, handsome Mike. She touched her lips briefly as she remembered kissing him. She couldn't stop seeing him shaking his head at her as he had pushed her away. He probably still thought she was a spoilt brat, miserable because she was no longer rich. Maybe he was even laughing to himself that morning about just how drunk she had been.

Her heart was broken. More so than it had been with Steve, she knew. Mike was worth a thousand Steves.

Maybe he had called or texted her. Even a message of friendship would be better than nothing. She felt a tiny flicker of hope as she picked up the evening handbag slung on the floor in the hallway where she had left it the previous night

But the screen on her phone showed only two missed phone calls from Caroline.

'Hi,' she said when Charley rang her back. 'How's the head?'

Charley slumped into her armchair. 'Like it's still trying to reject the rest of my body.'

'Good night, was it?'

'Far too much champagne.'

'No wonder I can't get hold of Julie either.'

Charley shook her head and then decided that was a very bad idea. 'She disappeared quite early on.'

'Any gossip I should know about?'

'I think she was with Wes.'

'Excellent!' said Caroline. 'But I meant you.'

'Nothing,' said Charley with a sigh.

'You're lying. But for now, tell me about the ice-cream. I've already had an email from Lady Beckenham to say how thrilled they were with the desserts.'

Charley closed her eyes, trying to hold back her emotions. It was all because of Mike that she had been given the business at Grove Castle in the first place.

'Hello?' called Caroline down the line. 'Did you hear what I said? You're going to be very busy from now on.'

Charley clutched her head. 'Can I have a couple of days off first to recover?'

'I don't see why not,' Caroline told her. 'You've been

405

working seven day weeks for months. Give yourself a bit of time off. Recharge the batteries before all the new orders come flooding in, especially after everyone hears about Lady Beckenham's recommendation.'

'That food critic from the newspaper was there too, apparently.'

'Okay,' said Caroline, sounding a little more unsure. 'Well, I'm sure that will be all right.'

'I hope so.'

Once Caroline had said goodbye, Charley shuffled into the kitchen once more to consider another piece of toast. She really hadn't eaten an awful lot at the Valentine's Ball, which might not be helping the head-ache disappear.

She clicked a piece of bread into the toaster and waited whilst it warmed up. She stared vacantly at the free local newspaper which had appeared the previous day on her front doormat and had only got as far as being thrown into the kitchen by Julie when she had arrived.

Charley picked up the paper to flick idly through the pages, anything to take her mind off Mike. But an envelope wafted on to the floor as she moved the newspaper.

Thinking it was probably one of those blank mail-shots, she gave it a cursory glance. But it was an official-looking letter, in a typed envelope addressed to her. It must have been hidden under the freebie newspaper the whole of the previous day. Charley bent down to retrieve it from the floor, her head imme-diately feeling like it would burst into flames.

She stared at the envelope as she straightened up. It looked official. Scary, even. God, she didn't need any bad news today.

But when she ripped open the envelope, she found

it was from the Official Receiver. The representative of the bankruptcy court had concluded his enquiries into her affairs and would file a notice of early discharge in court.

The court date was the following Tuesday. In two days' time, Charley would be free from the bankruptcy which had hung over her for nearly ten months.

She continued to stare at the letter, but the words swam before her as her eyes filled up with tears. The hangover was all but forgotten.

She was being given a new start. Any future financial mistakes would be down to her, but she knew she wouldn't be risking anything from now onwards. Financial insecurity had been a dreadful, debilitating feeling that had dragged her down for many months.

She glanced out of the kitchen window and saw brightly coloured crocuses beginning to appear in the ground outside. Spring was nearly here. A new season for a new start.

She just wished she had Mike to share it with.

Chapter Eighty-eight

'It's beginning to settle,' said Jeff, looking out of the patio window on Monday afternoon.

The sky was a grey infinity, filled with snow. On the ground, a dusting of white powder was beginning to change the landscape.

'Flora's going to want to play outside when she gets home,' he said. 'Where are her wellies?'

'She's staying at Molly's house for tea,' said Caroline.

Jeff spun round in surprise. 'I thought that was tomorrow?'

'It was,' replied Caroline. 'But my waters just broke.'

His mouth fell open. It was only then that he registered that his wife was wearing her coat.

'So I've rung Molly's mum and it's all sorted.' Caroline was cool and calm.

Jeff, on the other hand, was a bag of nerves as he rushed around the house, checking that the back door was locked and the door of the wood burning stove was shut tight.

Caroline waited patiently, sitting on the sofa until

he was ready. It had been exactly the same when Flora was born.

Eventually, her husband crashed to a halt in front of her, his breathing rapid. 'Okay,' he panted. 'The bags are in the car. The windows are locked. I've put the heating on low. I've got the car charger for the mobile. What else do I need?'

Caroline stood up. 'Me,' she told him, taking hold of his arm.

He held on to her as they made their slow and steady progress outside into the snow.

'It's so pretty,' said Caroline as she lowered herself into the car.

'God, I hope we don't get snowed in on the way,' moaned Jeff, getting into the driver's seat.

Caroline smiled. The hospital was only ten minutes away.

She found herself surprisingly relaxed these days. Flora's trousers had been muddy after their walk the previous day and it didn't faze her. Nothing did any more. Well, not the small things in life.

She rubbed her extended stomach, eager to meet her new son or daughter. She didn't care which sex the baby was. As long as he or she was healthy.

If the last nine months had taught her anything, it was that there was no point in worrying. The baby was coming and that was all that mattered.

The snow squeaked under Julie's wellington boots as they made their way through it the following morning.

'So your friend's okay?' asked Wes.

They had arranged to meet on the heath that morning for the dog walk.

'She's fine, thank goodness. Apparently all the

409

worrying symptoms disappeared now her son has arrived safely into the world.'

'Do you want a lift to the hospital later?' he said. 'My old Land Rover will be okay in the snow.'

'Thanks. That would be great.'

As they carried on walking, Julie watched Boris enjoy his first experience of snow. He was bounding about in the foot-deep downfall, leaping around as if on springs. Cadbury, Wes's brown labrador, was equally excited, catching the snowballs Wes threw for him. Both dogs' tails were wagging in unison.

Julie knew how they felt. She too felt excited about the future for the first time in years. Her house had been on the market only a day before a developer had snapped it up at a hugely inflated price. Despite the recession, the land in Upper Grove was still valuable. She had already spotted a small cottage overlooking the green in Little Grove which should leave her with only a tiny mortgage. The relief of having the financial burden lifted from her was palpable.

And then there was Wes. Perhaps her new start would include him too, if only as a friend. He was thoughtful, kind, and, most importantly in Julie's eyes, trustworthy.

He had even promised to help her move Uncle Sidney into a small bungalow in a retirement community village in Little Grove. Sidney had already offered the flat to Julie, who hadn't been able to take it because it was upstairs with no garden. But she thought it would be perfect for Charley to live in.

Because Julie wasn't moving anywhere without her beloved Boris. He was older now, nearly nine months old. He was almost fully grown in his body, but his brain and spirit were still pure puppy. His black eyes remained the same too, soulful, as if ringed by charcoal.

Boris was cuddly but clumsy. His tail could sweep everything from the coffee table in one movement. The house was covered with dog hair, but he was gentle with children. He was eager to please. And he just wanted to be with Julie, every hour of every day.

'This is awesome,' said Wes, staring around the heath. 'We never had snow Down Under.'

Julie shook her head. 'Never seeing snow? That's crazy.'

Yes, there was only one small cloud in her sunny world, she thought. For sure, Wes was lovely but they had only shared one slow dance a few nights previously. Afterwards he had behaved like a perfect gentleman and she really, honestly, appreciated it. But did it mean that he was happy just being friends?

'No snowball fights growing up,' carried on Wes. 'And what's this snow angel that everyone goes on about?'

'You don't know?' said Julie, in surprise.

'Not a clue.'

Julie glanced down at her jeans. Oh, well. She would just have to get changed when she was home. So she dropped to the ground on her back, the snow cold against her legs and back.

'What are you doing?' said Wes, laughing as he looked down at her.

Julie moved her hands and legs across the snow. 'Making an angel, of course.'

She jumped up and showed him the pattern in the snow where she had just been lying, brushing herself down.

'There you go. One snow angel!'

But Wes was shaking his head. 'Nope,' he told her. 'I can't see it. You'll have to show me again.'

Suddenly he grabbed Julie's hand before throwing himself on to the ground, pulling her down on top of him. She lay on her front, the whole length of their bodies touching, their faces inches apart.

'So how does this work again?' Wes asked, his tone husky as he stared deep into her eyes.

Then he reached out to touch the back of her head and pulled her down for a long, deep kiss.

When they finally drew apart, Julie was smiling. His kiss had told her everything she needed to know. His warm smile was everything she needed to see.

They were suddenly interrupted by the dogs throwing themselves on to their owners, desperate to join in this new game in a wet, cold assault of paws and swishing tails.

'Geroff!' said Julie, jumping up to shoo them away.

Wes stood up next to her, grabbing her hand to hold as they continued their walk.

Chapter Eighty-nine

Charley's week had been very quiet. Not only had the snow made driving impossible, the Mini was not exactly cut out for extreme road conditions. But her friends were also quite difficult to get hold of.

Of course, Caroline was in hospital most of the week until she and baby Joshua came home. But Charley also had difficulties talking to Julie whose conversation had become quite short, sweet and giggly. Charley was pleased for her friends but found herself alone once more.

There had been no further contact from Mike. Perhaps he was as embarrassed by her drunken behaviour as Charley was.

She had tried to rest and chill out in front of the television but couldn't stop thinking about him. So she spent the remainder of the week experimenting with new ice-cream flavours and ideas, anything to occupy her mind.

Charley had had a couple of trial runs at making iced margaritas and iced gin and lemon drink-desserts.

For the younger at heart, she had also experimented with putting a scoop of chocolate-coated ice-cream on the end of a cocktail stick, a sort-of miniature lollipop.

Throughout the week she played with pomegranates, orange water, nougat and anything else she could lay her hands on. With her music playing, the hours whizzed by until it was Monday morning once more and time to return to the shop.

Now that the snow had melted, Caroline had arranged to meet her there with the promise of lots of emailed orders. As Charley drew up to the small parking space at the back of the shop, she realised Julie had also joined them.

'Where's the baby?' asked Charley, as she got out of the Mini.

'At home,' replied Caroline, as they hugged. 'I thought we'd go there afterwards for a cuddle.'

'Hi,' said Julie, grinning from ear to ear.

'So why are we meeting here?' asked Charley. 'I don't understand.'

'You will,' Julie told her, turning the key in the back door.

Charley followed them into the kitchen but her friends didn't stop walking. So she let them lead her into the shop at the front. Except it wasn't the same any more.

'What have you done?' she asked, staring around.

Gone were the plain walls and dull interior. Instead the walls had been painted in a distressed, marble effect which matched perfectly the trompe l'oeil on the long empty wall. It showed a beautiful vista of some olive trees, a chair and table on a small patio and, beyond the trees and terracotta pots, the deep blue of the Mediterranean.

Instead of the old mismatched plastic tables and chairs, there was new wooden furniture with beautiful matching cushions and tablecloths.

'I managed to get most of the cushions done before the baby came,' said Caroline. 'But your mum and Aunty Peggy helped with painting the walls.'

'And your dad sorted out the terracotta pots for the tables,' said Julie.

Then they realised that Charley's eyes had filled with tears as she slowly took in the transformation.

'I–I can't believe it,' she stammered.

'Do you like it?' asked Julie.

'I love it,' she told them, in a wavering voice. 'I don't know how to thank you.'

They both came forward to put their arms around her.

'You don't need to,' said Caroline, her voice equally unsteady. 'That's what friends are for.'

'And everyone else helped?' said Charley. 'My family? Jeff and Wes too?'

Julie nodded. 'And Mike.'

Charley was astounded. 'Mike?' she whispered, her heart lurching at the sound of his name.

'He painted the trompe l'oeil,' Julie told her.

Charley was speechless.

'And that's not all,' said Caroline, grabbing a newspaper from one of the tables and thrusting it in front of her. 'Read that!'

The words swam in front of her eyes but Charley finally managed to establish that it was the food critic's review of the Valentine's Ball.

'Bland and tasteless fare,' she read aloud before looking up at her friends in horror.

'Not that part,' said Julie, tutting. 'She's talking about those dreadful canapés they served up.'

'This part,' said Caroline, pointing further down the page.

Charley finally focussed on the words. 'The rest of the food may have been a disaster but thankfully dessert saved the day,' she read aloud. 'It was a triumph of simple but stylish flavours, beautifully presented. If Miss Charlotte Summers' business doesn't achieve great success, I shall eat my hat. But I would much rather sample more of her delicious ice-cream.'

Charley's eyes filled with tears. She had done it. It had been a success.

Caroline and Julie began to talk about the flat upstairs as somewhere for her to live. But Charley was still mulling over the amazing changes that had occurred in her life. Two years ago she had been stuck in a marriage that had run its course, bored with her life. Almost a year ago she had been bankrupted, a wreck, barely able to get through each day without breaking down into tears.

Now here she was. She had a future doing something she really loved. She was ready for a new beginning, even if she was destined to remain single.

Charley began to smile through her tears.

Chapter Ninety

On the first Saturday in March, the shop was officially reopened. Charley walked around one last time, checking the ice-cream was still frozen, that the tables were clean and that they were ready.

Then she crossed the floor and turned the sign over on the door so that it read 'Open'. She turned back to survey the shop. Her shop. Or rather, their joint venture.

After all, they had each contributed in their own way. Caroline was not only taking care of newborn Joshua, she was also supervising the paperwork, which was under such tight control that it appeared to take care of itself, leaving her free to chill out and play as much as she liked with her new son.

Julie was due to move over the next couple of weeks and was going to continue working only part-time. She would help out in the shop on the odd afternoon, when she could leave her beloved Boris at the vet's where he could play with Cadbury and get lots of attention. The girls knew she would be okay. After all,

Caroline had already seen and approved of the engagement ring that Wes had shown her.

As Charley headed back behind the counter, Julie grinned at her. 'So . . . here we go again.'

The ice-cream selection was predominantly chocolate-flavoured, in reference to the approaching Easter holidays. There were even chocolate-coated egg-shaped lollipops for the children.

By lunchtime, the smile on Charley's face was genuine and relaxed. She was so proud of herself and everyone who had helped her. The shop was busy and the orders for ice-cream cakes and desserts for parties and social gatherings were flooding in.

The business was already bringing in enough money for to her to begin planning the first instalment of her repayment to her parents: £40,000 was still an awful lot of money but she was determined that they would be paid back in full, perhaps by the end of the following year.

Charley had also decided to move into the flat over the shop. She found she would be sad to leave her little damp-ridden, poky flat. It had been a safe haven, eventually. But she would be free to paint the new one and perhaps get some more furniture. Nothing extravagant, though. She would never again be reckless with her money.

There was a brief lull just before the mid-afternoon rush began and Charley took the opportunity to check the levels of ice-cream in the freezer cabinet. Seeing a pair of legs through the glass, she straightened up.

'Hi. How can I help you?'

The words trailed off as she found Mike standing at the other side of the counter.

'You can take this from me, if you like,' he told her.

He held out a small but perfectly formed lemon tree in a terracotta pot. 'I saw it the other day and thought it would do as a shop-warming present.'

Charley was thrilled. She took it from him and walked to the far end of the counter, where it looked right at home with the marbled walls and Mediterranean feel. She took some time to fiddle with the position, anything to give her cheeks time to lose some of their pink heat.

Finally she walked back to stand in front of Mike. 'Thank you,' she managed to stammer. 'It's lovely.'

But she kept her eyes down to avoid looking at him. She knew her own would betray her feelings.

'Charley?' he said in a soft tone. 'Please look at me.'

'Darling!' cried Maureen, suddenly arriving next to him. 'Hello, Michael. Isn't it super? I can't believe how well you've done, Charlotte.'

'Thanks, Mum,' replied Charley, finally daring to look at Mike.

He was glancing between mother and daughter, looking, to Charley's surprise, wound up about something. He opened his mouth to speak but missed the opportunity.

'It said on the radio that there's going to be another heatwave this summer,' announced her mother. 'So that'll be good for business, won't it?'

'Let's hope so,' replied Charley.

'That Wayne's not come back, has he? Dreadful little man. I said to Peggy, they were always the same that family . . .'

Charley stole another glance at Mike whose frown had deepened. His jaw was clenched. She desperately wanted to ask him if everything was all right but her mother was still wittering on.

'Did you know I went to school with his mother? Awful woman! The things she got up to would make the front pages of the *Sun* these days. Talking of which, did I tell you what happened at the knitting circle this week? Mrs Canfield told Gladys that . . .'

'I'm sorry, no! I can't take this any more!' Mike suddenly bellowed, causing the flow of gossip to grind to a halt.

Charley glanced across at her mother who was now staring up at Mike in amazement.

'Excuse me, but I have to talk to your daughter *right now*!' he told Maureen.

With that he marched around the counter, grabbed Charley's hand and dragged her out into the back room. He looked to his left, saw Julie checking the large freezer and kept walking through the kitchen and into the back courtyard.

Mike pulled her nearer to stand directly in front of him.

'I have to talk to you,' he almost shouted into her face. 'You're driving me crazy!'

He stopped and breathed in deeply, his chest going up and down.

Charley couldn't believe how upset he was. He looked so troubled that she actually found herself suppressing a giggle.

'I hope you realise that technically it's only staff who are allowed back here,' she told him, trying not to smirk.

He threw up his hands. 'Arrest me then. I'm past caring.'

'I may be reported to the Health and Safety Officer.'

Either he wasn't listening or he had completely lost his sense of humour. Instead, he grasped her arms and took a deep breath.

'I had this huge crush on you at school.'

She was shocked. 'You did?'

'Don't interrupt.' He softened his tone as he stared down at her. 'Please. I've just got to get this out, okay?'

Charley nodded in reply, stunned by his words.

'You broke my yellow pencil and I fell in love with you. Then you hooked up with Steve and broke my heart. I go to college, I see you in the village once in a while and I think, "I'm doing okay. I'm over you."' Mike dragged his hand through his hair. 'Then you crash back into my life, snapping and sniping about your bankruptcy and your miserable idiot of a husband. And I think, no, I can do this. I can be strong. I really am over you.'

She continued to stare up at him, trying to take in what he was telling her.

'Except I'm not,' he said, his voice catching. 'I can't stop thinking about you. I can't stop dreaming about you. I can't stop wanting to kiss you, every hour of every day. But the only time you seem to want to kiss me is when you're drunk on champagne.'

He stared down at her.

'I'm telling you here and now: I love you, Charlotte Summers.'

'You do?' she said, astounded.

He gave a heavy sigh. 'Yes. So you're stuck with me and it's too bad if you're not happy with that idea.'

Charley stared up into his face. The kind, generous face of a man who had helped, listened and cared when she had been as upset as he was now. He looked so distressed, so vulnerable, that she automatically reached up to stroke his cheek.

'I love the mural you painted for me in the shop,' she told him in a soft tone. 'I love all the words of

421

encouragement you gave me when I was really low. I love the fact that you got me home safely when I was off my head on champagne. I love the fact that I can trust you and feel safe with you.'

She pulled his face down close to hers. 'I love you, Mike Shearer.'

Then she kissed him. As the kiss grew deeper, she felt his body relax and he swept his arms around her, holding her close.

He drew back briefly to look at her. 'I will never hurt you.'

'I know.'

He bent down and kissed her again and it felt so sweet, so right. Finally she was in his arms, where she belonged.

Chapter Ninety-one

An attention-seeking cough from nearby made Charley and Mike draw apart from their embrace after many minutes.

'Sorry,' said Julie, beaming from ear to ear. 'Well, I'm not really. Thank God you two finally got your act together! But it's your mother, Charley. I can't put her off coming back here for much longer.'

Charley nodded, turned to give Mike one last lingering kiss on the lips and went back into the shop.

At that precise moment, her life had never felt better. She had built up a successful business, had survived the most horrendous year of her life and now she had the love of a very good man.

She knew she could cope on her own with whatever the future threw at her. But she was so very glad Mike was going to be with her. She found she couldn't stop the smile from showing on her face when she returned to stand behind the counter.

By now her mother was perched on a stool on the

other side of it. She took silent note of her daughter's happy expression and let a smile play over her lips.

'I'm having trouble deciding,' she said. 'Do I want the chocolate or the pistachio?'

Charley began to sort out the individual tubs and cones which had got in a bit of a muddle.

'Of course, nuts are a bit exotic,' said Maureen. 'Did you get them from the local farm? And did you hear what happened to Scott's Farm? Those squirrels can be little devils . . .'

Charley grabbed a pen and notepad, thinking that she would need to place another order for some more of the small plastic tubs in the next month.

'Of course, you don't get them out in Greece. I said to your father, it'll be the mosquitoes we'll have to worry about. We'll have to get those plug-in things for the night time. Never had this kind of trouble when we went to Torquay . . .'

Charley sucked on the end of the pen. She would have to keep a close check on the amount of ice-cream that was being sold. She must always make sure that there was some spare, just in case.

'But we might have to ask you to pop in to water the pots every evening. I won't have my petunias going to ruin just because your father's taken it upon himself to book us a fortnight in Crete.'

Charley was just counting up the boxes of wafers when her mind focussed on what her mother was saying.

She spun round. 'You're going on holiday?'

'Yes, silly. What do you think I've been talking about all this time? Two weeks in Crete at the end of the summer. Isn't it exciting?'

Charley nodded. 'Very. But how can you afford it?'

424

'Well, you won't believe it . . . I had the most marvellous piece of luck. Didn't I tell you?' Maureen frowned. 'No, that's right. You were too busy with all of this. I'm so proud of you, by the way.' She broke into a smile. 'And I'm so glad our nice Mike has finally got his act together. I never did get on with that Steve. I was always worried about his mother. You know how insanity can run in a family . . .'

Charley rolled her eyes. She knew. 'About the marvellous piece of luck?' she prompted. 'Has Cousin Sylvia finally died?'

'Lord, no! It'll be a good few years before I get my hands on her Japanese figurines. No, Peggy saw the advert for the *Antiques Roadshow* up at the castle. She wanted to take that blue vase of hers she's always bragging about.'

Charley stared at her mother. 'What was it? A Ming vase?'

Her mother laughed. 'No, silly! It was completely worthless. The chap doing the valuations was much more interested in the little bowl I took along. I had just grabbed it at the last minute, to take something with me. You know, the one with all the keys next to the telephone?'

'The green one?'

'Exactly. Well, it turns out that it was Chinese jade. Your grandfather must have got it in the war, I suppose. Anyway, this chap valued it at £20,000!'

Charley gaped at her mother.

'But he was wrong.'

Charley rolled her eyes. She had known it sounded too good to be true.

'It actually sold for £42,000 at auction last weekend. So you don't need to worry any more about that money you owe us.'

Maureen's face broke into a huge smile as she stared at her daughter's shocked expression.

'You know what? I think I'll have the vanilla. With chocolate sprinkles on the top.'